“We’ve been t
snow for almost
I looked, it wasn’t le

“I’d say it’ll be over before dark falls.”

“And then we go back down the mountain?”

She shot him an apologetic look. “Not after dark. Way too treacherous. We’ve got enough wood to keep us warm. We can stay here until daylight.”

Looking around the room, he spotted one narrow bed. “And sleep where?”

She looked at the bed and back at him. “You were saying something about body heat?”

His heart flipped a couple of times.

BLOOD ON COPPERHEAD TRAIL

BY
PAULA GRAVES

Published in Great Britain 2014
by Mills & Boon, an imprint of Harlequin (UK) Limited,
Eton House, 18-24 Paradise Road, Richmond, Surrey, TW9 1SR

© 2014 Paula Graves

ISBN: 978 0 263 91349 1

46-0214

Harlequin (UK) Limited's policy is to use papers that are natural, renewable and recyclable products and made from wood grown in sustainable forests. The logging and manufacturing processes conform to the legal environmental regulations of the country of origin.

Printed and bound in Spain
by Blackprint CPI, Barcelona

Alabama native **Paula Graves** wrote her first book, a mystery starring herself and her neighborhood friends, at the age of six. A voracious reader, Paula loves books that pair tantalizing mystery with compelling romance. When she's not reading or writing, she works as a creative director for a Birmingham advertising agency and spends time with her family and friends. She is a member of Southern Magic Romance Writers, Heart of Dixie Romance Writers and Romance Writers of America.

Paula invites readers to visit her website, www.paulagraves.com.

For the day job gang, Lisa, Amanda and Jessica,
for putting up with my distraction and all that writing
and editing I do during my lunch hour.

Chapter One

The trail shelter wasn't built for cold weather, but the three girls occupying the small wooden shed were young, healthy and warmly tucked inside their cold-weather sleeping bags. Overnight, the mercury had dropped into the mid-thirties, which might have tempted less-determined hikers off the trail and into their warm homes in the valley below. But youth and risk were longtime bedfellows.

He depended on it ever to be so.

Overhead, the moon played hide-and-seek behind scudding clouds, casting deep blue shadows through the spindly bare limbs of the birch, maple and hickory trees that grew on Copperhead Ridge. The air was damp with the promise of snow.

But not yet.

His breath spreading a pale cloud of condensation in front of his eyes, he pulled the digital camera from his pack. A whimsical image filled his mind. Himself as a mighty, fierce dragon, huffing smoke as he stalked his winsome prey.

The camera made a soft whirring sound as it auto-focused on the sleeping beauties. He held his breath, waiting to see if the sound was enough to awaken the girls. A part of him wished it would wake them, though he'd have to move now, rather than later, cutting short his plans. But the challenge these young, fit women posed excited him to the point that his carefully laid plans seemed more an impediment than a means to increase his anticipation.

Slow and steady wins the race, he thought. The experience *would* be better for having waited.

He snapped off a series of shots from different angles, relishing each composition, imagining them in their finished state. Despite the quick flashes of light from his camera, the princesses slept on, oblivious.

He stepped away from the shelter, punching buttons to print the shots he'd just snapped. They came out remarkably clear, he saw with surprise. He hadn't been sure they would.

Or maybe he'd been hoping he'd have to sneak over to the shelter again.

A clear acrylic box, cloudy with scuff marks from exposure to the elements, stood on a rickety wooden pedestal outside the shelter. It housed a worn trail logbook similar to those found farther east on the Appalachian Trail. The latest entry was dated that day. The girls had recorded their arrival and their plans for the next day's hike home.

He slipped the snapshots into the journal, marking the latest entry.

A snuffling sound from within the open-faced shelter froze him in place. He couldn't see the girls from where he stood, so he waited, still and silent, for a repeat of the noise.

But the only sound he heard was the cold mountain breeze shaking the trees overhead, the leafless limbs rattling like bones.

After a few more minutes of quiet, he slipped away, a dark shape in the darker woods, where he would bide his time until daybreak.

And the girls slept on.

"I'M NOT THE ENEMY." Though Laney Hanvey was using her best "soothe the witness" voice, she couldn't tell her efforts at calm reassurance were having any effect on the dark-eyed detective across the tearoom table from her.

"Never said you were." Ivy Hawkins arched one dark eyebrow, as if to say she saw right through Laney's efforts at handling her. "I'm just saying I don't know whether anyone besides Glen Rayburn was on Wayne Cortland's payroll, and the D.A. sending a nanny down here to spank our bottoms and teach us how to behave ain't gonna change that."

Laney didn't know whether to laugh at Ivy's description of her job or be offended. "The captain of detectives killed himself rather than face indictment. The chief of police resigned, an admission that he wasn't in control of his department. Surely you understand why the district attorney felt the need to send a public integrity officer down here to ask a few questions."

"We have an internal affairs bureau of our own."

"And I know how well police officers admire their internal affairs brethren."

Ivy's lips quirked, a tacit concession. "Why did you single me out?"

"Who says I did?"

Ivy looked around the airy tearoom of Sequoyah House, then back at Laney. "You're telling me you bring all the cops to the fanciest restaurant in town for pretty little cucumber sandwiches and weak, tepid dishwater?"

Laney looked down at the cups of Earl Grey in front of them and smiled. "You're laying on the redneck a little thick, aren't you?"

Ivy's eyes met hers again. "I'm not the one putting on airs, Charlane."

Touché, Laney thought.

Ivy's expression softened. "You've gotten better at your poker face. I almost didn't see you flinch. You've come a long way from Smoky Ridge."

"I didn't bring you here to talk about old times."

Ivy leaned across the table toward her. "Are you sure? Maybe you thought invoking a little Smoky Ridge sisterhood might soften me up? Make me spill all my deep, dark secrets?"

"I don't suspect *you* of anything, Ivy. I just want to pick your brain about whom *you* might suspect of being Glen Rayburn's accomplice."

"And I told you, I don't suspect anyone in particular." Ivy's mouth clamped closed at the end of the sentence, but it was too late.

"So you *do* think there may be others who were on Cortland's payroll."

"I think the possibility exists," Ivy said carefully. "But I don't know if I'm right, and I sure don't intend to toss you a sacrificial lamb to get you off my back."

"Fair enough." Laney sat back and sipped the warm tea, trying not to think of Ivy's description of it. But the image was already in her mind. She set the teacup on the saucer and forced down the swallow.

"The cucumber sandwiches weren't *too* bad," Ivy said with a crooked smile. "But I'm going to have to grab something from Ledbetter's on my way back to the cop shop, because I'm still hungry. Want to join me?"

An image of Maisey Ledbetter's chicken-fried steak with milk gravy flooded Laney's brain. "You're an enabler," she grumbled.

Ivy grinned. "I'm doing you a favor. You're way too skinny for these parts, Charlane. People will start trying to feed you everywhere you go."

"Laney, Ivy. Not Charlane. Even my mama calls me Laney these days." Laney motioned for the check and waved off Ivy's offer to pay. "I can expense it."

They reconvened outside, where Ivy's department-issue

Ford Focus looked a bit dusty and dinged next to Laney's sleek black Mustang.

Ivy grinned when Laney started to open the Mustang's driver's door. "I knew you still had a little redneck in you, girl. Nice wheels."

Laney arched her eyebrows. "Can't say the same about yours."

Ivy didn't look offended. "Cop car. You should see my tricked-out Jeep."

The drive from Sequoyah House to Ledbetter's Diner wasn't exactly a familiar route for Laney, who'd grown up poor as a church mouse and twice as shy. Nothing in her life on Smoky Ridge had ever required her to visit this part of town, where Copperhead Ridge overlooked the lush hollow where the wealthier citizens of the small mountain town had built their homes and their very separate lives.

The Edgewood part of Bitterwood was more suburban than rural, though the mountain itself was nothing but wilderness broken only by hiking trails and the occasional public shelter dotting the trails. People in this part of town usually worked elsewhere, either in nearby Maryville or forty-five minutes away in Knoxville.

Definitely not the kind of folks she'd grown up with on Smoky Ridge.

Ivy hadn't been joking. She pulled her department car into the packed parking lot of Ledbetter's Diner and got out without waiting to see if Laney followed. After a perfunctory internal debate, Laney found an empty parking slot nearby and hurried to catch up.

All eyes turned to her when she entered the diner, and for a second, she had a painful flashback to her first day of law school. A combination of academic and hardship scholarships had paid her way into the University of Tennessee, where she'd been just another girl from the mountains, one of many. But law school at Duke University had been so different. Even the buffer of her undergrad work at UT hadn't prepared her for the culture shock.

Coming back home to Bitterwood had proved to be culture shock in reverse.

"You coming?" Ivy waited for her near the entrance.

Laney tamped down an unexpected return of shyness. "Yes."

Ivy waved at Maisey Ledbetter on her way across the crowded diner. Maisey waved back, her freckled face creasing with a big smile. Her eyebrows lifted slightly as she recognized Laney, as well, but her smile remained as warm as the oven-fresh biscuits she baked every morning for the diner's breakfast crowd.

"I don't come back here to Bitterwood as often as I used to," Laney admitted as she sat across from Ivy in one of the corner booths. "Mom and Janelle have started coming to Barrowville instead. Mom likes to shop at the outlet mall there."

"Never underestimate the lure of a brand-name bargain." Ivy shoved a menu toward Laney.

Laney shoved it back. "Maisey Ledbetter never changed her menu once in all the time I lived here growing up. I don't reckon she's changed it now."

"Well, would you listen to that accent," Ivy said softly, her tone teasing but friendly. "Welcome home, Charlane."

The door to the diner opened, admitting a cold draft that wafted all the way to the back where they sat, along with a lanky man in his thirties wearing a leather jacket and jeans. He was about three shades more tanned than anyone else in Bitterwood, pegging him immediately as an outsider and one from warmer climes at that.

"Is that him?" Laney asked Ivy.

Ivy followed her gaze. "Well, look-a-there. Surfer boy found his way to Ledbetter's."

Laney stole another glance, trying not to be obvious.

Sooner or later, she was going to have to approach Bitterwood's brand-new chief of police in order to do her job, but it wouldn't hurt to take his measure first.

Her second look added a few details to her first impression. Along with the tan, he had sandy-brown hair worn neatly cut but a little long, as if he were compromising between the expectations of his new job title and his inner beach bum. He was handsome, with laugh lines adding character to his tanned face and mossy-green eyes that turned sharply her way.

She dropped her gaze to the menu that still lay between her and Ivy. "I haven't been able to set a meeting with Chief Massey yet."

"He's been keeping a low profile at the station," Ivy murmured. "I get the feeling he wants to get his feet under him a little, scope out the situation before he has a big pow-wow with the whole department."

"He's pretty young for the job." Doyle Massey couldn't be that much older than her or Ivy. "He's what, thirty?"

"Thirty-three," Ivy answered, looking up when Maisey Ledbetter's youngest daughter, Christie, approached their table with her order book. Ivy ordered barbecue ribs and a sweet tea, but Laney squelched her craving for chicken-fried steak and ordered a turkey sandwich on wheat.

When she glanced at the door, Chief Massey had moved out of sight. She scanned the room and found him sitting by himself at a booth on the opposite side of the café.

"Maybe you should go talk to him now," Ivy suggested. "While he's a captive audience."

Laney's instinct was to stay right where she was, but she'd learned long ago to overcome her scared-squirrel impulse to freeze in place if she ever wanted to get anywhere in life. "Good idea."

She pushed to her feet before she could talk herself out of it.

He saw her coming halfway across the room, his deceptively somnolent gaze following her as she approached, like an alligator waiting for his dinner to come close enough to snap his powerful jaws. She ignored the fanciful thought and kept walking, right up to the booth where he sat.

She extended her hand and lifted her chin. "Chief Massey? My name is Laney Hanvey. I'm an investigator with the Ridge County District Attorney's office. I've left you a couple of messages."

He looked at her hand, then back up to her. "I got them."

She was on the verge of pulling her hand back when he leaned forward and closed his big, tanned hand around hers. He had rough, dry palms, suggesting at least a passing acquaintance with manual labor.

He let go of her hand and waved toward the empty seat across from him in the booth. "Can I buy you lunch?"

Not an alligator, she thought as she carefully sat across from him. More like a chameleon, able to go seamlessly from predator to charmer in a second flat. "I'm actually having lunch with one of your detectives." She glanced at the corner where Ivy sat, shamelessly watching them.

Chief Massey followed her gaze and gave a little wave at Ivy.

Ivy blushed a little at being caught staring, but she waved back and then pulled out her cell phone and made a show of checking her messages.

"Good detective, from what I'm told." Massey's full mouth curved. "She's the one who broke the serial-murder case a couple of months ago."

"She didn't have much help from her chief of detectives."

Massey's green-eyed gaze snapped forward to lock with hers. "Let's just get things out in the open, Ms. Hanvey. Can we do that?" His accent was Southern, but sleeker than her own mountain twang she'd worked so hard to conquer.

He'd come to Bitterwood from a place called Terrebonne on the Alabama Gulf Coast.

"Get things out in the open?" she repeated.

"You may think you're here to ferret out the snakes in our midst. But you're really here because your bosses in the county government have been wanting the Ridge County Sheriff's Department to swallow up small police forces like Bitterwood P.D. for a while now. Ridge County could justify the tax increase they're wanting to impose if they suddenly had a bigger jurisdiction to cover."

Laney hid her surprise. For a guy who looked like all he wanted to do was catch the next big wave, Doyle Massey had clearly done his homework about Ridge County politics. "Technically, Ridge County Sheriff's Department already covers Bitterwood."

"If invited to participate in investigations," Massey corrected gently.

"Or if the department in question is under investigation," she shot back firmly. "Which you are."

He gave a nod of acceptance. "Which we are. But I don't see the point of fooling ourselves about this. You and I may both want to clean up the Bitterwood Police Department. But we're not on the same team."

"Maybe not. But if you think my goal here is to shut your department down, you're wrong. And if you think I'll go along with whatever my bosses tell me to do, you're wrong about that, too. I'm looking for the truth, wherever that leads me."

He lifted his hands and clapped slowly. "Brava. An honest woman."

She felt her lips curling with anger at his sarcastic display. She pushed to her feet. "I expect full cooperation from the police department in my investigation."

He rose with her. "You'll have it."

Frustration swelled in her chest, strangling her as she

tried to think of something to say just so he wouldn't have the last word. But the trilling of her cell phone broke the tense silence rising between them. She grabbed the phone from her purse and saw her mother's phone number.

"I have to take this," she said and moved away, lifting the phone to her ears. "Hi, Mama."

"Oh, Charlane, thank God you answered. I've been tryin' not to worry, but she was supposed to be home hours ago, and she's always been so good about being on time—" Alice Hanvey sounded close to tears.

"Mama, slow down." Laney dropped into the booth across from Ivy, giving the other woman an apologetic look. "Janelle's late coming home from somewhere?"

"She and a couple of girls went hiking two days ago, but they were supposed to be home this morning in time for her to get to school. I knew I should have insisted they come home last night instead."

"Hiking where?"

"Up on Copperhead Ridge. At least, that's what she said. I've been trying to encourage her to get out and do things with her friends, like you said I should. I know I can be overprotective, but you can't be too careful these days—"

"She's old enough to go hiking with some friends. What do you know about these girls she went with?"

"They're good girls. You know the Adderlys—they live over on Belmont Road near the church? Their daddy's a county commissioner. I think you may have gone to school with his cousin Daniel—"

"I know them. They were supposed to be back home in time for school?" Laney interrupted before her mother went through the whole family tree. She knew the Adderlys well, even socializing with them sometimes as part of her job with the district attorney's office.

"Joy and Missy are crazy about hiking club, and you

know Janelle's been walking up and down those mountains since before she could talk good, so I didn't think it would be a problem. She's so good about keeping her word—"

"You've tried calling her on her cell phone?"

"Of course, but you know how reception can be in the mountains."

"Are you sure there weren't any boys going with them? Or maybe they were meeting some boys up on the mountain?"

"She's been sort of dating Britt Lomand, but I already called over there, and Britt's home. He's just getting over the flu—his mama said he's been home all weekend."

"Missy Adderly has a boyfriend."

"They broke up a month ago," Alice corrected. "Should I call the police and report her missing? It was awful cold last night on the mountain."

Laney glanced at Ivy, who was watching her through narrowed eyes. "The police don't normally drop everything to look for a teenager who's a little late getting home, but I'll see what I can do."

"Please call me if you find out anything."

"You call me if you hear from her. I'll talk to you soon, Mama. Try not to worry too much. Jannie's probably just lost track of the time, or maybe she was running late and went straight to school."

"I never thought of that," Alice admitted. "I'll call the school, ask if she's showed up."

"Good idea. Call when you know something." She shut off her phone and met Ivy's curious gaze. "My sister went hiking up in the hills over the weekend with a couple of girlfriends, and she's late getting back home. She was supposed to be home in time to shower and dress for school."

"Cutting it close."

Laney saw the conflicted thoughts playing out behind

Ivy's expressive eyes. "Yeah, I know. At that age, they think they get to make their own rules. But Janelle's pretty levelheaded."

"Guess that runs in the family."

Laney wasn't sure whether Ivy meant the comparison as a compliment. Being thought of as a Goody Two-shoes wasn't exactly the goal of any high school student—she herself had chafed under the moniker through her high school years. Calling someone a good girl back then had been the same as calling her dull.

Maybe Janelle was rebelling against the perception herself by skipping school and making everybody worry?

She punched in her sister's cell phone number and waited for an answer. It didn't go immediately to voice mail as it usually did when Janelle's phone was out of range of a cell signal. After four rings, there was a click.

But it wasn't her sister's voice she heard on the other line. Nor was it Janelle's overly cute voice-mail message.

Instead she heard only the sound of breathing and, faintly in the distance, the rustle of leaves.

"Hello?" she said into the receiver.

The breathing continued for a moment. Then the line went dead.

"Did she answer?" Ivy asked.

Laney shook her head. "But someone was on the other end of the line—"

Ivy's phone rang, the trill jangling Laney's taut nerves. Ivy shot her a look of apology and answered. "What's up, Antoine?"

The detective's brow creased deeply, and she darted a look at Laney so full of dread that Laney's breath caught in her chest.

"On my way," Ivy said and hung up the phone. "I've got to run."

"What is it?" Laney asked, swallowing her dread as

Ivy dug in her pocket for money, carefully not meeting Laney's eyes.

"Someone called in a body. I'm heading to the crime scene to see what we can sort out." Ivy put a ten on the table. "Ask Christie to box up my order and put it in the fridge. I'll pick it up later."

Laney caught Ivy's arm. "Where's the crime scene?"

Ivy's gaze slid up to meet hers. "Up on Copperhead Ridge."

Chapter Two

"What's she doing here?" Doyle Massey asked Ivy Hawkins as she crossed to where he and Detective Antoine Parsons stood near the body.

On the other side of the yellow crime-scene tape, Laney Hanvey stood with her arms crossed tightly over her body as if trying to hold herself together. Her face was pale except where the hike up the cold mountain had reddened her nose and cheeks. Her blue eyes met his, sharp with dread.

Ivy looked over her shoulder. "Her sister went hiking up here over the weekend and didn't show up this morning when she was supposed to. I couldn't talk her out of coming."

He dragged his gaze from Laney's worried face and nodded at the body. "Female. Late teens, early twenties. Do you know what the sister looks like?"

Ivy edged closer to the body, trying not to disturb the area directly around her. "It's not Janelle Hanvey. It's Missy Adderly. No ID?"

"Not that we've found. We've tried not to disturb the body too much," Detective Parsons answered for Doyle.

"TBI on the way?" Ivy asked.

It took Doyle a moment to realize she was talking about the Tennessee Bureau of Investigation. He'd have to bone up on the local terminology. "Yeah."

Doyle found his gaze traveling back to Laney Hanvey's

huddled figure. He left his detectives discussing the case and crossed to where she stood.

She looked up at him, fear bright in her eyes. "Chief."

"It's not your sister."

A visible shudder of relief rippled through her, but the fear in her eyes didn't go away. "One of the Adderly girls?"

"Detective Hawkins says it's Missy Adderly."

Laney lifted one hand to her mouth, horror darkening her eyes. "God."

"Your sister was hiking up here with the Adderly sisters this weekend?"

Laney nodded slowly, dropping her hand. "They left Friday night to go hiking and camping. My mother said Janelle and the girls had planned to be back home first thing this morning so Jannie and Missy could get to school on time." Her throat bobbed nervously. "Jannie's senior year. She was so excited about graduating and going off to college."

"She's a good student?" he asked carefully.

Laney's gaze had drifted toward the clump of detectives surrounding the body. It snapped back to meet Doyle's. "A very good student. A good girl." Her lips twisted wryly as she said the words. "I know that's what most families say about their kids, but in this case, it's true. Janelle's a good girl. She's never given my mother any trouble. Ever."

There's always a first time, Doyle thought. And a good girl on the cusp of leaving home and seeing the world was ripe for it.

"Was it an accident?" There was dreadful hope in Laney's voice. Doyle felt sick about having to dash it.

"No."

She released a long sigh, her breath swirling through the cold air in a wispy cloud of condensation. "Then you may have three victims, not just one."

He nodded, hating the fear in her eyes but knowing he

would be doing her no favors to give her false hope. "We've already called in local trackers to start looking around for the other girls."

"I called her cell phone. Back at the diner. Someone answered but didn't speak." Laney hugged herself more tightly.

Doyle felt the unexpected urge to wrap his own arms around her, to help her hold herself together. "Could it have been your sister on the other end?"

"I want to believe it could," she admitted, once again dragging her straying gaze away from the body and back to him. "But I don't think it was."

"Did you hear anything at all?"

"Breathing, I think. The sound of rustling, like the wind through dead leaves. Nothing else. Then the call cut off."

"Anything that might give us an idea of a location?"

"I don't know. I can't think."

"It's okay." He put his hand on her shoulder, felt the nervous ripple of her body beneath his touch. She was like a skittish colt, all fear and nerves.

He knew exactly what that kind of terror felt like.

"No, it's not." She shook off his hand and visibly straightened her spine, her chin coming up to stab the cold air. "I know the clock is ticking."

Tough lady, he thought. "You said you heard rustling. What about birds? Did you hear any birds?"

Her eyes narrowed, her focus shifting inward. "No, I didn't hear any birds."

"What about the breathing? Could you tell whether it was a man or a woman?"

"Man," she answered, her gaze focusing on his face again. "He didn't vocalize, exactly, but there was a masculine quality to his breathing. I don't know how to explain it—"

"Was he breathing regularly? Slow? Fast?"

"Fast," she answered. "I think that's what was so creepy about it. He was almost panting."

Panting could mean a lot of things, Doyle reminded himself as a cold draft slid beneath the collar of his jacket, sending chill bumps down his back. It could have been a hiker who wasn't in good shape. Might not have been anyone connected to this murder or the girls' disappearance, for that matter. Maybe someone had found the phone, answered the ring but was too out of breath to speak.

Or maybe he was breathing hard because he'd just chased down three teenage girls like the predator he was.

He tried not to telegraph his grim thoughts to Laney Hanvey, but she was no fool. She didn't need his help imagining the worst.

"She's not alive, is she?"

"I don't know."

"But the odds are—"

"I'm not a gambler," he said firmly. "I don't deal with odds. I deal with facts. And the facts are, we have only one body so far."

"Who's out looking for the other girls?"

At the moment, he had to admit, no one was. It took time to form a search party. "We've put out the call to nearby agencies. The county boys, the park patrol, Blount and Sevier County agencies. They're going to lend us officers for a search."

"That's not soon enough." Laney turned and started hiking around the perimeter of the crime-scene tape, heading up the trail.

Doyle looked back at the crime scene and saw Ivy Hawkins looking at him, her brow furrowed. She gave a nod toward Laney, as if to say she and Parsons had the crime scene covered.

He was the chief of police now, not another investigator. While Bitterwood might be a small force, he didn't need to micromanage his detectives. They'd already proved they could do a good job—he'd familiarized himself with their work before he took the job.

Meanwhile, he had a public-relations problem stalking up the mountain while he waffled about leaving a crime scene that was clearly under control.

He ducked under the crime-scene tape and headed up the mountain after Laney Hanvey.

"I'M NOT GOING to be handled out of looking for my sister," Laney growled as she heard footsteps catching up behind her on the hiking trail.

"I'm just here to help."

She faltered to a stop, turning to look at Doyle Massey. He wasn't exactly struggling to keep up with her—life on the beach had clearly kept him in pretty good shape. But he was out of his element.

She'd grown up in these mountains. Her mother had always joked she was half mountain goat. She knew these hills as well as she knew her own soul. "You'll slow me down."

"Maybe that's a good thing."

She glared at him, her rising terror looking for a target. "My sister is out here somewhere and I'm going to find her."

The look Doyle gave her was full of pity. The urge to slap that expression off his face was so strong she had to clench her hands. "You're rushing off alone into the woods where a man with a gun has just committed a murder."

"A gun?" She couldn't stop her gaze from slanting toward the crime scene. "She was shot?"

"Two rounds to the back of the head."

She closed her eyes, the remains of the cucumber sandwich she'd eaten at Sequoyah House rising in her throat.

She stumbled a few feet away from Doyle Massey and gave up fighting the nausea.

After her stomach was empty, she crouched in the underbrush, battling dry heaves and giving in to the hot tears burning her eyes. The heat of Massey's hand on her back was comforting, even though she was embarrassed by her display.

"I will help you search," he said in a low, gentle tone. "But I want you to take a minute to just breathe and think. Okay? I want you to think about your sister and where you think she'd go. Do you know?"

She reached into her pocket and pulled out a tissue to wipe her mouth. Before she'd finished, Massey's hand extended in front of her eyes, holding out a roll of breath mints.

"Thank you," she said, taking one.

"I understand you don't live here in Bitterwood."

She looked up at him. "I live in Barrowville. It's about ten minutes away. But I grew up here. I know this mountain."

"But do you know where your sister and her friends would go up here?"

"I called my mother on the drive here. She said Jannie and the others were planning to keep to the trail so they could bunk down in the shelters. They're sort of like the shelters you find on the Appalachian Trail—not as nice, but they serve the same basic purpose." She waved her hand toward the trail shelter a half mile up the trail, frustrated by all the talking. "Has anyone looked up there?"

"Not yet." He laid his hand on her back, the heat of his touch warming her through her clothes. She wanted to be annoyed by his presumptuousness, but the truth was, she found his touch comforting, to the point that she had to squelch the urge to throw herself into his arms and let her pent-up tears flow.

But she had to keep her head. Her mother was already a basket case with fear for her daughter. Someone in the family needed to stay in control.

"Ivy called in the missing-person report on Jannie." She stepped away from his touch, straightening her slumping spine. "Has anyone contacted the Adderlys?"

The chief looked back at the crime scene. "No. I guess I should be the one to do it."

"No," she said firmly. "You're new here. You're a stranger. Let one of the others do it. Craig Bolen and Dave Adderly are old friends."

Massey's green eyes narrowed. "Bolen…"

"Your new captain of detectives," she said.

"I knew that." He looked a little sheepish. "I'll call him, let him know what's up." He pulled out his cell phone.

"You probably can't get a signal on that," she warned. "Go tell Ivy to call it in on her radio."

His lips quirked slightly as he put away his phone and walked back down the trail to the crime scene. He turned to look at her a couple of times, as if to make sure she wasn't taking advantage of his distraction to hare off on her own.

The idea was tempting, since she could almost hear the minutes ticking away in her head. She hadn't gotten a good look at Missy's body, but she'd seen enough of the blood to know that the wounds were relatively fresh. Even taking the cold weather into account, the murder couldn't have happened much earlier than the night before, and more likely that morning.

Which meant there might be time left, still, to find the other girls alive.

"Bolen's going to go talk to the Adderlys." Massey returned, looking grim. "He was pretty broken up about it when I gave him the news."

"He's seen the girls grow up. Everyone here did." She glanced at the grim faces of the detectives and uniformed cops preserving the crime scene as they waited for the Tennessee Bureau of Investigation crime-scene unit to arrive. "This place isn't like big cities. Nobody much has the stomach for whistling through the graveyard here. Not when you know all the bodies."

"I'm not from a big city," he said quietly. "Terrebonne's not much more than a dot on the Gulf Coast map."

"So this is a lateral move for you?" she asked as they started back up the trail, trying to distract herself from what she feared she'd find ahead.

"No, it's upward. I was just a deputy investigator on the county sheriff's squad down there. Here, I'm the top guy." He didn't sound as if he felt on top of anything. She slanted a look his way and found him frowning as he gazed up the wooded trail. She followed his gaze but saw nothing strange.

"What's wrong?"

His eyes narrowed. "I don't know. I thought—" He shook his head. "Probably a squirrel."

She caught his arm when he started to move forward, shaking her head when he started to speak. Behind her, she could still hear the faint murmur of voices around the crime scene, but ahead, there was nothing but the cold breeze rattling the lingering dead leaves in the trees.

"No birdsong." She let go of his arm.

"Should there be?"

She nodded. "Sparrows, wrens, crows, jays—they should be busy in the trees up here."

"Something's spooked them?"

She nodded, her chest aching with dread. All the old tales she'd heard all her life about haints and witches in the hills seemed childish and benign compared to the reality of what might lie ahead of them on the trail. But she couldn't turn back.

If there was a chance Jannie was still alive, time was the enemy.

"Let's go," she said. "We have to chance it."

"I'm not going to run into a pissed-off bear out there, am I?"

She could tell from the tone of his voice that he was trying to distract her from her worries. "It's not the bears that scare me."

"You don't have to go now. We can wait for a bigger search party."

She looked him over, head to foot, gauging his mettle. His gaze met hers steadily, a hint of humor glinting in his eyes as if he knew exactly what she was doing. Physically, there was little doubt he could keep up with her pace on the trail, at least for a while. He looked fit, well built and healthy. And she wasn't in top form, having lived in the lowlands for several years, not hiking regularly.

But did he have the internal fortitude to handle life in the hills? Outsiders weren't always welcomed with open arms, especially by the criminal class he'd be dealing with. Most of the people were good-hearted folks just trying to make a living and love their families, but there were enclaves where life was brutal and cruel. Places where children were commodities, women could be either monsters or chattel and men wallowed in the basest sort of venality.

She supposed that was true of most places, if you scratched deep enough beneath the surface of civilization, but here in the hills, there were plenty of places nobody cared to go, places where evil could thrive without the disinfectant of sunlight. It took a tough man to uphold the law in these parts.

It remained to be seen if Doyle Massey was tough enough.

"You want to wait?" she asked.

"No." He gave a nod toward the trail. "You're the native. Lead the way."

Copperhead Ridge couldn't compete with the higher ridges in the Smokies in terms of altitude, but it was far enough above sea level that the higher they climbed, the thinner the air became. Laney was used to it, but she could see that Doyle, who'd probably lived at sea level his whole life, was finding the going harder than he'd expected.

Reaching the first of a handful of public shelters through the trees ahead, she was glad for an excuse to stop. She'd grabbed some bottled waters from the diner when she and Ivy left, an old habit she'd formed years ago when heading into the mountains. She'd stowed them in the backpack she kept in her car and had brought with her up the mountain.

Now she dug the waters from the pack and handed a bottle to Doyle as they reached the shelter. He took the water gratefully, unscrewing the top and taking a long swig as he wandered over to the wooden pedestal supporting the box with the trail log.

She left him to it, walking around the side of the shelter to the open front.

What she saw inside stole her breath.

"Laney?" Doyle's voice was barely audible through the thunder of her pulse in her ears.

The shelter was still occupied. A woman lay facedown over a rolled-up thermal sleeping bag, blood staining her down jacket and the flannel of the bag, as well as the leaves below. Laney recognized the sleeping bag. She'd given it to her sister for Christmas.

Janelle.

The paralysis in Laney's limbs released, and she stumbled forward to where her sister lay, her heart hammering a cadence of dread.

Please be breathing please be breathing please be breathing.

She felt a slow but steady pulse when she touched her fingers to her sister's bloodstained throat.

"Laney?" Doyle's voice was in her ear, the warmth of his body enveloping her like a hug.

"It's Janelle," she said. "She's still alive."

"That's a lot of blood," Doyle said doubtfully. He reached out and checked her pulse himself, a puzzled look on his face.

"She's been shot, hasn't she?" Laney ran her hands lightly over her sister's still body, looking for other injuries. But all the blood seemed to be coming from a long furrow that snaked a gory path across the back of her sister's head.

"Not sure," he answered succinctly, pulling out his cell phone.

"Can you get a signal?" she asked doubtfully, wondering how quickly she could run down the mountain for help.

"It's low, but let's give it a try." He dialed 911. "If I get through, what should I tell the dispatcher?"

"Tell them it's the first shelter on Copperhead Mountain on the southern end." Laney's hands shook a little as she gently pushed the hair away from her sister's face. Janelle's expression was peaceful, as if she were only sleeping. But even though she was still alive, there was a hell of a lot of damage a bullet could do to a brain. If even a piece of shrapnel made it through her skull—

"They're on the way." Doyle put his hand on her shoulder.

But they couldn't be fast about it, Laney knew. Mountain rescues were tests of patience, and a victim's endurance.

"Hang in there, Jannie." She looked at Doyle. "Do you think it's safe to move this bedroll out from under her? We need to cover her up. It's freezing out here, and she could already be going into shock."

She saw a brief flash of reluctance in Doyle's expression before he nodded, helping her ease the roll out from beneath Janelle. She unzipped the roll, trying not to spill off any of the collected blood. The outside of the sleeping bag was water-resistant, so she didn't have much luck.

"Sorry to ruin your crime scene," she muttered.

"Life comes first." He sounded distracted.

She looked up to find him peering at a corner of something sticking out from under the edge of the bedroll. He pulled a handkerchief from his pocket and grasped the corner, tugging the object free.

It was a photograph, Laney saw, partially stained by her sister's blood. But what she could still see of the photograph sent ice rattling through her veins.

The photo showed Janelle and her two companions, lying right here in this very shelter, fast asleep.

Doyle turned the photograph over to the blank side. Only it wasn't blank. There were three words written there in blocky marker.

Good night, princesses.

Chapter Three

Doyle hated hospitals. He'd visited his share of them over the years, both as a cop and a patient. He hated the mysterious beeps and dings, the clatter of gurney wheels rolling across scuffed linoleum floors, the antiseptic smells and the haggard faces of both the sick and the waiting.

He hated how quickly everything could go to hell.

He sat a small distance from Laney Hanvey and her mother, Alice, a woman in her late fifties who, at the moment, looked a decade older. Mrs. Hanvey looked distraught and guilty as hell.

"I shouldn't have let her go camping. It was so stupid of me."

Laney squeezed her mother's hand. "You don't want to stifle her. Not when she's made so much progress."

Doyle looked at her with narrowed eyes, wondering what she meant. But before he'd had a chance to form a theory, the door to the waiting room opened and a man in green surgical scrubs entered, looking serious but not particularly grim.

"Mrs. Hanvey?" he greeted Laney's mother, who had stood at his entrance. "I'm Dr. Bedford. I've been taking care of Janelle in the E.R. The good news is, she's awake and relatively alert, but she's sustained a concussion, and given her medical history, we're going to want to be very careful with that."

Doyle looked from the doctor's face to Laney's, more curious than before.

"So the bullet didn't enter her brain?" Laney's question made her mother visibly flinch.

"The titanium plate deflected the path of the bullet. It made a bit of a mess in the soft tissue at the base of her skull, but it missed anything vital. We did have to shave a long patch of her hair. She wasn't very happy to hear that," Dr. Bedford added with a rueful smile, making Laney and her mother smile, as well.

Doyle couldn't keep silent any longer. "Does she remember what happened to her?"

The doctor looked startled by his question. "You are—?"

"Doyle Massey. Bitterwood chief of police. The attack on Ms. Hanvey took place in my jurisdiction."

The doctor gave him a thoughtful look. "She remembers hiking, but beyond that, everything's pretty fuzzy." He turned back to Laney and her mother. "She keeps asking about her two friends, but all we could tell her is that they weren't with her when she was brought in. Just be warned, she's in the repetitive stage of a concussion, so she may ask you that question or another several times without remembering you've already answered her."

"Were you able to retrieve a bullet?" Doyle asked.

"Actually, yes," Dr. Bedford answered. "The TBI has already put in a request for it. They're sending a courier."

"How soon do you think she can go home?" Mrs. Hanvey asked.

"Because of her medical history and the trauma of being shot, I'd really like to keep her here at least a couple of days. Even beyond her concussion, the path of the bullet wound is pretty extensive and we're going to work hard to prevent infection. We'll see how her injuries respond to treatment and make a decision from there."

"Can we see her?"

"She's probably on her way up to her room. Ask the nurse at the desk—she'll tell you where you can find her."

Doyle followed Laney and her mother out of the waiting room behind the doctor, trying to stay back enough to avoid Laney's attention.

He should have known better.

Laney whipped around to face him as her mother walked on to the nurse's station. "You're not seriously following us into her room?"

"I need to talk to her about what happened on the mountain."

"You heard the doctor. She doesn't remember."

"Yet."

Laney's lips thinned with anger. "I know it's important to talk to her. But can't you give us a few minutes alone with her? When we came here this morning, we weren't sure we were ever going to see her alive again."

Old pain nudged at Doyle's conscience. "I know. I'm sorry and I'm very happy and relieved that the news is good."

Laney's eyes softened. "Thank you."

"But there's still a girl unaccounted for. And anything your sister can remember may be important. Including what happened *before* they were attacked."

Laney glanced back at her mother, who was still talking to the desk nurse. She lowered her voice. "I don't think we'll find Joy Adderly alive. Do you?"

He didn't. But he hadn't expected to find Janelle alive, either. Not after seeing Missy Adderly's body in the leaves off the mountain trail.

"I think we have to proceed as if she's still alive and needs our help," he said finally. "Don't you?"

She looked at him, guilt in her clear blue eyes. "Yes. Of course."

He immediately felt bad for pushing her. Her priority

had to be her sister, not his case. "Look, I need to make some calls. I'll give you and your mother some time alone with your sister if you'll promise you'll come get me in an hour to ask her a few questions. Just do me a favor, okay?"

"What's that?"

"Try not to talk about what happened up on the mountain. Just talk about anything else. I don't want to contaminate her memories before I get a chance to talk to her."

"Okay." She reached across the space between them, closing her hand over his forearm. "Thank you."

He watched her walk to the elevator with her arm around her mother's waist. As they entered and turned to face the doors, she graced him with a slight smile that made his chest tighten.

The doors closed, and he felt palpably alone.

Shaking it off, he walked back to the waiting room and called the police station first. His executive assistant was a tall reed of a woman with steel-gray hair and sharp blue eyes named Ellen Flatley. Apparently she'd been assistant to two chiefs of police before him and would probably outlast him, as well. She saw the police station as her own personal territory and had a tendency to guard it like a high-strung German shepherd.

"There are two teams of eight searchers each on the mountains, but it's a lot of territory and slow going." She answered his query in a tone of voice that suggested he should have known these facts already. "Plus, the sun will be going down soon, and they'll have to stop the search. The coroner's picked up poor Missy Adderly's body, God rest her soul. He said he's going to call in the state lab to handle the postmortem, like you asked."

She didn't sound as if she approved of that decision, either, but he couldn't help that. Bitterwood had hired him to make those kinds of decisions. They'd hired Ellen to help him execute those decisions, not make them for him.

"Thank you, Ellen."

Her frosty silence on the other end of the phone told him he'd apparently made another breach of police-department etiquette.

"Can you give me the cell numbers for Detectives Hawkins and Parsons?" he asked.

She rattled off the numbers quickly, and he punched them into the phone's memory. "Will there be anything else, Chief Massey?"

"Yes, one more thing. Do you know if Bolen's been able to reach the Adderly family with the news about Missy?"

"He hasn't called in, but he headed over there about fifteen minutes ago, so I imagine he's told them by now." Her voice softened with her next question. "Chief, is there anything new on the other girl, Joy?"

"No, not yet. You'll probably hear as soon as I do, if not sooner. If you do hear anything, please let me know at once."

"Certainly, sir."

"Thank you, Mrs. Flatley, for your help."

There was a hint of a smile in her voice when she answered. "Just doing my job. Do you want me to forward your calls to your cell?"

"No, just take messages, unless it's urgent."

He ended the call, then dialed Ivy Hawkins's number.

She answered on the second ring, the connection spotty. "Hawkins."

"This is Massey. Catch me up."

"TBI crime-scene unit finally arrived. I sent some of them over to the trail shelter to get what they could find there, too. Parsons is with that crew. I'm sticking with the original scene, helping out with the grid search. But we're running out of daylight." Her voice tightened. "What's the news on Janelle Hanvey?"

"Better than we had a right to hope for." He outlined

what the doctor had told them, keeping it vague in deference to the girl's privacy rights. "She's awake and the family's with her."

"I can be in Knoxville in about thirty minutes if you'd like me to question the girl."

"I can handle it."

There was a thick pause on the other end of the line, reminding him of the frosty reception he'd gotten from Ellen Flatley earlier. "Okay."

"Is there a problem, Hawkins?"

"Permission to speak freely, sir?"

He grinned at the phone. "Please."

"The job of chief of police is primarily a political position. You supervise, schmooze, shake hands with the town bigwigs and basically present a nice, trustworthy face for the public. Witness interviews, though—"

"We're not a big city. We all have to wear different hats. The town council made that clear when they hired me. And how often do you get two violent-crime victims in one day?"

"Recently? More often than I like," she answered drily. "But, understood, sir. We're spread thin by this case already."

"Call me at this number if you need me." Ending the call, he looked at the round-faced clock on the waiting-room wall. After five already. But still thirty minutes before he could go to Janelle Hanvey's hospital room and ask the questions drumming a restless rhythm in his brain.

Patience, he feared, was not one of his virtues.

"WHAT ABOUT MISSY and Joy? Where are they?"

Laney squeezed her sister's hand gently. "I don't know, sweetie." She kept herself from exchanging looks with her mother, knowing that Janelle was bright enough to see the tension between them, even in her concussed state. "How about you? Head still hurting?"

Janelle smiled a loopy smile. "Not so much. The doctor said they stuck me with a local anesthetic, so the wound won't be bothering me for a while."

"Good."

Janelle drifted off for a few minutes, just long enough for Laney to give her mother a look of relief. Then she stirred again and asked, for the third time since Laney had entered the room, "Laney, where are Missy and Joy?"

She squeezed Janelle's hand again and repeated, "I don't know, sweetie."

There was a knock on the hospital-room door. Laney's mother went to answer it. She came back and touched Laney's shoulder. "Chief Massey would like to talk to you outside."

She traded places with her mother and opened the hospital-room door to find Doyle Massey leaning against the corridor wall. He didn't change position when he saw her, just turned his head and flashed her a toothy smile. "How's your sister doin'?"

Damn, but he could turn on the charm when he wanted to. "As well as can be expected, I think. She's still repeating herself a lot, but the doctor said that should pass soon."

"Has she said anything about what happened up there?"

Laney shook her head. "But she keeps asking about her friends. All we've told her so far is that we don't know where they are."

Doyle pushed away from the wall, turning to face her. He touched her arm lightly. "The coroner's picked up Missy Adderly's body and called in the state lab to conduct the postmortem."

"Has the family been contacted?"

"My assistant said Craig Bolen left to meet with them

about forty-five minutes ago. So I'm sure they know by now."

She shook her head, feeling sick. "Those poor people."

His gaze slid toward the door of her sister's hospital room. "She has a plate in her head?"

"Car accident when she was ten. It was bad." Laney tugged her sweater more tightly around her, as if she could ward off the memories as easily as she could thwart a chill. But she couldn't, of course. The memories of those terrible days would never go away. "The accident killed our brother." She released a long sigh.

"I'm sorry."

She looked up at him, seeing real sympathy in his eyes, not just the perfunctory kind. "I was a sophomore in college. I skipped a couple of semesters so I could come back home and help my mom deal with everything. Our dad had passed away from cancer only a year earlier. And then, so suddenly, Bradley was dead and Jannie was just hanging on by a thread—"

"Bradley was your brother?"

She nodded. "He was seventeen. Jannie had a softball game and Mama was working, so Bradley said he'd take her. He was a good driver. The police say there wasn't anything he could have done. The other driver was wasted, slammed right through an intersection and T-boned Bradley's truck. He was killed instantly, and Jannie had a depressed skull fracture. She had to relearn everything. Put her behind in school."

"How far behind?"

"Three years. Jannie's twenty. But she's only seventeen in terms of her maturity and mental age. There were a few years when we didn't think she'd ever get that far, but the doctors say she should develop normally enough from here on." She glanced back at the closed door. "Unless this sets her back even more."

"How does she seem?"

"Like herself," Laney admitted. "A little disoriented, but normal enough."

Doyle touched her arm again. It seemed to be a habit with him, a way to connect to the person he was talking to. Unfortunately, it seemed to be having a completely disarming effect on her. She'd just told him more about her family than she'd told anyone in ages, including the people she'd worked with now for almost five years.

Maybe he was a better cop than she had realized.

"You think it's okay for me to go in there and talk to your sister now?" His hand made one more light sweep down her arm before dropping to his side.

"I think so. They're not giving her anything like a sedative—they don't want her to sleep much while they're observing her for the concussion."

He looked toward the door. "Did the doctors tell you whether or not it would be okay to tell her the truth about Missy Adderly?"

Laney recoiled at the thought. "They didn't say, but—"

"I know you want to protect her, especially now. And if we didn't have a missing girl out there somewhere—"

"I know." She'd experienced only an hour's worth of sick worry about her sister's whereabouts. The Adderlys were still in that hell, made worse by knowing that one of their girls was dead. "Okay. But I want to be in there with you when you talk to her. I'm pretty sure my mother will want to be there, too."

"Fine. But you have to let me ask her the hard questions. You know we're working with a ticking clock."

She knew. If there was any chance Joy Adderly was still alive, time was critical.

Her sister was awake when they entered the hospital room. Laney introduced Doyle to Janelle, explaining he was there to ask her some questions. Her mother looked worried, but Janelle looked almost relieved. "Do *you* know where Joy and Missy are?"

Doyle pulled up the chair Laney had vacated, getting down to Janelle's eye level. "I know where Missy is, but it's bad news."

Janelle's eyes struggled to focus on his face. "She's dead, isn't she?"

"I'm sorry. We found Missy this morning, shortly before we found you."

Her eyes filled with tears. "Was she shot like I was?"

He nodded, his expression gentle with compassion and something else, some dark, private sadness hovering behind his green eyes.

Only the sound of Janelle's soft sniffles dragged Laney's gaze away from the sudden mystery the new chief posed. Laney grabbed a couple of tissues from the box the hospital supplied and handed them to her sister. Janelle wiped her eyes and cleared her throat. "What about Joy?"

"We haven't found Joy yet."

"You think she's alive?" Hope trembled in Janelle's soft voice.

"We hope she is," he answered. "We're looking for her. We have searchers up on the mountain right now."

"I wish I could remember." Janelle put her hand to her head. "It's like I have bubbles in my head that keep popping and fizzing. It's all I can hear or see."

Laney crossed to her sister's side and stroked her hair away from her face. "It's the concussion, baby. It'll clear up soon."

"What's the last thing you *do* remember?" Doyle asked.

"We were going hiking. It was Joy's twenty-first birthday, and that's how she wanted to celebrate." Janelle's pale lips curved in a faint smile. "That's so Joy. She loves the mountains more than anything. She just got hired by the Ridge County Tourism Board—did you know that? She's supposed to start work next Monday. If anyone can turn us into a tourism mecca, it's Joy."

Anger, fear and grief braided through the center of Laney's chest.

"Do you remember reaching the first shelter on the mountain?" Doyle asked.

"Yeah. Joy wanted to camp out in the open, but Missy and I—" Her voice broke, but she cleared her throat and continued. "Missy and I told her it was too cold to sleep out in the open. So we stopped at the shelter."

"Did you see anyone on the mountain before then? Other hikers?"

Janelle's brow creased. "I don't know. I remember reaching the shelter. I remember going to bed—that new sleeping bag Laney got me for Christmas was so warm, it was almost like being in my own bed." She shot a grin at Laney, but it faded as fast as it had appeared. "I think I was the first one to fall asleep."

"What about on the hike up—do you remember meeting anyone?"

"I think there might have been someone...." Janelle worried with the IV tube, wincing as it tugged the cannula in the back of her hand. "I can't remember. I can't." She closed her eyes, her forehead still wrinkled.

"Can't we let her rest?" Alice Hanvey had been quiet during Doyle's questioning, but she rose now, a mother tiger pouncing to her cub's defense.

"She can't remember right now," Laney agreed, putting herself in the narrow space between Doyle and her sister's hospital bed. She lowered her voice. "In ten minutes, she'll probably be asking us where Missy and Joy are, and we're going to have to tell her the truth this time. I wish she could help you. I promise you, I do. But she can't. Not yet."

"Maybe not ever," Alice warned in a half whisper. "The last time she had a head injury, she lost most of her memories. She had to relearn almost everything. We still don't know how much damage the concussion's going to do."

"It was worth a shot." Doyle stood, pinning Laney between his lean, hard body and the hospital bed. His eyebrows quirked as she took a swift breath.

He smelled impossibly good, given that he'd just hiked up and down a mountain. She herself felt rumpled and sweaty, but he smelled like the beach on a sunny day, all fresh ocean breezes and a hint of sunscreen.

"Join me outside a sec?" He cupped her elbow, nudging her toward the door.

"Ray," Janelle murmured from the hospital bed.

Doyle froze, his hand still on Laney's arm. "I'm sorry?"

Janelle's eyes drifted open. "The guy we met. I can't remember much about him, but he said his name was Ray." Her eyes fluttered closed again.

Doyle stared at her in consternation, clearly tempted to wake her back up and ask more questions. Laney tugged his arm, pulling him with her toward the door. He followed, frustration evident in the fierce set of his features.

"Do you know anyone named Ray?" he asked outside the room.

"There are a few men named Ray around here, but she knows them all. Didn't it sound as if she didn't know this guy?"

He nodded slowly, looking unsatisfied. "I'll run the information past my detectives. Maybe one of them will have an idea."

"Listen, I've been thinking." She glanced at the closed door to Janelle's room and lowered her voice. "The doctors say once they get Janelle out of the danger zone with the concussion, they'll probably start giving her pain medicine for the head wound, so I don't know how helpful it'll be for me to sit here at her side, hoping she tells us something solid we can use. I need to be doing something more active to help find Joy."

"You want to join a search party?"

"I'm a good hiker. I know the mountains as well as anyone up there."

"Good. Because I'm planning to join the search myself, and I don't know a thing about these hills. I could use someone to show me the way." He brushed his hand down her arm again, the touch almost familiar now. "But it won't be tonight. They'll shut down the search parties once the sun sets."

"I can be ready at sunup."

He smiled. "I'll be there."

Laney slipped back into the room, her heart catching as she saw her mother sitting with her head on Janelle's leg, tears staining her cheeks.

She sat up quickly, giving Laney a sheepish smile. "My baby," she said simply, fresh tears slipping down her cheeks.

Laney bent and gave her mother a fierce hug. "I'm going up the mountain to join the search for Joy in the morning, so I have to leave soon to get some sleep. Are you going to stay here tonight?"

Alice nodded, patting her cheek. "I'll be fine. Go find that girl. The Adderlys have lost enough already, don't you think?"

Laney kissed her mother's damp cheek. "Take care of our girl."

Remembering she'd driven her mother to the hospital, she pulled the car key from her key ring and handed it to Alice. "I'll see if I can catch the chief and get a ride with him. If you need anything, take my car."

Laney left her sister's room and hurried down the corridor toward the elevator bank. Doyle was still there, she saw with surprise. "Chief, wait up."

He turned to face her, a bleak look in his eyes. He was holding his phone with a tight-fingered grip.

Fear shot through her. "What's wrong?"

"The searchers found another body."

Chapter Four

Laney's face blanched at his blunt words, and Doyle quickly closed his hand over her arm, bending to level his gaze with hers. "It wasn't Joy Adderly. It's a male, and it looks like he's been up there awhile."

He saw a flicker of relief in those baby blues, quickly eclipsed by grim curiosity. "How long?"

"Weeks at least."

"Any ID?"

"Didn't have any on him. The searchers have cordoned off the spot and one of my deputies is on the way up there."

"There are only a couple of missing-persons cases outstanding in the county," she said, looking less pale and more in charge. She would know, he realized, being part of the county prosecutor's team.

"That part of the mountain is under Bitterwood's jurisdiction," he said firmly, in case she was thinking of starting a jurisdiction fight.

One side of her mouth curved. "I'm not sure the county sheriff will agree."

"Bitterwood is still autonomous at the moment," Doyle shot back, trying to keep his voice both light and firm. He didn't want to antagonize her, but he didn't want to let her walk all over him, either. Even though she had a way of getting under his skin without even seeming to try.

He'd always been a sucker for a pair of blue eyes and

a Southern drawl. And her mountain twang was just different enough from the girls he'd known back home in south Alabama to add a hint of the exotic to her appeal. It was a potent combination, especially added to her obviously quick mind. He was going to have to be on his guard around Laney Hanvey.

The job ahead of him was difficult enough as it was. The last thing he could afford was another complication. Especially a complication who could cost him his job with one word to her bosses.

"I need to leave the car for my mother," she told him as they stepped into the elevator together. "Think you could give me a ride?"

"To Barrowville?"

The look she sent blazing his way packed a punch. "To the crime scene."

"You're not a cop, you know." Doyle sounded somewhere between frustrated and amused.

Laney kept her voice even and, she hoped, nonconfrontational. "The county government's policies regarding public integrity investigations give me a great deal of leeway in police matters while your department is under scrutiny."

"Even ride alongs under duress?"

"I'm not sure I'd term this 'duress'—"

"You told me to shut up and drive," he drawled.

"I did no such—" She stopped short when she spotted the slight curve of his mouth. "You're a funny guy, Chief Massey. Real funny."

He turned up that hint of a smile to full wattage. If she were a lesser woman, she might find herself utterly dazzled by that grin. "Here's what I've learned about police work, Public Integrity Officer Hanvey. There ain't much to smile about, so you have to create your own opportunities."

He was right about one thing. There hadn't been much to smile about since she'd returned to Bitterwood to look into police corruption. Maybe the county administrator was wrong to think she was the best person for the job. There just might be too much history between her and this town for her to ever be fully objective.

"Think this body belongs to that missing P.I. from Virginia?" Massey asked a moment later, his grin having faded with her silence.

She didn't have to ask whom he meant. Peter Bell's disappearance was all tangled up with the police-corruption case she was investigating. "Depends on how long the body's been up there. Do you know?"

"At least a month, but probably not much more than three or four."

She nodded. "That fits the timeline for Peter Bell's disappearance. He was last seen in this area in late October of last year."

"Shortly after he observed Wayne Cortland meeting with Paul Bailey."

She slanted a look at him. "You know a lot about the Cortland case."

He met her gaze with a quirked eyebrow. "You think I'd take this job without doing my homework?"

Actually, she had figured him as the sort of guy who avoided homework every chance he got. But maybe she'd assumed too much about him based on his outward appearance and his laid-back attitude.

The road ended at the trailhead about halfway up Copperhead Ridge. Doyle parked his truck and turned to look at her. "I'm not a mountain goat. So go easy on me. Get me safely up that mountain and back."

She bit back a smile. "I'll do what I can. But those sea-level lungs may have a little trouble with the change in altitude."

At least he was appropriately dressed, in a fleece-lined weatherproof jacket and heavy-duty hiking boots. Her own attire was similar, as she'd changed clothes at Ledbetter's Diner before she and Ivy headed up the mountain earlier that day. Her travel bag was still in her car in the hospital parking deck.

With nightfall, the temperatures on the mountain had plunged below freezing, making the hike up the ridge trail a headlong struggle into a biting wind. Up this high, the tendrils of mist that shrouded the peaks turned into a freezing fog that stung the skin and made eyes water. Laney tugged the collar of her jacket up to protect her throat and lower face, squinting through tears.

"Damn, it's cold," Doyle muttered.

"Just wait till it snows again."

One of the search parties scouring the ridge had found the body about thirty yards east of the second trail shelter, about eight miles from where they'd found Missy Adderly's body. Since Laney was the native, Doyle let her lead the way. Despite his occasional self-deprecating comments about the hike, he didn't have any trouble keeping up, and his sea-level lungs seemed to be doing just fine at nearly five thousand feet. He seemed to be adapting quickly to his new surroundings.

They found some of the search-party members had remained on the mountain, huddled together under the shelter for warmth and a little respite from the freezing fog. Laney recognized a few of them, including Carol Brandywine and her husband, James, who ran a trail-riding stable. No horses out here tonight, Laney noted with grim amusement. The Brandywines wouldn't subject their precious four-legged babies to conditions like these.

"Delilah and Antoine are with the body." James pointed east, where blobs of light moved in the woods.

"Stay here if you like," Doyle told Laney, giving the sleeve of her jacket a light tug—a variation on his arm-touching habit, she thought. "That body's not likely to be pretty."

"I've spent time on the Body Farm at the University of Tennessee," she told him. "I've probably seen more bodies in various degrees of decay than you have."

His eyebrows lifted slightly, but he didn't try to talk her out of it when she fell into step with him as they headed toward the flashlight beams ahead. Halfway there, he murmured, "If I go all wobbly kneed at the sight of the body, promise you'll catch me?"

She glanced at him and saw the smile lurking at the corner of his mouth. "You think I overstated my credentials a bit?"

He looked at her. "No. But it's possible you've underestimated mine."

"Ridley County's not that big. And you weren't even the sheriff. You were a deputy."

"I was captain of investigations, with several years of experience as an investigator. I'm plenty qualified to lead a small-town department."

On paper, perhaps. But did he have the temperament to run a police department that had already been rocked by scandal?

"So serious," he murmured, as if reading her thoughts on her face. She tried to school her expressions to hide her musings, succeeding only in making him smile. "There are many ways to get things done, Public Integrity Officer Hanvey. Sometimes a smile is more useful than a frown."

And now he was implying she was a grim dullard, she thought with a grimace as they reached the clump of underbrush where Antoine Parsons and fellow Bitterwood P.D. detective Delilah Hammond stood a few feet from a pair of TBI evidence technicians examining the remains.

The body was clearly that of a male and, except for a few signs of predation, was in remarkably good shape, given how long it must have been in the woods. "Temps up here have been pretty cold since October," Delilah said when Doyle commented on it. "The TBI guys say the body's fairly well preserved."

"Looks like the only things that've been messing with the body were small carrion eaters like raccoons," Antoine added. "Could've been worse if the black bears weren't hibernating now."

Laney tamped down a shudder. She'd seen the kind of damage a black bear could do to a campsite. Her earlier bravado aside, she didn't want to know what one could do to human remains.

"No ID on the body?"

"Won't know for sure until the techs move him, but so far, no. No wallet, no watch, no jewelry, no nothing," Delilah answered. She glanced up and did a double take when she spotted Laney.

"Hi, Dee," Laney said with a smile, recognizing the look on the other woman's face. That look that said, "Don't I know you?" Delilah Hammond was five years older than Laney, and the last time they'd seen each other, Laney had been twelve years old, with a mouth full of braces and a pixie haircut. Delilah had been her idol, a smart, beautiful high school senior who'd volunteered to coach Laney's softball team.

Then Delilah's daddy had blown up the family home in a meth-lab explosion, burning Dee's brother Seth and killing himself. Delilah had left town soon after to go to college somewhere in the East. She hadn't been back to Bitterwood since, until she'd shown up a couple of months earlier and ended up taking a job on the Bitterwood detective squad.

"Laney Hanvey," she supplied, smiling as recognition sparked in Delilah's dark eyes. "Bitterwood Rebels—"

"Fight, fight, fight," Delilah answered with a wide smile.

"You remembered."

"How could I forget my star third baseman?"

"Third base, huh?" Doyle murmured, making it sound a little dirty. The fierce look she zinged his way triggered that half smirk again. But it disappeared quickly, and he transformed in an instant to the man in charge, shotgunning a series of questions at the two detectives.

In a few seconds, he'd gleaned a great deal of information about the body, from who had found it and whether or not they'd moved the body to the particulars of hair color, eye color and most likely cause of death.

"Defects in chest and head. Won't know until autopsy, but I think they'll turn out to be bullet holes," Delilah answered.

"Does he match the description of Peter Bell?"

"At first blush, yes. The Virginia State Police have Bell's dental records and DNA—his wife supplied both when she reported him missing. We should know one way or the other soon," Antoine answered.

There was a photo of Bell on the missing-persons wall at the Ridge County Sheriff's Department. Laney had seen it several times over the past few months. She stepped to the side, closer to where the busy evidence technicians worked methodically around the body, and tried to catch a glimpse.

Death was never pretty. Even the deceleration afforded by the colder temperatures up on the ridge hadn't spared the body the ravages of decomposition. It was impossible to compare the photo of a smiling, handsome, very much alive Peter Bell to this corpse.

She hated to think about Bell's wife looking at those remains and trying to recognize her husband in them.

As she stepped back toward the others, she felt the intensity of Doyle's gaze before she even lifted her eyes to meet his. "Recognize him?" he asked.

She shook her head. "Well preserved is not the same as lifelike."

"Do you think this death has anything to do with Missy Adderly's murder?" Antoine asked.

"I don't see how," Delilah answered. "If this is Peter Bell, he was probably killed because he caught Cortland conspiring with Bailey on video and someone found out about it."

Bell had been investigating lumberyard owner Wayne Cortland, a suspect in a drug trafficking and money laundering case the U.S. Attorney's office in Abingdon, Virginia, had been investigating. Tailing Cortland had led Peter Bell to Maryville, a small city near Bitterwood, where Bell had recorded a meeting between Cortland and a man named Paul Bailey on video.

Bailey had later proved to be the mystery man behind a series of murders for hire, which should have put Cortland in the crosshairs of a murder investigation. But Bell had disappeared somewhere in the Bitterwood area, and the video had vanished with him.

"If it's Bell," Laney said quietly, "what are the chances he hid a copy of that video he claimed to have?"

"Private eyes can be paranoid types," Antoine said, "but anybody who'd kill a man to get the video off his phone would probably be pretty thorough about shaking him down for any copies."

"Besides, both Paul Bailey and Wayne Cortland are dead," Delilah added.

"Cortland's body hasn't been identified yet," Doyle said.

All three sets of eyes turned to him.

"The confidence y'all show in my investigative abilities is touching," Doyle drawled. "Really, it is."

By the time the TBI technicians finished their work, midnight was fast approaching, along with a deepening cold that had long since seeped through Laney's coat and boots. Her toes were numb, her fingers nearly useless, and when Doyle told them to go home and get some sleep because the next day was going to be a long one, she nearly wilted with relief.

The walk back to the chief's truck got her blood pumping, driving painful prickles of feeling back into her toes and fingers. Doyle turned the heat up to high and gave a soft, feral growl of pleasure as warm air flooded the truck cab. "I think I've turned into a cop-sicle."

Laney couldn't stop a smile at his joke. "Regretting the job change already?"

He slanted a suspicious look her way. "Do you have some sort of bet riding on my job longevity?"

"Betting is a sucker's game."

"So it is." He continued looking at her, a speculative gleam in his eyes, which glittered oddly green from the reflected light of the dashboard display. His scrutiny went on so long, she began to squirm inwardly before he finally said, "I'm guessing you were an honor student. Straight A's, did all your homework without being told to, played sports because you're competitive but also because it helped round out your CV when it was time to get into a good college. UT for undergrad. I'd bet you went somewhere close by for law school—you haven't lost much of your accent. But somewhere prestigious because you were bright enough to score admission. Virginia, Duke or Vandy."

Her inward squirming nearly made it to the surface, but she held herself rigidly still.

"Duke," he said finally. "Vandy's too close. Virginia's not close enough to a big city. Durham's just right. Small-town–like in some ways, so you don't feel too much like a fish out of water. But those trips into Raleigh for the clubs and bars made you feel downright cosmopolitan."

She didn't know whether to be angry or impressed. She went with anger, because it was safer. "Nice parlor trick."

"I prefer to call it 'profiling.'"

"I chose Duke because they offered a scholarship. And I didn't go to clubs in Raleigh because I had to work two jobs at night to help pay for the rest."

"Avoiding the big school loans? Even smarter than I thought."

He sounded sincerely impressed, damn him. Just when she was working up a little righteous outrage, he had to go and say something nice about her.

"Sunrise is, what? Around eight?" He changed the subject with whiplash speed as he put the truck in gear.

"Thereabouts," she agreed. "But there'll be enough light for the search earlier. Maybe around a quarter till seven."

"There's a chance of bad weather tomorrow."

She knew. The local weathermen had been tracking something called a "cold core upper low" that had the potential to dump a lot of snow in the southern Appalachian mountains. "Hard to predict where it'll fall. All the more reason to get up on the mountain early and see if we can find Joy Adderly."

He nodded. "Wear your long johns."

THE CROWD GATHERED at the foot of Copperhead Ridge was larger than Doyle had expected, given the increasing probability of snowfall that had greeted him that morning when he turned on the local news. He'd made the call to assign all but a skeleton staff of patrol officers to the search, a decision that had seemed a no-brainer to him but had proved controversial among some of the staffers who were gathered for the search assignments. He made mental note of the grumblers for later; he wasn't going to put up with people who thought the job beneath them.

He'd put the Brandywines in charge of mapping out the

search grids, based on a suggestion from Antoine Parsons the night before when he'd called the detective from home to get his input on the next day's task. "The Brandywines take people up and down this mountain all the time on horseback. They know just about all the nooks and crannies. They can tell you the best places to look and the best ways to do it."

"Twenty-two people," Carol Brandywine said after a quick head count. "Let's split into groups of four where we can. I want an experienced mountaineer in each group."

James, her husband, went through the group quickly, pulling out the people he considered capable of leading a search team. He ended up with six people, including, Doyle noted with interest, Laney Hanvey. "The rest of you, pick a leader and team up. No more than four on a team."

Doyle went straight to Laney's side. Her blue eyes reflected the gray gloom of the clouds overhead. "Chief."

"Public Integrity Officer."

Her lips curved the tiniest bit, sending a little ripple of pleasure darting through his gut. She was just too damned cute for her own good.

Or for his.

He shouldn't have been surprised when the other searchers joined other leaders, leaving him and Laney in a group by themselves. Nobody, it seemed, was inclined to join a group that included the new chief of police.

"I took a bath this morning," he muttered to Laney, who wore a look of consternation. "Used deodorant and everything."

She looked up at him, her lips curving in a smile. "Maybe they figure, you being a flatlander and all, you'll hold 'em back."

He leaned closer, lowering his voice. "Poor you, stuck with the beach bum."

Her eyes flickered open a little wider, as if surprised

to hear him use the term that just about everyone in town was using to describe him. Did she think he was oblivious to the whispers?

"I know what they call me," he added softly. "I don't mind. I'd probably call you a mountain goat if you'd been voted sheriff of Ridley County. Nobody likes change."

"And yet it's inevitable." Laney turned away, taking a loosely sketched map from Carol Brandywine, who was handing out the search assignments. "Oh, goody. We get the boneyard."

He looked at the map. He could make little of the squiggles and lines drawn there, but she seemed to know exactly where they were supposed to go. He picked up his pack of supplies and caught up with her as she started toward the trailhead.

"What's the boneyard?" he asked, falling in step with her.

The look she darted his way was full of barely veiled amusement. "I thought you were the guy who did his homework."

"It's a graveyard?" he asked doubtfully.

"Well, sure, you could get that much from the name." Her voice lowered to a half whisper, an almost dead-on impression of his own teasing style of speech. "But not just any graveyard."

He played along. "Are we likely to run into haints?"

She grinned then, mostly at his less-than-successful attempt at a mountain twang. "Not just any haints. Cherokee haints. This land was their land first. They have a lot to be upset about."

"What should I expect from this boneyard?"

She lifted her flashlight, putting the beam just under her chin to light up her face in spooky shades of dark and light. "Terror," she intoned.

He grinned at her. "You got a good report from the hospital this morning."

Her grin morphed into consternation. "How do you do that?"

"Like you'd be playing haunted trail guide with me if things weren't better with your sister?"

She smiled. "If her vitals continue looking good, she'll go home tomorrow."

"Any progress on her memory?"

"Not so far. But my mom says she's a lot clearer about the things she *does* remember." Her smile faded as she looked up the mountain. "Uh-oh."

He followed her gaze, seeing only a pervasive mist that swallowed the top of the ridge. "What?"

"See that cloud?" She pointed toward the mist.

"Yeah?"

"It's not a cloud." She pulled her jacket more tightly around her. "Hope you like hiking in the snow."

Chapter Five

"Should I call off this search until the weather improves?"

Laney looked behind her. Doyle had been smart enough to bring a cap with him in his pack. It was keeping the snow off his head, though his uncovered ears blazed bright red from the raw cold. His weatherproof coat was covered with snow, and he looked cold, miserable and worried.

"We were assigned one of the highest points on the mountain, so we're the ones getting the snow. Most of the other parties are below the snow line. They're just getting mist and rain."

"Are you still okay? Warm enough?"

He seemed genuinely concerned rather than asking after her comfort as a way to express his own discomfort. She decided to show him some mercy and dug a spare set of earmuffs out of her pack. "Here. Put these on."

He looked at the bright green earmuffs for a second, his thought processes playing out candidly in his conflicted expression. On one hand, he wanted warm ears. On the other hand, sticking bright green fuzzy earmuffs on his ears would be an egregious assault on his masculinity.

Comfort won out. He took the earmuffs and put them on, replacing his cap. He looked ridiculous but warmer.

"Smokin' hot," she said under her breath.

"What?"

She shook her head. "Nothing."

He gave her a suspicious look.

She turned back to the trail, grinning to herself.

As they neared the Cherokee boneyard, she decided to keep that fact to herself. He wouldn't be able to see much from the trail with snow falling this hard. They were already struggling to stick to the trail as it was. They were in near whiteout conditions, and she was beginning to think he had been right to question the wisdom of trying to search the mountain in this much snowfall.

"Maybe we should go back," she said, turning to look at him.

But he wasn't behind her.

"Doyle?" She started back down the trail, her boots slipping on the snow-covered path. She couldn't see Doyle's tracks behind hers for several yards. Then she spotted a churned-up disturbance in the snow near a short drop-off.

She edged carefully to the lip of the drop and saw Doyle flattened out against the steep incline, inching his way back up to the trail. Had he called out to her when he'd fallen? The whistle of the wind and the sound-deadening effects of her earmuffs must have hidden the sound of his mishap. She took the offending ear protectors off.

"Doyle!" she called to him, wondering if the wind was carrying her voice away before it reached him below.

But he looked up at her, relief evident in his expression. "There you are!"

"Are you okay?"

He had his earmuffs hanging around his neck, she saw. Colder for his ears but better for hearing. "I'm not hurt, but climbing back up there is harder than it looks. The snow's got everything as slippery as a catfish."

"You're almost there." She crouched carefully near the edge. "Just a few more feet."

He inched upward, taking his time to get good footholds

and handholds. Soon he was close enough for her to flatten out on the ground and reach down to help him up the rest of the way. He dropped heavily on the snowy ground beside her, breathing hard. "Thanks."

"What happened?"

"I stepped on a stone and turned my ankle, which sent me toppling sideways." He pointed to the slanted stretch of ground where she'd spotted the disturbance in the snow. "I couldn't catch myself, and once I hit that patch, momentum drove me over the edge."

"Is your ankle okay?"

"Yeah, no harm done. But my radio's somewhere down there." He waved toward the drop-off.

"We'd better go back."

"We can try," he said doubtfully. "But I remember some pretty steep inclines on the way up, with drop-offs a lot scarier than that one. Going back down that way will be like skating downhill on a balance beam in places."

He was right. If she'd known how hard and fast the snow would fall up here, she wouldn't have agreed to the hike. But the weather reports had seemed fairly confident that the snow would be light.

What was falling now was more like a blizzard than anything the forecasters had discussed.

"Okay, we can't go back down the way we came."

"Is there another way to go?"

"We can keep going up. The trail tops off about a mile from here, and then there's an easier downhill stretch that's not nearly as steep or treacherous."

Doyle peered up the mountain, even though the snow was falling so hard that it was impossible to see more than a few yards ahead of them. "What if we can't make it down that way?"

"Then we're in serious trouble."

THEY WERE IN serious trouble. He could see the anxiety in Laney's blue eyes and the tense set of her jaw as they reached the peak and paused at the top of the trail, gazing down at what little they could see through the thick curtain of snowfall.

"Trees are down all over the place," he said aloud.

She nodded.

"It'll be worse downhill, won't it? We won't be able to see what we're heading into."

She nodded again. "Any luck getting a phone signal?"

He checked his phone again. "Nope. I just wish I'd held on to that radio."

A glance at his watch told him they had already been on the trail for five hours. He was in better physical shape than anyone around here seemed to give him credit for, but he was fast reaching the limit of his stamina.

"Where's the next shelter?" he asked. "I could use a rest break."

"Me, too," she said, "but there's not a shelter for another six miles, and it's way downhill from here. If we want to rest, we're going to have to go off the trail."

He looked at her, alarmed. "Off the trail? Will we be able to find our way back?"

She opened her backpack and pulled out a stack of slender orange vinyl strips with black plastic clips on the end. "Trail markers. They're reflective, so we can even find them in the dark if need be."

He hoped they wouldn't still be here by dark.

Laney looked around her as if she could actually tell what was out there in the fathomless wall of white that surrounded them on all sides. She headed to their right, which should be east. At least, he thought it must be east. Truth be told, he didn't have any idea.

The land flattened out a little, making for an easier hike, though the snow cover—already three inches and piling up thicker by the minute—obscured a lot of what lay underfoot. Laney marked the trail every twenty yards or so, making sure the last marker was still visible before she attached the next one to bushes and thin outcroppings to guide their way back.

"Where are we going?" he asked.

"There's an old cabin out there near the summit. It should be about a half mile ahead."

"Are you sure?"

"Well, it was still there last year when Jannie and I hiked up here. We just have to hope none of these trees have come down on it."

"Yeah, let's hope." He followed her forward, sticking close. They'd both left their earmuffs off, cold ears be damned. Better than one of them tumbling off a ledge again without the other one hearing.

When the cabin came into view, it seemed to simply appear, a hulking log-and-mortar structure sprawling like a slumbering bear in the middle of a snowy void. It was clearly old, but most of the mortar between the logs looked solid, and the logs were weathered but intact.

"How old is this place?" he asked as she climbed the one shallow step up to the porch. He followed, relieved to find the porch sturdy enough to hold their weight.

"About a hundred and fifty years old, but it's been shored up since. The Copperhead Ridge Preservation Society weatherizes it once a year."

"So we're about to shelter in a historical monument?"

The door didn't appear to be locked; all she did was pull the latch and the door creaked open with little effort. They hurried inside and closed the door against the snow.

The cabin was appreciably warmer, despite the lack of heat. Just getting out of the wind was a huge relief. With the grimy cabin windows blocking out most of what daylight remained, all Doyle could make out in the gloomy interior were blocky shapes he assumed to be furniture. As he reached into his pack to pull out his flashlight, Laney beat him to it, her flashlight beam scanning across the room to take in their surroundings.

"No critters," she said.

He wouldn't feel completely sanguine about that pronouncement until they had a chance to look beneath some of the furniture. But at least there *was* some furniture. Down in the gulf marshes where he'd grown up, old structures tended toward ruin rather than preservation, unless there was a pressing historical reason for keeping a structure from falling apart under the unrelenting pressures of humid salt air, hurricane-strength winds and adolescent vandalism. Anything like furniture would have been stripped away long ago by scavengers.

When he mentioned that fact to Laney, she laughed. "It happens like that everywhere. The only reason this cabin is still standing is that it was built by George Vesper, one of the town's founders. His great-great-granddaughter Anna Vesper Logan is the head of the Copperhead Ridge Preservation Society. You don't cross Anna Vesper Logan and live to tell it."

"I like her already."

"This woodstove should still work." She examined the cast-iron potbellied stove carefully, looking for obstructions or anything else that might prevent them from using it. "If there's any wood already chopped, it'll probably be in the bin on the back porch." She waved toward the door at the other end of the room.

"And if there's not?"

"Then I hope you know how to swing an ax."

Grimacing, Doyle tried the knob. Like the front door, it was unlocked. "Seriously, Anna what's-her-name notwithstanding, how do you keep thieves and vandals from stripping this place clean?"

"It's too high up the mountain," she answered. "Thieves and vandals are too lazy to hike up this far to scavenge some old furniture. Serious hikers tend to respect the history of the place."

The back porch was sheltered by a thin wooden overhang, but the blowing snow had whipped right through the opening, building a drift big enough to make opening the back door difficult. He shoved the snow out of the path of the door and looked around the back porch, spotting a wooden box a few feet away. Opening the lid, he was relieved to find several pieces of dry wood inside.

"How many pieces you need?" he called back into the cabin.

"Five pieces should be plenty," she answered. "Do we have enough?"

He brought in twice that amount, in case they'd need to refill the stove later. He handed her five pieces and put the rest where she directed, in a bin beside the stove.

"There should be some oil lamps in that cabinet over there." She waved toward a large pine armoire against the side wall. He opened it and found three hurricane lamps, all in good condition, along with a full bottle of lamp oil.

"God bless Anna what's-her-name." He filled and lit a lamp, spreading a warm, golden glow across the small one-room cabin.

Laney had the wood fire going by then, an answering glow radiating from the glass-front door of the cast-iron stove. "This place will warm up in no time, as small as it is."

"Now we should get naked and huddle for body heat," he suggested.

The look she threw his way made him grin. Her own lips curved, finally, in response. "You're not like any chief of police I've ever known."

"I like to think I'm an original."

"I suspect you like to think a lot of things." She softened the zinger with a widening smile, tugging off her gloves and splaying her fingers out in front of the stove. "Ooh, warm."

He pulled off his own gloves, laying them on the square table next to hers and joining her at the stove. The radiating heat felt like heaven. "How long do you think the snow will last?"

"The weather forecaster said the front would pass pretty quickly."

"We've been trekking through snow for almost five hours, and last I looked, it wasn't letting up."

"'Quickly' is relative. I'd say it'll be over before dark."

"And then we go back down the mountain?"

She shot him an apologetic look. "Not after dark. Way too treacherous. We've got enough wood to keep us warm. We can stay here until daylight."

Looking around the room, he spotted one narrow bed. "And sleep where?"

She looked at the bed and back at him. "You were saying something about body heat?"

His heart flipped a couple of times.

She grinned at him. "We can take the bedding off the bed and pull it up here by the fire. Huddle for warmth."

"Like a couple of refugees."

"Literally."

He crossed to the narrow wood bed, eyeing the construction. Good ol' Anna had apparently taken care to keep the cabin true to the time period. The bed was an old-fashioned rope cradle on a wooden frame, with a down-filled mattress covered with old quilts. The quilts were dusty and showed some wear and tear—they must be replicas, he realized. Not even a stickler for history would leave old quilts to molder up here on the mountain.

"The quilts aren't really valuable," Laney said, as if

reading his mind. "The historical society holds a quilting bee every year or two to replace them because they don't hold up well to the elements. Let's lay them down on the floor and put the mattress on top of them. It's not authentic to the period, either, but it's a lot harder to clean." She crossed to the armoire and opened one of the drawers in the bottom of the cabinet, revealing more quilts stored inside. She pulled out a couple, handing him one to lay atop the down mattress while she unfolded the other and held it in front of the woodstove to warm.

"Does the historical society care if you use this cabin for shelter?"

"Not as long as we leave it more or less how we found it," she answered, stripping off her jacket and folding it neatly over the seat of a nearby ladder-back chair. She looked back at Doyle, nodding toward his jacket. "You should take your jacket off. Or you won't feel warm in the morning when we go back outside."

He followed her lead, stripping down to the long-sleeved T-shirt he'd layered under the jacket and a heavier cable-knit sweater. His jeans were damp from his fall, but the woodstove was already beginning to dry them. He pulled off his boots and damp socks, laying them on another chair to dry, and replaced them with a dry pair of socks he'd stashed in his pack.

He looked up to find Laney doing the same thing. She met his gaze and grinned. "Boy Scout?"

"Girl Scout?"

She grinned. "Camp Fire Girl, actually. So your profiling wizardry can only take you so far, huh?"

"Far enough to know that your competitive streak makes you downright giddy that you were able to stump me."

She made a face and turned toward the glowing window of the woodstove, holding her hands out to the heat.

"Temperatures up here may go down into the low twenties tonight. I wish this place were a little better insulated."

"It's not too bad, considering how old it is." The cabin was drafty, but not egregiously so, and the rusted roof overhead was solid enough to keep out the snow. "How much snow do you think will fall?"

"From what the weatherman out of Knoxville was saying, it's hard to predict how much will fall in any given place, because a cold core upper low will do what it wants where it wants and without a whole lot of warning. So some places around here could see next to nothing, and other places could get several inches."

He pulled his knees up to his chin and scooted closer to the stove. "As you might imagine, my experience with snow is pretty limited."

"Don't see a lot of it on the Gulf Coast?"

"Not a lot. Though we probably see more snow than you see alligators, so there's that."

She chuckled. "Now who's being competitive?"

They fell silent for a few minutes, listening to the whisper of snow fall against the cabin windows. Doyle must have dozed off, because when Laney spoke again, her voice sent a jolt through his nervous system.

"Five inches," she said.

He roused himself and shot her a halfhearted leer. "Is this another competition? Because I can beat that."

She rolled her eyes. "I meant the snowfall, hotshot. I'm predicting five inches. What do you think?"

"I think it's cold and I'm hungry, and I ate my last protein bar about three hours ago. You're a mountain girl. Can't you go out there and kill me a possum for dinner or something?"

She grimaced. "Ugh. Opossum meat is greasy and, depending on their diet, can taste pretty horrible. With the park so close, they scavenge a lot of their food from trash cans, so, no."

"I don't know whether to be impressed or appalled that you know so much about possum meat."

She seemed to be torn between amusement and consternation. He supposed it wasn't fair to her to treat her like an interesting woman he'd met on vacation when she was a hard-nosed professional who'd been assigned to investigate his new department. But she was just so damned cute, it was hard to think of her as an opponent, no matter how worthy.

He let his gaze linger on her soft features, enjoying the way she looked in lamplight. The golden glow was forgiving, although Laney Hanvey wasn't a woman who required much forgiveness when it came to beauty. She had delicate features that, taken one by one, might not conform to some classical standard of beauty, but the combination could be damned near breathtaking if a man was to glance at her unprepared.

She had big, wide eyes, as blue as a clear summer sky. Unlike some blonds, her brows and lashes were brown, framing her eyes like a painting. Her nose was slender and small, a little too small for her face if one were inclined to be critical. Doyle was not so inclined. He liked the slight upward tilt and the way her nostrils flared with anger and laughter alike.

And that mouth. Wide and generous, prone to spreading in a grin that was instantly infectious. Right now, it was pursed as she gazed at him with suspicion.

He had trouble holding back a grin.

But as her mouth softened, her lips parting to speak, an unholy shriek ripped through the snowy silence outside the cabin, sending adrenaline racing through Doyle's nervous system.

Chapter Six

Despite the growing stiffness in his bruised and aching muscles, Doyle was on his feet in a second, reaching for his pistol. Laney jumped to her feet, as well, her nerves on high alert.

"Was that an animal?" Doyle asked.

"I'm not sure," she admitted, dismayed to hear her voice shaking. She cleared her throat and straightened her spine, even though her nerves were still rattling. "We don't have a lot of big predators on the mountains except bears. Maybe bobcats. But I've never heard either sound anything like that."

A gust of wind howled past the cabin, rattling the door and sending a blast of cold air shooting through the narrow spaces between the logs where time had worn away the cement holding them together. Laney shivered, moving closer to the wall of warmth that Doyle's body afforded.

They listened in breathless silence for another long minute, waiting for the scream to recur. But there was nothing but the sound of the wind and the whisper of snow falling steadily on the roof of the cabin.

"Whatever it was, I think it's gone," he said finally, turning to look at her. His eyes widened at how close she was standing, and she made herself take a couple of steps backward, even though it robbed her of his solid heat.

"You don't think it could have been—"

"Joy Adderly?" he finished for her. "I hope not."

She rubbed her arms, where goose bumps had scattered across the flesh beneath her sweater. "Should we go out and look?"

His brow furrowed, betraying the conflicts battling it out in his mind. She knew conditions outside were dangerous, and without knowing for certain what they'd heard, they'd probably be foolish to venture out into the snowy night.

But if that scream had belonged to a person…

"I'll go take a look around," Doyle said finally. "You stay here."

She shook her head. "No. If one of us goes out there, we both go."

"There's no point in us both getting cold and wet again."

"You could get lost very easily in the snow. I know this place. You don't."

His lips tightened, and she could tell that he wanted to argue. But he had to know she was right. "Okay. We'll both go. But if we don't see anything right around the cabin, we're coming back inside. Agreed?"

She nodded, already on the move to grab her coat and boots.

The snow had tapered off to a soft flutter of flakes from the glassy sky. Snow already blanketed the ground, hiding much of the underbrush around the cabin. Laney angled her flashlight around, looking for disturbances in the snow.

Next to her, Doyle uttered a low profanity as the flashlight beam settled on a churned-up path in the snow about ten yards east of the cabin, near the tree line. "Do you have a weapon?" he asked quietly.

"In my pack."

"Get it."

She hurried back to the cabin and pulled her compact SIG Sauer P227 from the built-in holster in her backpack.

She checked to make sure the magazine was full and returned to the porch, where Doyle was waiting, his gaze scanning the trees beyond the cabin.

"Could you tell where the sound came from?" he asked her quietly.

"East," she answered, nodding toward the path in the snow. "That way."

Doyle walked down the shallow steps of the cabin porch, his boots tamping down the snow beneath his feet. At least five inches had accumulated on the ground—not a huge snowfall for the area, but thick enough to be a problem hiking in the woods.

They stopped first near the disturbed snow, Doyle borrowing her flashlight to scan the perimeters of the path. The beam settled for a moment on a shallow depression at the edge of the snow. "What does that look like to you?" he asked.

"A boot print," she answered, her pulse pounding in her head. She tightened her grip on the P227, her gaze scanning the dark woods surrounding them. They seemed utterly still, save for the rustle of wind in the trees and the light snowfall.

Doyle moved forward, staying within the path in the snow. Laney stayed right behind him, more afraid of being left alone than of heading forward after whatever—whoever— had made the sound they'd heard.

The trail in the snow grew harder to follow once they were in the woods, as the cover of evergreen trees sheltered much of the undergrowth from snow cover. Only scabrous patches of snow lay in some parts of the woods, and if human feet had moved through in the past few minutes, Laney could see no evidence of it.

They faltered to a stop about fifty yards from the cabin. Here, the tree growth was thick, blocking almost all the snowfall. The limbs above sagged from the weight of the accumulated snow; Laney heard a limb crack and fall about twenty yards away, close enough that it made the hairs on the back of her neck prickle to attention.

"These trees are packed with snow." She grabbed Doyle's jacket as he showed signs of moving forward. "We can't even tell which way to go at this point, and the longer we stay out here, the more danger we're in of being hit by falling limbs."

Doyle looked up at the tree limbs trembling above them and then looked back at her. "Okay. Back to the cabin."

He made her wait just outside the door while he went inside and checked to make sure they hadn't received any unwanted visitors while they were out in the woods. But the cabin was empty except for their backpacks and the makeshift bed they'd made for themselves in front of the woodstove.

Doyle let her into the cabin and closed the door behind them. The door lock was true to the period, a wooden bar that fit into a latch to keep intruders from easily breaching the doorway. It wouldn't hold against a determined intruder, but it would give them time to react, at least.

Laney tucked her pistol into the holster in her backpack and shed her jacket and boots again, shivering as she settled on the floor by the fire. Doyle joined her there, wrapping one arm around her shoulders to pull her into the shelter of his body. "This okay?"

She'd be stupid to protest, given the situation. "Fine." She snuggled a little closer, and he brought his other arm up to enclose her in a warm hug.

"Who could be out there?" he asked, his breath warm against her temple.

"I don't know. The closest search-party group should be at least a mile south of here, if they're even still on the mountain in the middle of all this."

"Maybe they're looking for us?"

She shook her head. "That's not protocol. Each group had a seasoned hiker in it who'd know how to hunker down against the cold until morning light. So they'll wait until morning and better conditions to come looking for us."

Doyle fell silent for a little while, edging them both a little closer to the heat of the stove. After a few minutes, he murmured, "Maybe we were wrong about that print belonging to a human."

"It looked a lot like a boot to me."

"We didn't get a great look at it."

"True," she conceded. Her heart had been pounding and her body shaking from the cold too much for her to have been sure about anything they'd seen out there in the snow.

"Could that scream we heard have been a mountain lion?" Doyle asked.

"No mountain lions in these parts anymore."

He slanted a look at her. "Are you sure?"

"So says the park service, and they'd probably know."

"Maybe it was a ghost, then." He gave her arm a squeeze. "Maybe one of those Cherokee haints from the boneyard."

He was trying to ease the tension that had built during their outdoor trek. Even though her teeth were still chattering a little, she forced a grin. "That's probably it. Haints."

"Do you know all the stories about these mountains?" he asked a few minutes later, after her shivering.

"I don't know if I know all of them. I know a lot of them. My mother comes from a strong oral tradition. Her mother and her mother's mother before kept all the family stories and traditions, passing them down every generation. I could tell you about Jeremiah Duffy, my ancestor several generations back who was one of the first settlers in Ridge County."

"I was thinking of a little more modern history than that," he said.

She looked up at him. "You have something particular in mind?"

"What do you know about previous murders in these parts?"

"Going how far back?"

He shrugged, the movement tugging her a little closer to him. "Twenty or thirty years, maybe."

"Well, there have been murders along the Appalachian Trail for years, though statistically speaking, they're pretty rare. There was one guy who killed some hikers on the AT back in the early '80s, went to jail, got paroled about halfway through his sentence and ten years later tried to kill a couple of hikers he ran into in the same area."

"Our justice system at work."

"It's certainly not perfect," she conceded.

"What about the photograph we found with your sister yesterday—have you ever come across anything like that?"

"That," she said, "is actually interesting. There's an urban legend in these parts about hikers who spend the night in a trail shelter and, upon reaching the next shelter on the trail, find Polaroid photos of themselves asleep in the previous shelter. The legend is, if they don't turn around and go home, they disappear altogether, never to be seen again."

"How old a legend is that?" Doyle asked.

"It's got to go back years. At least the '70s, maybe earlier than that."

He fell silent for a while, and Laney found herself growing sleepy as the earlier adrenaline rush seeped away, leaving her drained. She tried to fight it, not sure they were actually safe in the cabin, given the disturbance they'd heard outside, but the long hike and the stress of her sister's attack conspired against her.

With the moan of the wind in her ears and Doyle's warm, solid body cradling her own, she drifted to sleep.

HE WAS IN a jungle, thick with mosquitoes and suffocating humidity. Rain battered the thatch roof of his shelter, drenching the world outside. But he remained dry, huddled with the mission workers who had gathered in the rickety supply hut to wait out the afternoon rainstorm.

The coastal country of Sanselmo didn't suffer the same heavy monsoon season as the Amazonian rain forests, but there was a definite wet season, and it was happening right now. August fifteenth. Several hundred miles to the south, on the other side of the equator, it was the heart of winter. But there was no winter in Sanselmo, only endless summer.

He didn't know the two girls sheltering with him. Only the man. Tall, lean, with gentle green eyes that reminded Doyle of his father. The green-eyed man was his brother, David, who'd broken the family tradition of working in law enforcement and had chosen, instead, to help people in a different way.

"The rain will end soon," David told him with a reassuring smile. "And then the steam bath begins."

No, Doyle thought. *When the rain ends, the bloodbath begins.*

He closed his eyes, willing the rain to keep falling. But nature had her own agenda, and soon—too soon—the patter of rainfall gave way to the soft hiss of steam rising from the jungle floor as the sun began to peek between breaks in the cloud cover and angle through the thick canopy of trees.

Already, he heard the sound of truck motors humming in the distance. They would arrive soon, and no one in this hut would survive.

No one but him.

Doyle jerked awake, his ears still ringing with the hissing sound of steam. It took a moment to reorient himself to reality, to replace the jungle of his imagination with the snowbound mountain cabin of his present dilemma.

"Good morning."

Laney's voice drew his gaze toward the table nearby. She was setting the table with stoneware mugs, he saw. The smell of hot coffee filled the cabin's one small room, coming from an old steel coffeepot sitting on the woodstove, fragrant steam rising from its mouth. More wood had gone into the stove's belly at some point overnight; it burned warm and bright in the gray morning light.

"Good morning," he replied, stretching his aching limbs. "I must have slept like a log once I drifted off. Where did you find coffee?"

"I always keep some in my backpack."

"The coffeepot, too?"

She flashed an adorably sleepy grin. "No. That came with the cabin. I melted some snow, washed it out with soap—"

"That you also carry in your backpack?"

"You never know when you'll need a good washup."

"Just how big is the inside of that backpack?"

Making a face, she crossed to the stove and poured coffee into one of the stoneware mugs. "Sorry, I don't have sugar or creamer."

"Slacker."

That comment earned him another grin. He was going to have to ration his quips, because a smiling Laney Hanvey was turning out to be quite the temptation. Their current camaraderie, built up by their forced togetherness and a common goal, wasn't likely to last beyond a return to civilization. She was still the public integrity officer Ridge County had sent to frisk his new department.

They didn't have to be enemies, of course, since they both wanted to see the Bitterwood Police Department function on the up-and-up. But as she represented people who wanted to disband the department altogether and bring the town under the county sheriff's jurisdiction, they were unlikely to be friends, either. Or anything more than friends.

No matter how tempting she was all sleep mussed and smiling.

She handed him the cup of coffee. "Chief—"

"Doyle," he corrected, even though he knew keeping a semblance of professional distance would have been a much safer plan.

"Doyle," she corrected, dimpling a little and making his insides twist pleasantly again. "Is Janelle still in danger?"

"Not as long as she's in the hospital," he answered. "I didn't mention this earlier, but yesterday morning I asked one of my officers to go to the hospital after work to keep an eye on things, now that the news of her survival is out in the press." He tried a sip of coffee. It was hot and strong, the way he liked it.

"Are you sure he can be trusted?"

"I'm sure she can. I assigned Delilah Hammond. I asked some people I know about her, and they all vouch for her integrity and also her skill as a bodyguard."

"I know Dee." Relief trembled in Laney's voice. "But I'd still like to get back to Jannie as soon as we can. Just to reassure myself."

He pushed to his feet, testing his muscles. A little achy in places from the long trek up the mountain the day before, not to mention the tumble off the trail. But nothing that should keep him from getting back down the mountain, as long as the weather allowed. "Snow melting yet?"

"Not yet. It's early. But the weather forecasters all agreed that even up here on the mountain, the temperatures should be above freezing by midmorning."

He looked through the grimy window next to the woodstove. Snow glistened diamond bright in the morning sunlight. "Sun will help, too."

She dug in her backpack and pulled out a protein bar. Breaking it in half, she handed a piece to him. "So you up for trying to get back down the mountain?"

"If you think it's safe enough now."

"The visibility should be tons better. You won't be as likely to wander off the trail." She shot him a look of amusement.

"I didn't wander off. I slid off. Big difference."

She just chewed her piece of protein bar and stifled another grin.

She was right about the visibility, Doyle had to admit an hour later, when they started back through the woods to the trail. The neon-orange trail markers Laney had left along the way glowed like beacons, returning them easily to the place where they'd left the beaten path behind. She stuffed the retrieved markers back in her pack, trading them for a pair of binoculars, which she lifted to her eyes.

"Gotta get me one of those packs," Doyle murmured, hoping for—and receiving—a grin in response.

"I'll give you a packing list for next time." She hooked the binocular straps around her neck, swung the pack onto her back and started moving along the snowy trail at a confident clip. He hurried to catch up.

About a quarter mile along the trail, she stopped, gazing down at the snow path ahead of them. "Look."

He followed the wave of her hand and saw nothing but snow. "What am I looking at?"

She crouched, bringing her eyes more level with the trail. "Someone's been through here."

He crouched beside her. "I don't see any prints."

"It was sometime during the snowfall," she said. "But after we came through here."

"How do you know that?"

"The trail is wide here, and we instinctively keep to the right side. Just like we are now." She waved her hand at where they stood, which was definitely on the right side of the trail path.

"Because we're raised to drive and walk on the right," he said.

"And to leave the left side open for others who might pass." She pointed to the two dips in the snow. The one on the left was shallow, the one on the right definitely deeper. "Someone came through here sometime last night. This path wasn't here when we came through, and it's a little deeper on the right here than the trail on the left we made on the climb up."

She was right. He'd have never noticed the subtle signs, or been able to read what they meant.

"It could have been one of the other search parties, couldn't it?"

"Maybe, but nobody else was supposed to be looking in this area. And I don't see signs that anyone came up here behind us."

He looked doubtfully at the snowy expanse ahead. "Not sure how you can tell that."

"The track would be deeper, like this one on the right. But it's not. It's only about three inches deep. Three inches is about how much snow there was on the ground when we came through, so these are our tracks. Whoever came through on the way back down tamped down more than three inches. About six inches fell in total, so whoever came through here came through when there was already five inches on the ground."

"The snow was around five inches deep last night when we went out in search of whoever made that sound," Doyle remembered.

"So maybe we were following in the wrong direction," she said, standing.

"Maybe they were heading back down the trail instead of away from it?"

She nodded, starting forward again. She kept clear of the trail she'd discovered.

He followed her lead, trying not to jump to any conclusions. Even if there had been someone outside the cabin last night, and someone hiking back down the trail after five inches of snow had fallen, they couldn't be sure that person was up to no good. It might have been another hiker, looking for shelter and shocked to find the cabin already inhabited.

Although why he wouldn't have knocked on the door and asked for help—or why he'd have screamed bloody murder—

"There's the second shelter." Laney pointed down the trail and he spotted the trail shelter about fifty yards ahead. "That means we're about eight miles from the staging area where we all gathered yesterday. If there are any search parties out looking for us, we should come across them soon."

"Mind if we stop a second? I keep feeling something in my boot. Maybe I picked up a pebble or something in the cabin." He'd been feeling it more sharply the longer they'd hiked, and he'd prefer not to keep going with whatever it was rubbing a blister on the bottom of his foot.

As he leaned against the wall of the shelter to take off his boot, Laney wandered over to the wooden pedestal that held the logbook box. "Maybe whoever was on the trail last night did us a favor and stopped to write something in the log," she said, her tone facetious.

Doyle found the offending wood chip that had gotten in his boot and dumped it out onto the dirt floor of the shelter. Shoving the boot back on and tying the laces, he was about to ask Laney if she'd found anything when she let out a profanity. "Doyle, come here!"

He quickly tied the knot and hurried outside, where she stood staring at the log box, a scowl creasing her brow.

Her blue eyes snapped up to meet his. What he saw there made his gut tighten.

"Look at this." She punched her finger at the logbook.

He crossed to her side and looked over her shoulder. The logbook was open to a page that was blank except for a square photograph and a single line of block lettering. "You're never really safe," the message on the logbook read.

The photograph showed two people sleeping half slumped inside a cabin, their features illuminated by the glow of a woodstove. The image was a little blurry, as if taken through a grimy, time-warped glass window.

Doyle felt as if he'd taken a punch to the gut.

"He was out there. Watching us." Laney sounded more furious than spooked.

Dragging his gaze from the photograph of the two of them in front of the stove, he darted a look around the woods surrounding them, wishing they were a whole lot closer to the bottom. "Laney, we need to get back down the mountain. Now."

Her anger elided into alarm. "You think he's still out here?"

The answer came with a sharp crack of gunfire and an explosive splinter of the wood wall just a few inches away from his head.

Chapter Seven

Doyle's body crashed into Laney's, slamming her to the ground before she had even processed the sound of the gunshot. Her heart cranked up to high gear, pounding like thunder in her ears, almost drowning out Doyle's guttural question.

"Where can we hide?"

She tried to gather her rattled thoughts into some semblance of order. There weren't a lot of places to hide on the trail, for obvious reasons. Nobody wanted to walk into an ambush, so the more open the trail, the better.

But there were places off the trail, and not just other structures like the cabin where they'd stayed the night before. None of them were that easy to get to, of course, but that might work in their favor.

She heard another crack of gunfire, felt the sting of wood splinters spraying against her cheek. Above her, Doyle let out a hiss of pain.

"Are you hit?" she asked.

The answer was a sharp concussion of gunfire, close enough to make her ears ring. Doyle was suddenly tugging her upward, his voice a muffled roar as he urged her to run.

She stumbled forward, forced to run in a crouch by Doyle's arm pinned firmly around her, keeping her low. She sprinted as fast as she could from that uncomfortable position, trying not to jump every time she heard Doyle exchange fire with whoever was shooting at them.

They were at a severe disadvantage, she knew, because the gunfire she was hearing from their pursuer was definitely a rifle, not a handgun. Rifles were far more accurate across much longer distances, although based on the misses so far, whoever was wielding the weapon wasn't exactly a crack shot.

Doyle pulled her out of the crouch and told her to run. "Zigzag!" he breathed, keeping his body between her and the shooter. "Don't give him a good target."

Gunfire continued behind them, at least four more shots, but they seemed to be coming from a greater distance now. Of course, with a scope, the rifleman could easily target them without having to leave his position, while they were already well beyond the distance at which Doyle's pistol or hers could return fire with any accuracy.

She spotted Old Man Pickens ahead, the enormous slate outcropping that looked like a wrinkled old man frowning at the woods, and remembered exactly where they were. She looked behind her, reaching for Doyle's hand, and almost stumbled over her own feet when she saw how much blood was flowing down the side of his face, staining the brown suede of his jacket.

He caught her as she faltered, pushing her ahead. She dragged her gaze forward again and darted around the side of the outcropping, trusting him to follow. From there, they would be out of the direct path of fire for as long as it took the gunman to shift positions and come after them.

The ground underfoot was only snow-free this far down the mountain, though the ground was soft in places from the rain. She dodged the muddy patches, trying to avoid creating any sort of trail, and edged her way closer to the rocky wall face that rose like a fortress to their right.

Somewhere along here, there was an opening, although

it was hard to spot in the ridges and depressions in the rock facing. If she hadn't already known it was there, she'd have never even thought to look for it—

There. It was almost invisible in the dappled sunlight peeking through the tree limbs overhead. She veered off the course, listening to Doyle's heavier footfalls following closely behind her, even though he had to be wondering why they were running straight for the stone wall.

The cave entrance appeared almost like magic in front of them, as the angle of approach revealed it in the shadow of a depression in the rock. It still didn't look like a cave, because the entrance to the deeper opening was off to the left, visible only once a person walked into the shallow depression.

Laney waited until they were several feet beyond the opening before she pulled her flashlight from her pack and clicked it on. The beam danced over the narrow walls of the cave, illuminating a small cavern about twenty feet long from the entrance to the farthest end. The walls themselves were only six feet apart, creating more of a tunnel with no outlet than a cave.

"No way out of here but back where we came?" Doyle asked, his breath a little ragged.

"No."

"So we could be sitting ducks."

"So could he," she said firmly, turning the flashlight on him.

He squinted against the light. "Give a guy a little warning."

"You're hurt." She reached for his head, trying to get a better look at where the blood was coming from.

"Shrapnel wound," he told her firmly. "It's not deep."

"It's a bloody mess." She nudged him toward the wall, where the stone had formed a shallow ledge about the size of a park bench. Hikers who'd found the cave over the years, herself included, had helped the natural formation along, chipping away at the slate to fashion the bench into a fun place to sit and tell ghost stories.

He sat on the bench, his gaze dropping to the obvious tool marks. "Is this a well-known hiding place?"

"Not that well-known," she assured him, hoping she was right. The cave had been largely untouched the first time she and some of her friends had discovered it when she'd been about fifteen. They'd been social outcasts of a particular sort, good students who fit in with neither the popular crowd nor the pot-smoking, moonshine-drinking misfits and were often targets of ridicule or abuse from both.

They'd made Dreaming Cave, as they'd called it, their own little haven. A secret clubhouse where they'd told scary stories and dreamed big dreams of life outside Ridge County and their insular little world.

She opened her backpack and found the first-aid kit stashed in a pocket near the top. Doyle sucked in a quick breath as she wiped his wound with an antiseptic cloth. She tried to be gentle, but if she didn't clean the scrape thoroughly, infection could easily set in.

"Will I live?" he asked, flashing her a grimace of a grin.

She smiled back, her heartbeat finally settling down to a trot from a full-out gallop. "I think so. The wound's long but not very deep. I just need to get this piece of wood." She wiped down the tweezers from the first-aid kit with an alcohol pad and eased out the splinter still embedded in Doyle's temple. It was about a half an inch in length and sharp as a needle. She showed the bloody bit of wood shrapnel to him, eliciting another grimace.

"That was in my head?"

She nodded. "Want to keep it as a souvenir?"

He shook his head. "No, thanks."

She placed three adhesive bandage strips over the wound to protect it from further contamination and went about gathering up the remains of her first-aid supplies. The simple act of cleaning up after herself seemed so normal, it went a long way toward calming her shattered nerves.

She packed away the kit and sat on the rock bench next to Doyle, wincing at how cold the rock was. "Yikes."

He slid closer to her, lending his body heat. "Kind of missing that woodstove about now."

"Yeah. Me, too."

"You're not hurt anywhere, are you?" He held out his hand in front of her. "Let me borrow the flashlight."

She handed it over. "I don't think I'm hurt."

He ran the beam of the flashlight over her, from head to toe, even making her stand up and turn around so he could check her back. Finally, he seemed to be satisfied that she hadn't sustained any injury and handed the flashlight back to her.

She settled next to him on the bench, consciously positioning herself so that their bodies were pressed closely together. She told herself it was for body heat, but when he slid his arm around her shoulders and pulled her even closer, the tingle low in her belly suggested her desire to be close to him wasn't entirely based on the need for warmth.

She ignored the ill-timed tug of her libido and concentrated on listening for any sign that the shooter was lurking outside.

"If the shooter is from around here, he may know about this cave," she warned, keeping her voice to a near-whisper.

"Don't suppose you and your fellow spelunkers left any cans or bottles in here, did you?" Doyle whispered back.

"Probably not," she answered. She and the other Dreaming Cave denizens had been the opposite of delinquents. Someone always made sure they left the cave the way they found it, like the compulsive rule-keepers they'd been.

But that didn't mean more recent cave visitors had been so conscientious. She took a chance and ran the beam of her flashlight across the cave's interior. To her consternation, the light revealed a pile of beer and soda cans in one dark corner of the cavern. "Bloody litterbugs," she whispered.

"Got any dental floss or thread in that pack?" Doyle pulled a compact multiblade knife from his pocket and flipped open a blade shaped like an awl.

"Matter of fact, I do." She pulled out a dental-floss dispenser and handed it to him.

"I need about five of those cans," he said, unspooling the dental floss. Laney fetched the cans and brought them back to the stone ledge, finally catching on to what he was up to.

"Just married," she murmured, drawing his sharp gaze. "Cans on a string, like you put on the back of the groom's car," she explained, earning a grin.

"Exactly. We'll string this across the entrance about ankle high and hide the cans out of sight." Using his knife, he punched holes in the bottoms of the aluminum cans and strung them like beads on the dental floss. "Anyone trips the string, we'll hear the cans clatter."

"Brilliant." She grinned at him.

He shrugged off his jacket and wrapped it around the string of cans. Handing the bundle to her, he edged quietly toward the cave entrance, listening. She slipped up behind him, putting her hand on his back to let him know she was there. His body jerked a little at her touch, the only sign that he might be as tightly strung as she was.

Edging through the cave entrance, he peeked around the stone wall that hid the cave from view. "Quick, while there's nobody out there."

He took the long end of the dental floss, while she gingerly placed the cans on the ground just inside the cave entrance. She edged the cans apart on the string to give them room to make a clatter and stepped back.

On the other side of the entryway, where the indentation ended not in a cave entrance but another wall of stone, Doyle found a small knob of rock jutting out about shin level. He looped the dental floss around the knob and tied a knot, adding a piece of surgical tape to help keep the knot from slipping off.

As he darted quickly back to where she stood, she felt along the rock wall for any sort of outcropping she could use to raise her end of the floss so that it stretched out adequately across the entryway. Her fingers collided with a small stone jutting out a little lower than the shin-level knob where Doyle had tied the other end of the floss. Not perfect, but it should do the job.

They stood back and looked at their makeshift intruder alarm.

"Think it'll work?" she whispered.

"We better hope it does." He picked up his jacket, caught her hand and tugged her back into the darkened cave.

They felt their way to the stone bench and sat, not risking the flashlight again. Without a fire or any way to warm themselves, it didn't take long for the damp cold within the cave to penetrate their clothing.

"Are you as cold as I am?" he asked, his teeth chattering a little.

"Yes," she whispered back.

He wrapped his arm around her shoulders again, tugging her close. She opened her jacket so that the heat of their bodies could mingle a little better. He did the same. It wasn't like sitting in front of the woodstove back in the cabin, but it was better than shivering alone.

She wasn't sure how much time passed before Doyle spoke again. Apparently enough time that she'd managed to drift into a light doze, for his voice in her ear jerked her awake, eliciting a soft, laughing apology from him.

"Sorry. I was just asking if we're still in the search quadrant we were assigned."

"No, we're south and east of our spot on the search map," she answered.

"So they may not even think to look for us here?"

"I imagine they'll search for us everywhere," she answered. "I just hope whoever's out there with that rifle doesn't start taking potshots at them, too."

"Your sister and Missy Adderly weren't shot with a rifle," he murmured.

"Doesn't mean it's a different killer."

"I think it does," he disagreed.

"What about the photo we found at the trail shelter?"

"It's not exactly the same, is it?" he countered. "We found the photo of Janelle and the Adderly girls under Janelle, not in the trail log."

"Maybe Janelle found the photo right before she was shot. The guy with the rifle started shooting at us not long after we found the photo."

"True."

"But serial killers do seem to be creatures of habit," she conceded. "Would it be likely he'd change weapons that way if he didn't have to?"

"When we get back to civilization, we'll let forensics take a look at the photo." He patted the pocket of his jacket. "They can probably tell us if it came from the same make of camera, or if the photo paper is the same."

They fell silent again for a long time. Laney didn't know what was occupying Doyle's thoughts, but all she could think about was that string of cans in the entrance of the cave, and how long it would be before they'd hear them rattle.

He touched her lightly on the arm before he spoke again. "How do you know about this cave? Was this some sort of hillbilly make-out spot?" He softened the slight dig with a smile in his voice.

"Some people may have used it that way, I suppose."

"But not you?"

She shook her head, her forehead brushing against his jaw. The rough bristle of his beard was pleasantly prickly against her skin. "No, my friends and I came here to plan our futures."

His hand on her upper arm squeezed gently. "Plotting world domination?"

"Something like that." She grinned at the thought. She and the other Dreamers, as they'd secretly called themselves, had been a motley crew, bonded not so much by their common interests as by their determination not to let the poverty and hopelessness of their surroundings stop them from believing they could make something out of their lives.

Not all of them had lived their dreams, but most of them had made it out of Bitterwood more or less unscathed. Tommy Alvin was a chiropractor in Cookeville. Gerald Braddock was in Nashville, singing backup in clubs and bars, still trying to sell his songs. Tracie Phelps got her master's and was teaching in a charter school in Georgia. And she herself had gotten her law degree and, while she wasn't exactly on the fast track for the Supreme Court, she was working a job she enjoyed, one that enabled her to give back to her mother and help take care of her sister.

"Was your childhood good?"

She could tell from the tone of his voice that he knew what life was like for so many people here in Appalachia. "Better than many," she answered. "I had parents who loved each other and were good to each other and to us kids. We weren't rich by any means, but we didn't starve and we had the things we really needed."

"You lost your father and your brother when you were in college, you said."

A familiar sadness ached in the back of her throat. "Yes. But we managed to get by. Dad had bought a cancer policy years before he got sick. Between that and his life insurance, my mother and sister were able to get through the worst of things. I think the secret is that my mom never, ever let any of us lose hope, no matter how bad a situation looked, that things would always get better eventually."

"It's a good attitude," he said approvingly.

"What about you?" she asked after a few minutes of silence. "What was your childhood like?"

"Idyllic," he said, a smile in his voice. "Sugar-white beaches as far as the eye could see, swamps to play in, no worries other than dodging the lazy old gators you might run into now and then. My dad was an Alabama state trooper. Mom stayed home with us kids—she was born for motherhood."

"Sounds wonderful," she whispered.

"It was." A hint of melancholy in his voice touched a dark chord still lingering from her own memories of loss. "Until?"

He was silent a moment, and she could almost feel the pain vibrating through him where their bodies touched. "Until my parents died in a car accident when I was twenty."

"Both of them?"

"Yeah." He released a soft sigh. "My sister, Dana, and I were both in college by then, and our brother, David, had just graduated high school. It was the first chance my parents had had in forever to go on vacation by themselves." He laughed quietly, though with little real mirth. "When they told us where they were going, we were surprised."

"Where were they going?" she asked.

"Right here," he answered. "Right here to Ridge County."

She could understand why he and his siblings had been surprised. "Nobody comes to Ridge County on purpose."

"I suppose I could have understood Gatlinburg or Pigeon Forge or somewhere like that. Or even if they'd told me they'd decided to hike the Appalachian Trail now that the kids had all flown the coop. But Ridge County was this tiny little nowhere spot on the Tennessee map, and my parents had enough money saved up that they could have gone to Hawaii or Paris or, hell, Australia if they'd wanted to."

"They had their accident on the way here?"

"No, the accident happened here. Their car ran off the road into a river gorge. The police said they must have missed the bridge in the dark and gone over the edge."

"Purgatory Bridge," she murmured. It was the only bridge over a gorge in the county.

"That's right."

"I think I remember that wreck," she said. "Nobody could figure out how they could have missed the bridge. It's not that dark there, because of the lights of the tavern just down the road." She didn't add that most people thought the driver must have been drunk.

"It was a mystery. My parents didn't drink and the coroner's report confirmed there were no drugs or alcohol in their systems. I guess maybe my dad fell asleep at the wheel." He shrugged, his body moving with delicious friction against hers.

"Is that why you took the job here?" she asked after a long silence. "Because it's where your parents died?"

"I don't know. Maybe." He fell silent again, as if pondering the idea.

Slowly, the air between them seemed to grow warm and thick with awareness. Even though she could barely see Doyle's face in the dim light seeping into the cave from the outside, she felt an answering tension in his body as he turned toward her, his chest a hard, hot wall against her chest.

His breath heated her cheeks as he bent his head until his forehead touched hers. "Tell me it's not just me," he whispered.

She didn't have to ask what he meant. She felt it, in the singing of desire in her blood and the languid pooling of heat at her center. "It's not just you," she answered, her words little more than breath against his lips.

He shifted until his mouth touched hers, just a soft brush at first. A foretaste.

Her fingers curled helplessly against the soft wool of his sweater, grabbing fistfuls as he lowered his mouth again for a longer, deeper exploration. She parted her lips, darting her tongue against his, delighting in his low groan of pleasure in response.

One hand dipped downward, fingers splayed across the small of her back, tugging her closer. The pressure of his mouth on hers increased, more command than request, and she parried with a fierce response that made his body shudder against hers.

Then, as shocking as a bucket of ice water in the face, came the loud rattle of aluminum cans from the mouth of the cave.

Something had tripped the alarm.

Chapter Eight

For a moment, there was no more sound at all, except the pounding of Doyle's pulse in his ears. He steadied the barrel of his Kimber 1911 Pro Carry II, telling himself that the .45 ammo would stop an intruder with a minimum of rounds. The intruder would be highly visible in the light coming through the opening, while he and Laney would be dark shadows in a dark cave, hard to target.

The lingering silence at the mouth of the cave suggested the intruder had come to the same conclusion. Either he'd retreated quietly or he was waiting in the cave entrance for them to venture out to see if he was gone.

Doyle shielded Laney's body behind him and waited, unwilling to make the first move. If the shooter wanted a standoff, Doyle was happy to give him one as long as he and Laney remained in the better tactical position.

He felt more than heard Laney's soft, rapid exhalations against the back of his neck. He didn't know if she'd pulled her own weapon, and he couldn't afford to turn around and check. The one thing he didn't worry about was her firing the gun by accident. If there was anything he'd learned about Laney Hanvey over the past couple of days, it was that she was almost radically competent.

The thunder of his pulse was nearly loud enough to drown out a distant shout coming from somewhere outside the cave. But he definitely heard the second shout, as well as the faint crunch of footsteps on the dirt-packed floor of the cave entrance. The cans didn't rattle again, and seconds later, the footfalls had faded into silence.

More shouts came, forming words he could make out. Someone was calling their names.

He felt Laney give a start behind him, but he reached back quickly, holding her still. "Not yet," he whispered.

The shouts came closer. "Laney!"

The female voice sounded familiar.

"That's Ivy," Laney whispered. "You know she's not the one who was shooting at us."

"I don't know anything," he whispered in response.

"I do," she said firmly. "Trust me on this, okay?"

He didn't want to lower his weapon, but now that she'd identified the voice calling outside the cave, he recognized it, as well. And from everything he'd heard about Ivy Hawkins since he'd agreed to take the job, she was one of the good guys.

He took a deep breath and let it out in a shout. "In here!"

He heard several voices, talking in low chatter as they came closer to the cave. Seconds later, two silhouettes filled the opening.

Doyle didn't drop his weapon. "Don't move any closer."

Both figures stopped. The one on the left was shorter and, despite the bulky clothing, identifiably more feminine. *Ivy,* he thought.

"I'm going to reach into my jacket pocket for a flashlight," Ivy's voice said. She moved slowly, her hand going into her pocket.

A moment later, a flashlight came on, the beam directed not at them but at herself, illuminating her features. "Chief, are you okay?"

"We're fine," Laney answered for Doyle. "Sorry for the caution. But someone was shooting at us less than an hour ago."

DOYLE BRUSHED ASIDE the offer to call in paramedics to check his shrapnel wound. "It's nothing but a splinter," he said dismissively, looking both frustrated and a little sheepish. Laney guessed he felt embarrassed at having to be rescued by the men and women he was supposed to be leading.

She was just glad to get off the mountain, however it had happened, and back to the hospital in Knoxville to check on her sister.

Delilah Hammond was still there guarding Janelle's room, though she'd clearly been in touch with her fellow detectives, for she stopped Laney for a quick postmortem of her experiences on the mountain.

"Must have been pretty scary up there," she said with sympathy before letting Laney enter her sister's room.

"Yeah, but do me a favor and don't let Jannie or my mom know how bad it was." She went on into the room, where her sister greeted her with a hug and a big smile. She was markedly better—more alert, more herself. She'd even put on a little makeup, looking far more put together now than Laney herself, who'd stopped at home only long enough for a hot shower and a fresh change of clothes before rushing to the hospital.

"Where have you been?" Her mother looked relieved to see her.

"I told you I was going to join a search party."

"All night?"

"Mom, you're talking to her like she's a teenager who broke curfew," Janelle said with a laugh.

Alice didn't smile back. "And look what happened the last time one of my daughters didn't show up on time."

Feeling guilty, especially given her ordeal over the past twenty-four hours, Laney gave her mother a fierce hug. "Sorry. I got snowed in up near the summit of Copperhead Ridge and had to overnight in the old Vesper cabin."

Janelle and her mother both exclaimed over her bad luck, and Janelle asked if she'd had to share the cabin with other searchers.

"Just one. I was with Chief Massey."

"Ooh," Janelle said with a smile. "He's cute."

Laney made a face at her sister, hoping she wasn't blushing. "Enough about my night in the snow. How are you? You're looking tons better."

"I'm feeling tons better," Janelle assured her. "I was running a fever last night, so the doctor won't sign off on letting me go. But I'm not even running a fever now." She looked frustrated.

"It won't hurt you to stay another night, just to be sure," Alice reminded her younger daughter. "Things could have been a lot worse."

Janelle's frown faded into sadness. "I know. When I think about what happened to Missy and what might be happening to Joy—"

Laney sat on the bed beside her sister, brushing away the tears falling down Janelle's cheeks. "We're not giving up on Joy yet. The police are back out there right now in the lower elevations, and as soon as there's some more melt-off up near the summit, they'll be heading back up there, too."

"I wish I could remember what happened. What if I saw or heard something that could help the police?"

"You can't worry about that right now," Alice told her. "You worry about getting better and the police will worry about what happened to Missy and Joy."

"Mom's right," Laney said. "You concentrate on you."

And I, she added silently, *will do everything I can to keep you safe.*

"IT LOOKS LIKE the same photo paper to me," Antoine Parsons told Doyle after taking a long look at the photograph of Doyle and Laney that Laney had found at the trail shelter. "I've sent some evidence techs up to that shelter to see if there's anything to be found." He didn't sound hopeful.

"Is there any way to be sure whether or not that photo and the photo of Janelle Hanvey and the Adderly girls came from the same camera?" Doyle asked.

"We'll send both photos to the crime lab in Knoxville to see what can be done about matching them." Ivy Hawkins was the one who answered his query. She and Antoine Parsons were the only ones with Doyle in his office at the Bitterwood Police Department, selected purposefully because they were two of the three people on the force that he felt, instinctively, he could trust.

The other person he decided he could trust was Delilah Hammond, based on the good word his old friend and former Ridley County deputy Natalie Cooper put in for the detective. Natalie's husband, J.D., was an on-call pilot for Cooper Security, where Delilah had worked before taking the job with the Bitterwood P.D. Natalie and J.D. both spoke highly of the woman and assured Doyle she could be trusted.

Delilah was currently in Knoxville, watching over their surviving witness. She'd called in a few minutes earlier to let him know that Laney had arrived safely to see her sister. Now all three of the Hanvey women were safely in one place and he could concentrate on his primary job.

"I think we go with the premise that you and Laney are targets," Ivy said, eyeing him warily as if uncertain how he'd react.

"Or that's what someone wants us to think," Doyle countered.

"Someone shot at you right after you found the photo. It seems that might be what happened with Janelle Hanvey and the Adderly girls, too," Antoine pointed out.

"They were shot with a pistol." Ballistics was still

looking over the bullets retrieved from Missy's body and
Janelle's head wound, but the technicians had already reported that the slugs had been .38s and had almost certainly
come from a semiautomatic pistol. "The guy shooting at
us was using a rifle."

"Maybe he's flexible about his weaponry." Antoine
shrugged. "I just don't think you can say it's two different assailants without more evidence."

"Maybe we should assign someone to guard Laney and
her sister full-time," Ivy suggested. "Although we're already shorthanded now that Craig Bolen's been moved to
chief of detectives."

Hiring a new detective to take Bolen's place had been
high on Doyle's list of priorities until this murder. Maybe
he needed to stop micromanaging the investigation and
wrap his head around the paper-pushing end of his job.

Natalie had warned him he might have trouble with the
transition from investigator to administrator when he'd
asked her advice on the job offer. "I know you, Doyle. You
like to get in there and get your hands dirty. It's not going
to be like that when you're the guy in the office making
hiring and firing decisions and worrying about whether
or not there's enough paper for the copier."

But small-town departments were different. It was the
only reason he'd decided to take the job. He could still get
involved in investigations, especially ones as high profile
as the murder of Missy Adderly and the apparent kidnapping of her sister. The townspeople would expect to see
his face in the newspaper and hear him on the local radio
shows.

"Chief, maybe you should guard Laney Hanvey yourself," Antoine said.

Doyle looked up at his detective, surprised. "You think
so?"

"Well, you're equipped to do it, obviously. But beyond

that, she's been sent here by the county to judge whether or not the Bitterwood Police Department even needs to exist anymore. I figure, it can't hurt to give her a firsthand look at how seriously and personally we take our jobs."

"You mean, offer myself as her bodyguard as some sort of PR stunt?"

Antoine made a face. "Well, when you put it like that—"

"You've already protected her," Ivy pointed out. "And you seem to be getting along okay now."

Doyle tried not to think about the kiss he and Laney had shared in the dark, cold recesses of the cave on Copperhead Ridge. He was pretty sure that kiss wasn't the kind of personal service Antoine was talking about. "Laney Hanvey doesn't strike me as a woman who'd appreciate being followed around by a cop all day."

"So don't let her know that's what you're doing," Antoine said.

"That'll never work," Ivy countered. "She's not stupid."

"Well, he's got to find a way to keep her from getting killed," Antoine argued, "because if we can't even protect the person sent to keep an eye on us, there's no way we're going to be able to convince the county we can pull our own weight."

"Patronizing her won't help anything," Ivy argued.

"You two figure it out and let me know what you decide." Doyle pushed to his feet and headed for the door.

"Where are you going?" Ivy asked, turning to watch him go.

"I haven't had a decent meal since breakfast yesterday." He grabbed his jacket from the coatrack by the door of his office. "I'm going to lunch."

LEDBETTER'S DINER WAS only a block down Main Street from the police department, an easy walk even with muscles as sore and tired as Doyle's. He'd taken his lunch hour early enough that the normal midday crowd had not yet filled the diner, so he had his choice of tables.

He picked one near the door and sat with his back to the wall, an old law-enforcement habit he'd picked up from his father long before he'd ever pinned on his first badge. Cal Massey had been an Alabama state trooper until his death, and he'd raised all three of his children as if they were going to follow in his footsteps.

"Never sit with your back to the door," he'd told them. "You need to always keep an eye on who's coming and who's going."

Doyle and his older sister, Dana, had both taken their father's lessons to heart. Only David, the youngest, had chosen another path.

Tragic, Doyle thought, that the only one of them who'd never strapped on a gun and a badge had been the one to die young.

The bell over the door rang, drawing Doyle's gaze up from the menu. His chief of detectives, Craig Bolen, entered the diner with a man and a woman in their late forties. The man was tall and heavyset, dressed in a dark suit. When he took off the sunglasses he was wearing, his eyes looked red-veined and tired.

The woman beside him wore a shapeless black dress and black flats. Her sandy hair was pulled back in a tight coil at the back of her head, her pale face splotchy from crying. Dark smudges beneath her eyes could have been the remnants of mascara, he supposed, but he suspected they were more likely the result of sleeplessness and grief.

These were the Adderlys, he understood instinctively. Dave and Margo.

He rose as they looked for a table, dreading what he knew he should do. Craig Bolen caught sight of him first, a glint in his eyes, and nodded a greeting.

"Mr. and Mrs. Adderly?" Doyle steeled himself against

the wave of sorrow he knew would flow from them. He may not have held the title of chief of police before, but he'd dealt with grieving families and knew what to expect.

Which was why the shifty look in Dave Adderly's eyes caught him flat-footed.

"Dave," Craig said, "this is Chief Massey—"

"I know who you are," Adderly said bluntly.

"I'm very sorry for your loss, Mr. Adderly," Doyle began.

"You have a funny way of showing it."

Margo Adderly put her hand on her husband's arm, a shocked look on her tear-ravaged face. "Dave."

Craig Bolen frowned at his friend. "Dave, Chief Massey has been out all night looking for Joy—"

"He's not out there now, is he?" Adderly walked stiffly to a table nearby, sitting deliberately with his back to Doyle. Margo Adderly darted a troubled look at Doyle and joined her husband, laying her hand on his arm. He shrugged the touch away.

Bolen looked apologetic. "He and Margo had to pick out a casket for Missy this morning."

"Understood." Doyle waved his hand toward the table, giving Bolen leave to join the Adderlys. He returned to his own table, his appetite gone. When the waitress came for his order, he settled for a grilled cheese sandwich and water, and asked for them to go.

As he left with his food, he glanced across the dining room at the Adderlys. Dave Adderly had turned in his chair to stare at him, his expression hard to read. It wasn't hostility, exactly, at least not the same blatant unfriendliness he'd displayed before. He almost looked as if he wanted to say something, but he finally turned back around and murmured something to his wife.

Doyle spent most of his walk back to the office trying

to figure out what that brief confrontation with Adderly
was all about.

"That was fast." Ivy was still in his office when he returned, in the middle of jotting a note. "I was just leaving
you a message."

"Anything important?"

"The TBI called with the results of the ballistics test on
the slugs from both Missy Adderly's body and Janelle's
head wound. Both came from the same weapon, and
they're pretty sure it's a pistol because of the polygonal
rifling and the size of the slugs. If we find the weapon,
they should be able to identify it."

"*If* we find the weapon." Doyle sank into the well-worn
leather of his inherited desk chair and set his food and
water on the desk. He eyed the brown paper bag without
enthusiasm. "I ran into the Adderlys at Ledbetter's Diner."

Ivy shot him a sympathetic look. "How were they holding up?"

"What do we know about the relationship between
Adderly and his daughters?" Doyle asked.

Ivy's eyes widened. "You mean, should we be looking
at him as a suspect rather than a grieving father?"

"Something about the way he responded to me this afternoon made me think he really, *really* doesn't want to
talk to me about the case. And if I were a father with
one daughter dead and another missing, I don't know that
there's anything else I would want to talk about besides
the case and what the police were doing to find my missing child." Doyle pushed the wooden letter opener lying
on his blotter from one side of the desk to the other. "Ever
been any rumors about that family?"

"You mean like sexual abuse? Never that I've heard."

"Some families go to great lengths to cover up that
kind of thing."

Ivy shook her head. "Both girls were well-adjusted. No

trouble in school, both good students and good kids. Definitely not typical of abuse victims."

"No," he conceded. "But I don't think I'm wrong about Adderly. There's something on his mind he does *not* want to talk about, especially with me."

"It might have something to do with his job," Ivy suggested. "He'll be voting on whether or not the county will attempt to take over the police department and move it under the Ridge County Sheriff's Department."

"Adderly's on the county commission?"

"You didn't know that?" Ivy sounded as if he'd looked up at the sky and somehow failed to notice it was blue.

"I'm new." He was only five days into the job. Surely he had a grace period before he'd be expected to know everybody's business the way the natives did.

Ivy shot him a grin, as if reading his mind. "Maybe we should put together a study book for you. Map out the family trees, outline all the deep, dark secrets."

"Yeah, you get right on that. After you go check on the progress of the search parties. They're supposed to reconvene at the staging area around one to get some food and take a breather. I need someone to gather all the status reports and compile them for me."

"I was going with Antoine to talk to some of Missy and Joy's friends."

"Antoine can grab one of the uniforms to go with him. Tell him to pick one who might be good as a detective. We still have a space to fill on the force, and I'm all for promoting from within."

"I thought you'd have wanted to talk to the searchers yourself."

"I would," Doyle agreed, rising from his desk. "But I can't be two places at the same time. So I need you to be my eyes and ears on the mountain."

"Where are you going?" Ivy asked, following him out of his office.

He shrugged on his jacket. "I'm going to go watch the back of a stubborn public integrity officer without her knowing it."

"LANEY." JANELLE'S VOICE was a soft singsong in Laney's ear. She opened her eyes to see the spring-green curtains of her sister's bedroom. Janelle sat on the bed beside her, writing in a bright blue spiral-bound notebook.

Laney lifted her face from the pillow, feeling cotton-headed. "I must have dozed off."

"That's what I thought, too. But then I realized I was just fooling myself." Janelle looked up briefly from her notebook and gave Laney a pitying look. "You'll have to come to the understanding yourself, though. I can't do it for you."

Laney cocked her head, confused. "What are you saying?"

"People don't get shot in the head and survive."

"Of course they do. You did. The bullet hit the plate in your head—"

"And people don't get shot at in the woods without getting hit." Janelle turned to look at the bright sunshine pouring through the bedroom window, revealing the gory mess where the back of her head should have been.

Laney's stomach lurched, and she clapped her hand over her mouth. When she pulled her hand away, it was coated with blood. She looked down and saw blood drenching her white blouse, still seeping from a large hole in her chest.

Fear seized her, flooding her emptying veins with panic.

"Laney. Sleepyhead." Janelle's voice filled her ears like a taunt.

Her body gave a jerk, and she was suddenly awake, really awake, staring up at her smiling sister. Gone was the bright bedroom, replaced by the muted glow of the light over Janelle's hospital bed. Laney pushed herself up to a sitting position, rubbing her eyes with the heels of her hands.

"Wow, you were dead to the world," Janelle said with a chuckle.

Laney shuddered at her sister's turn of phrase. "What time is it?"

"About one."

The last thing Laney remembered was the food-services aide bringing Janelle her lunch. Alice had taken advantage of Laney's presence to run home for a shower and a nap. Laney had taken over the chair by Janelle's bed and...that was the last thing she remembered.

"You should have awakened me earlier."

"Why? You looked tired. I wanted to watch TV anyway, so, win-win." Janelle grinned at her.

"Has the doctor come by yet?"

"Nope. I asked the nurse about it, and she said that if he hadn't come by to release me at this point, it probably meant he wanted to keep me one more day." Janelle grimaced. "I'm getting sick of this place."

"I know, sweetie, but you don't want to take chances with a head wound." The creepy sensation left over from Laney's strange dream began to dissipate. "And here, you've got an armed guard watching out for you."

"You mean Delilah?" Janelle asked. "She's not here anymore. She left about fifteen minutes ago."

Chapter Nine

Laney frowned. "Delilah left? Are you sure?"

Janelle nodded. "She came in while you were napping. Said she had gotten called back to the office and that there'd be someone taking her place in a little while. But nobody ever did."

Laney dug in her pocket for her phone, checking to see if there were any messages. Maybe there had been a break in the case and Doyle no longer thought there was any need for a guard. But she had no messages. "Did she say who called her?"

"She just said the chief wanted to meet with his detectives so she had to go."

Doyle had made sure Laney entered his cell number in her phone before they parted company that morning. She dialed it now.

Doyle answered on the first ring. "Massey."

"This is Laney. Did you call Delilah away from the hospital?"

There was a long pause. "No," he answered. "She's not there?"

"She told Janelle she'd gotten word you wanted her back at headquarters. She's been gone about fifteen minutes."

"Are you and Janelle okay?"

"We're fine. But I'd like to know who called Delilah."

There was a tap on the hospital-room door. Laney heard

Doyle's voice both on the phone and just outside the door. "I'm just outside. Can I come in?"

Relief jolted through her. "Please."

He was smiling when he entered, but Laney saw the weariness and concern hidden behind the smile. "Hi there, Janelle. How're you feeling?"

Janelle's dimples made an appearance, making Laney smile. "I'm much better. I hear you and Laney had an interesting night."

Doyle glanced at Laney, as if wondering how much she'd told her sister. "We did," he answered carefully.

"I told her about being snowed in," Laney said, flashing him a warning look. "Did you go in to the office?"

"Yeah. I had things to do."

"Should we worry about Delilah getting called away?" she asked.

"Might have been a mix-up on our end. I did ask for all the detectives to come in for a meeting, but I didn't mean Hammond." He walked to the side of the room and pulled out his phone, while Laney turned back to her sister, whose smile had faded into a look of worry.

"Is there something you're not telling me?" she asked Laney.

"We're just a little on edge because we still haven't found Joy or been able to figure out who shot you and Missy. I won't really be able to relax until we do."

"It's so crazy," Janelle said, wincing as she shook her head. "Ow. Pulled my stitches."

Laney helped her lie back against the pillows in a more comfortable position. "I know it's crazy. But there are a lot of folks out there looking for Joy."

"It was so cold last night up on the mountain. I don't know how Joy could have survived it if she's out there hurt and alone."

"Maybe she found shelter somewhere and all we have

to do is find her." Laney tried to sound hopeful, but she knew the odds of finding Joy alive decreased exponentially as the hours passed without any sign of her.

Doyle crossed back to Janelle's bedside. "I caught Hammond on her cell and told her to go on home and get some rest, since she was here all night. I'm going to stick around until I find someone to cover the evening shift."

"You really think I'm in danger?" Janelle asked.

"We're just taking precautions."

The nurse arrived to check Janelle's vitals, giving Laney a chance to pull Doyle aside. "Who pulled Delilah off guard duty?" she asked in a low tone.

"Don't know yet. Antoine's looking into it. Hammond said she didn't recognize the voice, but she's pretty new on the force and doesn't know all the dispatchers by voice. The number was blocked, but all the numbers from headquarters are blocked, apparently. A policy of the old chief. I'm going to have to look at his reasons for doing that and see if I concur."

"So it could have been anybody."

"Hammond says no. Dispatchers have to be able to give a clearance code on demand when they contact personnel on cell phones rather than the radio—so officers know they're not being hoaxed. Hammond said the caller gave the correct clearance code when she asked for it."

"Strange."

"Maybe it really was a miscommunication." Doyle put his hand on her arm, the now-familiar gesture making her stifle a smile. "Let's not borrow trouble when we have enough already."

The nurse finished with Janelle and left the room. Laney found her sister frowning fiercely at the IV cannula in the back of her hand. "My temp was one hundred. There's no way the doctor is going to let me go home today."

Laney brushed the hair away from her sister's forehead.

"If you're running a fever, this is where you need to be anyway, right? Where the doctors and nurses can make sure you get better instead of worse."

"I'm just tired of being here." Tears welled in Janelle's blue eyes. "I'd feel so much better in my own bed."

"I know." Laney glanced at Doyle, wondering if he was thinking the same thing she was. As much as she sympathized with Janelle's frustration at having to stay in the hospital another day, she felt relieved in a way. The extra layers of security the hospital afforded made it that much easier to keep Janelle safe. If she returned home to her mother's small house in the middle of Piney Woods, keeping her safe might become a more difficult proposition.

Doyle produced a deck of cards from the pocket of his coat and laid it on the rolling tray table at the foot of Janelle's bed. "Lucky for you, I came prepared."

Janelle gave the deck of cards a raised eyebrow. "What, you're going to do card tricks? I'm not twelve."

Doyle grinned. "I wouldn't let a twelve-year-old play this game." He pushed the tray table closer and sat on the end of the bed across from Janelle. "I have a friend—used to work with her, matter of fact. Anyway, she got married a while back and invited me to the wedding. She married into this big family—her husband has six brothers and sisters. And the night before the wedding, I got suckered into playing this game they play called Popsmack."

"Popsmack?" Laney mimicked her sister's earlier look of skepticism.

"The groom's twin brothers made it up, apparently."

"Why's it called Popsmack?" Janelle asked, curiosity getting the better of her grumpy mood.

"I'm told that when the brothers and sisters played the game when they were younger, they'd inevitably end up in a tussle. Hence the pop. And the smack."

Laney sat by Doyle at the foot of the bed, giving him

a stern look. "You're not suggesting that's the expected outcome. Because I don't think it would be very politic of a police chief to pop or smack a young woman in a hospital bed."

"I think we can keep it nonviolent," Doyle assured her with a grin. He nudged Laney's shoulder with his. "Three can play this game."

Based on the wicked gleam in his eyes, she wasn't sure playing Popsmack with him was a good idea. But the idea seemed to make Janelle forget about being stuck in the hospital for a while, at least, so what could it hurt?

"Okay," she said. "How do we play?"

"WHY, WHAT'S THAT? That's the queen of spades." Janelle shot Doyle a wicked grin that made him smile. He'd bought the cards in the hospital gift shop to give Janelle a way to pass the time, but his spur-of-the-moment brainstorm about playing Popsmack had turned out to be a mood changer for the patient. It even had Laney laughing, a delightful bonus.

Plus, thanks to the distraction, neither of the Hanvey women had protested having him stick around to play bodyguard.

He laid his card on the tray table. Ten of hearts. Janelle waggled her eyebrows at him.

Laney played her own card—jack of diamonds. She shot a grin at Doyle. "Guess you're in the hot seat, Chief."

"Hmm." Janelle seemed to give her question some thought. They'd been playing for half an hour already and had gone through the obvious questions—age, schooling, favorite food and color. If he were playing with Laney alone, he might have been inclined to cheat in order to get answers to a few of the more intimate questions he'd like to ask, but Janelle's presence put a damper on seduction by card game.

Maybe later, when he had to convince Laney to let him go home with her....

"How many brothers and sisters do you have?" Janelle asked.

He'd braced himself for the question earlier, but neither had thought to ask it before. "Two," he answered. "A brother and a sister."

He didn't clarify that only one of them was still alive.

"What are their names?" Janelle asked as he prepared to show his next card.

"Dana and David."

"Older or younger?"

"Dana's older by a year. David…" He stopped, realizing that if he stuck around Bitterwood long enough, they'd know all his secrets anyway, and it didn't seem fair to start out by hiding this one, inescapable truth about his life. "David was three years younger."

"Was?" Laney slanted a look at him.

"He was working with a charity group in South America when a drug cartel targeted the village where he was working. They wanted to make an example of people who tried to thwart them."

Janelle put her hand over her mouth, while Laney's expression was more grim than horrified. She worked for a county prosecutor, so she'd probably seen her share of brutality, though he doubted she'd ever seen the kind of carnage that had greeted the army patrol that had stumbled on the ruins of the tiny jungle village in Sanselmo.

"He was twenty-three."

"Your poor family." Laney's gaze drifted to her sister, and Doyle realized she probably understood what he'd gone through better than most people. She'd lost a brother herself, and almost lost her sister twice.

"My parents had died a few years earlier." Small blessings, he thought.

"But you and your sister—"

He nodded sharply, ready to move to a cheerier topic. He waved his next card at them. "We ready to deal again?"

Laney squeezed her sister's hand. "Sure."

He laid down a card, forcing a grin when he saw it was a king. "Y'all are in trouble now."

Janelle dealt a nine of hearts and grimaced. "Ugh."

Laney looked as if the last thing she wanted to do was play any more games, but she lifted her chin, smiled at her sister and put down a card. Three of clubs.

"Uh-oh." Janelle's grin was downright wicked.

Laney looked at Doyle, her blue eyes still soft with sympathy. Any thought of giving her a hard time vanished, and he tossed her an easy question. "Loony Tunes or Disney?"

"Loony Tunes," she said emphatically.

"Mickey Mouse scared her," Janelle said with a grin.

"Oh?" Doyle quirked his brows at Laney. "What was it? The big ears? The white gloves? The enormous shoes?"

"It wasn't Mickey Mouse as such," she answered, glaring at her sister. "If you have to know, it was the movie *Fantasia*. Mom took me to see it when I was really little, and I guess it was too intense for me. I'm told I woke from a few nightmares screaming about Mickey Mouse trying to kill me."

Doyle bit back a smile. *Fantasia* had scared him the first time he saw it, too. Only later had he come to appreciate its magic. "So, Mickey gives you the heebie-jeebies?"

"I got over it," she defended quickly. "Mickey's the man and all that. Yay, Disney!"

"She hates to admit having any weaknesses," Janelle said with a sisterly shrug. "It can be annoying, but what can you do?"

The fact that he found Laney more endearing than annoying was starting to scare him. He wasn't quite sure what it was about the pretty blue-eyed mountain girl that had gotten under his skin, but there wasn't much point in denying the fact that he found her damned near irresistible.

Considering the power she held over his job, any sort of personal relationship between them was risky as hell. He should be running hard and fast the other way, but he couldn't exactly do that now, could he? Not with someone targeting her and her sister.

A knock on the door sent a jolt down his spine, and he reached for his holster, not relaxing until the door opened a few inches and Ivy Hawkins stuck her head through the opening. "Everybody decent?"

"Depends who you're asking," Doyle said with a smile.

Ivy grinned at him as she entered the room. She was carrying a folder, which she handed to Doyle before turning her smile on Janelle. "Hey there, Jannie. You're looking a lot better than the last time I saw you."

"I'm feeling better," Janelle assured her. "Although my stupid doctors won't let me out of here."

"The doctors are not stupid." Laney's voice held a hint of sternness that Doyle recognized from his own dealings with his bossy older sister. He let the sisters sort things out between them while he opened the folder Ivy had given him.

Compiled inside, he saw with a glance, were typed reports from the search parties on Copperhead Ridge. He flipped through them, looking for anything new but seeing more of the same. The searchers had so far stuck mostly to the trails, but there were no signs of the missing girl.

He supposed soon they'd have to send searchers off the beaten paths, as dangerous as that might prove to be. For all any of them knew, the girl could be miles away from Bitterwood by now, assuming she was even still alive.

And he was fast losing any hope that she could be.

"Thought you might want these today," Ivy said in a quiet tone.

"Thanks. You still on duty?"

Ivy glanced at her watch. "My shift ended on the way here, but you know we're always on call. You need something?"

He nodded toward the door, and she walked with him over there so they could talk without Janelle overhearing. Doyle felt Laney's gaze follow him across the room, as tangible as a touch.

"I doubt Laney's eaten anything since we came off the mountain. I thought I'd take her out for dinner, but I need to arrange for another guard for Janelle."

Ivy frowned. "Yeah, I heard someone lured Delilah away. Strange."

"It might have been a misunderstanding," Doyle told her, though the more he thought about it, the less he was inclined to think so. Dispatchers didn't normally take it upon themselves to interpret a vague mention of wanting to gather his detectives as an order to call one of them off a guard assignment.

"You want me to keep an eye on Janelle while you take Laney out on a date?" Ivy asked, her expression neutral but her dark eyes twinkling.

"Insubordination, Hawkins," he warned, but he couldn't put much authority behind the words, since she was mostly right.

"If you need someone to take the night shift, I could call Sutton and see if he could do it," Ivy suggested. "He had a late shift at the detective agency last night, but he was off today and is off tomorrow. He napped earlier today, so he should be rested and alert. He could stay until we can pull someone else off the job to take over guard duty."

"I can't pay him," Doyle warned.

"He'd do it for free. We've known Laney and her family for years. She's from up on Smoky Ridge," she added, as if that meant something to Doyle. It clearly meant something to her.

"I've got to see who would be available. Mind if I pass the names by you? I want to make sure whoever we assign to guard Janelle is someone I can trust. And right now, there are only a few people here I know well enough to trust."

"I'm honored to be considered one of them." Her eyes narrowed slightly. "I *am* one of them, right?"

"You are." He smiled. "Even if you're incorrigibly sassy mouthed and prone to meddling in your superior's personal business."

"I'll call Sutton and get him here for the evening shift. That'll give you time to assign someone overnight. Meanwhile, I'll stay until you and Laney finish your, um, dinner." She stopped there, but he still saw the gleam of humor in her eyes.

He had to be careful, he thought. His laid-back style of police work had made him a favorite on the Ridley County Sheriff's Department back in Alabama, even with some of the criminals he'd dealt with, but he knew it might not serve him well as a chief of police. He didn't need to become friends with the people under his supervision, even if it was his inclination to do so. In some cases, too much familiarity could definitely breed contempt.

But he also didn't believe that authoritarianism for its own sake was an effective management style.

He'd have to figure it out on the fly, he supposed.

He stepped back into the hospital room. "Laney, when was the last time you ate anything?"

She looked up, surprised by the question. "I had some crackers around noon."

"Grab your coat," he said. "We're going out to dinner."

"THIS BOSSY STREAK of yours is a little disconcerting," Laney commented as she and Doyle left behind the warmth of the Thai restaurant and headed across the street to where he'd parked his truck. She'd figured when he coaxed her out of Janelle's room for dinner that they'd grab something in the hospital cafeteria. But he'd insisted on getting all the way out of the hospital, assuring her that Ivy would take good care of her sister.

She'd been the one to suggest the Thai place, half expecting he'd be reluctant. Or maybe she'd been hoping for it, for some sign that he was unsuitable as an object of the desire she was having more and more difficulty ignoring.

But he'd foiled her hopes, ordering with ease and even coaxing her into trying one of the more exotic dishes she'd never had the guts to sample before. *Pla sam rot* tasted much better than it looked; the fish—fried whole, head and all, and served in a spicy sweet tamarind sauce—had been delicious.

"I spent some time in Thailand after college," he'd told her. "A college pal's father worked for Chevron in Thailand, and he invited me to visit awhile. We taught English in one of the smaller cities for about a year. It was an adventure."

So much for dampening her interest in him. Now he was more intriguing than ever.

When he slid his arm around her shoulders as she shivered in the cold wind, she couldn't have kept herself from snuggling closer to him if she'd wanted to. "Bossy, huh?" he asked. "I'm practicing my people-handling skills. How am I doing?"

"Not bad," she admitted.

"Brrr." He made a show of shivering as he dug in his pocket for his truck keys. "How long before spring?"

"By late April, it'll be a lot less chilly," she promised. "I guess you're used to warmer weather down on the gulf."

"It gets cold, but not like this." He helped her into the cab before he walked around and slid behind the steering wheel. He turned to look at her, his expression thoughtful. "You thought I'd balk at Thai food, didn't you?"

She couldn't have felt more naked if she'd been literally free of clothing, standing in the middle of the street. Either he was uncannily perceptive or she needed to do a little work on her poker face.

"I was hoping you would," she admitted.

"Why?" The glint in his moss-green eyes suggested he already knew the answer, but he seemed intent on making her admit it.

She sighed and tugged her coat more tightly around her. "I don't need a complication in my life."

"And I'm a complication?"

"Yes." A big, good-humored, impossibly sexy complication.

"If it makes you feel any better, I'm not really looking for complications, either." But even as he said the words, he leaned closer to her, the heat of his body washing over her, his eyes glittering with feral intent.

"No?" she breathed, her chest tight with anticipation.

"No," he answered, his lips brushing hers.

Her fingers curling in his hair, she tugged him closer, her body humming with pleasure. He leaned in, ignoring the console that sat inconveniently between them. He grumbled as his rib cage hit the gear shift, but he didn't stop kissing her, and she felt her control slipping away in a heated rush.

It took a second to realize the vibration against her hip came from her phone. Groaning, she pulled away and tugged the offending instrument from her pocket. Recognizing the number as her sister's hospital-room extension, she put her hand on Doyle's chest and pressed the answer button. "Jannie?" She sounded as breathless as if she'd run a race.

"Please come back, Laney. Please." Janelle sounded teary.

"On my way, sweetie. Has something happened?"

"I don't know. Maybe." Janelle's voice turned into a soft wail. "I think I remember what happened that night."

Chapter Ten

Janelle looked pale and red eyed, but Doyle was glad to see she hadn't fallen apart completely while waiting for them to return from dinner. She held out her arms to Laney, who gave her younger sister a fierce, protective hug while Ivy and Doyle stood a few feet away, allowing the sisters a moment.

Laney cradled Janelle's face between her hands. "Are you okay, baby?"

"Yes. I just—" Janelle closed her eyes tightly, as if she could shut out whatever it was she'd remembered. "I'm glad you're back."

Laney exchanged a quick glance with Doyle. He gave her an encouraging smile as she turned back to her sister. "I'm right here. Tell me what you remembered."

"The aide brought my dinner just after you left, and you know I get sleepy after I eat—" Janelle cut herself off abruptly, as if she realized she was stalling. She took a deep breath. "I dreamed about the camping trip. It was so real. And then I remembered his face."

"Whose face?" Laney asked.

"The man who shot Missy." Janelle's throat bobbed with emotion. "The man who shot me."

Laney looked at Doyle again, her blue eyes haunted. He stepped forward, pulling a chair closer to the bed, near enough to Laney to touch her if he wanted. But he kept his hands to himself, despite the urge to offer his comfort.

Janelle looked at him. "I can tell you what he looks like, but I don't know who he is."

"He's not someone from around here, then?"

"No." Her fingers tightened around Laney's, her knuckles whitening. "He was older, like in his forties or fifties. He had blond hair, or maybe it was blond with gray. Thinning but not completely bald." She closed her eyes a moment, as if trying to conjure up the picture from her memory. "I think he had blue eyes, or maybe gray. It was early morning, and still kind of dark, so I can't be sure."

"And you're sure this is a memory and not just a dream?" Laney asked.

"I'm sure. I was getting my gear together—we had to get a move on if Missy and I were going to make it to school on time. Missy was outside the shelter, about to write something in the logbook when she started cussing."

Doyle glanced at Laney and saw that she was making the same connection he was. He wasn't surprised by Janelle's next words and neither was Laney.

"She'd found this photograph of the three of us sleeping in the shelter." Janelle shuddered. "Someone must have taken it the night before. It was so creepy. Missy showed it to me and then, suddenly, he was there."

"The older man?" Doyle asked.

"Yes." Janelle's face crumpled. "He aimed the gun at Missy and sh-shot her. I think he must have just wounded her the first time, because she started to run away."

"And he chased after her?"

Janelle shook her head, her whole body shaking. "Not then. First, he came into the shelter and aimed his gun at me."

Doyle heard Laney's soft intake of breath, but he didn't let himself be sidetracked by his concern for her. Janelle needed to tell him what she remembered as much for herself as for his case. "Is that when he shot you?"

"Yes," she whispered through her tears. "I think I must have turned away, to try to get up and run." She wiped her eyes with the edge of her bed sheet. "That's the last thing I remember."

"You said before that you girls met someone on the trail earlier. Someone named Ray—"

"Stop." Laney's hand snaked out and grabbed his arm. She turned fierce blue eyes on him. "Enough. Leave her alone."

"We need to know everything she can recall," Doyle said with quiet urgency, understanding her need to protect her sister but not willing to let it stop him from getting the information he needed. Janelle may have been injured and traumatized, but she was going to live.

He wanted to give Joy Adderly the same chance, if she had any chance at all.

"I'm tired," Janelle murmured, closing her eyes. He could feel her starting to withdraw behind the comfort of forgetfulness.

"Janelle, please, I need just a little more information."

She ignored his quiet plea, and Laney slid off the hospital bed, standing firmly between him and her sister. "I think you need to go now."

He stared at her, angry and frustrated. "I'm not the enemy."

Laney's expression softened, but only slightly. "I know. I'm just asking you to give her a little time to recover."

He nodded toward the door, where Ivy stood guard. Laney frowned, obviously reluctant to follow him, but when he moved, she followed.

"Please go to Jannie," she murmured to Ivy as Doyle led her outside the room. "She's upset."

Ivy squeezed Laney's arm. "Okay."

"Come get me if she needs me."

Doyle led Laney down the hall to the waiting area, which was empty, since visiting hours wouldn't be over until nine. He waved toward one corner of the room, where a couple of chairs sat half facing each other. When she sat, he pulled out his chair so that he faced her directly. "I'm sorry for pushing."

She seemed surprised by the apology, and just a little suspicious, as well. "I know you're doing your job."

"I am. And what your sister just told me is a huge break in the case, you know. I need to know everything she remembers."

She pushed her hair back from her pale face, looking tired and sad. "I know. I just hated watching her relive it."

He put his hand over hers. "She's starting to remember things, though, and that's good. Not just for me and this case but for her, too."

She shook her head. "I don't see how remembering someone trying to kill you could be a good thing."

"She already knows it happened. Remembering it helps to demystify what happened. She can't make it any bigger in her mind than it was."

"She can't make it any smaller, either."

He didn't know what to say in response. Laney was right. The more her sister remembered, the more she'd have to deal with emotionally.

But remembering could be the difference between finding Joy Adderly alive or bringing her home in a body bag.

"I think we should consider hypnosis."

Laney looked at him as if he'd just suggested torture. "No."

"I know it's not admissible in court, and I'm not even sure how reliable recovered memories are, but I do think hypnosis could help Janelle work through her fears. There are things she may not be remembering because she's afraid to, and hypnosis could help her control her fears enough to allow herself to get a clearer picture of what happened."

"She had a pretty clear picture of the man who shot her," Laney countered, rising to her feet and pacing across the room until she reached the wide picture windows that normally looked out on the mist-shrouded mountains to the east. But nightfall had turned the windows into large mirrors, reflecting Laney's conflicted expression and the concern in his own eyes.

"I know." He needed to call it in to his office, he realized, to see if the description rang any bells for his officers. He also needed to see if the department had access to a sketch artist who could come to the hospital and work with Janelle on a composite.

"You don't know what it was like before." Laney's breath fogged the glass of the window. She ran her finger through the condensation, making a streak. "When she was in the accident, I mean. We'd lost Bradley and the doctors weren't giving us a lot of hope for Jannie. She was so little." Laney lifted her hand to her mouth briefly, then dropped it to her side. "So many tubes and bandages. Her face was bruised and swollen—I remember the first time I saw her that way, I told my mother the paramedics had made a mistake. That wasn't Jannie."

He touched her shoulder, let his hand slide lightly, comfortingly down her back. She met his gaze in the window reflection, her lips curving in a faint smile.

"But it was, of course."

"She was ten, right?" He thought that was what she'd told him before.

"Yeah. Smart as a whip, and full of crazy energy. A pistol ball, my daddy used to call her. God, he loved her so much. She was his comfort when he was dying. His little pistol ball."

He wrapped his arms around her, tugging her back against his chest. She rested her temple against his cheek. "How long did it take for her to recover?"

"She lost two years of forward movement, basically. When she woke up from the coma, she had to learn everything all over again. The doctors weren't sure she ever would get all her functions back, but they didn't know Jannie."

"She can't remember anything from the first ten years of her life?"

"No. She doesn't really remember Bradley or Dad. Only the stories we told her about them once she was able to understand everything that had happened."

He thought about his own parents, about the brother he'd lost, and the idea of not remembering them was so wretched he felt tears sting his eyes. He kissed the top of Laney's head. "I'm sorry."

"Maybe it was easier, not remembering what she'd lost." There was a wistful tone in Laney's voice, a reminder that whatever memories Janelle had lost had remained vivid and painful in her older sister's memories.

"I'm not sure avoiding the pain is worth losing the memories," he murmured.

She turned around to look at him. "Is that your way of saying I'm being stubborn about the hypnosis?"

"No, I'm just saying I'd hate to lose my memories of my parents and David. Even if I also lost the memory of losing them."

She looked at him thoughtfully for a long moment. He didn't know if he'd convinced her he was right about Janelle, but at least she seemed to be considering what he'd said.

"I'd like to go down to the gift shop and find something to cheer Jannie up."

He nodded. "Okay. I'll come with you."

She pressed her hand against his chest. "No. I need to be alone for a little while. To think about everything you said."

He frowned, remembering why he'd come to the hospital in the first place. "I'm not sure I like you wandering around here by yourself."

She gave him an odd look. "You're never really alone in a hospital."

"I know, but—"

"You're thinking about that photograph."

"I don't think it was some coincidence."

"Obviously not. But it also doesn't mean someone's going to hunt me down in a busy hospital and try to shoot me."

He knew she was probably right. And she was right about the hospital being a place where a person was never really alone. Between patients, visitors and staffers wandering around the halls at all hours, privacy was about the last thing a person was able to find in a place like this.

And there were security guards on the first floor, where the gift shop was located—he'd seen them as he entered earlier that evening.

"Okay. I'll go back and make sure Ivy and Janelle are doing okay."

"Have you arranged a guard for tonight?" she asked as he walked with her into the hallway.

"Ivy asked Sutton Calhoun to fill in until I can find a replacement. He's probably on his way here by now."

She nodded with approval. "Sutton's a good guy."

He bent and pressed his lips to hers, the touch undemanding. But he felt a pleasant rush of heat pour through him even so. "Hurry back."

He headed down the hall toward Janelle's room, sparing a look back down the hall over his shoulder as he reached the door. Laney stood near the elevator alcove, her gaze on him. Her lips curved in a brief smile, then she turned and walked into the alcove, disappearing from sight.

He went into Janelle's room and found her napping, while Ivy and a tall, dark-haired man conversed, head to head, in quiet tones near the window. They both turned at the sound of the door opening, their hands dropping to the weapons holstered at their waists. They relaxed when they saw who had entered. Ivy caught the tall man's hand and tugged him with her toward Doyle.

"Chief, this is my fiancé, Sutton Calhoun. Sutton, this is Doyle Massey."

"Nice to finally meet you," Sutton said with a smile of greeting. "I know a couple of friends of yours—J.D. and Natalie Cooper."

"Oh, right," Ivy said. "I forgot you worked with Natalie down in Terrebonne."

"Worked with J.D. once, too."

"Where's Laney?" Ivy asked.

"She went to the gift shop to get something for Janelle." He glanced at the hospital bed and lowered his voice. "How is she?"

"She drifted off soon after you left," Ivy answered quietly. "Shouldn't you have gone with Laney? What happened to being her bodyguard?"

"She needed some time alone," he answered, hoping he hadn't made a mistake. "I figured, since there's security here in the hospital, she'd be okay."

Ivy didn't disagree, but she also looked concerned, which made him second-guess his decision to let Laney go to the gift shop alone.

Fifteen minutes, he decided. He'd give her that long to get the gift and return to the room. If she wasn't back in fifteen minutes, he'd go look for her.

What could happen in fifteen minutes?

LANEY ALMOST TURNED back to her sister's hospital room when she reached the first floor and found that the normally busy hospital lobby was nearly empty. Even the employee who normally manned the front desk was missing in action. If she hadn't known better, she might have thought the hospital had been abandoned.

But she shook off her nerves and walked down the silent corridor until she reached the gift shop. It was mostly empty, too, but a woman with curly gray hair stood behind the counter and greeted her with a smile when she entered, making her feel less vulnerable and alone.

She needed to get her emotions under control. Janelle needed her to be strong and unflappable. She couldn't fall apart every time she heard some new detail about her sister's ordeal. She needed to be the sane one. The one her sister could depend on to be her rock.

As she searched for something to cheer her sister up, her mind wandered back to the question of who had called Delilah Hammond off her guard assignment. From what Doyle had told her, it almost had to be someone familiar with the Bitterwood P.D.'s procedures. Possibly even someone in the police department itself.

She'd been assigned to look into corruption in the department before her sister's injury and Missy Adderly's murder had distracted her. Maybe it was time she got back to the job assigned to her.

She had an idea where to start.

Down the second small aisle of the gift shop she found a plush pony the color of copper pennies. It reminded her of Sugar, Janelle's favorite horse at the Brandywines' trail-riding stable. Even though a stuffed toy was far too juvenile a gift for a young woman of twenty, she bought it anyway. At least it was cute and, if nothing else, Janelle could concentrate on feeling miffed at being treated like a baby rather than thinking about the details of her ordeal.

She paid for the stuffed horse, waved off the cashier's offer of a bag and headed back to the elevators. The doors nearest to her slid open with a dinging noise, and Doyle stepped out, nearly running into her.

He put his hand on her arm to steady her, looking down at the stuffed horse she held tucked under one arm with a quirk of his eyebrows. "Nice pony. I didn't realize your sister was still twelve."

She made a face at him. "How is she?"

"Sleeping. Sutton Calhoun's up there watching over her with Ivy. And your mother arrived as I was leaving."

"You're going home?" She hadn't meant the question to sound as needy as it had come out.

If he noticed the desperation in her voice, he didn't show it. "I came to look for you. Your mother said you would try to stay here tonight and that I should try to talk you out of it."

She looked up at him skeptically. "Do you always do what people tell you to do?"

"Only if I agree." He ran his hand slowly down her arm, from shoulder to elbow. "How much sleep have you had since we left the cabin this morning?"

"I napped in Jannie's room."

"For what, an hour?"

"Something like that."

"Let's get you home."

The temptation to do as he suggested was more powerful than she'd expected. The truth was, she was exhausted, her exertions of the day before conspiring with her lack of sleep during their long, cold night in the cabin to wipe out most of her stamina.

"Okay, but there's one thing I want to do first. Two

things, actually. At some point, I need to take Sugar here up to Jannie."

"But first?"

"First, I'd like to go talk to hospital security."

THE HOSPITAL SECURITY office consisted of one small room with six video monitors, two of which covered the lobby and the parking entrance full-time, and the other four rotating between cameras in the elevator alcoves of each of the hospital's eight floors.

"We don't cover the hallways so much, since there are nurses and other personnel on duty at all times," the head of security, Roy Allen, explained. "We mostly cover the ways in and out so we have a record of who's coming and going at any given time."

A security technician manned the live feeds at all times. The one on duty now continued doing so, while Roy Allen, who had told them he was a retired police sergeant as if he felt the need to provide his bona fides, had pulled that day's video covering Janelle's floor and set it to play for them at double speed on a smaller monitor set apart from the live feeds.

"There." Doyle pointed to the security monitor as a man in dark green scrubs walked into view of the security camera positioned in one corner of the elevator alcove. He had shaggy brown hair, a thick mustache and horn-rimmed glasses, and he kept his head down as if aware of the camera. "Why does that guy look familiar?"

"He doesn't," Laney said, frowning at the screen. "Does he?"

Doyle frowned, wondering why the man had caught his eye. Something about the curve of the head, maybe.

About ten minutes later in the recording, Delilah Hammond appeared on the surveillance camera and entered the elevator.

"There goes Delilah," Laney said. "Have you heard anything from the station about who might have called her?"

"None of the dispatchers have copped to it. Delilah's pulling the records for her cell phone to see if we can get a number, but that could take a while." He paused as the camera image running across the monitor caught the same man with the mustache heading into the elevators a few minutes after Delilah's departure. He looked the same as before, but there seemed to be something dark sticking out from the pocket of his pants. "Pause the video," he said.

Allen hit Pause. "Back it up?"

Doyle nodded. "To where the man steps into the picture. Can you run it at a slower speed?"

"Sure." Allen backed up the video to where Doyle had asked. The man in the scrubs came into view.

"Pause," Doyle said.

Allen pushed a button and the video froze.

"What's that in his pocket?" Laney asked, bending closer to the monitor.

The video picture wasn't clear enough to tell. But whatever it was bulged in the pocket, suggesting it had some size to it. It was too big and bulky to be a cell phone. Not the right shape to be a pistol.

"Maybe a camera?" Roy Allen suggested.

Doyle and Laney exchanged a look. He saw excitement, liberally tinged with worry, shining in her blue eyes. He knew they were both remembering that Polaroid photo they'd found on the mountain. Someone had targeted Laney, in a very personal and specific way.

Could this be the same man? The man who'd taken the photos on the mountain? The man who'd killed Missy Adderly, tried to kill Janelle and done God only knew what with Joy Adderly?

"Maybe we should get a screen grab of the best shot we have of the guy," Laney suggested. "We could show it to the desk nurse, see if anyone saw the guy lurking outside Janelle's room."

"Good idea." Doyle looked at Roy Allen, who immediately told the technician to get them a screen grab of the best image and print it out. Ten minutes later, they left the security center with a large printout of the man in the green scrubs, his face partially lifted toward the camera, enough to make out shaggy brown hair, a thick brown mustache and glasses with brown plastic rims.

So far, none of the desk nurses could tell them anything about him, though one remembered seeing him. "I just figured he was a new orderly," she'd said without much interest. "His badge looked right. I didn't look closely, though."

Doyle made a mental note to check if any of the hospital's regular employees was missing a badge, and went with Laney back to Janelle's room to show the photo to Ivy, Sutton and Laney's mother, Alice, who joined them near the door to hear what was going on. None of them had been there when the man showed up on the video feed, but Doyle hoped maybe one of them would recognize him.

"Never seen him before," Ivy commented when Doyle showed them the image. Alice Hanvey shook her head, as well.

"Doesn't that look like a disguise?" Sutton asked.

They looked at the image again. Doyle realized Sutton was right. "It does."

Alice's blue eyes searched her daughter's face. "Are you okay, Charlane? You look a little shaky."

Doyle looked from Alice's concerned expression to Laney's pale face, where spots of red had risen in her cheeks. Charlane, he thought. So that was what *Laney* was short for.

"I'm fine," Laney answered. "Just tired."

Alice gave her arm a squeeze and headed back across

the room to the chair by Janelle's bed, leaving Doyle and Laney with Ivy and her fiancé.

"Nice horse." Sutton reached out and flicked the tail of the stuffed horse still tucked under Laney's arm, a teasing light in his eyes.

Laney gave his arm a light punch. "I know where you can get one if you need a cuddle buddy."

His gaze slanted toward Ivy. "Oh, I've got one of those already."

"Too much information," Doyle drawled. He glanced at the bed, where Janelle lay with her back to the door. "How's Janelle?"

"She's been asleep most of the time you were gone," Ivy answered just as quietly. "Although if my calculations are correct, she's due for another visit from the nurse, so she won't get to sleep much longer."

She might as well have cued the nurse's arrival, for within seconds, a smiling licensed practical nurse came through the door with her machine to check Janelle's temperature, blood pressure and oxygen level. After she left, Janelle frowned at the four of them huddled in the doorway of her room.

"What's going on?" she asked, sounding a little groggy.

Laney went to her sister's side. "Everything's fine. I brought you something." She handed over the stuffed horse.

Janelle pulled a face. "Oh, look. A baby toy."

"I thought she looked like Sugar."

Janelle's expression softened. "Okay, in that case…" She took the stuffed horse and hugged it to her, looking more like a scared kid than a twenty-year-old. Doyle supposed, after all she'd been through, she was allowed a little bit of emotional regression.

But he needed her to be grown-up for just a few minutes longer. He took the screen-grab printout from Sutton and crossed to Janelle's bedside. "Janelle, do you think you could take a look at this and tell me if you've ever seen this man before?"

Laney shot him a look of displeasure, and even Alice seemed surprised that he would bring up the subject, but he couldn't let their overprotectiveness stop him from doing his job. He handed the printout to Janelle, who looked at it intently, her brow furrowed.

"It's not a great picture," she said after a few seconds of consideration, "but it might be him."

"Might be who?" Laney asked.

"Ray." Janelle handed the photo back to Doyle. "Remember? I told you about him. The guy we ran into on the trail the day before..." Her words faltered, her expression darkening. "Before the shootings."

Laney caught her sister's hand, her tone urgent. "Are you sure?"

"No, not entirely. This guy looks a little older, but the glasses and mustache are the same. And the hair. My memory isn't exactly running on all cylinders."

"This isn't the guy who shot Missy, is it?" Doyle asked.

"No." She seemed certain about that much. "That guy was a lot older. Looked entirely different—he was nearly bald, for one thing. No mustache or glasses." Her mouth flattened. "I'd definitely remember the shooter if I saw him again."

Doyle and Laney exchanged glances.

"Where did you get that picture?" Janelle asked. "Is that in the hospital?"

"Yes," Laney answered. "Just down the hall, as a matter of fact."

Janelle looked suddenly excited. "Did you get to talk to him? Maybe he saw or heard something on the mountain—"

"We haven't located him," Doyle answered.

"But how did you get the picture?"

"We were looking into something else," Laney answered before Doyle could. "Something unrelated, and we happened across this photo."

"Did I describe him to you before? Is that how you recognized him?"

She hadn't described him before, Doyle realized. Laney had been so intent on rushing him out of Janelle's hospital room that first day that all he could remember about someone named Ray was that the girls had run into him on the trail at some point before the shootings.

He should have followed up, but they'd found the other body, and then he and Laney had gotten caught in the snowstorm and ended up hiding in a cave from a gunman. He'd been a little distracted.

So why had he thought the man looked familiar?

Chapter Eleven

After taking the photo back from Janelle, Doyle handed it to Ivy, who was pulling on her jacket in preparation to leave. "Can you run this back to the station on your way home? We need to get an APB out on this guy."

"On what grounds?" Ivy asked quietly as he and Sutton walked out of the room with her. "Walking through the hospital with a camera? That's not against the law. And this isn't even our jurisdiction."

"He was on the mountain the day before the shootings. That means he might be a material witness. He could have seen someone else on the mountain."

"Good point." Ivy turned to Sutton and rose to kiss him lightly. "See you when you get home."

Sutton released a long, slow breath through his nose, his gaze following Ivy's small, curvy form down the hall.

"You two have a date set yet?" Doyle asked.

Sutton dragged his gaze away from his fiancée's backside and looked at Doyle. "Next weekend, we're driving to Gatlinburg and doing the quickie-wedding thing. Her mama was getting kind of nuts with the planning and my dad isn't exactly the 'going to the chapel' kind anyway. So we're going to take Seth and Rachel as our witnesses and just go ahead and get hitched."

"Seth is Detective Hammond's brother? The former con man?" Doyle asked, trying to place the names.

"Right. And Rachel is Rachel Davenport."

"Ah, the trucking-company heiress." A few months ago, threats to Rachel had exposed the dark underbelly of the Bitterwood P.D., causing the upheaval that had brought Doyle to town in the first place. "And Seth and Rachel are together now, right?"

Sutton grinned. "Ivy and I may end up racing them to the altar. Seth's always been pretty competitive."

"Thanks for filling in for us here tonight. We're spread pretty thin these days to begin with, and I don't want to pull people off the mountain search to guard Janelle."

"Happy to do it," Sutton assured him.

Doyle went back into Janelle's hospital room and found Janelle had already started to doze off again. Alice and Laney had their heads together, Alice's expression firm and Laney's tinged with a hint of rebellion.

Alice looked up at Doyle as he came closer. "Tell her she needs to go home and get some sleep."

"I'm fine," Laney said.

Doyle sighed. She was half-asleep, only worry and stubbornness keeping her upright. "I know you're fine," he said, adding an exaggerated leer to his voice, eliciting, as he'd hoped, a roll of her weary blue eyes. "But nothing's changed since we agreed earlier that it was time for you to go home."

"Of course things have changed," she disagreed.

"I've put out an APB for our mustachioed friend. Sutton's out there, looking like a grizzly guarding this room. Your mama's here to give your sister all the TLC she can handle," he added, earning a smile from Alice. "It's time to get you home and into bed."

Laney's eyebrows lifted at his choice of words, but with her mother listening, she said nothing in reply. But he could see her thinking up at least six sassy retorts she'd have shot back at him if they were alone.

"Okay, fine. I know when I'm outnumbered." She turned to give her mother a hug and a kiss. "I'll be back in the morning to spell you."

"Take care of yourself, Charlane. I don't want to have to split my hospital time between my girls."

Laney didn't question Doyle when he walked her to her car, though he saw her looking around the parking deck for his truck. "Are you going to follow me home, too?"

He nodded, taking her keys from her and unlocking her car door. "Got a problem with that?"

Conflicts played out behind her eyes. "Yeah, sort of. But not enough to kick up a fuss." She took the keys back from him and sat behind the steering wheel, looking up at him as he continued to stand there with the door open. "You want me to wait outside the pay booth?"

"I do," he said. "Will you actually wait?"

That earned him a whisper of a smile. "Maybe."

He leaned into the car, brushing her temple with a light kiss. "If you wait, I might be talked into tucking you in and reading you a bedtime story."

Her blue eyes blazed up at him. "Tease."

Smiling, he dropped another kiss on her forehead and backed out of the door, letting her close it. His truck was up a level; he bypassed the elevators, taking the stairs two at a time.

He held his breath as he steered toward the final turn at the parking-deck exit, peering through the shadowy dusk past the toll booth until he spotted a pair of taillights about ten yards beyond the tollgate. He paid the parking charge, drove under the rising gate and pulled up behind her little black Mustang, trying not to think too long or too hard about what he planned to do when they got to Laney's place in Barrowville.

He'd seen promise in her eyes, but also a bone-deep weariness that had sounded an echo in his own tired body.

The spirit might be willing to see where the night might take them, but he had a feeling the flesh might not be up to it.

And that was okay, he realized, even though his sex life was in the middle of a bit of a drought these days. It was a mostly self-imposed bout of celibacy, a combination of the recent upheavals in his professional life and a lack of interesting women in his personal life.

Laney Hanvey was the first woman who'd sparked his imagination in a long time. Just his luck, the first woman he'd really wanted in a long time was one of the last people in the world he should pursue.

"It could use a little dusting." Laney cast a critical eye over her cozy living room, trying to see it through Doyle's eyes. The house was a Craftsman-style bungalow on a small cul-de-sac near the southern edge of town, chosen as much because it cut five minutes off her drive to Bitterwood as for its quaint charms. She had converted one of her two bedrooms to an office, but she did most of her work from home in the living room, her laptop perched on a small tray table so that she could work from her comfortable armchair in front of the fireplace.

"It's fine." Doyle closed the door behind them, shutting out the cold wind whistling past her eaves.

"It's cold in here." Laney rubbed her arms, telling herself it was the cold, not her rattled nerves, that sent shivers dancing up and down her spine. She busied her trembling hands with firewood from the bin beside the hearth, tossing a couple of logs atop the half-burned remains of her last fire.

Doyle took the last log from her hands, dropping it into the fireplace. He caught her hands in his. She looked up at him, trapped between wariness and a slow burn of desire that had taken up residence at her core. "Nothing has to happen tonight," he whispered, even as his face moved closer, his eyes dipping to her lips.

She tightened her grip on his hands. "I know. I'm not sure what I want."

"There are very good reasons why I should walk out that door," he agreed. "And at least one good reason I should stay."

"Doyle…."

He eased away from her, though he still held on to her hands. "If the man at the hospital was the same man who took the photos on the mountain—"

"He's not. You heard Janelle. That's not the man who shot them."

"I believe that was a camera in his pocket."

She shook her head. "You think it's possible, maybe, but you couldn't tell anything from that video grab. It was too blurry. You could be seeing what you expect to see."

"It's no coincidence that the man from the mountain showed up near your sister's hospital room."

"Maybe he saw news stories about the attack on her. Maybe he thought he'd drop by and see how she was, then realized he didn't really know her well enough for that and didn't want to scare her."

"Do you really believe that?" Doyle looked skeptical.

No, she had to admit, at least to herself. She didn't really believe it. "He didn't do anything to Laney while Delilah was gone."

"You were there."

"I was asleep part of the time," she admitted, a flutter of anxiety shimmering through her brain when she recalled waking up at her sister's side. She'd dreamed something, she remembered, although the details of the dream were gone, leaving only a bitter aftertaste of unease.

He brushed his knuckles down her cheek, his brow

furrowing as if he picked up on her disquietude. "You need sleep."

"So do you."

"Yeah, I do. Mind if I crash on your sofa?"

Her gaze, which had drifted down to the curve of his full lower lip, snapped up to meet his. "The sofa?"

"You have another suggestion?" His voice was as warm as a flannel blanket, wrapping itself around her like a snare.

Part of her wanted to tell him to go home and leave her in peace, but beneath the sexy heat of his voice, she heard a darker thread of concern. He might be willing to go as far as she allowed his gentle seduction to take them, but he was here primarily as a wall between her and whoever had been out there in the woods gunning for them.

"You've assigned yourself as my bodyguard."

He didn't deny it. "Two birds, one stone," he murmured, bending closer until his lips brushed lightly over hers.

She groaned deep in her throat. The sound sparked an answering growl that rumbled through Doyle's chest as he pulled her closer, his mouth moving over hers with stronger intent.

He felt good, she thought, sliding into the curve of his arms as if she belonged there, as if she'd come into the world in that strong, hot embrace and any time spent away from it was time wasted.

She was loopy, she thought, even as she slipped her cold hands under the hem of his sweater and sought out the hot silk of his skin beneath.

He hissed against her mouth. "Cold hands."

"Hot body," she answered, flicking her tongue across his lower lip.

He smiled against her mouth as he started to walk her toward the sofa. "Thank you."

They stumbled over the corner of the coffee table and

landed with a soft thud onto the sofa's overstuffed cushions. Doyle shifted until he was half lying across the sofa and positioned her over him. "Comfy?"

"Be careful. If I get too comfy, I might doze off."

He caught her face between his hands as she bent to kiss him again. "I'm okay with that, you know."

She looked deep into his gaze and saw the truth there. "You mean, you'd be willing to just cuddle all night?" she asked, her voice tinted with humor.

"I could do that."

"Could you cuddle naked all night?" she asked, mostly to wipe that suddenly serious look off his handsome face.

"Um, no." He rewarded her with a glint of humor in those mossy eyes.

"Okay, so that's ground rule number one. No nakedness without intent."

He pulled his head back as she once again started to dip her mouth to his. "Ground rules? We have ground rules?"

"Of course. Rules are important, you know. They tell you the limits of your boundaries."

He cocked his head, humor still lighting up his eyes. "What if you don't like your boundaries to have limits?"

"Then you're an anarchist and you're dangerous as hell."

"Dangerous can be good." He lowered his voice, dropping his eyelids until he gazed at her through his dark eyelashes. "Dangerous can be sexy."

"Danger is usually destructive," she answered.

His mouth curved. "You are so damned sexy when you're prim."

She pushed against his chest. "I'm not prim."

He tugged her back against him. "But you are. Prim and decent and so very controlled." He slid his hand down her side, letting it come to a rest against the curve of her hip. "Makes a man want to see what it takes to break that control."

Not very much, she thought, her heart jumping as his thumb played slowly over the ridge of her hip bone, moving dangerously close to her center with each light stroke. Her body felt combustible beneath his touch.

When Doyle spoke again, his voice was hoarse. "You were talking about ground rules."

"What ground rules?" she murmured against his throat. She slid her hands under the front hem of his sweater this time, her fingers tangling in the coarse thatch of hair that grew in a line up his belly. She traced the path upward, flattening her fingers across the hard muscles of his chest.

He kissed her deeply, intently, his fingers going still against her hip as if he wanted to concentrate all of his focus on her mouth. The last of her resistance seemed to melt away, until she felt boneless against him, helpless to contain the wildfire of desire filling every cell of her body.

The trill of a cell phone jarred through her body like an electric shock. Doyle growled a curse against her mouth and gently set her away from him, sitting up to pull the phone from his pocket.

"I'm sorry," he murmured as he punched the button. "Massey."

He listened for a second, his brow furrowed, then waved his hand toward the television. "What channel?"

Laney read his gestures and pulled the television remote from a drawer in the coffee table. She turned on the television. "What channel?"

"Nine," he answered. The look of concern in his eyes was starting to scare her.

She switched the channel to the Knoxville television station. The evening news was on; a still image of a man's face filled the screen. Below the picture, a caption read, "Ridge County man found dead in Knoxville."

The grainy image of the man seemed to be a driver's

license photo blown up to fit the screen. He looked to be in his fifties, with thinning fair hair and light-colored eyes.

Laney's phone rang, giving her a start. She saw a Knoxville number on the screen and realized it was her sister's hospital room. "Hello?"

"It's him, Laney." Janelle's voice was shaky and full of tears.

"Who?"

"The man on the TV. Are you watching? It's him."

Laney looked at the screen just as the image switched to a live shot from outside a Knoxville restaurant, where the reporter was standing just outside a taped-off crime scene. Within the yellow tape, police had cordoned off a rectangular section of the restaurant building, where a dark blue Dumpster sat near the wall.

"The restaurant owner found Richard Beller's body in the Dumpster at six this morning, but police say the body could have been there for as long as a couple of days, as the restaurant has been closed the past week for renovations. Mr. Beller, age fifty-eight, who lived in Melchior, Kentucky, until recently, had not been reported missing. Police are investigating his death as a homicide."

"That's him," Janelle repeated through the phone, her voice strangled. "That's the man who shot Missy."

Chapter Twelve

"Richard Beller, age fifty-eight. Formerly of Melchior, Kentucky. His priors include stalking, animal cruelty, assault and gun charges." Doyle stuck an enlargement of Beller's driver's license photo on the bulletin board in the small detectives' bull-pen area, where all his investigators, along with several county lawmen and even a pair of detectives from Knoxville, had congregated to hear what he'd come up with over the past thirty-six hours.

One of the county representatives was Laney, who sat near the back, her arms folded and her brow furrowed. He hadn't had much of a chance to talk to her since he'd dropped her off at the hospital Wednesday evening so she could comfort her distraught sister.

He'd arranged with a private security firm out of nearby Purgatory—the same one Sutton Calhoun worked for—to provide guards for Janelle Hanvey at the hospital and, since her release yesterday, at her mother's home on Smoky Ridge. He wasn't quite sure how he was going to explain the expenditure to the people who paid the department's bills, but he'd figure that out later. Janelle's safety was a top priority, and he couldn't spare any of his own officers.

He needed all his people on deck, because this murder case had just taken a drastically unexpected turn.

"He was shot in the back of the head, execution style. The coroner's initial report states that he was probably killed sometime Monday morning and dumped in the large trash container outside Mama Nellie's BarBQ within a few hours after. His body remained there until Wednesday morning, when the proprietor showed up to ready the restaurant for its grand reopening on Thursday."

"Which means he was killed shortly after he killed Missy Adderly and shot Janelle Hanvey," Antoine drawled.

"Looks that way."

"So where is Joy Adderly?" Delilah Hammond asked.

"That's the question, isn't it?" He picked up a stack of paper and gave it to Ivy to hand out to the rest of the people in the room. "These are copies of a map of Copperhead Ridge, supplied by the Copperhead Trail Association. It shows the major and minor hiking trails as well as the general terrain of the mountain. The last map we gave searchers only showed the trails because that's what we asked the Brandywines to supply. Much of the area off trail is largely overgrown, but clearly, we're going to have to push our search boundaries outward to include these areas, as well."

Ivy finished handing out the maps, keeping one for herself and handing the leftovers to Doyle. He took one for himself and put the rest on the table next to him. He looked out over the small crowd.

"Other than the Adderly sisters and Janelle Hanvey, we know of only one other person who might have been on the mountain besides Richard Beller the weekend of the attacks. We think it was this man." He picked up the photograph of the man with the mustache and glasses, the man Janelle had called Ray. "A man who looked like this met the girls on Sunday. Janelle said he seemed friendly enough but didn't linger. However, this same man showed up on surveillance video at the Knoxville hospital where Janelle Hanvey was being treated until yesterday."

Most of the people in the room turned to look at Laney.

She went a little pink at the scrutiny but kept her eyes on Doyle. He smiled at her, earning a slight curve of her otherwise solemn mouth.

"We don't know the connection, if any, between this man and Richard Beller. Nor do we know if he had any hand in the attacks on the girls. But he's a material witness in the Copperhead Trail shootings. So keep a lookout for this man as you're searching. Any more questions?"

The lawmen in the room with him shook their heads.

"Your search assignments are on the back of the maps. Contact headquarters as soon as you find anything of interest. And assume that anyone you meet on the trail could be armed and dangerous. Be safe out there."

While everyone else departed for their search assignments, Laney remained, rising from the table where she'd perched at the back of the room and walking slowly to where he stood at the front. "My name isn't on any of the search lists."

"I know. I have a different assignment for you." He nodded his head toward the door to his office, not waiting for her to follow. He entered the room and smiled at the two women sitting there, bracing himself for Laney's reaction.

"Mom," she said, her voice rising with surprise. "Jannie?"

Her mother crossed to give Laney a hug, while Janelle remained seated in the chair across from Doyle's desk.

"What's going on?" Laney directed the question to Doyle.

"I had a talk with Janelle last night. She's ready to help with the investigation."

Laney's eyes narrowed. "Help you how?"

Janelle stood and caught her sister's hands in her own. "Laney, I think I may be able to remember more about what happened to me if I go back up the mountain and try to retrace my steps."

Laney looked horrified. "Jannie, you just got out of the hospital. You're in no shape to climb a mountain."

"The Brandywines agreed to let us take three of their horses up the trail," Doyle said.

Her blue eyes met his sharply. "I'd like to speak to you alone."

He'd expected her rebellion. He was ready for it. Mostly. "If you'll excuse us," he murmured to Alice and Janelle, escorting Laney through the door into the now-empty detectives' bull pen.

"Have you lost your mind?" she asked, blue eyes blazing. "Jannie's recovering from a gunshot to the head! She still has stitches and a doctor's excuse to keep her out of school another week."

"She wants to do it, Laney."

"I don't care!"

He reached out to touch her arm, hoping to soothe her, but she jerked her arm away and glared at him, her sharp little chin stabbing the air in front of him.

"We're not taking her up the mountain," she said.

"That's my decision." Janelle's voice was soft but firm behind Doyle. He turned to find her standing in the open doorway, her squared shoulders and stubbornly jutted chin a mirror image of her sister's. "I want to do this, Laney. I *need* to do it. I have to remember so we can find out what happened to Joy."

Laney crossed to stand in front of her sister, her expression full of equal parts love and fear. "Are you sure you're up to it?"

Janelle nodded. "I can do this."

Behind Janelle, Alice looked both terrified and proud. "I'll take Janelle home to get ready for the ride. Give us about an hour."

Laney watched them go, her heart shining in her eyes. Doyle felt a coiling sensation in the center of his chest, as if someone had taken his heart and given it a painful twist. Taking Janelle up the mountain had been his idea, and he'd known that Laney probably wouldn't like it. But he hadn't realized until this moment just how deep her fear for her sister went.

If something happened to Janelle because he'd convinced her she needed to take this ride up the mountain—

The door closed behind Alice and Janelle, and Laney whirled around to face him, her blue eyes wide with anxiety. "Tell me this isn't a mistake."

His answer stuck in his throat.

She stared at him a long moment, then looked down at her feet, slumping into a nearby chair. "We've spent the past couple of days with an armed guard protecting her, and now we're taking her up the mountain on a horse to the place where she damned near died. Have we all lost our minds?"

He sat in the chair beside her, reaching across to take her hand. "I thought it was a good idea. Janelle seemed eager for it, but—"

To his surprise, she squeezed his hand and slanted a quick smile at him. "You can't talk Jannie into something she doesn't want to do."

"You and I will be there with her. We'll both be armed, right?"

She nodded quickly. "Damned straight."

He smiled at that. "How much do you hate me right now?"

Her blue eyes lifted, a hint of humor in their depths. "Enough to want to smack you upside the head, but not enough to actually do it."

Putting his hand over his chest in mock relief, he smiled at her. "Maybe this'll give us a good excuse to kiss and make up."

She tried to look stern, but the curve at the corner of

her lips gave her away. "That is not what my boss sent me here to do, Chief Massey."

He leaned closer, lifting his hand to her cheek to brush aside the wisp of hair that had fallen out of her neat pony-tail. "What he doesn't know won't hurt him."

She caught his hand and pulled it away from her face. "Don't make this harder, Doyle. You know it's a conflict of interest for me."

Clearly, he realized, the time they'd spent apart had given her the chance to shore up her crumbling defenses against him. Gone was the sweet and willing temptress he'd tangled with on her sofa the other night. She was fully armed this morning and showed no signs of melting again.

That wasn't to say, however, that he couldn't give it a go anyway.

"Technically, since I'm brand-new on the job, anything you find of any interest to you or your boss really can't be held against me. I wasn't here for it." He ran his thumb over the back of her hand and lowered his voice. "And in case you've forgotten, we crossed that line by a mile the other night."

She gave him a look full of exasperation. "Doyle, is this just a game to you? It's not a game to me. I take my job seriously."

He stopped grinning. "I take my job seriously, too. But I've learned the hard way that if you don't laugh now and then, you go crazy. And believe me, a crazy cop is not someone anyone around here wants to deal with."

She stared at him for a long, silent moment, consterna-tion vibrating in her expression, as if she were trying to put together a jigsaw puzzle that didn't have all its pieces. Other people had told him, over the years, that he was a hard guy to figure out. He'd never thought of himself that way, but maybe there was some truth to what those other people had said.

He supposed he had a tendency to keep his real feelings, the hard-to-deal-with feelings, buried under the smiles and laid-back charm he doled out with abandon. Apparently, in the middle of that very serious attempt at seduction the other night, he hadn't made his intentions clear enough. Maybe because he was still trying to figure out those intentions himself.

Did he want something long-term with Laney? Or, more to the point, perhaps, did he really intend to let Laney Hanvey drift out of his life without his putting in the effort to keep her?

As she turned toward the door, he caught her hand, pulling her back into his orbit. Her eyes blazed up at him, setting fire to his blood.

"I'll tell you what I don't care about," he said in a gravelly growl. "I don't care what the county commission thinks about what you and I do in our private lives. I don't believe for a second that your boss would accuse you of looking the other way just because you and I happen to find each other attractive, because if he's spent ten minutes with you, he knows integrity is your most enduring and incorruptible quality."

Her eyes softened at his words, melting into warm, blue pools. "Doyle." Her voice came out soft and almost pleading.

He bent his head slowly, taking his time as he kissed her, giving her room to run if she wanted. But she lifted her face to his, drinking in his kiss and giving it back with a fierce passion that rocked him off his internal axis. He tugged her with him into his office and closed the door, pressing her up against it as he deepened the kiss. Her arms snaked around his neck, her breasts flattening against his chest, and he found himself suddenly light-headed, dizzy from the burst of passion she'd kept in check since that night at her house.

Laney finally pushed him back from her, gazing up at him with midnight eyes as she let out a soft *whoosh* of breath.

He grinned at her soft exhalation. "Am I still a puzzle to you?"

She cocked her head slightly, one corner of her kiss-stung lips curving upward. "Yes. But I must admit, I'm a little more invested in solving you now."

"We'd better get changed for our trek up the mountain." He'd dressed for the office today, complete with tie, because of the bull-pen meeting. Laney's suit was business-casual, better for the office than a search party. "I have a change of clothes here."

"I have clothes in my car," she said, her gaze dipping briefly to run the length of his body before rising again to meet his eyes. He stifled a grin—and the urge to ask her if she liked what she saw—and nodded for her to get moving. She dragged her gaze away and headed out his door, closing it behind her.

He dressed quickly, exchanging the suit for jeans, a sweater and a thick leather jacket. His dress shoes went in his office closet, replaced by sturdy Timberland boots. The pistol and holster stayed, of course, hidden beneath his jacket. He considered adding a second weapon in an ankle holster but decided having a pistol there might interfere with the stirrups on the saddle.

He ran into Laney near the front desk, on her way out to the parking lot. She'd dressed in slim-fitting, faded jeans, a heather-brown sweater and a brown leather jacket. Her shoulder-length hair was pulled back into a tuft of a ponytail at the base of her neck, and she hadn't bothered reapplying any of the lipstick he'd kissed off of her in his office.

He was tempted to grab her and get rid of what little remained.

"Want to drive up together?" she asked.

"You mean, you don't trust me driving in the mountains."

"Well, you *are* a beach boy." She shot him a sparkling grin that suggested she'd given some thought to his earlier arguments against keeping their distance from each other and was beginning to lean in his favor again.

Her smile faded when they reached her small black Mustang, her gaze flicking his way. "This may not be car enough for all three of us."

He sighed, knowing he'd been bumped in favor of sisterly devotion. "I'll meet y'all on the mountain."

She caught his hand as he started to walk away, her eyes shining with delicious promise. "See you soon."

He grinned as he headed for his truck, feeling like a teenage kid in the throes of his first crush.

"Does he know how to ride?" Janelle asked doubtfully as she and Laney watched Doyle unfold himself from the front seat of his truck.

"I guess he does, since he suggested it." Laney watched Doyle cross to where they stood by the Brandywines' horse trailer. He smiled a greeting.

"Do you know how to ride?" Laney whispered as the Brandywines outfitted Janelle with a hard-shelled riding helmet and led her horse from the trailer.

"Yes," he answered. "Do you?"

The look of indignation she shot his way elicited a grin, and she realized sheepishly that all he'd done was turn her mildly insulting question around on her. She wiped her scowl away with a grin. "I deserved that."

"I realize that when it comes to mountain living, I'm a novice. But they do have things like horses and hiking and camping in other places."

"I reckon I've been givin' you a hard time about your strange, flatlander ways." She laid on her drawl pretty thick.

"You have. You really have." He flattened his hand against the small of her back, the touch deliciously possessive. "Lucky for you, you're too damned cute for me to take offense."

She glanced at the Brandywines and her sister, wondering if they had overheard.

Doyle bent his head closer, dropping his voice to a whisper. "Are we keeping this thing between us secret?"

She darted a look up at him. "For a little while."

"Until your work with the Bitterwood P.D. is done?"

"I think that would be wise."

He nodded and edged away from her, robbing her of his body heat. The morning chill flooded in to take its place.

"How good are you with horses?" James Brandywine asked Doyle. "How much riding have you done?"

"I played polo for several years back in Terrebonne," he answered, a hint of a smile curving his lips. "Did a lot of trail riding as a kid. One of my fellow Ridley County deputies owned horses and I'd ride with him and his wife and kids pretty regularly. I know how to ride."

"Then you can take Satan." With a grin, James handed over the reins of a powerfully built black gelding. "I brought extra helmets. You don't have to wear one, but it's probably a good idea."

"Better safe than sorry." Doyle took the helmet.

Janelle had already mounted the gentle chestnut mare Sugar, her favorite horse in the Brandywine Stables and the namesake of the stuffed horse Laney had given her at the hospital. Carol led the third horse, a bright-eyed Appaloosa, down the ramp. "This is Wingo," she told Laney.

Laney recognized Wingo from her last trip to the Brandywine Stables almost a year earlier. Wingo seemed to recognize her, nuzzling her hand when she patted his velvety nose. While James closed the trailer, Carol gave

Laney a leg up into the saddle. "We'll wait down here with the trailer until you get back."

"I hope we're not keeping you from work," Laney said, apology in her tone.

"It's our off-season—too cold for trail riders this time of year. Come spring and the warmer weather, we'll be swamped. But our grooms can handle things back at the stables for now." Carol patted Wingo's side. "Y'all be careful up there." She lowered her voice. "Don't let Jannie get too worked up."

Laney wasn't sure she could prevent it. This trip was about Janelle trying to recover some terrible memories her mind had, so far, not allowed her to access. Success almost guaranteed that Janelle would get worked up.

It was Laney's job to make sure things didn't go too far.

The sun was peeking over the top of the ridge by the time they reached the first trail shelter. Janelle, who'd ridden ahead a bit with the eagerness of youth and the excitement of being out of the hospital, pulled her horse up as she reached the shelter, her expression going from pink-cheeked energy to pale apprehension.

Laney drew Wingo up beside her, reaching across to touch her sister's shoulder. Janelle's startled jerk elicited a nervous response in her mount; the chestnut twitched sideways for a couple of steps before Janelle brought her back into control. "You sure you want to do this?" Laney asked.

Janelle nodded, swinging her leg over the saddle to dismount. Holding the reins, she walked the horse to the front of the shelter, where there was no fourth wall. She gazed inside, her lip curling as she seemed to remember something.

Laney dismounted, as well, walking Wingo over to the post that held the logbook, looking for somewhere she could tie the reins. But she stopped midstep as she saw a triangle of white sticking out of the logbook.

She flipped open the acrylic cover that protected the logbook from the elements and tugged the triangle from between the pages of the book. It was a photograph, she saw with a sinking heart. A photo of a woman lying in a hospital bed, asleep. And another woman sitting in a chair beside the bed, her hand entwined with that of the woman in the bed. She was asleep, as well, her blond hair tousled and her face soft with sleep.

Someone had taken a photo of Laney and her sister at the hospital and left it here in the logbook for her to find.

Chapter Thirteen

Janelle's already pale face whitened further as she looked
away from the trail shelter and met Doyle's concerned
gaze. "I was reaching into my pack for my camp knife,"
she said in a strained voice. "I don't know why I thought
a knife could be any sort of protection against a man with
a gun. Just instinct for survival, I guess."

She leaned her head against the horse's neck. The chestnut mare snuffled softly but didn't move away.

Doyle looked at Laney to gauge her reaction. But Laney
wasn't looking at her sister. Instead, she was looking at
something she held in one shaking hand, her face as pale
as her sister's.

Dismounting from the black gelding, he crossed to her
side and looked at what she was holding. It was another
photograph. Of Laney and her sister in the Knoxville hospital.

"I want this son of a bitch taken down," she growled,
shoving the photo at Doyle and walking her horse over to
Janelle's side.

He and Laney were both wearing gloves, but he still
held the photo by the edges in case the photographer had
left fingerprints, though the other two photos had been
clean of any prints or trace evidence. He took a closer look,
realizing the photo had to have been taken during the pe-

riod of time between Delilah's departure from the hospital and his arrival. Laney had mentioned falling asleep then.

That was the time the man in the scrubs had shown up on the hospital security cameras. The man he was now certain had been carrying a camera.

"What's wrong?" Janelle picked up on the sudden tension.

"Nothing," Laney said. "This was a bad idea. Let's go home."

Janelle pulled away from her sister and crossed to Doyle. He briefly considered hiding the photograph from view, but doing so would only upset her more, as she'd wonder what they were keeping from her.

"Doyle," Laney warned as he started to show the photograph to Janelle.

He ignored her, feeling a certain kinship with Janelle. The accident that had killed his parents was still, to this day, something of a blank space in his memory. He hadn't been there, of course, but even the secondhand version of their accident was a blur in his mind. He'd been twenty, just like Janelle, old enough to join the army if he'd wanted to, or get his own place, but the authorities had glossed over so many of the details that he wasn't even sure, to this day, what had really caused his parents' car to go off Purgatory Bridge into the river gorge below.

"She has a right to know everything that's happening to her," he said. "Good or bad. She's old enough to make a choice how she wants to handle it."

Janelle stared at the photograph, her lower lip trembling. "Who could be doing this now? Richard Beller is dead. We saw him on television."

"I don't think Richard Beller has been doing anything since shortly after he killed Missy and shot you," Doyle confessed.

Janelle's look of horror made his stomach squirm, but

he held her gaze. Laney muttered a low profanity and hurried to her sister's side, grabbing the photograph away from Doyle and wrapping a protective arm around her shoulders.

Janelle shrugged her sister's arm away. "I'm not a baby. And this is crazy. Where the hell is Joy? If Beller's gone, why haven't we found her?" She pushed away from Laney and mounted Sugar, giving the mare a light kick in the ribs that spurred her into an uphill canter.

"Jannie, what are you doing!" Pocketing the photo before Doyle could get it back from her, Laney hurried to catch the reins of her own mount, which was sidestepping energetically as if ready to sprint off after the mare.

Doyle grabbed the reins of the black gelding before Satan could dart off after them. Hauling himself on the horse's back, he tried to catch up, but despite his assurances to the Brandywines earlier that morning, he wasn't nearly as good a horseman on uphill, rocky trails as he was on flat land. Satan seemed to be sure-footed as he navigated the winding mountain path, but Doyle's own unease with the terrain kept him moving at a slower pace than Satan wanted to go.

Laney and Janelle seemed to have no such caution, putting distance between themselves and him at an alarming pace. He lost sight of them where the trail curved around a large shale boulder, and by the time he rounded the outcropping, they had disappeared from sight completely, though the trail ahead was visible for several hundred yards.

He looked off the path and thought he caught a glimpse of Janelle's bright orange riding helmet, but the trees on this part of the mountain were young growth evergreens, survivors of the blights and pests that had hit so many of the trees in the Smoky Mountains. How Janelle and Laney were even riding through this thicket, he had no idea.

"Laney!" he called, but the ever-present wind blowing down the trail seemed to whip his voice backward into his face.

He tried to lead the black gelding off the trail, but the big horse balked, as if he knew he wasn't supposed to wander off track. Growling a curse, Doyle dismounted and wrapped the gelding's reins around a nearby tree. "If you run off, you stubborn piece of rawhide, I'll have you arrested. You hear me?"

Satan rolled his eyes with annoyance, clearly unimpressed with Doyle's show of authority.

Doyle started to thread his way through the underbrush, trying to follow the trail of broken twigs and flattened plants Janelle and Laney had left in their wake, but no matter how far into the woods he walked, he never seemed to catch sight of them. Worse, he began to question his own tracking skills, which had been honed in swamps and marshlands rather than a rock-infested alpine rain forest.

He'd lost sight of the hiking trail longer ago than he liked to think about, and if he didn't start backtracking, he might end up lost in these woods for hours if not days. Unlike Laney, he hadn't thought to bring trail markers, nor had he dropped any bread crumbs to show him how to get out of the woods. He was, to his utter dismay, a complete greenhorn when it came to hiking the Smokies.

But he did have the map he'd stuck in the pocket of his jeans before they left the police station, he remembered with relief.

As he reached into his pocket to retrieve the map, he felt two sharp stings in his back and his right thigh. Simultaneously his whole body seized up, every muscle bunching in a symphony of pain. Losing all control of his limbs, he fell forward into the underbrush, hitting the ground face-first with a thud, saved from a bone-shattering impact only by the bill of his riding helmet.

He screamed with pain, except he was pretty sure that

the cry ringing through his brain hadn't made it out of his mouth. Then, after what seemed a lifetime, the cramping, zapping pain went abruptly, blessedly away.

But he still couldn't move.

Taser, his buzzing brain deciphered.

But knowing what had just hit him didn't help. He knew from past experience that his limbs might not work for another few seconds, and that was all his attackers needed.

First, rough hands jerked him up by the collar of his shirt, nearly choking him as they pushed off the riding helmet and shoved a musty-smelling cloth sack over his head. A different set of hands grabbed his limp arms and secured his hands over his head. His tingling limbs wouldn't cooperate with his attempt to fight back, twitching more than moving in response to his brain's commands.

By the time the feeling came back to his body, he was trussed up and being dragged through the bushes. His shouts earned him a sharp kick to his ribs, knocking the breath right out of him as pain blasted through his side.

By the third kick, he decided to bide his time and see where his captors were taking him. He just hoped, wherever he was going, Laney and her sister were far, far away.

"WHY DID YOU do that?" Laney tried not to shout at her sister, but after hurtling headlong into the thick woods, more adrenaline than blood seemed to be pumping through her veins. "Have you lost your mind?"

Janelle had finally pulled the mare to a stop, sobbing like a hopeless child. She slid from the panting horse's back and met Laney halfway, wrapping her arms around her sister's waist and pressing her tearstained face against Laney's neck. "I'm sorry. I just—I freaked. I'm sorry."

Laney stroked Janelle's hair, murmuring soothing words as she tried to figure out just how far off the trail they'd come. Fortunately, they were still in the middle elevations, a long way from the snowy top, and a cursory glance at their surroundings convinced her they hadn't come nearly as far as she'd thought from the hiking trail. She saw Widow's Walk, the bald rock face near the summit, and estimated they were a good three miles from there. Widow's Walk faced south, so if she kept moving due west, they should find the trail sooner or later.

"Who killed Richard Beller?" Janelle asked a few moments later, as her tears subsided. "And if Beller's dead, who left that photo of us?"

"I don't know," Laney admitted. "Right now, we need to get back to the trail and find Doyle." She forced a smile. "You know he's a flatlander. He might be lost and need us to find him."

"Nah, Satan won't let him go off trail," Janelle said confidently, wiping her eyes and grabbing Sugar's reins.

Laney gave her sister a leg up to the saddle. "I forgot about that. You're right. He's probably stuck on the trail with that stubborn horse, cussing us both."

Sure enough, when they reached the hiking trail, Satan was still there, his black coat dappled by the midday sun peeking through the trees overhead.

But apparently Doyle hadn't let Satan's recalcitrance stop him, because he was nowhere in sight.

"Uh-oh," Janelle murmured, slanting an anxious look at her sister.

Laney looked around, spotting only the tracks of their own horse ride into the woods. But if Doyle had gone in search of them on foot, he'd have probably tried to stick to their trail, wouldn't he?

Then why hadn't they run into him on the way back?

"Should we go look for him?" Janelle asked.

Laney glanced at her sister, alarmed to see that her face was pale, dark circles forming under her eyes. "He'll have to fend for himself for a while," Laney said, even though her guts were starting to twist with worry. "It's time to get you back home and in bed for some rest."

"I'm okay," Janelle said, but she wasn't able to infuse her protest with any conviction.

"You just got out of the hospital. You're going home. Carol and James can run you by the house on their way back to the stables."

"So we're taking Satan with us?"

"Yes." No point in leaving the horse up here, Laney thought. If Doyle made it back to the trail, he was strong enough to walk back down the mountain. And if he didn't make it back to the trail, Satan standing there tied to a tree would do him no good.

Carol and James were surprised to see Laney and Janelle return with three horses and no chief of police, but Laney's terse explanation sent them into action. "Should we contact the other search teams?" Carol asked as she settled Janelle into the front seat of the truck while James started leading the horses into the trailer.

"Not yet," Laney answered after a brief pause for thought. She didn't know for sure that Doyle was in trouble. He was just, for the moment, lost. And the last thing he needed, as the new chief of police, was to become the butt of jokes around the watercooler at the police station. "He may still be out looking for us. If I don't run into him pretty soon, I'll call for help."

She crossed to the truck to talk to Janelle while Carol went to help James with the other horses. Her sister sat with her head back against the car seat, her eyes closed. She looked up when she heard Laney's footsteps nearing the truck. "You're going back to look for him." It wasn't a question.

Laney nodded. "Flatlanders," she said with a forced smile.

Janelle wasn't smiling. "You're in that photo, too, Laney. You shouldn't be out there by yourself."

"I'll be okay."

"You can't know that."

Laney didn't bother arguing. Janelle was right. She couldn't know whether or not she'd be okay. She only knew that Doyle was out there somewhere in the woods, quite possibly lost. On the mountain, it was easy enough to step off a blind drop and break an arm or leg or, God forbid, a neck. He could run across a bear up early from its winter slumber. Or step on a copperhead or a timber rattler.

She turned to Carol, who was approaching the truck. "If I don't call you in two hours, contact the search teams and tell them what's going on. Tell them I'm looking for the Bitterwood chief in the woods off the hiking trail just past the first trail shelter. But give me two hours, okay?"

Carol looked alarmed but nodded. "You sure you don't want James or me to go up there with you? Or maybe keep one of the horses?"

She might be slower without the horse, but she could go more places on foot. And neither Carol nor James was nearly as good a hiker as she was. They'd just hold her back. "I need y'all both to take care of Jannie. If there's not a policeman parked outside my mom's house, please go check with my mom to find out why. And don't let Jannie go in by herself. One of y'all walk her in."

"Laney, for Pete's sake," Janelle grumbled.

"Humor me, okay?" She squeezed Janelle's arm through the open window, then looked at Carol. "Two hours."

"Got it."

Laney gave Carol's arm a quick squeeze, as well, realizing only after she was heading back up the trail that she'd unconsciously mimicked one of Doyle's people-handling habits.

He's just lost, she told herself as she headed up the trail at a clip.

But deep in her gut, she didn't quite believe it.

By the time Doyle's captors finished hauling him uphill, he was bruised all over and his ears were still ringing from a particularly vicious kick delivered by whichever of his captors was holding his arms. The man at his feet let go of his legs without warning, letting them thump painfully to the ground.

"Who the hell are you?" Doyle asked, not raising his voice this time, since yelling seemed only to piss off his captors and drive them to greater violence.

There was no answer, only the sound of the wind rushing through the trees, making a clattering noise that sounded for all the world like rattling bones, reminding him of Laney's tale of the Cherokee boneyard on their earlier hike up the mountain. Just three days ago, he thought with surprise. It felt like another lifetime.

Hands still held his wrists, keeping his torso partially upright. He tried to use his feet to push to a standing position, but they seemed to be bound together, and his effort earned him a quick, hard slap to the side of his face.

"Cut it out!" he growled, giving a hard jerk of his hands. They came loose from his captor's grasp, but he wasn't prepared, and all his insubordination got him was a hard thump on the back of his head when it hit a pair of steel-toed boots.

"Shut up." It was the first time either man had spoken. Doyle didn't recognize the voice, but he had been in Bitterwood only a few short days. There were several people in his own department he'd met maybe once so far. He certainly couldn't have picked their voices out of a crowd.

Hands grabbed his wrists again and started tugging him backward through the underbrush. Rocks dug into his bottom and the backs of his thighs, sharp in places and cold as a tomb, sending shivers rolling up his spine in waves. He tried to dig his heels in, to make it harder for the man with the hard hands to do whatever he was trying to do.

Nobody tried to pick up his feet or stop his kicking attempts at rebellion. Had the second person left after dropping Doyle's feet?

That would make the odds more even, but as long as he was hog-tied and hooded, he was still at a huge disadvantage. And too many more clouts to the head like the last one might make it even harder for him to fight back if the opportunity ever presented itself.

The pain of being dragged backward over the ground increased as the rough terrain started putting rips in his jeans, exposing his bare skin to the sharp-edged rocks littering the ground beneath him. He tried using his feet to lift his backside off the ground but couldn't get enough of a foothold to make much difference. He nearly wept with relief when darkness descended, and the ground beneath his bottom smoothed out.

The man who'd been dragging him let go of his hands again. This time, however, Doyle anticipated the move and was able to stop his head from slamming into the ground. He heard footsteps moving away from him, and he struggled to roll over onto his stomach, hoping to get his knees under him enough to push to a standing position. To his surprise, nobody tried to stop him.

The footsteps receded. There was a loud creaking noise, and what little light had been filtering through the bag over Doyle's head disappeared completely.

He lifted his hands to his neck, his gloved fingers coming into contact with something holding the hood in place. Duct tape, he realized as he gave a clumsy tug and the adhesive pulled the skin on his neck. But a little pain was worth the effort, and within a few seconds, he'd pulled the offending bag from his head and had his first look around.

There was nothing but darkness, any direction he looked.

No, he thought a few seconds later. That wasn't quite true. Behind him, in the direction where his captor had disappeared, he thought he could make out dots and slivers of light, faint but tantalizing. But his first attempt at moving in that direction landed him facedown again, his hobbled feet giving him no way to balance.

He rolled onto his back this time and sat up, using his teeth to pull off his gloves. His fingers ached in response to the damp cold, but they were far more agile bare, and he made much quicker work of the duct tape wrapped around his ankles than he had the tape around his neck.

He pushed to his feet again and walked over to the whispers of light his adjusting eyesight had spotted. Reaching out, he felt the rough wood of a door. Following the surface, he found the door ended on either side in damp, solid rock.

A cave with a door? Or was he in an abandoned mine shaft?

Even when he found the handle that should have opened the door, he couldn't make the slab of wood move. It must be locked on the outside.

Okay. So he was stuck here for a little while. Not exactly good news, but at least he was still alive. He wasn't sure why, exactly, his attackers hadn't shot him dead instead of subduing him with a Taser, but he decided not to waste time trying to figure it out. Small victories were better than none.

Using his hands to explore the contours of his dark prison, he decided he was in a cave, not a mine. Someone had apparently put a door into the cave entrance to shut people out, and judging by how far he'd been dragged uphill through the underbrush, this place wasn't anywhere near a well-beaten path.

The men who'd tied him up had frisked him first, he remembered, the hazy memories of those mind-numbed moments after the Taser attack starting to roll back into his brain. They'd taken his Kimber 1911 for sure. Had they taken his keys, too? He tried his right jeans pocket, where he usually kept the keys. Nothing.

He tried his left pocket, half hoping he'd put the keys there for some reason he couldn't remember. He hadn't, but to his surprise, he felt the contours of his cell phone, which he normally kept in his back pocket. He'd put the phone there, he remembered, rather than sit on it while in the saddle and risk butt dialing everyone on his contact list.

Though he knew there was no chance of a phone signal inside this mountain cave, he tugged the phone from his pocket and hit the power button. The display lit up, casting a dim blue glow in the area directly around him. But he could do better than that, he thought with a grin of triumph. He slid his fingertip across the face of the phone and opened a flashlight app. Seconds later, bright light flowed from the tiny flashbulb beneath the phone's camera lens.

Playing the light around the cave, he saw that it was roughly circular, the walls ending about ten feet from where he stood. Only a second sweep of the light revealed a dark opening that suggested another cavern lay beyond that back wall. He crossed there slowly, his legs still feeling rubbery after the dual ordeal of the Taser shock and the skin-shredding drag through the woods. The dark opening was narrow but large enough for him to slip through easily. Beyond, there was another, smaller chamber, with the same damp brown walls and slightly slanted floor.

But this room was different in one important respect.

It was already occupied.

She was curled up against the far wall, her knees up to her chest and her face averted from the bright light. Her hair was dirty and tangled, her cold-weather clothing grimy and torn in places. She made soft mewling noises of pure fear that ripped a new hole in Doyle's heart.

Her own mother might not recognize her if she saw her, he thought, but he'd been looking at her photograph enough over the past few days to know exactly who she was. Directing the light away from her eyes, he slowly approached, crouching as he neared her. Keeping his voice gentle, he said her name. "Joy."

She looked up at him, her eyes wide with fear. She'd cried a lot over the past few days. He saw the evidence in her puffy, red-rimmed eyes.

"That's your name, isn't it?" he asked. "You're Joy Adderly, right?"

"What do you want?" she whimpered, looking away.

"The same thing you do," he answered. "To get us out of here."

Chapter Fourteen

At some point since Laney had last passed this way, some-one had beaten a highly visible path through the under-brush just off the trail where she had followed Janelle off into the woods. There were broken twigs, crushed leaves, all indicators that someone had been through on foot with-out worrying about leaving signs.

The problem was, there were almost too many trails to follow, going off one way or another, and following each of them, she ended up losing the trail altogether.

Where in blazes had Doyle gotten off to? How far would he wander before realizing he was lost? Would he know to stop where he was and wait for people to find him rather than to continue to wander about, getting more and more lost?

Of course he would, she scolded herself. He was a flat-lander, not stupid. He'd been a deputy and had, no doubt, participated in his own share of search parties. He'd know the rules to abide by if he found himself lost.

All she had to do was find him.

The sound of movement coming through the underbrush behind her had her whirling around, reaching instinctively for the zipper of her jacket to get to her pistol. Only when she recognized the tall, thin-faced man with sharp blue eyes did she still her movements, relaxing. "Detective

Bolen," she said, dropping her hand over her pounding heart. "You scared me."

Craig Bolen smiled his greeting. "You're a ways off the trail, aren't you?"

She started to explain why but stopped when she thought about the position she'd be putting Doyle in, exposing his mistake to one of his top cops. "I was up here earlier with my sister, and I think I dropped a bracelet," she fabricated.

"And came back up here alone, with what all's been happening out here?" Bolen looked surprised.

"What are *you* doing off trail?" she asked.

"The chief told me to take a few days off—since I'm so close to the Adderlys—but I hated missing out on the search party." Bolen looked haunted. "I can't putter around the house all day if there's any way to find Joy Adderly alive."

Of course, Laney thought. Bolen must be devastated by what had happened to Missy and Joy. He and the Adderlys were close.

"I'm so relieved your sister is okay," he added with a warm smile.

"Thank you."

"You want to join me in searching?" he suggested, waving his arm toward the wide-open wilderness around them. "Since we're both here? We could keep an eye out for your bracelet, too."

"That's a great idea," she agreed quickly, feeling a ripple of relief. She hadn't exactly been able to relax and focus on the job of searching for Doyle when she'd spent half the time jumping out of her skin every time she heard a strange noise. Craig Bolen was the Bitterwood P.D. chief of detectives. She could hardly have picked a better bodyguard for her search.

And since Bolen knew the Adderlys well, he might even

have some insight about where Joy Adderly would go if she'd somehow managed to get away from her captors.

"I guess you heard about Richard Beller," she said as they started walking east up the incline toward the summit of Copperhead Ridge.

"Richard Beller?" Bolen sounded confused.

"The man who shot Missy and Janelle. A guy in Knoxville found his body in a Dumpster up there. Jannie identified him as the one who shot her and Missy."

"I was fishing up on Douglas Lake the past couple of days," he said quickly. "I haven't watched the news since I left." His brow furrowed. "She's sure it's the same fellow?"

"She identified him from his driver's license photo."

"So, the man who killed Missy is dead." Bolen looked satisfied. "Do her parents know?"

"I'm not sure they've been told yet. The police wanted to be sure."

"If he's dead, where's Joy?" Bolen's eyes met hers, full of challenge. "Do you think she's still alive?"

"We all hope so," Laney answered, her gaze snagged by a glitter of sunlight glancing off something lying in the underbrush ahead. She crossed to the spot and saw, with surprise and no small bit of alarm, a set of car keys lying half-hidden in the jumble of leaves, vines and rocks underfoot. Crouching, she picked them up, recognizing the "Visit Gulf Shores" key ring belonging to Doyle.

"Find your bracelet?" Bolen called.

She started to tell him about the keys but stopped, seized by a sudden rush of caution. Were the keys dropped accidentally or as a bread crumb to mark Doyle's trail into the woods?

She pocketed the keys and turned to look at him. "Yes. Hope we can find Joy just as easily."

Bolen smiled at her, but she couldn't quite bring herself to smile back at him. The keys felt heavy in her pocket, a tangible reminder of something she hadn't let herself think about during her search for Doyle.

Something was wrong. Very wrong.

Whatever had happened to Doyle, it couldn't be good.

"ARE YOU INJURED?" Doyle edged closer to Joy Adderly, taking care not to scare her any further. She trembled like a windblown leaf, her limbs wrapped around herself as if she could roll into a cocoon and shut out the cruel world.

"Joy," he said when she didn't respond, "I need to know if you're hurt."

She finally lifted her gaze, squinting at the light, even though he took care not to direct the phone flashlight directly at her face. "They're going to kill me."

"Believe it or not, it's a pretty good sign that you're still alive after all this time."

"Have they told anyone what they want with me?" She was crying, a soft, helpless bleat that made his heart break. He carefully reached his bound hands toward her, but she scuttled away from his touch.

He dropped his hands in front of him with a sigh. "I'm not sure. But if you'll help me out a little, maybe I can get us both out of here."

She slanted a suspicious look at him. "Help you how?"

He held up his hands, which were still bound by duct tape. "I don't suppose you could help me get this off?"

She stared at him for a long time, as if she suspected a trick. "If you're a cop, how did they get you?"

"Shot me with a Taser and tied me up while I was still incapacitated."

He couldn't tell if she believed him or not. But before he became desperate enough to pull up his shirt and show her the Taser marks, she reached for his hands and started tugging the tape from around his wrists.

Her fingers, he saw with horror, were bruised and bloody,

the nails torn nubs as if she'd tried to claw her way out of here. Hell, she probably had, he realized. If she'd seen what had happened to her sister and Janelle, she'd be desperate to get away before the same thing happened to her.

Although, the person who brought her here couldn't have been Richard Beller, the man who'd shot Missy and Janelle. Unless Janelle had been mistaken about Beller....

"Joy, did you see what happened at the trail shelter?"

Her fingers twitched against his wrists. "Yes." Her voice was guttural, full of inner torment. "That man killed them. He killed them both."

"I'm really sorry about your sister. I wish I could tell you she'd survived. But there is a small bit of good news. Janelle Hanvey is going to be okay."

Her gaze whipped up. "No. I saw him shoot her."

"He did," Doyle agreed. "But that titanium plate in her head deflected the bullet. She had a concussion but she's already out of the hospital."

"The plate in her head." To Doyle's consternation, Joy started laughing, the sound manic and out of control. She turned and started beating against the wall of the cave, her laughter ringing off the damp stone.

He used his teeth to tear through the few slivers of tape she hadn't removed and reached for her, wrapping his arms around her flailing body. She felt tiny in his arms, tiny and frail, and as her laughter turned to sobs, he rocked her like a child, vowing silent vengeance against the men who'd turned her into this broken thing, huddled in a dank, dark cave, waiting for someone to finish killing her.

Hours seemed to go by while he waited for her to calm down, though a glance at his cell phone revealed that only a few minutes had passed. She finally subsided against him, letting him comfort her as she snuffled a few times before falling silent.

"Can you tell me what the man who shot Missy and Janelle looked like?" he asked after a few more minutes.

"He was older. Maybe close to sixty." As she described Richard Beller in detail, Doyle felt a ripple of relief, although confirmation that the man who'd shot the girls was dead opened up a whole new set of questions.

Like, who had just trussed him up and thrown him in a cave?

"That man is dead," he told Joy.

"I know. Craig killed him."

Doyle's body went still with surprise. "Craig?"

She pushed her way out of his grasp, her body shaking again, but this time with anger rather than fear. "Craig Bolen. My father's best friend."

"Craig Bolen, the chief of detectives?"

"He was in the woods. He shot Beller as he was about to kill me. I thought—I thought he was there to save me."

"But he wasn't?"

"No." Joy's anger was starting to work on her like a stiff drink, settling her nerves and adding a little steel to her spine. She met his gaze without blinking. "He helped Ray bring me here. He thinks I didn't see him, but I did. I got away once, during the big snowstorm. I got so close to a hiding place—"

"The Vesper cabin?" he guessed, remembering the scream he and Laney had heard.

"How did you know?"

"We heard you. We were holed up there against the storm. But when we looked for you, you weren't out there."

"They grabbed me and dragged me back to this cave."

"Why would Bolen help someone imprison you like this?"

"I think they want something from my father." A hank of Joy's tangled hair fell into her face. She pushed it back behind her ear with a quick, angry jab. "Some sort of ransom. I haven't found out what."

"But that's good news, isn't it?" he pointed out. "It's why you're still alive."

"Craig Bolen has been like an uncle to me. Why would he do this? How could he betray my family this way, especially after what happened to Missy?"

"I don't know," Doyle admitted, a new, uneasy line of thought entering his mind. "You have no idea what he's asking of your father?"

She shook her head. "They haven't told me anything."

"What do you know about this person named Ray?"

"He wears a disguise. I thought it might be so when we first met him on the trail the day before the shootings. Now I'm sure of it."

"What can you tell me about him?"

"He's the one who interacts with me. I think Craig still thinks he can convince my father that I imagined his being there in the woods, so he's careful to stay clear of the cave. But his voice carries. I know it like I know my own." Her voice lowered. "I saw him in the woods. I saw him kill that man. I know he's the one who carried my feet after Ray overpowered me and tied me up."

"Put a hood over your head?" he asked, still feeling the claustrophobic sensation of the sack over his own face.

"Yes. You, too?"

"Yeah." He looked back toward the cavern opening. "I guess you've had no luck trying to tear down that door out there?"

She lifted baleful eyes toward him and raised her bloodied hands. "No."

"Does Ray come back here much? Does he come in here?"

"Yes, but he's always armed."

"There may be a way to get around that," Doyle said quietly. "And the sooner, the better."

Joy gave him a curious look. "What do you have in mind?"

He held out his hand, daring her to take it. She looked at it for a long moment, then let him help her to her feet. He walked her through the narrow opening that led into the larger cavern as he explained in quick, simple terms what he had in mind. She looked skeptical but finally nodded. "I can do that."

He knew her skepticism was warranted. They were both unarmed. She was hungry and demoralized, and he was still feeling the occasional tingling aftershocks of his encounter with the Taser.

But he had to get out of here, and soon.

Because the second Laney found Satan tied up to the tree by the trail, she'd know Doyle was out there somewhere. She'd probably assume he'd gotten lost, knowing her opinion of his mountain-hiking skills. And she'd look for him. He knew that about her if he knew nothing else in the world.

But she wouldn't be out there alone. Ray was out there somewhere. And even worse, so was Craig Bolen.

She knew Craig. Probably even trusted him.

She'd have no idea that encountering him in the woods might be the last thing she ever did.

He was going to get out of this damned cave, whatever it took. He'd never been one to worry too much about the future, but there was one thing he knew in this sharply distilled moment of crisis: he wanted his future to include Laney. In his bed, in his home, in his life.

He'd be damned if he'd sit here like a trapped animal while someone tried to stop that from ever happening.

LANEY AND CRAIG BOLEN had covered almost a square mile, moving through the woods with methodical thoroughness, and other than the keys and a couple of pieces of torn denim that might or might not match the jeans he'd been wearing that morning, they'd come across nothing to suggest Doyle had come this way.

Of course, the keys were evidence enough. But she hadn't yet told Craig Bolen about finding them. She wasn't sure why.

Was she making a mistake, trying to protect Doyle this way? What if keeping information from Bolen put Doyle in greater danger?

She was on the verge of speaking up, trying to figure out a reasonable explanation for why she'd kept her find to herself, when Craig came to a halt and turned to look at her. He wiped a film of sweat from his forehead with the sleeve of his jacket and shot her an apologetic smile.

"I'm getting older than I think," he admitted, sliding the straps of his backpack off his shoulders. He unzipped the pack, reached inside and pulled a blue-tinted bottle from his backpack. "Let's take a water break. You need one?"

She pulled a bottle of water from her own pack. "I'm good." After a couple of long swigs, she replaced the cap and started to tuck the bottle back into her pack when her eyes fell on the photograph she'd slipped inside one of the backpack's inner pockets to protect it.

With a glance toward Bolen to make sure he wasn't paying attention, she pulled the photograph from the pack and stepped into a nearby shaft of midday sunlight pouring down through the trees. Shifting the image to get rid of the glare, she took a closer look, not at the image of her sister and herself this time but at the window just beyond the bed. Earlier, when she'd found the photo back at the trail shelter, she'd thought she'd seen something strange in the background, but her sister's rush into the woods had sidetracked her.

After scanning the image a couple of times, her eyes

finally made out a faint reflection in the window. Not of herself and Janelle, as she might have assumed, but the mirror image of a man holding a camera in front of him.

The cameraman had inadvertently taken a photograph of himself.

He was holding the camera about chest high, slightly out in front of him. His face was bent toward the image screen so he could focus the shot the way he wanted, but not so much, she realized with a ripple of shock, that she wasn't able to make out his features. It was the man in the mustache and bad wig, but he'd taken off the glasses, probably because they kept him from being able to see well through the camera's viewfinder.

And that one small change in his appearance, the removal of the glasses, brought his features more sharply into focus, even in that window reflection, than the best shot from the security camera had.

Her heart lurched and seemed to stop for a second before it started racing like a thoroughbred. Despite the adrenaline flooding her system, she made herself move slowly, taking time as she slipped the photograph back into her pack and turned to look at Craig Bolen.

He was looking at her now, a bemused smile on his face. But his gaze was sharp and curious. "Is something wrong?" he asked.

She shook her head, trying not to panic. "No. Ready to go again?"

For a breathtaking moment, he seemed reluctant to answer. But finally, he nodded, smiled and waved his arm as if to say, "You first."

She walked ahead of him, the skin on her back crawling.

It had been Craig Bolen, complete with wig and fake mustache, who'd shot the photo at the hospital.

Chapter Fifteen

Okay, think.

Laney trudged ahead of Bolen, wondering why she hadn't insisted on going back down to the staging area. If she kept going much farther with Craig Bolen, she'd be a fool, even though he hadn't shown any sign of aggression toward her.

But running down to the staging area and calling for help wasn't going to get her very far, either. What could she say—"Hey, look, he disguised himself to take a photo of my sister and me without our permission and left it in the trail-shelter logbook"? What if nobody else saw the resemblance she'd seen?

She needed to figure out what to do and fast. Before they went much farther.

"Do you have a map of the search-party assignments?" Bolen's friendly query sent another shudder down her spine.

"Uh, yeah." She stopped and opened her backpack again, digging around inside for the map she'd folded and stuck in one of the pockets. She pulled it out, wincing as the Polaroid snapshot snagged in the folds and flipped out of the pack onto the ground at her feet.

She bent and picked it up, trying to be nonchalant as she dropped it back into her pack. She darted a look at Bolen and found him looking not at her but at the woods behind her, his eyes slightly narrowed.

Suddenly, pain shot through her hip and side, exploding into agony so all-encompassing that she felt as if her whole body was a giant, raw nerve. She wasn't aware of falling until she hit the ground with a thud.

"Why'd you do that?" Faintly, through the buzzing sensation that had begun to replace the pain, she heard Craig Bolen's soft query. "She didn't suspect anything!"

"New plan," the other voice, deep and unfamiliar, answered. "We wanted to scare her off the job. Now we'll just get rid of her altogether."

"Then why didn't you just shoot her?" Bolen asked.

"Because we need her help first."

"WHAT TIME IS IT?" Joy Adderly's voice was barely a whisper, but in the taut silence they'd been maintaining for the past hour, it sounded like thunder, making Doyle's already rattled nerves shimmy in reaction.

He checked the time on his phone, wondering how much longer his battery would last. "Just after noon."

The phone itself was useless as a means of communication. Picking up signals this far up Copperhead Ridge was difficult in the best of situations, and inside a closed-off cave? Impossible. Probably why they hadn't bothered taking the phone off him when they took his pistol and keys.

"He usually brings me something for lunch," she said. "It's how I kept time. Breakfast, lunch and dinner."

Anger boiled up in him again, joining the clamorous chorus of emotions vying for top billing in his mind. Fear was there, raw and unsettling, and also determination, fed by the fear. Anger was the ever-present heat source, bubbling never far from the surface. "When he comes, we'll be ready."

"He'll have a weapon."

"I know."

She fell silent for a long moment. "I'm studying law enforcement in college. Did anyone tell you that?"

"No," he admitted. "What year?"

"Sophomore."

"What college?"

"Brandon College, up near Purgatory. It's a private four-year college."

"Pricey."

"Scholarship," she said with a smile in her voice.

He turned on the flashlight app and flashed it her way. This time, instead of wincing, she shielded her eyes and flashed a half smile, half grimace his way. "Give a girl some warning!"

Her change in demeanor gave him hope that her ordeal hadn't broken her. He hadn't been so sure when he'd first found her. "Joy, we're getting out of here. And you're going to get a chance to say goodbye to your sister."

Her smile faded. "Oh, God. Sweet little Missy."

"I lost my younger brother to violence. It's unfair and all kinds of wrong, and I wish it hadn't happened to you. I'm so sorry."

"How are my parents taking it?"

He thought about his one brief meeting with the Adderlys at the diner. Remembered Dave Adderly's strange behavior, the way he'd looked as if he'd been keeping secrets.

He'd been with Bolen that morning, Doyle remembered. Had someone already given him his ransom instructions?

And if so, what were they?

"I haven't seen a lot of your parents," he answered.

"Let me guess. Craig's been handling them?"

She was smart, he thought. She might just make a good cop. Now that she was no longer stuck in this dark hellhole alone, she seemed to have found her nerve and came across as a completely different young woman than the one he'd found cowering in the back of the cave. He just hoped she wouldn't let this horrific experience destroy her dreams once they got out of here.

"Do you really think they'll let us out alive?" she asked.

"I think the plan has always been to let you out alive," he said, not sure if he believed it but saying it anyway, because she needed the hope. "You said Ray wears a disguise, and Craig Bolen has been careful not to let you see him."

"I heard him, though."

"He doesn't know that."

She didn't answer.

The sound of footsteps outside the cave penetrated the ensuing silence, spurring them both into action. As they'd planned, Joy stood in the middle of the main cavern, her feet planted apart so that she could dodge or run the second she sensed direct danger. Doyle, meanwhile, hurried all the way to the front, waiting in the shadows for whoever was bringing the food that afternoon. Joy had told Doyle that she'd started hiding in the back of the cave after Ray had told her the more she saw of him, the less likely she'd be to live.

They were hoping her presence near the doorway would lure him inside.

But when the door opened, it wasn't Ray who entered. In fact, the door opened just enough for a shadowy figure to stumble through the opening and land with a moan against the nearest wall. The door closed again without anyone else coming through, keys rattling in the lock and the footsteps receding quickly.

Doyle pulled out his cell phone and engaged the flashlight app. The beam of light played across a slender female figure, hands and feet bound with duct tape and a sack taped around her head.

The clothes, the shape—Doyle didn't have to see the face beneath the hood to know who it was.

Laney.

His chest tightening, he ran across the mouth of the cave and knelt by her side, pulling away the tape around her neck. She tried to fight, but her movements were loose limbed and flailing.

"No, sweetheart, it's me." He removed the rest of the tape and pulled the hood off, revealing her wide, scared eyes and dirt-smudged face. He pressed his mouth against her forehead, felt the cool dampness of perspiration and residual tremors and knew what had happened to her. When he ran his hands lightly over her body, her soft whimper when he reached her back confirmed his speculation.

"That bastard Tasered me," she growled.

He bit back a smile of relief. If she could still curse, she was going to be okay. "How long ago?" he asked, removing the tape around her wrists.

"Time was kind of fluid there for a little while." She struggled up to a sitting position, squinting as he ran the beam of light across her to check for any other injuries. "I found your keys."

The non sequitur threw him for a second. "Where?"

"In the woods." As he removed the last of the duct tape around her ankles, she made a move to stand, and he helped her to her feet, keeping his arm firmly around her waist while she found her bearings. "And you'll never guess who took that picture of Jannie and me in the hospital."

"Let me guess," said Joy Adderly from behind them. "Craig Bolen?"

Laney's gaze swung to the sound of Joy's voice, her eyes narrowing as she tried to see into the gloom beyond the circle of light created by Doyle's cell phone application. Doyle shifted the beam to reveal Joy, and Laney gasped before pushing to her feet and stumbling toward the other girl.

Joy opened her arms for a fierce hug. "Is Jannie really going to be okay?"

"She is. And she's going to be so glad to see you!" Laney turned to look at Doyle, a wide smile on her grimy face. "You found her."

He laughed. "I had very little to do with it."

"Don't let him fool you," Joy said, her arm still firmly around Laney's waist. She was helping hold Laney up, Doyle realized, seeing the tremors that were rocking Laney's slender frame. She must have been zapped recently, he thought.

"There are two of them," Laney said. "They put that bag over my head so I didn't see them, but of course, I know Bolen's one of them.

"The other one is the guy we know as Ray," Doyle told her.

"Why did they grab us?" Laney asked. "Why not just kill us?"

"I don't know," Doyle admitted. "Keeping us alive certainly doesn't fit what they've done so far."

"I think they may be trying to get my father to pay a ransom," Joy said.

"But they're not the ones who shot Missy and Janelle, right?" Laney asked. "Jannie was very sure it was a guy named Richard Beller."

"She's right," Joy answered. "At least, I guess that was Richard Beller. I described the shooter to the chief here, and he seems to think it's the same guy."

Laney looked at Doyle for confirmation, and he nodded, watching her lean on Joy and feeling a battle of emotions raging inside him. He'd spent the past couple of hours worried sick about Laney being out there somewhere, with no idea that Craig Bolen was one of the bad guys. But as glad as he was to know she was okay, at least for the moment, he wished she were safely home, far away from this dank cave prison.

"Oh," Laney said suddenly, slapping her hand against her right side.

"Are you hurt?" Doyle hurried over, flashing the light toward her side. He didn't see any blood on her jacket, but her injuries could be internal, if they were as rough on her as they'd been on him while dragging her to the cave.

She unzipped her jacket, grinning up at him. "Those stupid, sexist idiots."

He followed her gaze and saw what her captors had missed.

She was still armed.

LUNCH TURNED OUT to be a couple of peanut-butter sandwiches and two juice boxes. Doyle had found them in a paper sack near the mouth of the cave when it became clear their captors weren't going to return with food. Apparently the small sack of supplies had been tossed in along with Laney, overlooked in the spectacle of her arrival.

Doyle shared his sandwich and juice with Laney, agreeing with her silent assessment that Joy needed food more than either of them, after several days in captivity. She also needed sleep, having been largely sleep deprived since her abduction, too fearful of the unknown to be able to sleep for more than an hour at a time. She'd nodded off after eating, and Laney had followed Doyle from the interior cavern to the larger one near the entrance in order to speak without disturbing her.

"I didn't think we'd find her alive," she confessed in a whisper, leaning against Doyle as they settled with their backs to the cave wall.

He wrapped his arm around her, lending extra warmth. "Neither did I."

"What do they want from her father?"

"I've been thinking about that. He's on the county commission, right?"

"Yeah." She nestled closer, wishing they had something warmer to sit on than the grimy cave floor. "You think it has to do with the upcoming vote on the status of the Bitterwood Police Department?"

"From what I understand, he may be the deciding vote. Everyone else on the commission seems pretty set on a particular course."

"So swinging his vote one way or another could be a viable goal."

"But which way do they want to swing it?" Doyle asked. "For Bitterwood P.D. or against?"

"I think it has to be for," Laney said after a moment's thought. "If Craig Bolen is corrupt—and I think we can conclude he is, at this point—he'd be inclined toward preserving his job, wouldn't he? Maybe he was working with Glen Rayburn on Wayne Cortland's payroll."

"He was Rayburn's direct underling," Doyle agreed. "Obvious choice for chief of detectives, taking Rayburn's place after Rayburn's suicide."

"But here comes the new chief, threatening to upset the order of things," Laney murmured.

"And a county public integrity officer's suddenly assigned to the department for extra scrutiny," Doyle added.

"So they have reason to want us out of the way," she agreed. "But why keep us alive?"

Doyle took a deep breath, as if bracing himself for what he had to say. "Until you dropped in on us, I thought there was a real chance they were going to let Joy live. The only face they think either of us saw was Ray's, and I think we all agree he's wearing some sort of disguise."

"But I saw Craig Bolen."

He nodded, his cheek brushing against her temple. He

tightened his hold on her. "Now I wonder if I was just being naive, thinking they'd let Joy live."

"Still gets us back to the question at hand—why are they keeping us alive?"

"The vote doesn't happen for another three days," he answered.

"And they might need Joy alive as leverage, in case her father demands to see her," Laney said. "But if they kill her, won't her father just tell the world what he was forced to do?"

"Maybe, but who's he going to blame? I'm damned sure he doesn't know Bolen's behind all this. I saw them together the other day, and he didn't show the slightest antagonism toward Bolen. He seemed more angry at me."

"Because you're part of the reason his daughter was taken, in his mind," Laney said, understanding the thought process even though she knew it was deeply unfair. "He's being forced to maintain your job. Maybe he even wonders if you could be behind his daughter's kidnapping."

Doyle sighed. "I wonder if maybe I'm being set up as the fall guy."

She turned toward him, even though there was far too little light in the cave for her to be able to make out more than the faintest outline of his profile. "How?"

"Maybe Bolen's been hinting to Adderly that I could be behind the kidnapping. Maybe that's what's behind the hostility I noticed."

"But why would he believe that? It's ridiculous."

"Is it? I'm new in town. An outsider. A flatlander. I came from a sheriff's department that had its own issues with corruption. I showed up just days before the girls were shot. I have a vested interest in keeping the Bitterwood P.D. alive and kicking. And now I've gone AWOL, along with you. The woman the county sent to spy on me."

"I wasn't sent to spy on you."

"You know what I mean."

"You think Bolen or Ray plan to use your weapon to kill Joy and me," she said with a sinking heart.

"They have it. They took it off me when they Tasered me."

"I guess maybe they didn't think I'd be packing," she murmured.

"Lucky for us." He'd taken over her pistol and holster, with her blessing, after a quick grilling established that he was the more experienced shooter.

"It would tie up a lot of loose ends. Plus put Bolen in prime position to step into the chief's job," Laney admitted.

"He'd be next in line. The only reason he didn't get it this time was that the county commission wanted to look outside the area for their next chief."

"But if you turned out to be even worse than Rayburn, they might not feel that compunction a second time."

"Exactly."

Laney rubbed her gritty eyes. "This is so crazy."

"What I don't get," Doyle added a few moments later, "is how this connects to Wayne Cortland. If Bolen was working for Cortland, and Cortland is dead, what's his plan now?"

"Maybe that's where Ray comes in."

"Maybe. He could be Cortland's successor, although the feds didn't think there was such a person. They thought the whole cartel died with him."

"Well, clearly the pieces of that whole are still around. What if they've found a new leader?"

"A new leader who can pull all those mismatched pieces together?" Doyle sounded skeptical.

He was probably right, she knew. The prevailing theory about Cortland's criminal enterprise was that Cortland's ruthless control had held the disparate groups involved together. Militia groups, meth dealers and anarchist hackers hardly made ideal partners, but Cortland had somehow brought those groups together, massaging egos and convincing each group that their goals would be met if they went along with his plans.

But could someone else maintain that delicate, improbable balance?

"Maybe not," she admitted. "Probably not."

"Doesn't mean someone isn't trying," Doyle countered.

Laney pushed the stem of her watch, lighting up the dial. Just after three o'clock. Based on what Joy had told them, their captors would bring them something to eat around five, as daylight was beginning to wane.

"What if all they do is throw the food in here?" she asked Doyle. "What good does it do to have a weapon if we can't get close enough to use it?"

"Joy and I had a plan before you arrived." His voice was a rumble in her ear, sending a shudder of feminine awareness dancing down her spine despite the less-than-ideal situation. "She was going to scream bloody murder near the back of the cave to lure someone inside. I'd be hiding near the door, ready to jump."

"Dangerous."

"Desperate times," he said, a shrug in his voice.

"What if they both come in?" she asked.

"Then it gets a little more difficult."

WHEN LANEY FELL SILENT, her head drooping against Doyle's shoulder, he was loath to move, even though his legs were starting to cramp from sitting in one position so long. Time was ticking toward their next chance to make an escape, and if she needed a nap to restore her strength, he didn't want to disturb her.

So he was surprised when she sat up abruptly and said, "Oh."

"Oh what?" he asked when she didn't say anything else.

"I think I know what this place is."

"Yeah?"

She looked over at the heavy wood door closing them in. "When we were kids, my mother used to tell us every Halloween before we went out trick-or-treating, 'Y'all be careful, or Bridey Butcher'll get you!'"

"Bridey Butcher?" he asked, pricked by déjà vu.

"Yeah. Bridey Butcher was a big, strappin' mountain girl who lived up this way back during Prohibition. She and her daddy ran a moonshine still and scared off a lot of the other moonshiners with a little well-applied violence and threats of more. Anyway, one day a city slicker from over Knoxville way came up here looking to employ some men on a public works project, and for Bridey, it was love at first sight."

Listening to Laney's accent broaden as she warmed to the tale, Doyle's sense of familiarity bloomed into memory. "But he did her wrong."

Laney paused in her story. "That's right. He led her on, made her think he was going to marry her and take her out of these mountains, but when the time came to go, he told her he had a girl back in Knoxville."

"And Bridey lured him up here for a goodbye, or so he thought," Doyle continued, the story coming to life in his mind, as if his mother were whispering in his ear. "She and her daddy had built a door in the mouth of a cave where they hid their still from the revenuers. But she'd moved the still somewhere else, and when she lured her lover inside the cave, she'd knocked him out and locked him inside. She left and never came back, leaving her lover to die slowly, the same way he'd killed her love."

"How do you know that story?" Laney asked, her eyes wide with surprise.

"My mother used to tell it," he said. "I'd forgotten. When I was old enough to be thinking about girls, she told me about the girl done wrong and how she got her revenge. But she never said what mountain."

"I bet you were afraid to date after that," Laney said.

He smiled back at her. "For a while. I'm pretty sure that was my mother's intention."

"How did your mother know about Bridey Butcher?"

He shrugged, not sure. "I know she was from somewhere in eastern Tennessee. Maybe she heard the story there."

"It's pretty specific to Bitterwood, since it actually happened here—" Laney stopped short, her face turning toward the doorway. "Footsteps," she whispered.

Doyle clicked on his phone and saw that it was only three-thirty. Their captors were way too early to be bringing their evening meal.

He had a sick feeling that time had just run out.

Chapter Sixteen

Doyle nearly dumped Laney onto the floor of the cave in his haste to get to his feet, though he held her arm to make sure she didn't fall as she scrambled up. She felt his tremble of hesitation, then suddenly he was handing her the pistol she'd given him earlier.

"What are you doing?" she whispered.

His response was to flatten himself against the wall closest to the door.

What had been the plan? Joy was going to scream, right?

But Joy wasn't awake.

Laney scrambled back deeper into the cave, trying to get out of the line of sight. She wasn't much for scream-ing, but if that was what it took—

The door opened and she saw a silhouette enter the cave, shorter than Craig Bolen. Leaner, with a headful of hair that Craig Bolen would have envied even ten years earlier. The wig, she thought. Ray's disguise—and Craig's disguise, too, that one time in the hospital.

That was why Janelle hadn't been quite sure the man in the hospital was the same man she'd seen on Copperhead Trail, she realized. Because they'd been different men in the same disguise.

In one hand Ray held a pistol, in the other a flashlight.

He flicked on the light, piercing the gloom of the cave with its bright beam.

Shoving her own pistol behind her back, she squinted, turning her head away from the blinding light.

Suddenly, from the back of the cave came a soul-piercing howl. It filled the cavern, rang along the walls and sent tremors racing up Laney's spine, as if the earth had opened up and the agony of a thousand souls filled the still air of the cavern.

She heard a scuffle of footsteps moving toward her from the front of the cave, punctuated abruptly by a bone-rattling thud of body meeting body.

The flashlight crashed to the floor of the cave, the beam extinguished. It rolled toward Laney, but she ignored it, her gaze fixed on the struggling silhouettes backlit by the open doorway.

Doyle and Ray were struggling for Ray's pistol, a tangle of grappling arms and kicking legs. The hard lines of the deadly weapon were easy to distinguish, so she kept her eyes on that particular silhouette, aware that whoever had the gun had the upper hand.

She left her own weapon where it was, tucked behind her back, knowing it was useless to her while Doyle and his opponent were locked by battle into a single, writhing organism.

Ray pulled free for a moment, and he swung the gun toward Doyle.

Laney brought her own weapon in front of her, ready to shoot.

Then Doyle launched himself at Ray, slamming him into the wall by the open door. The gun went off, the bullet ricocheting against the hard stone wall. Laney pressed herself flat against the door, praying Joy wasn't standing in the open, then dared another look.

The men were no longer inside the cave.

And the door was slowly swinging shut.

Laney raced forward, catching the heavy door before it closed. It pinched her left hand hard enough to make her cry out in pain, but she gritted her teeth and pulled the door open with her uninjured hand.

Outside, the sunlight was blinding, the pain of her contracting pupils almost eclipsing the agony of her smashed hand. She heard the sound of fighting long before she could open her squinted eyes enough to see what was happening only a few yards away.

At first she could make out only dark figures, locked in a fierce battle of crashing fists and tangling legs. Then, as her eyes adjusted to the brightness, she saw details. Doyle's bloody mouth. The gash across Ray's cheek. His wig was hanging half off his head; Doyle's next blow knocked it to the ground, revealing short blond hair that had hidden beneath the brown wig. The glasses he'd worn were gone, as well.

Neither man seemed to be holding the pistol. But the danger was greater than ever, Laney realized with a jolt of alarm, for their fight had taken them dangerously close to what looked like a steep drop-off. The tree line ended feet away, with nothing but sky and the velvet blue outlines of distant mountains stretching out beyond.

Ray threw himself at Doyle with a vicious head-butt. Doyle's head snapped back, and suddenly they were teetering at the edge of the bluff.

"No!" Laney cried, pushing her sluggish feet into action.

But it was too late.

Both men tumbled over the side and disappeared.

IN HIS THIRTY-THREE YEARS, Doyle had felt the cold finger of death on the back of his neck twice before. Once, at the age of nine, when he had gone swimming in the Gulf of Mexico and ignored an undertow warning. He'd made it back alive, though there had been several minutes of choking on salt water and praying for deliverance before that had happened.

The second time, he'd been in the swampy woods of Terrebonne, the sleepy little town in south Alabama where he'd spent most of his life. He'd been on a manhunt for a drug dealer the coast guard had chased ashore. He'd ended up pinned down between well-armed and ruthless Colombians and an equally well-armed and ruthless group of DEA agents. Bullets had rained from the sky in all directions, ripping to shreds the fallen log behind which he'd taken cover. When the battle ended, he'd been bloody from splinters but, by some miracle, untouched by gunfire.

Today, death came in the form of a fifty-foot drop down the side of a mountain.

He clawed at the rocky side of the bluff, trying not to hear the bone-cracking thuds of Ray's body bouncing down the incline below him. Doyle's own fingers had caught on an exposed tree root, keeping him from following, but his feet dangled below him, gravity and his own weight conspiring to wrench him free of his desperate hold on life. He tried to go completely still, to stop his body's swaying movements, and that was when his ankle cracked against something hard embedded in the side of the bluff.

Ignoring the sharp sting of pain, he glanced down and saw the flat, narrow outcropping of shale just above his dangling feet.

He bent one knee, putting his foot on the outcropping, and pushed down, expecting the rock to crumble under the pressure. But it held.

Lifting the other foot, he put more weight on the ledge. No give. The rock was solid, and it seemed to be firmly embedded in the side of the bluff.

"Doyle!" Laney's voice rang above him. He looked up

and found her pale face and wide blue eyes staring back at him.

"Are you okay?" Her gaze slid past him to focus on something below.

He dared a quick look downward and saw that Ray had finally stopped tumbling, his crumpled body lying motionless against the outcropping that had stopped his descent.

Footsteps scurried above, and he looked up to see Joy Adderly crouching next to Laney. Her breath caught at the sight of Doyle hanging precariously on the steep side of the bluff.

"How's your foothold?" Laney asked. Doyle could tell she was struggling to stay calm and focused, but she couldn't hide the fear in her eyes or the tremble of her voice.

"My feet are on a narrow ledge," he told her. "It seems to be holding pretty well, but I can't get any leverage to climb. You don't happen to have a rope, do you?"

"In my backpack. Which those bastards took." Her lips pressing to a grim line, she stripped off her jacket. Her body immediately trembled—whether from cold or fear, Doyle didn't know. Holding one sleeve of the sturdy jacket, she flung the coat toward him.

Sucking in a deep breath, he let go of the rock beneath his right hand, ignoring the resulting sensation of falling backward, and caught the other jacket sleeve, understanding what she had in mind.

"You sure this will hold?" he asked.

"No," she admitted. "You sure you can hold on long enough for me to go down the mountain for help?"

The thought was enough to make his insides shrivel. "No."

She put her left hand on the sleeve she held, but the second she closed her fingers around the fabric, the muscles in her jaw tightened to knots.

"What's wrong with your hand?" Doyle asked, seeing a long purple streak of incipient bruising across the back of her hand.

She took her hand off the jacket, shaking it with a wince. "My hand got caught in the door."

Joy reached for the jacket, gripping it above the sleeve seam with both hands. "Let's give it a try now."

You can do this, Doyle told himself as he prepared to take his hand away from the tree root he'd been holding on to for dear life. *Just grab the jacket. You won't fall.*

His gaze slid downward toward the steep drop below, but he quickly forced his eyes back upward, where they locked with Laney's baby blues.

"You can do this," she said with soft urgency. In her eyes, he saw a blaze of emotion that stole his breath.

His heart pounding with a surge of adrenaline, he released his grip on the side of the mountain and closed both hands on the jacket sleeve. Pushing off with his legs, he used the leverage of the jacket to claw his way upward until his torso hung partially over the edge of the bluff.

Laney grabbed the waistband of his jeans with her uninjured hand and pulled, falling backward as she hauled him the rest of the way up. He sprawled forward, his body landing over hers. She was soft and warm and perfect beneath him, and even as relief washed over him like a tidal wave, he wanted to stay there cradled in her fervent grasp forever.

He held her face between his hands, wanting to kiss her so much it was a physical ache. But a blast of icy wind rolled down the mountain, sending a shudder of cold through her slender body, and he pushed his own desires back under control, rolling off of her and reaching for her coat.

It had somehow survived its brief role of makeshift rope. He wrapped it around her shivering body as she sat up. "Thank you," he said.

That fierce emotion still blazed back at him from her eyes. "You're welcome."

He reached for her bruised hand and gently manipulated the fingers, feeling for any sign of a break. "How badly do you think you're hurt?"

Her jaw tightened with pain, but she shook her head. "I think it's just a bad bruise."

He didn't feel any obvious fractures, but the angry purple color was spreading. "It's swelling a little," he warned.

She pulled her hand away, her chin lifting. "It'll be okay until we get down the mountain."

He bent and kissed her forehead. "Okay." He turned to look at Joy. "Thank you, too."

She was watching them with eyes narrowed almost to slits. The light was hurting her eyes, Doyle realized. She'd been in that cave for days; daylight probably felt like needles in her brain.

"I wish I had a pair of sunglasses for you," he told her. He'd had a pair in his backpack, but the bag had disappeared at some point after the Taser attack.

"I'll be okay." Joy pushed to her feet, looking weary but determined. "I just want to go home."

Doyle rose, holding out his hand to help Laney to her feet. His body creaked a little, the aftereffects of his fight with Ray making themselves known in twinges and aches. He took a quick assessment of his injuries—a bloody scrape on one cheekbone, puffy skin around his right eye that felt sore to the touch, a split lip and all sorts of muscle twinges—but he would survive.

He wandered back to the edge of the bluff and looked down. Ray hadn't moved.

"Is he dead?" Joy asked.

"He fell a long way," Doyle answered.

"We can send for help when we get down the mountain," Laney said firmly, grabbing Doyle's arm and pulling him away from the drop-off.

"I left something in the cave," Joy said. "I'll go get it."

Doyle caught her arm as she started toward the entrance. "Don't go back in there."

Joy's expression hardened to a dogged scowl. "I pulled a leather patch off Craig's coat when he put me in the cave. Apparently he realized it was missing, because Ray kept asking me to give it to him. I lied and told him I didn't know what he was talking about. He even searched the cave, but he didn't find where I hid it. It's proof that Craig was part of my kidnapping."

"Tell me where you hid it and I'll get it," Doyle said.

"No," Laney said firmly, handing him her pistol. "I'll go with Joy to find it. You keep guard."

Doyle started to argue, but she had a point. Ray might be out of commission, but Craig Bolen was still around here somewhere. Gripping the pistol with resolve, he nodded, walking with them to the mouth of the cave.

He handed Laney his phone. "The battery's close to giving out, but it should give you enough light to find the patch and get back here."

Laney took the phone and disappeared into the cave with Joy.

Doyle watched until they reached the outer edge of the ambient glow coming through the open doorway. Laney turned on the phone flashlight and followed Joy deeper into the cave, both of them disappearing from sight.

Doyle turned away from the doorway and studied the woods around him, alert for any sign of movement. He heard the rustle of wind in the leaves, the distant twitter of birdsong and the thudding drumbeat of his own pulse.

No sign of Craig Bolen.

But he was still out there somewhere, dangerous as hell.

LANEY FOLLOWED JOY through the narrow passageway to the deeper room of the cave, flashing the light toward the wall of the cave where Joy directed her. It looked no different from the other stony walls surrounding them, but Joy went directly to a particular spot and started tugging at a piece of stone embedded there, waist high.

As Laney shifted to direct the light from Doyle's phone toward Joy's hands, she saw a flicker of movement out of the corner of her eye. She started to turn, expecting to find that Doyle had followed them inside.

A hand snaked out of the gloom behind her, tangling in her hair and jerking her backward. She hit a thick body and felt hot breath on her neck. The fist in her hair twisted, sending pain ripping through her scalp.

"Don't say a word," Craig Bolen growled, pressing something hard and cold against her temple.

Joy whirled around, her expression shifting from surprise to terror in the span of a second. Hatred curling her lip, she spit out a profanity.

"Just give me the patch," he told her, his voice expressionless. But Laney thought she heard a hint of dismay hidden beneath Bolen's stoic tone.

"You don't want to hurt Joy," she said. "You've seen her grow up. You killed that man to save her."

He jerked her hair, making her gasp. "I told you not to talk."

She ground her teeth against the pain and tried to think. She'd heard no sound of a struggle from the front of the cave, meaning Bolen hadn't gotten in here through Doyle. He must have slipped inside to try to retrieve the patch Joy had hidden while the rest of them were outside dealing with the fight and the fall off the mountain. "Doyle's not going to let you take us out of here."

"Shut up!"

"You can't get out of this now, Craig," Joy said. "We

know about your part in all this. What are you going to do—kill us all?"

"If I have to."

Laney couldn't tell if he was bluffing or not. She had to err on the side of caution, she decided. Bolen had a gun. She didn't. "Let Joy go. Use me as a hostage. I can get you off the mountain."

"Joy stays. None of this works without her."

"Your pal Ray is dead."

"Shut up," he snapped.

Joy moved suddenly, racing toward the passageway to the bigger part of the cave. Laney took advantage of the distraction to start struggling against Bolen's grasp.

He cracked the butt of his pistol against the side of her head, making her reel. She sagged against him, losing her grip on Doyle's phone. Darkness deepened, and the world reeled around her.

Bolen tightened his grip around her waist, keeping her upright. "Guess it's just you and me, Charlane."

JOY BURST OUT of the doorway into the cave, shouting Doyle's name. He shook off the aches and pains from his fight with Ray, instantly on alert.

"Craig's in the cave," she cried. "He has Laney!"

His heart skipped a beat, but somehow he kept his head. "Joy, you have to go for help. Can you do that?"

She nodded quickly, though her eyes were bright with fear.

Hoping he still had the search-party map, he dug for it, relieved when he found it hanging half out of the torn back pocket of his jeans. It was ripped in places, but the map was still visible. "Antoine Parsons and Delilah Hammond are searching there." He showed her on the map. "Near the boneyard. Can you find it?"

She nodded frantically. "Please get her out of there, okay? Don't let Craig get away with what he's done."

Doyle gave her a swift hug. "Find Antoine and Delilah and tell them where we are."

Joy started running east through the underbrush, her weariness showing. Doyle watched until she disappeared from view, hating that she had to make her way back to civilization alone.

But Laney was in that cave with a man who'd killed before. What would Bolen be willing to do to get off this mountain?

Doyle edged toward the mouth of the cave, trying to hear what was going on inside. But only silence greeted him.

"Bolen?" he called. "You're not going to get out of this. Joy knows you're one of the people who kidnapped her and kept her prisoner. I know it, too. All you're doing is prolonging this whole mess. Give yourself up. You killed the man who killed Missy and shot Janelle—Joy can tell everyone what you did. You might even come out a hero."

He waited for Bolen's answer. But there was only silence.

"If you give up without a fight, I can help you. I can make things go a whole lot easier on you."

Bolen's voice rang from deep in the cave. "I've got Charlane, Massey. I don't want to hurt her, but I will. Back off and call off your search parties. I'll let her go when I get to a safe place."

"You know I can't do that. And you'll only be prolonging the inevitable."

"I'll take my chances." Bolen's voice seemed closer.

"Laney?" Doyle called, his heart seeming to freeze in his chest as he waited for her to answer.

"I'm okay," she called. But she didn't sound okay. She sounded weak and woozy.

"My gun is against her head," Bolen called. He was very close now. Peering into the cave opening, Doyle spotted a dark silhouette just beyond the rectangle of daylight painting the cave floor.

Bolen took a few steps forward, shoving Laney in front of him. Doyle bit back a gasp as he saw blood flowing from a gash in the side of Laney's head. It spilled down over Bolen's wrist and dripped onto the cave floor.

"I don't want to hurt her," Bolen repeated.

"I don't want you to, either," Doyle agreed, backing up to give him room to emerge from the cave.

Bolen kept Laney between them, shielding himself from Doyle's weapon. "Put down the pistol." He gave his own weapon a jab toward Laney's head, making her gasp in pain.

Doyle was a pretty good shot with a handgun, but not good enough to risk Laney moving the wrong way at the wrong second. Slowly, he bent and lowered the pistol to the ground.

Without warning, Bolen's pistol barked fire. Doyle felt the bullet whistle past his head and, at the last second, retrieved his pistol and rolled away, looking for cover.

All he found was a leafy bush about ten feet from the cave entrance. It offered more camouflage than cover, but Doyle took what he could get.

Bolen took a second shot at him, the bullet rattling the limbs of the bush, driving Doyle farther toward the outer wall of the cave.

He was pinned down, with nowhere else to go.

Chapter Seventeen

Bolen's gun fired. Doyle went down.

Laney cried out his name and struggled harder against Bolen's grasp. "He did what you said!"

"Shut up!" Bolen tightened his grip around her neck, squeezing the breath from her.

She pulled at his arm with her uninjured hand, fighting to breathe. Dark spots appeared in her vision, and she stomped desperately at his feet. She couldn't inflict much damage on his sturdy boots, but he loosened his grip enough for air to flow into her lungs again. The dark places in her vision diminished and she could see once more.

How long had Joy been gone? Was there anyone close enough to their position to hear the gunfire and come to investigate?

Doyle's voice came from behind a bush a few yards in front of them. "Bolen, there are police all over this mountain. You can't get out of here. But so far, you haven't killed anyone who didn't need killing. It's a point in your favor."

"You know it doesn't work that way!" Bolen dragged Laney closer to the bush, his pistol outstretched, as if he was ready to shoot at the first sign of movement.

"Maybe not. But know this. So far, you've killed a serial killer who shot two defenseless girls. You shoot me, it's cold-blooded murder."

"You think they'll let me walk after all of this?"

"No. But you won't fry."

"Not good enough." Bolen had dragged Laney only a couple of feet away from the bush behind which Doyle had disappeared. Another few steps and they'd have him cornered.

She couldn't let that happen.

Balling her hand into a fist, she shifted her body to the right and slammed her fist into the soft vulnerability of Bolen's groin.

His grip loosened. Not completely, but enough for her to wriggle free of his grasp. She grabbed his gun hand and swung it wide as he started to fire into the bush again.

The kick of the pistol slammed his fist into her face. She stumbled backward, crashing into the outer wall of the cave. Bolen swung the gun toward her, his eyes full of pain and rage.

Suddenly the bushes exploded next to them, and Doyle tackled Bolen, knocking him to the ground. The older man's hand hit the ground hard and the pistol skittered free from his grasp, sliding toward the mouth of the cave.

Laney dived for it, sweeping it into the cavern and pushing the door closed. Rolling over, she saw that Doyle had pinned Bolen to the ground and held him there with her pistol pressed against the rogue cop's neck.

He met her gaze, his green eyes afire with anger. But under the fury she saw something softer, something deeper that made her breath catch in her chest. She sat up and gazed back at him, wondering if he could read her thoughts.

A slow, sexy smile crossed his face, and she realized he could.

"His name isn't Ray." Bolen didn't meet their eyes across the interview-room table. His anger had subsided the moment Doyle had belted his hands behind his back and told him, with a few salty terms that had made Laney's eyes widen with surprise, that trying to move was a very bad idea. "I guess you'd call it a nom de guerre."

His battle name, Doyle thought, and made a guess. "I suppose he spelled it *R-e-y,* then? With an *e?*"

Bolen lifted his gaze for the first time, a hint of respect gleaming there in his narrowed eyes. "King of all he surveyed," he murmured.

"What's his real name?" Doyle asked, half his mind wandering back up the mountain, where they'd left the fallen man's body while they returned to the police station with Joy. She had arrived within fifteen minutes with reinforcements in the form of Delilah Hammond, Antoine Parsons and a pair of uniformed deputies from the county sheriff's office. They'd apparently been only a couple of miles from the cave when they'd heard gunfire and headed toward the sound to investigate.

Doyle and his detectives had left the deputies to await the mountain rescue unit. He hadn't heard anything about the status of the extraction by the time they arrived back at the police station, but he assumed they'd figure out a way to get Rey's body up the mountain, sooner or later.

"Merritt Cortland." Bolen answered Doyle's question. "Not legally Cortland, of course, but that's who he was."

Doyle glanced at Delilah Hammond, who sat beside him across from Bolen. She didn't react visibly, but he knew the name *Cortland* had to give her a start. Wayne Cortland had tried to kill her only a couple of months earlier—and damned near succeeded.

"Yeah," Bolen said, reading their expressions. "*That* Cortland. Merritt was his son."

Delilah shook her head. "Cortland didn't have any children."

Bolen's smile was a sneer. "None he claimed."

Doyle shifted in his chair, hiding a wince of pain as

the bruises in his rib cage twinged. "Was the kidnapping his idea or yours?"

He saw Bolen considering how to answer.

"The truth will serve you better than lies," Doyle warned.

Bolen's lips pressed to a thin line. "Mine. But I wouldn't have even thought about it if he hadn't been blackmailing me."

"With what?" Delilah asked.

He shot her a black look. "He knew I was Rayburn's man."

"We had a feeling the corruption didn't end with him," Delilah murmured. "How deep does it go?"

Bolen shook his head. "I'm not a snitch."

Doyle and Delilah exchanged a look. She gave a slight shake of her head, which he read as a suggestion that he move on past the subject of police corruption. They could deal with that problem another day.

"How did Merritt know you were Rayburn's man?"

"He'd been dogging his father's business for years, ever since his mama told him who his daddy was," Bolen answered. "He got a job at the sawmill. Wormed his way into the business without Cortland ever knowing he'd hired his own kid. He made copies of all the keys and snuck around finding out his daddy's business. He wanted to be the heir to the throne." Bolen's teeth bared in another bitter smile. "Got a little impatient."

Delilah reacted that time, her body shifting forward toward Bolen. "You're saying Merritt killed his father?"

"You always figured the bombs were an inside job," Bolen answered, meeting her gaze with a knowing look. "You were right."

"What about his father's files?" Doyle asked.

Bolen shrugged. "He said he had made copies of everything he needed. He was planning to take his daddy's place."

"And Wayne Cortland never suspected Merritt was his son?" Delilah asked.

"Oh, he knew," Bolen answered. "Merritt told him. Damn fool was thinking his father would welcome him into the fold and give him his due as his son."

"But he didn't."

Bolen shook his head. "Fired him instead. But it was too late. Merritt had the keys to the kingdom by then."

And blew it to smithereens, Doyle thought.

"Why kidnap the girls?" Delilah asked. "I assume that's what you were after, right? Kidnapping the Adderly girls and Janelle Hanvey?"

"Just the Adderly girls," Bolen answered. "Not Janelle. She was in the wrong place at the wrong time."

"What were you going to do with her?" Doyle asked, an image of Janelle's sweet smile flickering in the back of his mind.

Bolen's silent stare told him the answer. Rage flared in the center of Doyle's chest as he remembered the depth of Laney's fear and pain when they'd found her sister's unconscious, bleeding body in the trail shelter. He gripped the seat of his chair to keep his hands from balling into fists and slamming his former chief of detectives to the floor.

"What were you after?" Delilah asked. "Ransom?"

"Coercion," Doyle answered for Bolen. "Right? You wanted to influence Dave Adderly's county commission vote on whether or not to dissolve the Bitterwood Police Department."

Once again, Bolen's gaze held reluctant respect. "Merritt needed the Bitterwood P.D. to stick around."

"We're a long way from Travisville, Virginia," Doyle said, referring to Wayne Cortland's home base. "What does Bitterwood offer that's so important to Cortland's enterprise?"

"It's like a chain," Bolen said. "Break a link and everything can fall apart."

"So there are more links in this chain."

It wasn't respect Doyle saw in Bolen's eyes that time. "Cortland owned these mountains, all the way from Abingdon to Chattanooga. He'd co-opted meth mechanics and militia groups the feds don't even know about. But keeping them on the chain is a precarious business."

"And if Bitterwood P.D. fell?"

"There wasn't any way to be sure the people he had in place were going to be able to get jobs on another force. Or that they'd have the access and influence he needed to keep investigations into his business from going anywhere," Bolen answered without emotion.

Doyle could tell he hated telling them the truth, but that was the bargain his former chief of detectives had struck. They weren't going to charge him with murder in the death of Richard Beller in exchange for his confession.

But so far, he hadn't given up any of the people in the police department he might have been working with.

"How many other departments in the area?" Doyle asked.

"Most of them," Bolen replied. "But Merritt said his father never was able to penetrate the Ridge County Sheriff's Department. If they took over our jurisdiction—"

"A link would break," Delilah finished for him.

Bolen looked at her without answering.

"Did Dave Adderly know who was blackmailing him?" Doyle asked.

Bolen shook his head. "He told me about it, begged me for my help." To his credit, he looked sickened by his betrayal of his old friend. "We didn't figure on a sicko like Beller coming along and screwing up our plans. I swear to God, I wouldn't have let Merritt hurt those girls."

Doyle didn't remind him that he'd terrorized one of

those girls, throwing her in a dark, cold cave and traumatizing her for a long time yet to come.

"What were you and Merritt planning to do with Laney and me?"

Bolen's lips pressed to a thin line and he didn't answer.

"Were you going to try to pin this on me?" Doyle guessed.

Bolen's gaze whipped up to meet his.

"I had some time to think about it, in the cave," Doyle continued. "There was no reason to keep me alive when you two ran into me on the mountain. No reason to shoot me with a Taser instead of bullets. You had to have a reason you needed me alive."

"Merritt said it would kill two birds with one stone," Bolen mumbled.

"What two birds?"

"He was going to set you up to be the bad seed in the police department. We knew you already suspected there might be someone in the department involved in Joy's abduction. We knew you weren't going to let up searching the mountain until you found her. You and Laney Hanvey. You took it personal because of her sister."

"Everyone took it personally."

Bolen didn't argue. "He was going to have you kill Joy and then I was going to kill you. He told me so, after we left the cave." He leaned forward toward Doyle. "I swear to God, I went back there to stop him, but you reached him first. And then I thought, while y'all were distracted, I'd go in the cave and hunt for that patch that got pulled off of my jacket. I'd already scoured the woods looking for it without any luck."

"You knew it would tie you to Joy's abduction."

"Nobody knew I was involved. I took care not to let Joy see me."

"She saw you," Doyle said. "She knew the whole time it was you."

Bolen looked genuinely stricken.

"What made you think people would believe I would be in on the abduction?" Doyle asked.

"You had a lot to lose if the county shut down the Bitterwood P.D. You just took the job. You'd moved your whole life here."

"I don't exactly have a reputation for corruption."

"Maybe not down there on the beach where you came from, but you're a Cumberland. Cumberlands are crooks and swindlers. Hell, they're baby killers. People around here would have found you guilty just by association. No good ever came from a Cumberland in these parts."

Cumberland had been his mother's maiden name. Doyle had never known it until her death. She'd never talked about her family or where she'd come from. But his mother had been the most good-hearted, honest-dealing person he'd ever known. Why would Bolen think people would hold Doyle's mother against him?

Before Doyle could ask another question, a knock on the interview-room door sent a jolt through his nerves, sparking irritation. He shot a look at Delilah and she went to the door, slipping outside. She came back into the room almost immediately and bent to speak into Doyle's ear.

"Merritt Cortland's body is gone."

THE X-RAYS CONFIRMED Laney's assessment that her hand was not broken, only badly bruised. The doctor at the urgent-care clinic had a nurse wrap her hand in a compression bandage and suggested ice packs for the swelling and acetaminophen for the pain.

Doyle had called her mother to meet her at the clinic while he went with his detectives to take Bolen in and book

him. Alice was still in the clinic's large waiting area when
Laney walked out of the exam area.

But she was not alone.

Doyle rose at the sight of her, his expression hovering
somewhere between relief and an emotion she couldn't
quite discern. He crossed the room and wrapped his arms
around her, his cheek pressed tightly against hers, trans-
mitting the unidentified emotion straight to her own nerve
center.

Fear. He was afraid.

She looked up into his mossy eyes. "What's wrong?"

He whispered the answer in her ear.

LANEY'S FIRST THOUGHT had been for her sister, not for herself. Doyle hadn't been surprised when she'd grabbed a
fistful of his sweater with her uninjured hand and asked,
"Is Jannie in danger?"

He'd assured her that they didn't think she was. "She
was always collateral damage, and we have enough evidence against him that going after her won't change his
situation."

He'd offered to drive Laney home, allowing her mother
to go check on Janelle, who'd stayed with the Brandywines
while her mother had gone to the clinic to be with Laney.
They were five minutes past the Bitterwood city limits
before he dropped the rest of the bomb.

"His real name is Merritt Cortland."

Her gaze snapped up to his face. "As in Wayne Cortland?"

He told her what Bolen had revealed. "He'll be looking
to keep all those links intact."

"So my job at the Bitterwood P.D. has just begun," she
murmured.

He slanted a look her way. "Looks that way."

She pressed her lips together, looking thoughtful. "I'm not sure I'm the person for the job anymore."

"Oh?"

"I don't think I can be objective where you're concerned."

He had to keep his eyes on the road as it twisted its way to Barrowville. "Is that good news or bad news?"

"Is that a serious question?" She sounded a little annoyed.

"I guess I mean, are you glad about it? Or does it bother you?"

"Oh." She sounded surprised by his question, as if it hadn't occurred to her that he might have doubts about her feelings or intentions. "Glad, I suppose. I mean, I'm a little annoyed by the thought of having to hand over the case to another investigator, but not enough to wish things were different."

This time he was the one who shot a look her way. "That's flattering. I guess."

She grinned at him. "Just drive and I promise, when we get to my place, I'll flatter the hell out of you."

She hadn't been exaggerating. They hadn't gotten all the way through the front door of her bungalow before she flattened him against the wall, her mouth slanting hard and hungry against his.

"As flattered as I am," he murmured around her lips, "I need to check this place for possible intruders." He pushed her away gently and unsheathed his recently recovered weapon while he walked around her house, room to room, until he'd assured himself they were safely alone.

She'd locked the door behind them and was in the kitchen when he finished his safety check, scooping coffee into a filter. "You like your coffee strong or wimpy?"

"Strong," he answered with a grin.

She poured a carafe of water into the machine and set

the empty pot on the burner. Coffee started trickling from the reservoir almost immediately, filling the kitchen with a heavenly smell.

"So," she murmured as she slid her arms around his waist, "where were we?"

"You know, at the risk of having to turn in my man card, I have to ask your intentions, Ms. Hanvey."

She arched her eyebrows at him. "My intentions?"

"I mean, beyond the next hour or so," he added as he saw the wicked glint in her eyes. "I realize you might not have gleaned this from my devil-may-care persona, but I have a soft and fragile heart."

She turned her head to one side, giving him a suspicious look. "Uh-huh."

He gave her a serious look that wiped the hint of humor from her expression. "I've never been very good at relationships. Probably why I'm still single at my advanced age."

"Yeah, you're ancient."

"I've never had a long-term relationship work out. I've barely ever had a long-term relationship, period. And you know, I've been okay with that so far."

"Oh." He could feel her retreating, first emotionally and then physically, taking a step back until her spine hit the kitchen counter.

He caught her face between his hands, making her look at him. "I'm not warning you of anything," he said firmly. "Except I guess, maybe, I'm warning you that if you're looking for something temporary, I don't think I'm your man this time around."

Her eyebrows notched upward again. "So what, exactly, are you looking for?"

"Forever would be kind of nice. If we could make it work."

She covered his hands with hers, the nubby texture of

her compression bandage tickling his wrist. "That sounds like a challenge, Chief Massey."

"And you like a challenge?"

She rose on her tiptoes and pressed her lips to his ear. "I love a challenge."

* * * * *

Don't miss the next two books in award-winning author Paula Graves's miniseries BITTERWOOD P.D., *on sale in March and April 2014.*

Desperation had the muscles in her face rigid as she stood in front of him, moving closer. A red heat climbed up her neck.

"I can't let you lie." He smiled. "Besides, you're no good at it. And the evidence will clear us."

Defiance shot from her glare. Her stubborn streak reared its head again. "You don't get to decide."

Her gaze was fiery hot. Her body vibrated with intensity as she stalked toward him.

He readied himself for the argument that was sure to come, but she pressed a kiss to his lips instead, shocking the hell out of him.

"There's been enough fighting for one day. I need something else from you."

He locked onto her gaze. "Are you sure this is a good idea?"

"No. Not at all. But I need to do it anyway."

RANCHER RESCUE

BY
BARB HAN

Published in Great Britain 2014
by Mills & Boon, an imprint of Harlequin (UK) Limited,
Eton House, 18-24 Paradise Road, Richmond, Surrey, TW9 1SR

© 2014 Barb Han

ISBN: 978 0 263 91349 1

46-0214

Harlequin (UK) Limited's policy is to use papers that are natural, renewable and recyclable products and made from wood grown in sustainable forests. The logging and manufacturing processes conform to the legal environmental regulations of the country of origin.

Printed and bound in Spain
by Blackprint CPI, Barcelona

Barb Han lives in North Texas with her very own hero-worthy husband, has three beautiful children, a spunky golden retriever/standard poodle mix and too many books in her to-read pile. In her downtime, she plays video games and spends much of her time on or around a basketball court. She's passionate about travel, and many of the places she visits end up in her books.

She loves interacting with readers and is grateful for their support. You can reach her at www.barbhan.com.

The chance to work with the incredibly talented
Allison Lyons is a thrill beyond measure.
Thank you for sharing your editing brilliance
and giving me the chance to learn from you.

To my agent, Jill Marsal, for all your guidance,
encouragement, and patience.

To Jerrie Alexander, my brave friend
and critique partner.

To Brandon, who is strength personified; Jacob,
who is the most courageous person I know; and Tori,
who is brilliant and funny, I love you.
This one is for you, Babe.

Chapter One

Katherine Harper pushed up on all fours and spit dirt. "Don't take him. I'll do whatever you say."

The tangle of barbed wire squeezed around her calf. Pain seared her leg.

"She got herself caught." The man glared down at her. He glanced toward the thicket, sized up the situation and turned to his partner. "She's not going anywhere."

The first man whirled around. His lip curled. Hate filled his eyes. "Leave her. We have the boy."

"Kane won't like it. He wants them both."

"No. Please. My nephew has nothing to do with any of this." She kicked. Burning, throbbing flames scorched her ankle to her thigh. "I'll give you whatever you want. I'll find the file."

"We know you will. Involve the police and he's dead," the second man warned. "We'll be in touch."

Noah screamed for her. She heard the terror in his voice. A wave of hopelessness crashed through her as she struggled against the barbs, watching the men disappear into the woods with her nephew. *Oh. God. No.*

"He's sick. He needs medicine," she screamed through burning lungs.

They disappeared without looking back.

Shards of pain shot up her leg. Fear seized her. The thick

trees closed in on her. Noah had been kidnapped, and she was trapped and helpless.

"Please. Somebody."

The thunder of hooves roared from somewhere in the distance. She sucked in a quick breath and scanned the area. Were more men out there?

Everything had happened so fast. How long had they been dragging her? How far into the woods was she?

All visual reminders of the pumpkin patch were long gone. No open fields or bales of hay. No bursts of orange dotting the landscape. No smells of animal fur and warmth. There was nothing familiar in her surroundings now.

Judging from the amount of blood and the relentless razor-sharp barbs digging into her flesh, she would bleed to death.

No. She wouldn't die. Noah needed her to stay alive. *Noah.*

Anger boiled inside her, heating her skin to flames. Katherine had to save him. He had no one else. He was probably terrified, which could bring on an asthma attack. Without his inhaler or medication, the episode could be fatal.

Forcing herself to her feet, she balanced on her good side and hopped. Her foot was slick with blood. Her shoe squished. Her knees buckled. The cold, hard ground punished her shoulder on impact.

She scrambled on all fours and tried to crawl. The barbed wire tightened like a coil. The ache in her leg was nothing compared to the agony in her heart.

Exertion wasn't good. Could she unwrap the mangled wire? Could she free herself? Could she catch up?

Panic pounded her chest. Her heartbeat echoed in her ears.

The hooves came closer. Had the men sent company? Had her screaming backfired, pinpointing her location?

Autumn foliage blanketed the ground, making it difficult to see if there was anything useful to use against another attacker. She could hide. But where?

The sounds of hooves pounding the unforgiving earth slowed. Near. She swallowed a sob. He could do whatever he wanted to her while she was trapped. Why had she made all that noise?

She fanned her hands across the ground. Was there anything she could use as a weapon? The best one encased her leg, causing a slow bleed. She needed to think. Come up with a plan. Could she use a sharp branch?

Biting back the pain, she scooted behind a tree and palmed a splintered stick.

The thunderous drumming came to a stop. The horse's labored breath broke through the quiet.

An imposing figure dismounted, muttering a curse. His low rumble of a voice sent chills up her neck.

Her pulse raced.

His boots firmly planted on the ground, Katherine got a good look at him. He was nothing like her attackers. They'd worn dark suits and sunglasses when they'd ambushed her and Noah. Everything about this man was different.

He wore jeans, a button-down shirt and a black cowboy hat. He had broad shoulders and lean hips. At his full height, he had to be at least six foot two, maybe more.

A man who looked genuine and strong like him couldn't be there for the wrong reasons, could he? Still, who could she trust? Couldn't murderers be magnetic?

"What in hell is going on?" A shiver raced up her spine as he followed the line of blood that would lead him right to her.

He took a menacing step toward her. Friend or enemy, she was about to come face-to-face with him.

Katherine said a silent protection prayer.

Her equilibrium was off. Her head light. She closed her fingers around the tree trunk tighter. Could she hold on long enough to make her move?

A dimpled chin on a carved-from-granite face leaned toward her. Brown eyes stared at her. She faltered.

Nope. Not a hallucination. This cowboy was real, and she was getting weak. Her vision blurred. She had to act fast.

With a final push, Katherine stepped forward. Her knees buckled and she stumbled.

IN ONE QUICK motion Caleb Snow seized the stick being jabbed at his ribs and pinned the woman to the ground.

She was gorgeous in her lacy white shirt. Her sea-green skirt hiked up her thigh far enough to reveal a peek of her panties. Pale blue. He swallowed hard. Tried not to think about his favorite color caressing her sweet little bottom as he wrestled to keep her from stabbing him. The rest of her was golden skin and long legs. She had just enough curves to make her feel like a real woman, sensual and soft. "What's wrong with you?"

The tangle of chestnut hair and limbs didn't speak.

Was she afraid? Of him? Hell no. He took the stick and tossed it. She kicked and punched.

"Hold still. I'm trying to help."

"No. You're not."

"I will as soon as I'm sure you won't try to poke me with that stick."

He'd turned his horse the moment he'd heard the screams that sounded half wild banshee, half horror-film victim expecting to help, not be attacked.

"You're hurting me," she yelped.

The tremor in her voice sliced through his frustration. Her admission tore through him. The thought he added to her pain hit him hard. "Stop trying to slap me, and I'll get up."

Her lips trembled. She looked at him—all big fearful eyes and cherry lips—and his heart squeezed.

Those violet eyes stared up at him, sending a painful recollection splintering through his chest. She had the same look of terror his mother always had right before his father'd raised a hand to her. Caleb buried the memory before it could take hold.

"Listen to me. I'm not going to hurt you." Her almond-shaped face, olive skin and soft features stirred an inappropriate sexual reaction. Skin-to-skin contact was a bad idea. He shifted more of his weight onto his bent knee.

Her breaths came out in short gasps. "Then let me go. I have to find him before they get away."

"As soon as I know you're not gonna do something stupid, I will. You're not going anywhere until I get this off your leg. You want to tell me what the hell's going on? Who's getting away?" Her actions were that of a wounded animal, not a crazed murderer. He eased more weight off her, scanning her for other injuries.

She recoiled. "Who are you?"

"Caleb Snow and this is my ranch." He picked up the wire to untangle her. Her pained cry pierced right through him. "Sorry about that." He eased the cable down carefully. "Didn't mean to hurt you."

She'd seriously tangled her long, silky leg in barbed wire. She'd lost a lot of blood. He couldn't have her going into shock. "The more you fight, the worse it'll get. You've done a number on yourself already."

Her eyelids fluttered.

Based on her pallor, she could lose consciousness if she didn't hold still. He stood and muttered a curse.

Her wild eyes looked up at him, pleading. "Some men took my nephew. I don't know who. They went that way." She motioned toward the McGrath ranch. Her voice cracked and he could see she was struggling not to cry. Tears fell anyway.

"The wire has to come off first. Then we'll take a look. Don't watch me. It'll only hurt worse. Tell me your name." A stab of guilt pierced him at the pain he was about to cause. The weight of her body had impaled the rusty steel barbs deep into her flesh.

Her head tilted back as she winced. She gasped but didn't scream, her eyes still radiating distrust.

"Hold on. I have something that can help." He pulled wire cutters and antibiotic wipes from his saddlebag. He tied a handkerchief below her knee to stem the bleeding.

"Promise you won't leave me here?"

"Now why would I do that?" One by one, he pulled the barbs out of her skin, giving her time to breathe in between. "Tell me more about the men."

"They. Were. Big." The words came through quick bursts of breath.

He pulled the last barb and stuck his hand out, offering a help up.

Hers felt soft and small. A jolt of electricity shot up Caleb's arm. Normally he'd enjoy feeling a sexual spark. This wasn't the time or place.

"I need to go that way." She pointed north, grasping at the tree.

"You're hurt. On my property, that means you don't go anywhere until I know you're okay. Besides, you still haven't told me why you're out here to begin with."

"Where is here?" she asked, dodging his question.

"The TorJake Ranch." How did she not know where she was? A dozen scenarios came to mind. None he liked. He took a step toward her. She was too weak to put up a fight. He wrapped his arm around her waist for support. "You aren't going anywhere like this. Start talking and I might be able to help. I have medical supplies at the house. But you'll explain why you're on my land or I'll call the sheriff. We clear?"

"Please. Don't. I'll tell you everything." He'd struck a nerve.

He should call Sheriff Coleman. No good ever came from a woman caught in a situation like this. But something about her made Caleb wait.

"My name is Katherine Harper. I took my nephew to a pumpkin patch." She glanced around. "I'm not sure which way."

"The Reynolds' place." Was it the fear in her eyes, or the tremble to her lips that hit him somewhere deep? He didn't care. He was intrigued.

"Sounds right. Anyway, two men in suits came from nowhere and grabbed us. They dragged us through the woods…here…until I got caught up. Then…"

Tears streaked her cheeks. "They took off with him."

The barbed wire had been cut. The McGrath ranch was on the other side of the fence. He'd have to ask about that. Of course, he preferred to deal with creatures of the four-legged variety or something with a motor.

"We'll figure this out."

Caleb assessed her carefully.

Her vulnerable state had his instincts sounding alarm bells.

Chapter Two

Noah was gone. Katherine was hurt. Her only chance to see her nephew again stood next to her. The cowboy's actions showed he wanted to help. He needed to know the truth. She couldn't pinpoint the other reason she felt an undeniable urge to confide in the cowboy. But she did.

"My nephew was kidnapped for a reason." *Oh. God.* It was almost unbearable to say those words out loud.

His thick brow arched. "Do you know these men?"

She shook her head. "They wanted me to give them a file. Said they knew I had it, but I don't. I have no idea what they're talking about."

The cowboy's comforting arm tightened around her. Could he really help? Noah was gone and she was desperate.

He pulled out his cell phone.

"I'm calling my foreman, then the sheriff. We'll cover more ground that way."

"No police. They insisted. Besides, there's no time. Let's use your horse. We might be able to catch them. Noah needs medicine." She moved to step forward. Pain nearly buckled her knees. Her vision blurred.

"Hold on there," he said, righting her again with a firm hand. "We'll find him, but I'm bringing in the law."

"They'll hurt—"

"I doubt it. Think about it. They'd say anything to back you off. There's no chance to find him otherwise." He turned to his call. "Matt, grab a few men and some horses. We have a situation. A boy's been taken. Looks like they might've crossed over to the McGrath place with him. I want every square inch of both properties scoured. And call the sheriff." His gaze met Katherine's, and her heart clutched. He was right. They were most likely bluffing.

She nodded.

"There are two men dressed in suits. Could be dangerous." His attention shifted to her. "How old is your nephew?"

"Four." With reinforcements on the way, she dared to think she could get Noah back safely before the sun went down.

A muscle in the cowboy's jaw ticked. "You heard that, right?" A beat later came, "Somebody cut the fence on the north corner. Jimmy's been running this side. Ask him how things were the other day when he came this way."

Katherine looked at the barbed wire. The last bit of hope this could have been a bad dream shriveled and died.

"Tell the men to be careful." Caleb took more of her weight as he pocketed his phone. "I've got you."

"I'm fine." Katherine struggled to break free from his grip. Her brain was scrambled. She'd been dragged through this area thinking it had been a random trail, but how could it be? They'd cut the fence in advance. Everything about them seemed professional and planned. But what kind of file could she possibly have for men like them?

The cowboy's strong grip tightened around her as she fought another wave of nausea. "I think I'll be fine once I get on your horse."

"My men are all over this. Matt's phoning the sheriff as we speak. I need to get you home where I can take care of your injuries. The sheriff will need to speak to you for his report."

"The longer I wait, the farther away Noah will be." She had no purse, no ID and no money. Those had been discarded along with his medicine. Everything she'd had with her was scattered between here and the pumpkin patch.

His brow arched. "You won't make it a mile in your condition."

"I can. I have to." Katherine tried to put weight on her foot. Her knee buckled. He pulled her upright again with strong arms. He was powerful, male and looked as though he could handle himself against just about any threat.

Caleb shook his head. "Hell, I'd move heaven and earth if I were in your situation. But you're hurt."

"He needs me. He's little and scared. You can't possibly understand." Her voice hitched.

The lines in the cowboy's forehead deepened. "We'll cut through the McGraths' on the way to the house. How's that?"

His arms banded around her hips. Arms like his would be capable of handling anyone or anything they came across. He lifted her onto the saddle with no effort and then swung up behind her.

"I need to make sure you're going to be around long enough to greet him. You let infection set in and that leg will be no use to you anymore."

She didn't argue. Fatigue weighted her limbs, drained her energy. If he could fix her leg, she could find Noah.

Taking the long way around didn't unearth any clues about Noah's whereabouts. The sky was darkening. Night would fall soon.

The house coming into view was a white two-story Colonial with a wraparound porch and dark green shutters. An impressive set of barns sat behind the house. There was a detached garage with a basketball hoop off to the side. This was a great place for kids.

Katherine hadn't stopped once to realize this man probably had a family of his own. The image of him cradling a baby edged its way into her thoughts. The contrast between something so tiny and vulnerable against his bare steel chest brought shivers up her arms.

Did he have a son? His reaction to Noah's age made more sense.

She prayed Noah would be home in bed before the sun vanished. Was he still panicked? Could he breathe? Did he have time before the next attack? Did she?

What would happen when the men came after her again if she couldn't produce the file?

She shrugged off the ice trickling down her spine. Police would need a description of the attackers. She had to think. The last thing she remembered was being hauled through the woods. She ran so long her lungs burned. The next thing she knew, she was facedown in the dirt. The men had disappeared. She'd lost everything.

"Lean toward me. I'll catch you." Caleb stood next to the horse.

One of his calloused but gentle hands splayed on the small of her back. He carried her inside as if she weighed nothing and placed her on the sofa in the front room. He lifted her bloody leg to rest on top of the polished knotty-pine coffee table.

The smell of spices and food warming sent a rumble through her stomach. How long had she been dragged? She wouldn't be able to eat, but how long could Noah go without food? Was he hungry?

"Margaret, grab my emergency bag," Caleb shouted before turning to Katherine. "Margaret helps me out with cleaning and cooking. Keeps me and my boys fed."

So he did have children. Katherine figured a place with this kind of space had to have little ones running around. Noah would have loved it here.

A round woman padded into the room. A salt-of-the-earth type with a kind face, she looked to be in her late fifties. Her expression dropped. "What happened?"

Caleb gave her a quick rundown before introducing them. "I'll need clean towels, a bowl of warm water and something for Katherine to drink. Some of these gashes are deep."

Margaret returned with supplies. "If anyone can find your nephew, it's this man."

Margaret's sympathetic expression melted some of Katherine's resolve. "Thank you."

"You look like you're in pain. Tell me where it hurts."

"My head. Stomach." Her hand pressed against her mid-section to stave off another round of nausea. "But I'll be fine."

"Of course you will. You're in good hands." She set a cup of tea next to Katherine. "This'll help."

She thanked the housekeeper, smiled and took a sip. "Tastes good."

"Would you mind grabbing the keys to my truck? Call the barn, too. I rode Dawn again. Ask Teddy to put her up for the night." Caleb patted one of Katherine's gashes with antibiotic ointment.

She gasped, biting back a scream. "Now that I'm okay, we're going to find them ourselves, right?"

"I'm taking you to the E.R."

"No." Shaking her head made everything hurt that much worse. "I can't leave. Your guys will find Noah and bring him here, right?"

"Yes."

"Then the only reason I'd walk out that door is to help

search for him. I won't leave here without him. He needs me and his meds."

She expected a fight but got a nod of agreement instead.

Caleb went back to work carefully blotting each gash without saying another word. Trying to distract herself from the pain, Katherine studied the room. The decor was simple. Substantial, hand-carved wood furniture surrounded the fireplace, which had a rust-colored star above the mantel. The cushions were soft. The place was more masculine than she figured it would be. There had to be a woman somewhere in the picture. A protective, gorgeous man like Caleb had to have a beautiful wife. And kids. She'd already envisioned him holding his child. She could easily see him with two or three more.

There was one problem. Nothing was out of place. She knew from spending the past week with Noah, kids left messes everywhere. "I hope your wife doesn't get the wrong impression when she sees a strange woman on your sofa."

Caleb didn't look up. "I'm single."

Had she met him under other circumstances, the admission would've caused a thousand tiny butterflies to flutter in her stomach. But now she could only think about Noah.

"Do you want to call Noah's parents and let them know what's going down?"

"No. There's no one else. His mother died. I'm all he's got." *The poor kid.*

Her sister, Leann, had always been the reckless one. Everything had been fun and games and risk for her. Now she was gone and Noah was in trouble.

A hundred questions danced across Caleb's intense brown eyes. To his credit, he didn't ask any of them.

Katherine figured he deserved to know the truth. "She died in a climbing accident at Enchanted Rock a week ago.

She was 'bouldering,' which apparently means you don't use safety equipment. You're supposed to have people spot you, but she didn't."

Caleb's jaw did that tick thing again. She'd seen it before when he'd seemed upset and held his tongue. Did he have something he wanted to say now?

"Sorry for your loss. This must be devastating for you. What about Noah's father?"

"She…the two of them…lived in Austin alone. She never told me who his father was. As far as I know, no one else has a clue, either. My sister may have been reckless with her actions but she could keep a secret." Katherine wondered what else she didn't know about Leann.

"Be easy enough to check out the birth certificate."

A half-laughed, half-exacerbated sigh slipped out. "She put down George Clooney."

If Caleb thought it funny, he didn't laugh.

Katherine cleared her throat. "I doubt if the father knows about Noah. Leann never told anyone who she dated. Not even me. I never knew the names of her boyfriends. When she spoke about them, they all had movie-star nicknames."

"There must've been a pattern to it."

Katherine shrugged. "Never gave it much thought before. Figured it was just for fun."

His reassuring nod comforted her.

"You two were close?"

"Our relationship was complicated, but I'm…was… fiercely protective of her." Katherine squeezed her elbows, not wanting to say what she really feared. Her sister had shucked responsibility and become involved with something or someone bad, and now both Katherine and Noah were in danger. Things had been turning around for Leann. Why would she do it?

Katherine tamped down the panic rising in her chest. No one could hurt Noah.

She had to believe he would come home safely. Even though every fiber in her being feared he was already panicked, struggling to breathe. What if she found him and couldn't help? Her purse was lost along with his medicine.

One of Caleb's eyebrows lifted. "What about her friends?"

"I don't have the first idea who they were. My sister was a free spirit. She moved around a lot. Took odd jobs. I don't know much about her life before Noah. It wasn't until recently she contacted me at all." Had Leann known something was about to happen? Was she connected to the file?

Caleb didn't look at her. He just went back to work on her leg, cleaning blood and blotting on ointment.

Oh, God. Bile rose in her throat. Acid burned a trail to her mouth. "No news is definitely not good news."

"There aren't a lot of places to hide. If your nephew's around here, we'll find him. My men know this property better than they know their own mothers."

His comfort was hollow. A wave of desperation washed through her. If the men got off the property with Noah, how would she ever locate him?

"You hungry?"

"You know, I'm starting to feel much better." She tried to push up, but her arms gave out.

"Eat. Rest. The pain in your leg is only beginning. You must've twisted your ankle when you fell. It's swelling. Stay here. Keep it elevated. I'll check in with my men."

Caleb disappeared down the hall, returning a moment later with a steaming bowl in one hand and a bag of ice in the other. He'd removed his cowboy hat, revealing sandy-blond hair that was cut tight but long and loose enough to curl at the ends.

He set down the bowl before placing a pillow behind her head and ice on her ankle. He pulled out his cell while she ate the vegetable soup Margaret had prepared.

There was a knock at the front door. Katherine gasped. Her pulse raced.

CALEB'S EYES MET Katherine's and the power of that one look shot straight to his core. Her on his couch, helpless, with those big eyes—a shade of violet that bordered on purple in this light—made him wish he could erase her pain.

He let Sheriff Coleman in. The officer's tense expression reflected Caleb's emotions. "Your coming by on short notice is much appreciated."

Coleman tipped his hat, a nod to the mutual respect they'd built for one another in the years Caleb had owned the ranch.

"My men are out looking as we speak. I'll need more details to file the report."

Caleb introduced Coleman to Katherine. "This is the boy's aunt. He was with her at the Reynolds' pumpkin patch when it happened."

Sheriff Coleman tilted his head toward Katherine. His lips formed a grim line. "Start from the beginning and tell me everything you remember."

She talked about the pumpkin patch.

"Do you have a picture we can work with?" he asked, looking up from his notepad.

Her head shook, her lips trembled, but she didn't cry. "No. I don't. Lost them along with my purse and everything else I had with me. Not that it would do any good. He's only been living with me for a week. We haven't been down to clean his mother's apartment yet. I don't have many of his things. A few toys. His favorite stuffed animal."

She rambled a little. Not many women could hold it together under this much duress. Her strength radiated a flicker of light in the darkest shadows of Caleb. Places buried long ago, which were best left alone.

"Let's go over the description then," Coleman suggested.

"Black hair. Big brown eyes. Three and a half feet tall. About forty pounds. He's beautiful. Round face. Full cheeks. Curly hair. Features of an angel."

"And the men who took him?" he pressed.

"One of them had gray eyes and a jagged scar from the left side of his lip. He had a dark tan."

"How big was the scar?"

"Not more than a couple of inches. It was in the shape of a crescent moon." She sobbed, but quickly straightened her shoulders and shook it off.

The sheriff glanced away, giving her a moment of space. Caleb dropped his gaze to the floor, respecting her tenacity even more.

"He mentioned the name Kane. He said 'Kane wouldn't like it.'"

"We'll run the name against the database."

"I'm sorry. It's not much to go on. My nephew is alone. Sick. Scared. If he gets too upset, he could have an attack. Without his inhaler or medication, he won't be able to breathe."

Silence sat in the air for a beat.

Coleman cleared his throat. If Caleb didn't know any better, he'd say the sheriff had moisture in his eyes. In this small town, they didn't deal with a lot of violent crime.

"We'll do everything we can to bring him back to you safe and sound. That's a promise," Coleman said.

"Thank you."

"What's Noah's last name?"

"Foster."

"You said you haven't had a chance to clean out his mother's place. Where's that?"

"Austin."

"That where you're from?"

She shook her head. "I live in Dallas."

Caleb could've told the sheriff that. She had a polished, city look. The jeweled sandals on her feet were one of the most impractical shoes she could wear to the country aside from spiked heels.

"When's his birthday?"

"March. The seventeenth."

Caleb looked at her. He could see the tension in her face muscles and the stress threatening to crack, but to her credit, she kept her composure. Probably needed to be strong more than she needed air. Caleb knew the feeling for reasons he didn't want to talk about, either.

He'd known she was different from any other woman he'd met when he'd showed up to help her and she'd thanked him with a makeshift knife to his ribs. Hell, he respected her for it now that he knew the circumstances. She'd probably believed he was working with whoever had taken Noah and that he'd showed up to finish the job. She'd bucked up for a fight.

When she pushed herself up, it took everything in him not to close the distance between them and pull her into his arms for comfort. No one should have to go through this alone.

If Katherine Harper wanted to do this her way, he wouldn't block her path.

The sheriff asked a few more routine-sounding questions, listening intently to her answers. "You fight with anyone lately? A boyfriend?"

Caleb tried not to look as though he cared about the answer to that question. He had no right to care.

Katherine looked down. "Nope. No boyfriend."

"What about other family?"

"None. My parents died during my freshman year of college."

He didn't want to think about what that would do to a person.

Coleman asked a few more questions about family. Katherine looked uncomfortable answering.

"I'll notify my men to keep an eye out for your belongings. What were you doing out here with your nephew?"

"I wanted to take his mind off things. Get him out of the city. We planned our trip all day yesterday. He'd never seen a pumpkin patch. He loved the open space. I didn't think much about letting him run around. We've been in my small apartment all week. Didn't look to be anything or anyone else around for miles. He followed a duck out to the tree line. When I went over to take pictures, two men came from nowhere and snatched us. I panicked. Couldn't believe what was happening. I remember thinking, 'This can't be.' I fought back. That's when I ended up tangled in the barbed wire and they took off. If only I hadn't been so stubborn. If I hadn't fought."

"Don't blame yourself for this," Coleman said quickly.

"They told me if I came any closer or called the police, they'd kill him."

The sheriff nodded, but Caleb caught a flash behind Coleman's eyes. Caleb made a mental note to ask about that when they were alone.

"Ever see them before or hear their voices?" Coleman's gaze was trained on his notepad as he scribbled.

"No. Nothing about them was familiar. They asked for

a file, but I don't have the first clue what they were talking about. Wondered if they'd confused us with someone else."

Katherine continued, "I don't remember tossing my purse or jacket, but I must've ditched them both somewhere along the way. Noah needs his medicine."

"We'll check between here and the Reynolds' place." The sheriff glanced at his watch. "Should have another half hour of daylight to work with."

"My car's still over there. Can't move it until I find my keys." She made a move to stand.

Caleb took a step toward her. The real estate between them disappeared in two strides. "You're too weak. Matt can get your car as soon as we find your purse. For now, I'll give the Reynolds a call. Make sure they don't have it towed."

Caleb phoned his neighbor and gave a quick rundown of the situation. He asked if anyone had reported anything or found a purse.

They hadn't.

Caleb finished the call solemnly. There wasn't much to go on, and time ticked away.

"I feel like I should be doing something besides sitting here," Katherine said to the sheriff.

"Best thing you can do is wait it out. Let my men do their work. I'll put out an AMBER Alert." Sheriff Coleman shook her hand and then walked to the door. "In the meantime, sit tight right here in case I have more questions. Let me know if anything else suspicious happens or you remember anything that might be important."

If Caleb heard things right, he'd just picked up a houseguest. Couldn't say he was especially disappointed. "You'll call as soon as you hear anything, right?"

"You bet."

Caleb thanked the sheriff and walked him out the door.

Outside, Caleb folded his arms. "What do you think?"

Coleman scanned his notes. He rocked back on his heels. "Not sure. Kids are most often taken by a family member. Don't see many kidnappings. Especially not out here."

"Doesn't sound good."

The sheriff dropped his gaze for a second and shook his head.

"What are the chances of finding him alive?"

"The odds are better if he was taken by a relative. Doesn't sound like the case here." Coleman broke eye contact. "That's a whole different ball game."

The words were a sucker punch to Caleb's chest.

"I'd appreciate hearing any news or leads you come across firsthand." Last thing Caleb wanted was for Katherine to learn what had happened to her nephew over the internet or on the news.

"Of course. There's always the possibility he got away and will turn up here. The first twenty-four hours are the most critical."

The thought of a little boy wandering around lost and alone in the dark woods clenched Caleb's gut. "Why'd they threaten to kill him if she called the police?"

"They probably want to keep this quiet. To scare her. Who knows? She's not a celebrity or politician. Why would someone target her? We need to find her phone. In the meantime, have her make a list of enemies. Ask her if she's gotten into a fight with anyone lately. Could someone have a problem with her or her sister? Without her cell, we don't know if anyone's trying to contact her to make demands."

Caleb shook Coleman's hand before he got in his cruiser and pulled away.

He stood on the porch for a long moment, looking out

at the landscape that had kept him from getting too rest-less for years. He couldn't imagine living anywhere else. This was home. And yet, an uneasy feeling crept over him.

Chapter Three

Matt's black pickup roared down the drive. Caleb walked to meet his foreman. "Find anything?"

"There's nothing around for miles. Whoever did this got away fast."

The whole scenario seemed calculated, ruling out the slight possibility this was a case of mistaken identity. "You checked with the McGraths?"

Matt nodded. "They haven't seen or heard anything all day. Gave us the okay to search their property and barn. I sent Jimmy and Greg over to the Reynolds', too. Not a trace. No one saw anything, either. There's nothing but her word to go on." Worry showed in the tight muscles of his face. "I gotta ask. You think it's possible she could be making this up?"

Caleb ground his back teeth. "This is real. She has the bumps and bruises to prove it."

"It was a crappy question but needed to be asked. There's no trail to follow. No other signs she's telling the truth. Could the marks be from something else?"

"You didn't see her. The terror in her eyes. The blood. I had to cut her free from the fencing. Dig barbs out of her leg."

"Stay with me for a minute. I'm just sayin'. Where's the proof she even has a nephew? How do we know all the mechanical stuff upstairs is oiled and the cranks are working with her?"

The point was valid. If he hadn't been the one to find her, he might wonder if she was crazy, too. But he had been the one. Her tortured expression might haunt him for the rest of his life. She'd faced the hell in front of her with her chin up. He didn't doubt her. "I hear you and I understand your concerns. I do. But you're off base."

"How can you be so sure?"

"I just know."

Matt cocked one eyebrow. "Okay…how?"

"Call it gut instinct."

"Then I'll take your word for it. I'll give her a ride wherever she wants to go." He took a step toward the house.

"Sheriff wants her to stick around."

Matt hesitated. His doubt about the situation was written all over his face. To his credit, he seemed to know when to hold his tongue. He turned toward the barn. "Be careful. You have a tendency to get too involved with creatures that need saving. I'll check on the boys out back."

It would be dark before too long. The sun, a bright orange glow on the horizon, was retreating. "I'll put on a pot of coffee."

As soon as Caleb walked inside, Katherine hit him with the first question.

"What did the sheriff say?" She stroked the little yellow tabby who had made herself at home in her lap.

"How'd you manage that?" He inclined his chin toward the kitty.

She shrugged. "She hopped on the couch and curled up. She's a sweet girl. Why?"

"Claws has been afraid of people ever since I brought her into the house."

"How'd she lose her leg?"

"Found her like that when I was riding fences one day. She was in pretty bad shape. Vet fixed her up, and she's been my little shadow ever since. Scratched the heck out of Matt the first time he picked her up. Usually hides when I have company."

Claws purred as Katherine scratched under her chin. "Can't imagine who would hurt such a sweet girl." She paused, and then locked gazes. "You were going to tell me what the sheriff said."

"That he'd contact me if they found anything. Do you remember what else you were doing before the men showed up?"

"We'd bought a jar of local honey. We were picking out pumpkins to take home with us."

"Anything else?"

"That's it. That's all I remember."

Caleb moved to the side table and picked up the empty soup bowl. "You drink coffee?"

"Yes."

"Give me five minutes. In the meantime, sheriff wants a list of names. Anyone who might've been out to hurt your sister. Or you."

He put down the bowl, took a pen and paper from a side table drawer and placed it next to her before moving into the kitchen.

She was making scribbles on the sheet of paper when he returned and handed her a cup. "Wasn't sure how you took yours."

"Black is fine." She gripped the mug. "What's next? How long does the sheriff expect me to sit here and do nothing?"

"Waiting's hard. Believe me, everything that can be done is happening. The authorities have all their resources on this. My men are filling the gaps. It's best to stay put until the sheriff calls. Give yourself a chance to heal. How's your leg?"

"Better. Thank you."

His bandage job looked to be holding. "What was the last thing you remembered before Noah was…" Damn. He hated saying the word *taken* out loud.

"I don't know. After the pumpkins, we were going on a hayride. I'd gone over to tell him. He was playing with the really big ones on the edge of the patch. Near the woods. I took pictures of him climbing on them. If we can find my phone, I can supply the sheriff with a recent photo."

"Think you might have captured the guys on your camera?"

"It's possible."

"I'll notify the sheriff."

Caleb phoned Coleman and provided an update. The hunt for her belongings intensified. They might find answers. At the very least, Matt would believe her if she could produce a picture of her nephew. Why did that seem so important?

"Think they saw you snapping shots?"

She shrugged. "Don't know."

"Did Noah scream?"

"They covered his mouth at the same time they grabbed him around the waist. Didn't bother once we got out of range." Sadness, desperation, fear played out across her features. "Please tell me we'll find him. I don't know what they want. If I can't produce a file, I'm afraid they'll take it out on him."

Caleb moved from his spot on the love seat to the couch and draped an arm around her. "We won't allow it. We'll figure it out."

"I wish I'd been thinking more clearly. I panicked.

Dropped everything. If I had those pics now, we might have a direction."

Five raps on the door—Matt's signature knock—came before the door sprang open. His foreman rushed in holding a black purse.

Claws darted under the sofa.

Katherine strained to push off the couch. "You found it."

"The boys did." Matt's gaze moved from Caleb to Katherine. His brow furrowed and a muscle along his jaw twitched.

"Any luck with my phone?"

"This is all we got before we ran out of daylight. All the men in the county are involved. A few want to keep going. The rest will pick up the search tomorrow."

Matt handed the bag to Katherine. She immediately dumped out the contents, palming Noah's pill bottle and inhaler.

"Did you let Coleman know?" Caleb asked.

Matt nodded. "Sure did. There's something else you should know. Thanks to that little bit of rain we got the other day, one of the boys located four-wheeler tracks on the McGrath farm on the other side of the fence near where you said you found her."

Matt couldn't deny she'd told the truth now.

Katherine was already digging around the large tote, tossing snack bags and juice boxes onto the sofa. "It all happened so fast. I can't even remember where I put my phone. I just remember taking photographs one minute, then the world spinning out of control the next. I wouldn't even believe any of this myself if it hadn't happened to me. I keep feeling like all of this is some kind of bad dream, and I'll wake up any second to find everything back to normal. Noah will be here with me. My sister will be alive."

As if shaking off the heavy thoughts, Katherine jammed

her hand back inside her bag. Blood soaked through one section of the gauze on her leg.

"If you won't let me take you to the hospital, you'll have to listen to what I say. We have to keep this elevated." Caleb curled his fingers around her calf and lifted, watching for any signs he hurt her. Based on her grimace, her darkening eyes, she was winning the fight against the pain. When the shock and adrenaline wore off later, she'd be in for it. He didn't like the idea of her being home alone in Dallas when it happened.

"You're right. I'm sorry. I'm not thinking clearly. This whole ordeal has me scattered. Waiting it out will drive me insane."

Caleb didn't even want to think about the possibility of not finding her nephew.

Big violet eyes stared at him. "It's gone. I must've still been holding it. They have no way to contact me. What if they've called already? What if they've…"

"Sleep here tonight." Caleb ignored Matt's sharp intake of breath. He hadn't planned to make the offer. It just came out.

"I'D GET IN your way. Besides, you have plenty to do to keep busy without me underfoot," Katherine argued without conviction.

"If you stay here, I'll be able to keep an eye on your leg and get some work done."

Going back to her one-bedroom apartment was about as appealing as sleeping alone in a cave. Her keys were in her purse, but she doubted she could drive. Even though Noah had only been there a week, she couldn't face going home without him. Staying at the ranch, being this near Caleb, provided a measure of strength and comfort.

His warm brown eyes darkened. "I can have Margaret

turn down the bed in the guest room. Doesn't make sense for you to go anywhere."

"I don't want to be rude. I just…"

Frustration, exhaustion was taking hold. It had been three long hours since the ordeal began.

"No reason to leave. This is best place to be for now."

Caleb seemed the type of guy who took care of anyone and everyone he came across. Cowboy code or something. Still, she didn't want to abuse his goodwill. "Thank you for everything you've done so far, but—"

"It's no trouble."

Matt ran the toe of his boot along the floor. "Think they'll call her house?"

"I saw no need for a landline."

The cowboy sat on the edge of the coffee table. "Then it's settled. You stay. Agreed?"

"For tonight."

Matt quickly excused himself and disappeared down the hall. What was that all about?

The cowboy followed.

Her heart gave a little skip at the satisfied smile on his face. She refocused on the sheet of paper. Who would want something from Leann? What file could she possibly have? A manila folder? Computer file?

Why on earth would they think Katherine had it? If they knew Leann at all, they'd realize she could keep a secret. The last thing she would do was confide in her sister.

Maybe a trip to Austin would help? She could start with Leann's computer.

She rubbed her temples to ease the pounding between her eyes. Other than playing with the pumpkins, had Noah spoken to anyone? Had she?

There had to have been at least a dozen other people around. Were any of them in on it? A chill raced up her spine.

Caleb reappeared, holding a crutch. "I should take another look at that ankle before you put any weight on it."

"I just remembered something. There was a man talking to me while I was in line to buy tickets for the hayride."

His rich brown eyes lifted to meet hers and her heart faltered.

"He could've been there to distract you."

Panic at reliving the memory gripped her. She buried her face in her hands. "I'm so scared. What will they do to him?"

He cupped her chin, lifting her face until her eyes met his. "You can't think like that."

"He has to be terrified. He's so vulnerable and alone. I'm praying they haven't hurt him. He's been through so much already. I was supposed to take care of him. Protect him. Keep him safe."

"If he's half as strong as his aunt, he'll be all right." She could tell by his set jaw he meant it.

She almost laughed out loud. Little did he know how weak and miserable she felt, and her heart was fluttering with him so close, which could not be more inappropriate under the circumstances. "I promised on my sister's grave I would look after him. Look what I did."

The weight of those words sat heavier than a block of granite. Panic squeezed her chest. Her breath labored.

Brown eyes, rich, the color of newly turned fall leaves, set in an almost overwhelmingly attractive face stared at her. Before she could protest, his hand guided her face toward his shoulder.

"Don't blame yourself," he soothed. "Talk like that won't bring him back." His voice was a low rumble.

This close she could breathe in his scent. He smelled

of fresh air and outdoors, masculine and virile. His mouth was so close to hers she could feel his cinnamon-scented breath on her skin.

She'd felt so alone, so guilty, and then suddenly this handsome cowboy was offering comfort.

Caleb pulled away too soon. Her mind was still trying to wrap itself around the fact a room could be charged with so much tension in less than a second, and in the next she could feel so guilty for allowing herself to get caught up in it.

The sounds of boots scuffling across tiles came from the other room. He inclined his chin toward the kitchen. "Sounds like we have company."

He stood and held out his hand.

By the time Katherine limped into the kitchen with Caleb's help, the table was filled with men. As soon as they saw her, chatter stopped and they stood. There were half a dozen cowboys surrounding the table.

"Ma'am." Matt tipped his hat.

She smiled, nodded.

Caleb led her to the sink to wash her hands and blot her face with a cool, wet towel.

"Take my seat," he said, urging her toward the head of the table.

Matt leaned forward, staring, lips pinched together.

As soon as she thanked the cowboy and sat, conversation resumed.

He handed her a plate of ribs and beans. She smiled up at him to show her gratitude.

He brought her fresh iced tea before making his own fixings and seating himself at the breakfast bar.

She looked down the table at the few guys. These must be the boys he'd referred to earlier.

Yep, he took care of everyone around him, including her.

WHEN DINNER WAS over, Caleb excused himself and moved to the back porch. Remnants of Katherine's unique smell, a mix of spring flowers and vanilla, filled his senses when he was anywhere near her. He had to detach and analyze the situation. He needed a clear head. He could think outside.

Katherine had clearly been through hell. An unexpected death and a kidnapping within a week?

Before he could get too deep into that thought, the screen door creaked open and Matt walked out.

"Tough situation in there," he said, nodding toward the house.

"You believe her now?"

"Hard to dispute the evidence." He held his toothpick up to the light. "I didn't mean to insult her before. I didn't know what to believe."

"Can't say I wouldn't be suspicious, too, if I hadn't seen her moments after the fact."

"I know you're planning to help, and it's the right thing to do, but is there something going on between you two?"

He clamped his mouth shut. Shock momentarily robbed his voice.

"No. Of course not. I met her five minutes ago. What makes you think otherwise?"

"You have a history of getting involved with women in crisis."

"I'd help anyone who needed it."

"True."

Matt didn't have to remind him of what he already knew. He had a knack for attracting women in trouble. Did he feel an attraction to Katherine? Yes. Was she beautiful? Yes. But he knew better than to act on it. The last time he'd rescued a woman, she'd returned the favor by breaking his heart. She'd let him help her, but then deserted him. He needed to keep his defenses up and not get involved with Katherine the way he did with the others. Period.

That being said, he wouldn't turn away a woman in trouble. Did this have something to do with his twisted-up childhood? He was pretty damn sure Freud would think so.

Tension tightened Matt's face. "Just be careful. When the last one walked out, she took a piece of you with her. You haven't been the same since."

"Not going to happen again."

Matt arched his brow. "If I'm honest, I'm also bothered by the fact there's a kid involved."

Figured. Caleb knew exactly what his friend was talking about. "My ex and her little girl have nothing to do with this."

"No? You sure about that?"

"I don't see how Katherine's nephew being kidnapped has anything to do with my past," Caleb said. Impatience edged his tone.

"A woman shows up at your door with a kid in crisis and you can't see anything familiar about it? I've known you a long time—"

"You don't have to remind me."

"Then you realize I wouldn't come out of the blue with something. I think your judgment's clouded." Matt's earnest eyes stared into Caleb. His buddy had had a ringside seat to the pain Cissy had caused when she'd walked out, taking Savannah with her. Matt's intentions were pure gold, if not his reasoning.

"I disagree." He couldn't deny or explain his attraction to Katherine. It was more than helping out a random person in need. He could be honest with himself. He probably felt a certain amount of pull toward her because of the child involved. No doubt, the situation tugged at his heart. But he'd only just met her. He'd help her. She'd leave.

Whether she was wearing his favorite color on her underwear or not, they'd both move on. He had no intention of finding out if the pale blue lace circled her tiny waist. He was stubborn, not stupid. "Nothing else matters until we find that little guy."

"Saw the sheriff earlier." Matt's hands clenched. "Heard about the boy having a medical condition. What kind of person would snatch a little kid like that?"

Matt didn't use the word *monster,* but Caleb knew his buddy well enough to know he thought it.

"That's what I plan to find out."

"You know I'll help in any way I can. Then she can go home, and you can get on with your life."

Caleb chewed on a toothpick. "How are the men taking everything?"

"Hard. Especially with Jimmy's situation. He's still out searching."

"Meant to ask how his little girl's doing when I saw him tonight."

Matt shook his head. "Not good."

Damn. "Send 'em home. They need to be with their families."

"I think most of them want to be here to keep searching. Jimmy made up flyers. A few men headed into town to put the word out. Everyone wants to help with the search. They're working out shifts to sleep."

"Tell 'em how much I appreciate their efforts. We'll do everything we can to make sure this boy comes home safe. And we won't stop looking for him until we do."

Matt nodded, his solemn expression intensifying when he said, "You be careful with yourself, too."

"This is not like the others."

"You don't know that yet," Matt said, deadpan.

Caleb bit back his response. Matt's heart was in the

right place. "Tell Gus I can't meet tomorrow. I know the buyer wants to stop by, but I can't."

"This is the third time he's set up a meeting. You haven't liked anyone he's found so far."

"Can't dump my mare on the first person that strolls in."

"Or the second...or third apparently. Every time we breed her, the same thing happens. It's been three years and not one of her foals has lived."

"Which is exactly the reason I don't want to sell her. What will end up happening to her when they realize she can't produce? Besides, she's useful around here."

"How so? The men use four-wheelers so it won't do any good to assign her to one of them. I have my horse and you have yours."

"I'll find more for her to do. Dawn's getting older. I'll use both. Not all lost causes are lost causes."

Matt's eyebrow rose as he turned toward the barn. "We'll see."

CALEB HAD BEEN buried in paperwork for a couple hours when Katherine appeared in his office doorway, leaning on the crutch.

"Mind some company?"

She wore an oversize sleep shirt and loose-fitting shorts cinched above the hips. Even clothes two sizes too big couldn't cloak her sexy figure. Her soft curves would certainly get a man fantasizing about what was beneath those thin threads.

"Sure. Where'd you get the clothes?"

"Margaret put these on the bed with a note saying they belonged to her daughter. Even said I could borrow them as long as I needed to. I managed to clean up without getting my leg wet. I took a nap. I'm feeling much better."

Katherine sat in the oversize leather chair Caleb loved.

It was big enough for two. Claws hopped up a second later, curling in her lap.

"Any word from the sheriff yet?"

"No. I put in a call to him. Should hear back any minute. If your leg is feeling better in the morning, I thought we could head to Austin."

"I want to stay here and search for my phone."

"We'll look first. Then we'll head out. Any chance you have a copy of your sister's keys?"

"Afraid not."

"We'll get in anyway."

She cocked her head and pursed her lips. "Tell me not to ask why you know how to break in someone's house."

Caleb cracked a smile as he rubbed his temples. "Misspent youth. Besides, some secrets a man takes to his grave." He chuckled. "I've been thinking. You have any idea if Noah's father knew about him?"

Katherine heaved a sigh, twirling her fingers through Claws's fur. "I should but don't. My sister's relationships were complicated. Especially ours."

"Families can be tricky," Caleb agreed.

"When our parents got in the car crash my freshman year of college, I resented having to come home to take care of her." Katherine dropped her gaze. "I probably made everything worse. Did everything wrong."

"Not an easy situation to be thrown into."

Katherine's lips trembled but no tears came.

"Leann had always been something of a free spirit. Her life was lived without a care in the world. I was the one who stressed over grades and stayed home on Friday nights to study or to help out around the house. My parents owned a small business and worked long hours. I was used to being alone. Leann, on the other hand, was always out with friends. The two of us couldn't have been more opposite. Sometimes I wished I could have been more like her. Instead, I came down on her hard. Tried to force her to be more like me."

"You had no choice but to be serious. Sounds like you were the one who had to grow up." She was a survivor who coped the best way she could.

"What about your parents?" She turned the tables.

"My mom was a saint. The man who donated sperm? A jerk. Dad, if you can call him that, didn't treat my mother very well before he decided to run out." Caleb's story was the same one being played out in every honky-tonk from there to the border. "I rebelled. I was angry at her for allowing him to hurt her when he was here. Angry with myself for not jumping in to save her. Mom worked herself too hard to pay the bills. Didn't have insurance. Didn't take care of her diabetes. Died when I was fifteen." The familiar stab of anger and regret punctured him.

"Did you blame yourself?"

"I know a thing or two about feeling like you let someone down. Only hurt yourself with that kind of thinking, though. I found the past is better left there. Best to focus on the here and now. Do that well and the future will take care of itself."

"Is that your way of saying I should let go?"

"I did plenty of things wrong when I was a child. You could say I was a handful. Dwelling on it doesn't change what was."

She studied the room. "Looks like you're making up for it now."

Pride filled his chest. "Never felt like I belonged anywhere before here." He'd been restless lately though. Matt had said Caleb missed having little feet running around. The wounds were still raw from Cissy leaving. Another reason he should keep a safe distance from the woman curled up on his favorite chair. She looked as though she belonged there. "TorJake is a great home."

"I love the name. How'd you come up with it?"

"My first big sale was a beautiful paint horse. The man who'd sold him to me when he was a pony said he tore up the ground like no other. He'd been calling him Speedy Jake. I joked that I should enter him over at Lone Star Park as ToreUpTheEarthJake. Somehow, his nickname got shortened to TorJake, and it stuck. Had to geld him early on to keep his temperament under control. He had the most interesting, well-defined markings I've ever seen. Sold him to a bigwig movie producer in Hollywood to use filming a Western. The sale allowed me to buy neighboring farms and eventually expand to what I have now."

"Was it always your dream to own a horse ranch?"

"I figured I'd end up in jail or worse. When I landed a job at my first working ranch, I fell in love. A fellow by the name of Hank was an old pro working there. He taught me the ropes. Said he saw something in me. He never had kids of his own. Told me he went to war instead. Became a damn good marine. Special ops. He taught me everything I know about horse ranches and keeping myself out of trouble."

"Where is he now?"

"He passed away last year."

"I'm so sorry." Her moment of distraction faded too fast, and he knew what she was thinking based on the change in her expression. "You don't think they'll hurt him, do you?"

He ground his back teeth. "I hope not. I don't like this situation for more than the obvious reasons. This whole thing feels off. Your sister dies a week ago. Now this with Noah. Could the two be connected somehow?"

Katherine gasped. Her hand came up to cover her mouth. "I didn't think about how odd the timing is."

"Maybe she got in a fight with Noah's father. Was about to reveal who he was. He could be someone prominent. Most missing children are taken by family members or acquaintances, once you rule out runaways, according to the sheriff."

"Then what about the file?"

"I was thinking about that. Could be a paternity test."

"If his father took him, at least Noah will be safe, right?" Katherine threaded her fingers through her hair, pulling it off her face.

"It's possible. I don't mean any disrespect. Do you think it's possible your sister was blackmailing him?"

"He didn't pay child support. That much I know. I paid her tuition. She enrolled in a social program to help with Noah's care. Got him into a great daycare. I was planning to move to Austin in a few months to be closer. I work for a multinational software company scheduling appointments for our trainers to visit customer sites, so it doesn't matter where I live. I wanted to be close so I could help out more. I can't help wondering what kind of person would hurt the mother of his child."

"I'm probably grasping at straws. We'll start with trying to figure out who he is. See what happens there."

"She was reckless before Noah. I thought her life was on track since his diagnosis. She got a part-time job at a coffee shop and enrolled in community college. She reconnected with me."

His ring tone cut into the conversation. "It's Matt." He brought the phone to his ear. "What's the word?"

"Jimmy found two things out at the Reynolds' place.

A stuffed rabbit and a cell. I told him to meet me at your place."

"I appreciate the news. We'll keep watch for you."

Caleb hit End and told Katherine what his ranch hand had found.

"I hope I got a shot of someone. They wore dark sunglasses, so their faces might be hard to make out, but maybe I captured someone else involved. Like the man who distracted me."

"Either way, we'll know in a minute." Wouldn't do any good to set false expectations. And yet, hope was all she had.

Looking into her violet eyes, damned if he wasn't the one who wanted to put it there.

A knock at the door had him to his feet faster than he could tack a horse, and tossing a throw blanket toward Katherine.

Caleb led Jimmy and Matt into the study. After a quick introduction, Jimmy advanced toward Katherine, carrying a phone. "Found this along the tree line by the Reynolds' place. Look familiar?"

"Yes, thank you. That looks like mine." Katherine's eyes sparkled with the first sign of optimism since Caleb had found her in the woods. She checked the screen. "Seven missed calls and a voice mail."

Another knock sounded at the door. Caleb walked Sheriff Coleman into the study a moment later, before moving to her side. The hope in her eyes was another hint of light in the middle of darkness and blackness, and every worst fear realized.

"Put it on speaker."

"I'm praying the message is from the kidnappers, but I'm scared it's them, too."

Caleb tensed. "Whatever's on that phone, we'll deal with it."

Her gaze locked on to his as she held up the cell and listened.

"What's wrong with the boy? You have twenty-four hours to help me figure it out and get me the file. I'll call back with instructions. No more games. Think about it. Tick. Tock."

Click.

Caleb took the phone and scanned the log. "Private number." He looked at Coleman. "There any way to trace this call?"

"Doubt it. They're probably smart enough to use a throwaway. We'll check anyway." Coleman scribbled fresh notes. "You mentioned the file before. Has anything come to mind since we last spoke?"

Katherine shook her head. "I've been guessing they mean a computer file, but I'm not positive. It could be anything."

Outside, gravel spewed underneath tires. Caleb moved to the window. Two dark SUVs with blacked-out windows came barreling down the drive. "Sheriff, you tell anybody you were coming here?"

Coleman shook his head. "Didn't even tell my dispatcher."

Katherine's eyes pleaded. She wrapped the blanket around her tighter, clutching the stuffed rabbit Jimmy had handed her. "I don't have the first clue what file they're talking about. As soon as they realize it, they'll kill us both. Don't let them near me."

"Dammit. They must've followed someone here. The sheriff can cover for us." Caleb pulled Katherine to her feet as she gripped her handbag. He moved to the kitchen door, stopping long enough for her to slip on her sandals before looking back at his men.

"Can you cover me?"

Chapter Four

Caleb's arm, locked like a vise around Katherine's waist, was the only thing holding her upright.

The barn wasn't far but any slip, any yelp, and the men would barrel down on them. The lightest pressure on her leg caused blood to pulse painfully down her calf. She breathed in through her nose and out through her mouth, slowly, trying to keep her breaths equal lengths and her heart rate calm.

Could the darkness cloak them? Hide them from the danger not a hundred yards away?

Katherine squinted.

The glow from lamplight illuminated the parking pad. There were two men. Dark suits. A wave of déjà vu slammed into her like a hard swell.

They weren't close enough to make out facial features. Only stature. They looked like linebackers. Had the man with the jagged scar etched in his overly tanned face come back to kill her? He would haunt her memory forever.

Her pulse hammered at the recollection. "Even if you have a car stashed here somewhere, they'll never let us get past them."

"Don't need to."

"If you have another plan besides trying to barrel

through them, or sneak around them, I'm all ears." She glanced at her bad leg and frowned.

"You still have your keys?"

She nodded, tucking the rabbit into her purse.

"Then we'll take your car."

"How will we do that? It's too far. I doubt I could get there unless you carried me." He seemed perfectly able to do just that.

"Won't have to. You'll see why." Caleb leaned her against the side of a tree near the back door of the barn. "Wait here."

She didn't want to be anywhere else but near him.

A moment later he pushed an ATV next to her. A long-barreled gun extended from his hand. A rifle? Katherine wouldn't know a shotgun from an AK-47. She only knew the names of those two from watching TV.

"This'll get us there." He patted the seat.

She glided onto the back with his help.

He slid a powerful leg in front of her and gripped the bars. "I think we're far enough away. The barn should block some of the noise. Hang on tight just in case they hear us."

Katherine clasped her hands around his midsection. His abdominal muscles were rock-solid. Was there a weak spot on his body? She allowed his strength to ease the tension knotting her shoulders. His warmth to calm her shaking arms.

"Why would they come looking for me? They said I had twenty-four hours. Why come after me before that?"

"Might be afraid you'll alert the authorities, or disappear. Plus, they must've figured out your nephew needs medication since they asked what was wrong with him."

"How did they find me?"

"There weren't many places to look other than my ranch."

"Good point." She hated the thought of putting Caleb and his men in danger. At least the sheriff was there to defend them. He would have questions for the men in the SUV. He'd slow the plans of any attackers and keep Caleb's crew safe. A little voice reminded her how the kidnappers had warned her about police involvement. She prayed Sheriff Coleman's presence didn't create a problem for Noah.

The trip was short and bumpy but allowed enough time for her eyes to adjust to the dark. Caleb cut the engine well before the clearing as she dug around in her purse for the keys.

"They might be watching your car, so we'll need to play this the right way." His earnest brown eyes intent on her, radiating confidence, were all she could see clearly in the dark.

A shiver cycled through her nerves, alighting her senses. It was a sensual feeling she was becoming accustomed to being this close to him. It spread warmth through her, and she felt a pull toward him stronger than the bond between nucleons in an atom. His quiet strength made her feel safe.

Caleb's powerful arms wrapped around her, and she wanted to melt into him and disappear. *Not now.* She canceled the thought. Noah needed her. No amount of stress or fear would make her shrink. She would be strong so she could find him. Sheer force of will had her pushing forward.

"Wait here." Caleb moved pantherlike from the tree line. Stealth. Intentional. Deadly. His deliberate movements told her there wasn't much this cowboy had faced he couldn't handle.

Katherine scanned the dark parking lot. She couldn't see far but figured even a second's notice would give Caleb a chance to react.

There was no one.

Nothing.

Except the din of the woods behind her. Around her. Surrounding her. A chilling symphony of chirping and sounds of the night.

Silently she waited for the all-clear or the telltale blast of his gun. For a split second she considered making a run for it. Maybe she could give herself up and beg for mercy before it was too late? Maybe the men would take her to Noah, and she could get his medicine to him now that she had her purse back?

Maybe they would take what they wanted and kill her?

They'd been ruthless so far. She had no doubt they would snap her neck faster than a branch if given the chance. Without his medicine, Noah would be dead, too.

All her hopes were riding on the unexpected hero cowboy, but what if he didn't come back? What if he disappeared into the night and ended up injured, bleeding out or worse?

Caleb was strong and capable, but he had no idea what kind of enemy they were up against. A bullet didn't discriminate between good and evil.

When the interior light of her car clicked on, she realized she'd been holding her breath. Caleb's calm voice coaxed her.

Another wave of relief came when she slid into the passenger side and secured her seat belt. He put the car in Reverse and backed out of the parking space. The sound of gravel spinning under tires had never sounded so much like heaven.

"You did good." His words were like a warm blanket around her frayed nerves.

"Thank you. Think it's safe to call the ranch?"

He nodded, stopping the car at the edge of the lot. The phone was to his ear a second later. He said a few uh-huhs into the receiver before ending the call and getting on the road. "Everyone's fine. Two men showed up, asking questions."

"What did they want?"

"They flashed badges. Said they were government investigators following a lead on a corporate fraud scheme."

A half laugh, half cough slipped out. "Leann? She didn't even have a normal job. She worked at a coffee shop."

"They didn't ask for your sister. They asked if someone matching your description had been seen in the area."

Fear pounded her chest. "Me? Corporate fraud? I don't have the first idea what they're talking about. I'm a scheduler for a software company. That's a far cry from a spy."

"Coleman took their information and plans to follow up through proper channels. Maybe the trail will lead somewhere."

"I hope so. Where do we go in the meantime?"

"Your sister's place. What's the address?"

Katherine scrolled through her contacts and read the details while he programmed the GPS in her car.

"We can check her computer and talk to her friends. Maybe we'll find answers there."

"Or just more questions. I told you. Knowing my sister, this won't be easy. I'm not sure who she hung around with let alone what she might've gotten herself into that could lead to this."

"Maybe the sheriff will come up with something. Good thing he was there. Might make these men think twice before they do anything else."

"Or…" She could've said it might make them kill Noah but didn't. No police. They'd been clear as day about it. Had she just crossed a line and put her nephew in more danger? Damn.

"They won't hurt him," Caleb said as though he read her thoughts.

"How can you be so sure?"

His grip tightened on the steering wheel. His jaw clenched. His gaze remained steady on the road in front of them. "We can't afford to think that way. First things first, let's get to Austin. We'll take the rest as it comes. Send Coleman the photos you took of Noah earlier."

"I almost forgot I had these." She scrolled through the pictures from the pumpkin patch. Noah smiled as he climbed on top of a huge orange gourd and exclaimed himself "king." Tremors vibrated from her chest to her neck. A stab of guilt pierced her. She scrutinized other details in the picture. Nothing but yellow-green grass and brown trees. A frustrated sigh escaped. "No good. I can't make anything out on the small screen except him and a couple of large pumpkins."

"Look up the last number I dialed, and send Coleman every shot you took today. He can blow them up and get a better view."

Her heart lurched as she shared the pictures one by one. When she was finished, she shut her eyes.

Caleb took her hand and squeezed. Warmth filled her, comforting her. When was the last time a man's touch did that?

She searched her memory but found nothing. No one, aside from Caleb, had ever had that effect on her.

"Think you can get a little shut-eye?"

Katherine was afraid to close her eyes. Feared she'd relive the horror of seeing a screaming Noah being ripped from her arms over and over again. "Probably not."

"Lean your seat back a little."

She did as she watched out the window instead. Interstate 35 stretched on forever. Every minute that ticked by was a reminder Noah was slipping away. Waco came and went, as did a few other smaller towns. The exhaustion of the day wore her nerves thin. Sleep would come about as fast as Christmas to June, but she closed her eyes anyway, praying a little rest would rejuvenate her and help her think clearly. Maybe there was something obvious she was overlooking that could help her put the pieces together.

Had Leann said anything recently? Dropped any hints? Given any clue that might foreshadow what was to come?

Nothing popped into Katherine's thoughts. Besides, if she knew one thing about her sister, Leann could keep a secret.

Sadness pressed against her chest, tightening her muscles. Leann must've known something was up. Why hadn't she said anything? Had she been in trouble? Maybe Katherine could've helped.

Katherine tried to remember the exact words her sister had used when she'd asked if Noah could come to Dallas for a week. Katherine could scarcely remember their conversation let alone expect perfect recall. How sad was that?

Her sister was dead, and Katherine couldn't even summon up the final words spoken between them. Guilt and regret ate at her conscience. Wait. There'd been a tornado warning, which was odd for October. When she joked about not being able to trust Texas weather, Leann had issued a sigh.

Katherine sat upright. "She knew something bad was going to happen."

"I figured it was the reason she sent Noah to stay with you."

"That means everything she did was premeditated. Maybe she'd gotten mixed up in a bad deal she didn't know how to get out of. But what?"

"Drugs?"

"No. She might have been a handful, but she didn't even drink alcohol."

Caleb shrugged. "My mind keeps circling back to the father."

"I guess it could be. I can't think of anyone else who would have so much to lose. Then again, I didn't know my sister very well as an adult. I believe she realized something was about to happen. That's as much as I can count on." Would Leann have blackmailed someone? Didn't sound right to Katherine. Her sister had always been a bit reckless, but not mean-spirited.

She was untrustworthy. Katherine had never been able to depend on her sister. A painful memory burst through her thoughts....

Leann was supposed to watch Katherine's dog, Hero, while Katherine had been away on a school trip. Leann had sneaked him to the park off-leash to catch a Frisbee after Katherine had said no. He'd followed the round disc far into the brush and never come back out. The whole time Katherine had been gone, she'd had no idea her dog was missing.

He'd been gone for three days by the time Katherine returned home. She hadn't cared. She'd looked for him anyway. She'd searched the park, the area surrounding the open field, and the woods, but he was nowhere to be found.

Losing Hero had delivered a crushing blow to Katherine.

It was the last time she'd allowed her sister around anything she cared about.

She sighed. When it came to Leann, just about anything was possible.

"We don't have any other leads. It's a good place to start."

She wanted—no, needed—to believe her sister wasn't

capable of spite. Leann had always been a free thinker. She was Bohemian, a little eccentric, not a calculated criminal. Especially not the type to hold on to hate or to try to hurt someone else.

Desperation nearly caved Katherine.

"We'll find the connection and put this behind you." Caleb's words were meant to comfort her. They didn't.

They would be at Leann's place soon and there had to be something there to help them. Get to the apartment. Find whatever it is the men want. Exchange the file for Noah. Mourn her sister. Try to forget this whole ordeal happened. *If only life were so easy.*

The hum of the tires on the highway coupled with the safety of being with someone who had her back for once allowed her to relax a little. Maybe she could lay her head back and drift off. Adrenaline had faded, draining her reserves.

She closed her eyes for at least an hour before the GPS told them to turn left. "Destination is on the right."

Katherine's heart skipped. In two hundred feet, a murderer might be waiting. Or the ticket to saving her nephew. Oh, God, it had to be there. Otherwise, she had nothing.

Caleb pulled his gun from the floorboard as he drove past the white two-story apartment building.

The GPS recalculated. "Make the next legal U-turn."

He pressed Stop. "We better not risk walking in the front door. We don't know who might be waiting on the other side."

Good point. "There's a back stairwell. We can go through the kitchen entrance."

Even long past midnight on a weekday, the streets and sidewalks teamed with college students milling around. Activity buzzed as groups of twos and threes crisscrossed the road into the night. Music thumped from backyards.

Lights were strung outside. It would be easy to blend into this environment.

He put the car in Park a few buildings down from Leann's place. "We can walk from here. But first, I want to check in with Matt."

Katherine agreed. She had no idea what waited for her at her sister's. Her stomach was tied in knots.

"Matt's voice mail picked up." Caleb closed the phone. "I'm setting my phone to vibrate. You might want to do the same."

"Great idea." Katherine numbly palmed her phone. She stared at the metal rectangle for a long moment, half afraid, half daring it to ring. In one second, it had the power to change her life forever and she knew it. *Think of something else. Anything.*

Caleb took her hand. She followed him through the dark shadows, fighting against the pain shooting through her leg.

He stopped at the bottom of the stairwell and mouthed, "Stay here."

"No." Katherine shook her head for emphasis.

"Let me check it out first. I'll signal when it's okay."

"What if someone's out here watching?" Katherine didn't want to let her cowboy out of her sight. She'd never been this scared, and if he broke the link between them, she was certain all her confidence would dissipate. "I want to go with you. Besides, you don't know what you're looking for."

His eyes were intense. Dark. Pleading. "I don't like taking risks with you."

She couldn't let herself be swayed. They might not have much time inside, and she wouldn't wait out here while he did all the heavy lifting. "Either way, I'm coming."

Looking resigned, Caleb's jaw tightened. "You always this stubborn?"

"Determined. And I've never had this much on the line before."

His tense stance didn't ease. Instead he looked poised for battle. His grip tightened on her hand. His other hand was clenched around the barrel of a gun.

"Then let's go," he said.

Katherine stayed as close behind as she could manage, ignoring the thumping pain in her leg.

Caleb turned at the back door and mouthed, "No lights."

The streetlight provided enough illumination to see clearly. He turned the handle and the door opened. It should have been locked.

Hope of finding anything useful dwindled. Of course, the men would have come here first.

If there was anything useful around, wouldn't they have found it already? They couldn't have, she reminded herself. Or she and Noah would be dead.

She moved to the dining space. The small corner desk was stacked with papers. A photo of Leann holding baby Noah brought tears to her eyes. She blinked them back, tucking the keepsake in her purse. The laptop Katherine had bought Leann for school was nowhere in sight.

Caleb's sure, steady movements radiated calm Katherine wanted to cling to. She dug through the pile of papers neatly stacked on the dining-room table while Caleb worked through the room, examining papers and objects.

Luck had never smiled on Katherine. She had no idea why this capable cowboy appeared. She needed him. The feeling was foreign to her and yet it felt nice to lean on someone else for a change. He looked every bit the man who could hold her up, too.

The realization startled her.

She knew very little about him, and yet he'd become her lifeline in a matter of hours. She could scarcely think about doing this without him and she wasn't sure which thought scared her the most. Katherine got through life depending on herself.

"Find anything useful?" he asked from across the room.

"No. It's hard to see in the dark though. You think whoever was here got what they wanted?"

Caleb moved to her. "Hard to say. You haven't been here since before the funeral, right?"

Katherine nodded. "I offered to pick up Noah, but she said no. Come to think of it, she's the one who mentioned meeting halfway. She'd never suggested that before. She wanted to meet in Waco this time in a restaurant that was way off the interstate. I figured it was just Leann being herself. Wanting to try something new."

"Looking back, did she act strange or say anything else that sticks out?"

"When we met she looked stressed. Cagey. I thought the responsibility of caring for Noah might be getting to her. Don't get me wrong, she loved that little boy. But caring for any kid, let alone one with medical needs, is stressful. Even so, she was a better parent than I ever would be."

She could feel his physical presence next to her before his arm slipped around her shoulders. "You would have been fine. And you will be, once we get Noah back safely."

Easy for him to say. He didn't know her. She didn't want to dwell on her shortcomings. Not now. She'd have time enough to examine those later when this was all over and her nephew was safe. "I thought she needed a break. The responsibility was becoming a burden. And then I didn't even think twice when I found out she'd had an accident climbing. I just assumed she'd been reckless." A sob escaped. "What does that say about me?"

"That you're human."

"Or I'm clueless. No wonder she didn't trust me with the truth. She must've known how little faith I had in her."

He guided her chin up until her gaze lifted to meet his.

"When people tell you who they are, it's best to believe them."

"What if they change?"

"Only time can tell that. Besides, it never does any good chasing what-if. You have to go on the information you have. Move from there."

"I guess."

"Look. You're strong. Brave. Determined. You were doing right by your sister. She trusted you or she never would have sent Noah to stay with you. As for the restaurant, she might've been worried she was being followed. She might've had a hunch there'd be trouble. I'm guessing she didn't bet on anything of this magnitude. She must've thought with Noah safe, she could handle whatever came her way."

His words were like a bonfire on a cold night. Warm. Soothing. Comforting.

Katherine reached up on her tiptoes and kissed his cheek.

A LIGHT TOUCH from those silky lips and a hot trail lit from the point of contact. Caleb's fingers itched to get lost in that chestnut mane of hers. She slicked her tongue over those lips and his body reacted with a mind of its own. His blood heated to boiling. He swallowed hard. Damn.

One look into Katherine's eyes and he could see she was hurt and alone. He wouldn't take advantage of the situation even though every muscle in his body begged to lay her down right then and give her all the comfort and pleasure she could handle. Another time. Another place. Might be a different story?

Then again, he'd never been known for his timing. He'd taken Becca in when she'd showed up at his door in trouble. Anger still flared through him when he thought about the bruises on her face and her busted lip. No way would he turn away a woman who looked as though she'd been abused. Caring for her and giving her a place to stay until she got on her feet had been the right thing to do. Having a relationship was a bad idea.

He'd opened his home and developed feelings for her. *Look how that turned out,* a little voice in his head said. She'd left after a year, saying she needed time to figure herself out.

Katherine faced a different problem. She was being brave as hell facing it rather than running and hiding. "Let's see what else is here."

"While I'm here, I should find some clothes and change."

Caleb walked away. If he hadn't, he couldn't have been held responsible for his actions. His body wanted Katherine. He was a man. She lit fires in him with a slight touch. A spark that intense couldn't lead to anything good. He could end up in a raging wildfire of passion. Weren't wildfires all-consuming? And what did they leave in their wake? Devastation and tragedy.

The image of walking into the kitchen and finding Becca's Dear John on the counter wound back through his thoughts as Katherine entered the room.

Caleb refocused and searched for something that might be significant. A medical file. A sealed envelope. A scribble on a piece of paper. He kept an eye on Katherine. Her tightly held emotions were admirable. Pride he had no right to own filled a small space inside him.

An hour into the search, her expression told the story.

Eyes, dark from exhaustion. Lips, thin from anger. Muscles, tense from frustration.

He moved behind her and pressed his palms to the knots in her neck, ignoring his own rising pulse.

"I know I haven't painted a good picture of my sister, but I can't imagine what she could've gotten herself into that would cause this. She could be irresponsible, but she had a good heart. Whatever she did would have to have been an accident. Something she fell into. She wouldn't have caused this much damage on purpose. She was sweet. Harmless. She isn't—wasn't—the type of person who'd do something malicious."

"What happened between the two of you?" He doubted she'd tell him but he took a chance and asked anyway.

Katherine sat for a moment. She leaned forward, allowing him to deepen the pressure on her neck and move his hands to her shoulders.

"She was fifteen. Rebellious. There was this one time I specifically told her not to go out. I needed her home to let a repairman in. She didn't listen and left anyway. Probably out of spite. We had to go the night without A/C in the middle of a Dallas summer. I'd been in class all day and then worked the afternoon shift as a hostess. I was hot. Miserable. I decided to wait up for her. The minute she waltzed through the door, I blew up. Told her she was a spoiled brat."

"You had every right to ask her to pitch in more. It wasn't like you asked her to gut a hog."

"I didn't 'ask' anything. I demanded she stay home. I thought it was my job to tell her what to do with our parents gone, not that she made it easy. She didn't want to listen and was never there when I needed her. I resented her. I learned pretty fast that I couldn't depend on her and had to learn to do things on my own."

"You should be proud of yourself."

"I could've been more sympathetic. But Leann did what she did best—disappeared. When she came home, I noticed she'd been drinking. I came down on her too hard."

Caleb knew all about self-recrimination. Hadn't he been beating himself up with worry since his last girlfriend left? Hadn't the ache in his chest been a void so large he didn't think he'd ever fill it again?

Caleb increased pressure, working a knot out of Katherine's shoulder.

A self-satisfied smile crossed his lips at the way her silky skin relaxed under his touch, and for the little moan that escaped before she could quash it. "You always this tough on yourself?"

Katherine hugged her knees into her chest. "A week later when she left, she didn't come back. I didn't hear from her for years."

Caleb couldn't imagine how difficult it was for Katherine to say those words out loud. She couldn't be more than twenty-six or twenty-seven, and seemed keenly aware of all her misjudgments now. A few years younger than him, she bore the weight of the world on her shoulders. The knots he'd been working so hard to release tightened. "Your sister was old enough to know better. You were trying to do what was best. I'm sure she knew that on some level."

"No. I had to close myself off because it was too painful repeatedly being disappointed by her. We stopped speaking. I didn't hear from her again until this year. Noah had barely turned four. I didn't even know I had a nephew before then."

Caleb moved to face her and took a knee, reaching out to place her hand in his. Her skin was finer than silk, her body small and delicate. The point where skin made contact sent a jolt of heat coursing through him. "Life threw you for a loop, too. Besides, you did what any good person would. You stepped up to fill impossible shoes and did your best. Because you weren't perfect doesn't mean you failed. You're an amazing woman."

He looked at her, really looked at her. There was enough light to see a red blush crawl up her neck, reaching her cheeks. Her skin glowed, her eyes glittered. The fire in her eyes nothing in comparison to the one she lit inside him.

He studied the soft curves of her lush mouth and then let his gaze lower to the swell of her firm, pointed breasts. All he felt was heat. Heat and need. Her jeans, balanced low on slim hips, teased him with a sliver of skin between the edge and the bottom of her T-shirt. Damn that she was even sexier when she was hurting. He pulled on all the strength he had so as not to take her lips right there… then her body.

Caleb needed to redirect his thoughts before he allowed his hormones to get out of hand. She made it difficult to focus on anything but thoughts of how good her body would feel moving beneath his. Alter the circumstances and things might have been different. Last thing Caleb needed was to get tangled up with another woman who showed up at his door with a crisis. He pushed all sexual thoughts out of his psyche.

"Since there's nothing here, we'd better go. I'm actually surprised no one's been watching the place."

Her gaze darted around the room. "Where do we go next? We can't go back to your ranch, can we?"

"No. I don't want to put my men at risk any more than we already have. What about your place? Any chance Leann passed a file to you in Noah's things?"

Hope once again brimmed in her shimmering eyes. "I hadn't thought of that. It's a possibility."

Caleb glanced at his watch, ignoring the ache in his chest for her. "If we leave now, we'll make it before daylight."

He preferred to move under the cover of night anyway.

She pulled back as they started toward the door. "Wait."

Caleb eased more of her weight on him, ignoring the pulsing heat on his outer thigh at the point of contact. "What is it?"

"I want to grab more medicine and something from Noah's room first." Katherine pushed off him to regain balance.

Her phone vibrated and she froze.

"Take a deep breath and then pick up," Caleb said.

She exhaled and answered.

"Is he breathing?" She paused. "Good. He has asthma. There's an inhaler he uses and I have medicine. I can bring them wherever—"

The guy on the line must've interrupted because Katherine became quiet again and just listened. "What time?"

Her expression vacillated between anger and panic.

"Where?" She signaled to Caleb for a pen and paper.

He retrieved them and watched as she jotted down "Sculpture at CenterPark" and then ended the call.

Her wide-eyed gaze flew up to him. "They want to meet tomorrow afternoon."

"Did they mention anything about the file we're looking for?"

She shook her head. "They only said to bring it to NorthPark Center."

"Good, it's out in the open. What time?"

"Three o'clock."

Caleb glanced at his watch. "We have plenty of time to check it out first."

"They told me to come alone." Determination thinned her lips before she turned and walked away.

He wouldn't argue as he closely followed her, ready to grab her if she faltered. She was determined to walk on her own; he'd give her that. The way she did "stubborn" was sexy as hell. Now was not the time for the conversation he needed to have with her. The one that said no way in hell was he allowing her to go by herself.

"Before we leave, is there any place we haven't looked? Did she have a secret hiding spot?"

"None she would share with me." As she moved behind the sofa, she stopped suddenly. "I didn't think about this before, but it makes perfect sense. We might not find anything, but it's worth checking out."

Katherine limped down the short hall and into the master bedroom.

She stopped in the middle of the room and looked up at the ceiling fan. "She had a small diary when we were kids that she hid by taping it to the top of one the blades. I found it when I was helping my parents spring clean once." A hint of sadness darkened her features. "Found out just how much she was sick of me when I peeked at the pages."

Caleb righted a chair that had been tossed upside down and settled it in the center of the room. "Let me look."

Even on the chair, he couldn't see the tops of the half-dozen blades.

Puffs of dust floated down when he wiped the first. More of the same on the second. His hand stopped on a small rectangle on the third. "I found something."

"Can you tell what?" Her voice brightened with hope.

"It's secure." He didn't want to take a chance on damaging it by ripping it off. His fingers moved around the smooth surface. Tape? He peeled the sticky layer off the item. "I'll be damned. It's a cell phone."

"Thank God, they missed it."

"I don't recognize the brand," he said as he palmed it. "Think it works?"

He pressed the power button. "It's dead. If we can find a store that sells these, we can buy a new cable or battery. We'll look up the manufacturer when we get back in the car."

"Okay." She spun around. "Oh, and I need to find something else."

He followed her down the hall to Noah's bedroom.

"I know it's here somewhere," she said, tossing around toys and clothes.

"What are you looking for? I'll help."

"No. I found it." She held up a stuffed reindeer. "It's Prancer. One of Noah's favorites. He apparently used to sleep with it all the time. Now he's into the rabbit. I was just thinking he'll need as many of his things as possible to make my place feel like home." She gathered a few more toys from the mess.

"Prancer? Seems like an interesting choice for a name. I mean, why not Rudolph?" He examined the stuffed animal.

"Noah thinks the other reindeer get overlooked. Said Rudolph gets all the glory," she said, melancholy.

Caleb couldn't help but crack a smile. "How old did you say he is?"

"Four."

"Sounds like a compassionate boy." He tucked the stuffed animal under his arm. "We'll keep Prancer safe until he's back with Noah."

When Caleb looked at her, his heart dropped. A dozen emotions played across her delicate features. Fear. Regret. Anxiety.

He walked to her and took her hand in his.

"We'll find him. I promise."

Before he could debate his actions, he tilted his head forward and pressed his lips to hers gently. The soft kiss intensified when she parted her lips to allow him access. His mouth covered hers as he swallowed her moan.

Both his hands cupped her cheeks, tilting her face until his tongue delved more deeply, tasting her.

She pulled back long enough to look into his eyes.

"I believe you mean that," she said, her voice like silk wrapping around him, easing the ache in his chest.

Caleb always delivered on his commitments. He hoped like hell this time would be no different.

Chapter Five

Exhaustion dulled Katherine's senses, but she managed to follow Caleb back to the car. The visit hadn't produced any real optimism. All their hopes were riding on a dead phone.

And what if there's nothing there? a tiny voice in the back of her mind asked.

What then?

Hot, burning tears blurred Katherine's vision. Her mantra—*Chin Up. Move Forward. Forge Ahead*—had always worked. She'd survived so much of what life had thrown at her repeating those few words. Hadn't she been stronger because of it?

Then how did she explain the hollow ache in her chest? Or the niggling dread she might live out the rest of her days by herself. Everyone let her down eventually. Who could she lean on when times got tough? Who did she really have to help celebrate life's successes?

Before meeting this cowboy, she'd never realized how alone she'd truly been. She gave herself a mental shake as she opened the car door and buckled in.

Caleb found her cable-knit sweater in the back and placed it over her as she clicked the seat belt into place.

She slipped the sweater over her shoulders and closed her eyes, expecting to see the attackers' faces or to hear their threats replaying in her mind. She didn't. Instead she saw Caleb and relaxed into a deep sleep.

KATHERINE DIDN'T OPEN her eyes again until she heard Caleb's voice, raspy from lack of sleep, urging her awake. For a split second she imagined being pressed up against him, snuggled against the crook of his arm, in his big bed. She'd already been introduced, and quite intimately, to his broad chest and his long, lean, muscled thighs. He'd left no doubt he was all power, virility and man when his body had blanketed her, pinning her to the ground. Her fists had pounded pure steel abs. Warmth spread from her body to her limbs, heating her thighs.

The reality she was curled up in her car while running for Noah's life brought a slap of sanity.

"Where are we?"

"Dallas. If the address on your license is correct, we're a couple blocks from your house." He glanced at the clock. "Don't worry. We have plenty of time before the drop."

She sat up and rubbed sleep from her eyes. They were at a drive-through for a local coffee shop.

Coffee.

There couldn't be much better at the moment than a good cup of coffee save for finding Noah and having this whole nightmare behind her.

Caleb handed her a cup and took a drink from his while he pulled out of the parking lot.

"I ordered black for you."

"Perfect." Katherine took a sip of the hot liquid. The slight burn woke her senses. A blaze of sunlight appeared from the east. "You've been driving all night. You must be exhausted."

Caleb took another sip from the plastic cup. "I'm more worried about that leg of yours. At some point, we need to take another look. Didn't want to disturb you last night while you looked so peaceful."

"I'm surprised I slept at all." Katherine stretched and yawned. She glanced down at her injuries. Blood had soaked through a few of the bandages and dried. Most were intact and clear. All things considered, they were holding up. "You dressed these well. My ankle feels better already."

She touched one, then two bandages. "I think they'll hold awhile longer. At least the bleeding has stopped."

"That's the best news I've heard all day." He cracked a sexy little smile and winked. "We'd better park here." He cut the engine. "We'll walk the rest of the way."

"Do you think they're watching my apartment?"

"A precaution," he reassured her. His clenched jaw belied his words.

"Why didn't they stop us last night? They could've waited at Leann's and shot us right then."

"I thought about that a lot on the drive. They want you to find what we're looking for. And fast."

"I didn't say anything about the file on the last call. I was too focused on Noah. They must realize I don't have it." She glanced toward her purse where the cell phone had been stashed.

"Stores don't open until ten o'clock. We have to wait to find a charging cable until then." He took a sip of coffee. "I'm guessing Noah's breathing problems must've forced them to ask for a meeting before they were ready. I think they'd rather let you locate the evidence, and then snatch you. Once they're convinced you have it, I have no doubt the game will change."

He watched over their shoulders a few times too many for Katherine's comfort, as they did their best to blend with pedestrians.

"Wait here while I scout the area." They were a few hundred feet from the front door of her apartment. He pointed toward the row of blooming crepe myrtles. There hadn't been a cold snap yet to kill the flowers. Fall weather didn't come to Dallas until mid-November some years. This was no exception.

"Okay."

A few minutes later he returned. "Looks fine from what I can tell. If they're watching, they're doing a good job of hiding. Either way, keep close to me."

She had no intention of doing anything else as she unlocked the door and followed him inside. "I wish we knew what kind of file we were looking for."

Her office had been temporarily set up in the dining room so Noah could occupy the study. From where she stood, she could see they'd taken her computer. "First Leann's laptop is missing. Now my computer. I'm guessing we're looking for a zip drive or other storage device."

"If it wasn't at your sister's place and it's not here, where else could the file be?"

"I work from home, so there's no office to go to. All I need to schedule appointments for my trainers is a computer and a phone. I keep everything here. I'll check the study where Noah's been sleeping. You might be right about Leann slipping it into his things." Katherine moved to the study that had been overtaken by her nephew. Toys spilled onto the floor. She stepped over them and rummaged through his things. No red flags were raised.

This approach wasn't working. If she were going to get anywhere, she had to figure out a way to think like Leann. Where would she stick something so incredibly valuable? Maybe Noah's suitcase? She could have removed part of the lining and tucked a file inside.

Katherine dug around until she located the small Spider-

Man suitcase Noah had had in his hand when she'd met up with them. That and the rabbit he'd tucked under his arm were all the possessions he'd brought.

The Spider-Man suitcase had several pockets with zippers. Katherine checked them first. Empty. The lining was a bit more difficult to rip open but she managed without calling for help. *Sorry, buddy.* She hated to destroy his favorite bag.

Nothing there, either. Katherine tore apart the seams. Zero.

The clock ticked. The men would expect her to produce the file soon. She had nothing to give them and still no idea what it was she was looking for. Damn.

When she returned to the living room, Caleb stood sentinel.

"No luck," she said. "She might've sent it over email."

Katherine dug around in the back of her coat closet to find her old laptop. She held it up. "This might still work."

"Your sister brought Noah to you. He was the person she most prized. Have you thought she might not have involved you because she was trying to shelter you both?"

Katherine hadn't considered Leann might be protecting her. It softened the blow. "We'll see."

A soft knock at the door kicked up Katherine's pulse.

Caleb checked through the peephole. His expression darkened. His brow arched. "Gray-haired woman. Looks to be in her mid-sixties, carrying a white puff ball."

"Does she look angry?"

"More like sour."

"Annabelle Ranker. She's my landlady, and that's her dog, Max. Big bark, no bite for the both of them." Katherine got to her feet and his strong arm was around her before she could ask for help to walk.

Caleb cracked the door open. Ms. Ranker cocked her

eyebrow and looked him up and down. An approving smile quirked the corners of her lips. When Caleb didn't invite her in, the skeptical glare quickly returned.

No doubt, the bandages and blood wouldn't go unnoticed. Nor would the fact Katherine was gripping her old laptop as though it was fine crystal.

"Are you all right?" Her gaze traveled to Katherine's hurt foot.

"I'm fine. Got into some trouble in the woods. Turns out I'm not a nature girl. Caleb owns a nearby ranch where we visited the pumpkin patch yesterday."

"That's right. You said you were taking Noah out of the city for the day."

"We got lost in the woods. Caleb found us and helped me home." Katherine could feel heat rising up her neck. No one would ever accuse her of being a good liar. She'd kept her story as close to the truth as she could so her whole face wouldn't turn beet-red.

Ms. Ranker seemed reassured by the answer. "I wanted to check on you and the little boy. Where's Noah?"

Katherine swallowed a sob. She couldn't afford to show any emotion or to invite unwanted questions. "I'm sorry. He couldn't sleep…nightmares. We were…playing army most of the night. I've been trying to keep him busy since his mother…" Katherine diverted her eyes.

"Such a shame." Ms. Ranker shook her head, obviously moved by Leann's passing. "Is he home? I'd be happy to take him off your hands while you rest that foot."

"He's napping. Tuckered out from our adventure," she said quickly. A little too quickly.

The answer seemed to appease the landlady. She nodded her understanding. "I almost forgot. A package came for you while you were out. I went ahead and signed for it since you didn't answer."

Katherine had scarcely paid attention to the FedEx envelope Ms. Ranker held in one hand. Her other arm pressed her prized six-year-old Havenese, Max, to her chest.

"For me?" Katherine asked, lowering her gaze to the fur ball on Ms. Ranker's arm. "Hey, big guy."

She patted his head, stopping short of inviting them in; Ms. Ranker's arched brow said she noticed. Last thing Katherine needed was a long conversation. Besides, she wasn't prepared to discuss her situation with anyone. Except Caleb. And she'd told him things about her relationship with her sister she'd never spoken aloud to another soul. It was probably the circumstances that had her wanting to tell him everything about her. It was as if she wanted at least one person to really know her. The feeling of danger and the very real possibility she might not be alive tomorrow played tricks on her emotions. "Who's it from?"

The well-meaning Ms. Ranker held out the envelope. No doubt she wanted to know more about the handsome cowboy. Plus, it wasn't like Katherine not to invite her landlady inside or to be so cryptic.

She cleared her throat and tugged at the envelope.

A slight smile was all she could expect by way of apology as the older woman loosened her grip enough for her to take possession.

Katherine's gaze flew from the return address to Caleb. The letter was from Leann. Katherine pressed it against the laptop she was still clutching.

Out of the corner of her eye, she saw the door across the courtyard open. A long metal barrel poked out. A gun?

A shower of bullets descended around them at the same time Katherine opened her mouth to warn them. A bullet slammed into the laptop. Before she could think or move, she felt the impact against her chest.

Ms. Ranker's eyes bulged before she slumped to the ground.

In the next second Caleb was on top of Katherine, covering her, protecting her.

"Are you hit?" he asked.

"I don't think so. Can't say the same for my computer." She'd dropped it the moment a bullet hit and then embedded. The hunk of metal she'd clasped to her chest had just saved her life.

He angled his head toward the kitchen. "Go. I'll fire when they get close enough."

Before she could respond, he'd urged her to keep moving as he pulled the gun to his shoulder.

When bullets exploded from the end of it, her heart hammered her chest.

Didn't matter. No time to look back. If Caleb thought she'd get out through the side window, she was in no position to argue. She clawed her way across the taupe carpet until she reached the cold tiles of the kitchen.

A moment later he was lifting her through the opened window and she was running.

Her heartbeat painfully stabbed her ribs.

Why were they shooting? They must've been watching the whole time. Did they think she'd found what they were looking for?

Oh. God. Noah. What would happen to him?

Her legs moved fast. She barely acknowledged the blood soaking her bandages. She had to run. Get out of there.

Caleb guided her to the sedan. "Get in and stay down."

Katherine curled up in a ball on the floorboard. If the bad guys knew where she lived, wouldn't they recognize her car, too?

What about Ms. Ranker? Katherine had been so busy ducking she didn't even look. "Is my landlady…?" Katherine couldn't finish the sentence.

Caleb shook his head. "I'm sorry."

"Max?"

"I think he got away."

Katherine gripped the envelope, fighting against the tears threatening to overwhelm her. Release the deluge and she wouldn't be able to stop. "Maybe this is what they're looking for." She held up the envelope that had cost Ms. Ranker's life.

His focus shifted from the rearview to the side mirrors. "Might be."

She ripped open the letter and overturned it on the seat. A CD fell out.

"A file?"

"Sure looks like it." Caleb glanced around. "Stay here and stay low. Do not look up until I get back."

Before she could ask why or argue, he disappeared.

Katherine made herself into the smallest ball she could, praying for his safe return.

She couldn't even think of doing any of this without him. And yet, didn't everyone flake out on her eventually?

Even her parents.

The memory of standing on stage, alone, her senior year of high school pushed through her thoughts. The anticipation of seeing her parents' smiling faces in the crowd as she'd competed in the academic fair filled her. She'd worked hard all year and qualified with the best score her school had ever received. She'd sacrificed dates and socials to stay home and work quiz after quiz. On stage, her pulse had raced and she'd felt tiny beads of sweat trickling down her neck. She remembered thinking that if she could just see someone familiar, she'd be okay.

The curtain had opened and she'd scanned the crowd. No one.

Disappointment and fear had gripped her. Panic had made the air thin. She'd struggled to breathe.

By the third round, she'd choked and given the wrong answer.

When she'd arrived home that evening, her parents had told her how sorry they were. They'd come home from work, opened a bottle of wine, turned on the TV and forgotten. Again.

Katherine had worked to suppress the memory from then on. She'd learned another important lesson that day. If she was going to get anywhere in life, she had only herself to depend on.

Her heart squeezed when she heard quick footsteps hustling toward her. She held her breath until Caleb's face came into view. He slipped into the driver's seat and handed over Max, his white coat splattered with red dots. He was whimpering and shaking. "Is he hurt?"

"No." Caleb turned the key in the ignition and pressed the gas. "Just scared."

Was Max covered in his owner's blood?

Katherine looked to Caleb. He dropped his right hand to his side. It was covered in blood.

"You're shot?"

"Just a flesh wound. Bullet grazed my shoulder. I'll be fine." Caleb hoped what he said was true. Based on the amount of blood he was losing, he couldn't be certain. He wouldn't tell Katherine though. Didn't need her to panic.

She made a move to get up, and winced.

"I'll pull over in a minute and examine us both."

Caleb glanced through his rearview, checking traffic

behind them. The usual mix of sport utilities, Ford F-150s and luxury sedans sped down the North Dallas tollway.

His cell vibrated. He instructed Katherine to retrieve it from his pocket and put the call on speaker.

Matt didn't wait to speak. "My coverage has been spotty. I tried to reach you last night but couldn't."

"Everyone all right?"

"Us? We're fine. I'm concerned as hell about you."

Caleb kept watch on the road. "So far, so good here."

"Has Katherine mentioned anything about being involved in corporate espionage?"

"Of course not. I would've told you something like that. She has no idea what they're looking for."

"I guess she wouldn't tell you," Matt said. "Especially if she's involved from the get-go."

Caleb grunted but didn't speak. He had no plans to repeat himself.

"Well, ask her. The men who showed up yesterday claimed to be government officials. They asked questions about a brown-haired woman who had been seen in the area. Said she was involved in a little family business that stole and sold corporate secrets. They'd been tracking her for days before you helped her get away."

"They knew we were there?" Caleb asked. "And I don't have to ask Katherine. You're on speaker."

The line was quiet. "No. But I'm saying—"

"I already know the answer."

"You can't ignore the possibility she's involved," Matt quickly interjected.

"She's not."

"How do you know, dammit?"

"I just do."

Matt let out a frustrated hiss and a string of cuss words Caleb heard plainly through the phone.

"You just met her yesterday, and you're willing to vouch for her already? What do you know about her? You haven't met any of her people. She could've been hurt while running from the government for all we know."

"I told you once so I won't repeat myself. What else did they say?"

"One thing is sure. She shows up then suddenly we have official-looking men coming out of the woodwork. All we have to go on is her word. She claims there was a kidnapping, but did you actually see the kid?"

No, he hadn't seen the boy. That didn't mean there wasn't one. He'd seen the pictures of him. Had been there moments after Noah had been taken. He'd seen kid toys at her sister's place and at Katherine's. Besides, Caleb had seen the sheer terror on her face. He could still see the agony in her violet eyes. This conversation was going nowhere. He needed to redirect. She most definitely did not make this up, and he hated the fact she had to hear his friend's accusations. "The kid has a name. Noah. Did you speak to Coleman?"

"Sheriff doesn't know what to believe. Said he'd follow up through proper channels to see if the men were legit, but it could take a while. He doesn't exactly have ready access to the kinds of people who can verify something like this. Those men who showed up looked serious to me. They flipped badges, too."

"Doesn't mean anything."

"That's exactly what Coleman said. They looked pretty damn official from where I stood."

"Can Coleman find out if there is a 'Kane' involved in a federal investigation?"

"He's trying but he said not to hold out a lot of hope."

"Anything else?" Caleb tensed against the pain in his shoulder.

"Take her to the nearest government building and turn her in, Caleb. Before this gets even more out of control."

"You know I won't."

"I don't think it's safe for you here at the ranch," Matt said quietly.

"I won't put my men at risk. I won't come home until this is settled."

There was a long silence.

"Then for God's sake, be careful," Matt warned.

"Got it covered."

"I'll keep things working here until you get back."

"Always knew I could count on you." The pressure in Caleb's chest eased. His men would be covered until his return.

"How's Jimmy's little girl?"

"Not good. They scheduled surgery for her in Dallas."

"They found a donor?"

"Seems like it."

"That's good news."

Jimmy's daughter would get the chance she deserved. He'd ensure Katherine did, too.

Caleb asked Katherine to end the call.

She looked at him deadpan. "Why didn't you tell me Matt thinks I'm involved?"

"He's not sure what to believe." Caleb glanced down at her. She looked helpless and small. His protective instincts flared. He wanted to guard her from Matt's accusations as much as the men chasing her. Those full cherry lips and chestnut hair stirred him sexually. Caleb would swim with caution in the emotional tide.

"What about Jimmy's daughter?"

"She was born with a bad heart. They found a donor. Her surgery is scheduled in a few days." Caleb hoped like hell he'd be around for it.

Katherine frowned. "Children should get to grow up before they have to give up their childhood. They shouldn't have to deal with sickness or death at such young ages. It seems so unfair."

"Agreed."

Her back went rigid as she took in a breath. "Okay. What's next?"

"We need to find a laptop or computer to figure out what's so important on the disk. Coleman's checking into the other. If the men who showed up turn out to be government, there could be anything on that CD."

"And now you don't believe me, either?"

"When did I say that?"

Katherine set the CD down on the seat next to Max. Anger and resentment scored her normally soft features. "You didn't have to. I was putting myself in your shoes."

"Don't."

"What if they do work for the government but whoever's behind this is paying them off?"

"There could be one bad egg. Not this many. Besides, Coleman doesn't think they're legit. He's expecting to find ghosts as he investigates. We can give him a call."

"Would he sit on this kind of information?"

"No. He'd contact me right away."

"Whatever's on this CD caused my nephew to be kidnapped. I want to find the bastard who did this and make him pay. He deserves to be in jail."

"You're right." Caleb pulled over, and then concentrated on his phone. The map feature produced three coffee shops and an internet café nearby. "There's a place a few blocks from here we might be able to go into."

He'd have a chance to inspect their injuries. Caleb's shirtsleeve was soaked. He needed to stop the bleeding.

Chapter Six

Katherine fumbled for her cell as it buzzed for the second time. The screen read Private.

Caleb parked the car in a crowded lot as she answered before the call transferred to voice mail, hoping she might recognize the voice if she heard it again.

"Did you find what you've been looking for?" His tone was smooth and practiced, and she detected a slight accent. His cool and calm demeanor made the hairs on the back of her neck prickle.

Frustration got the best of her. "What do you think you'll accomplish by hurting me? Not to mention the fact I can't find anything for you if I'm dead. You didn't have to kill an innocent person to get what you want. I'll gladly give it to you when I find it." Could she ask about the government men without giving Caleb away?

"Are you saying you don't have the file?" the even voice said.

"That's not answering my question. Who were those men you sent to kill me?"

"Let's just say I have very loyal employees."

Damn him for being so composed when her world had crumbled around her. She gripped her sister's CD tighter. Anything could be on there. She hoped this was the file they wanted, but she couldn't be sure. Besides, if she said yes and was wrong, she'd be signing a death warrant for Noah. She had to stall them. "Tell me what I'm looking for. I want to help you. I want Noah back and I want this nightmare over."

"What was in the envelope?"

"I don't know what you're talking about." Fire crawled up her neck at the lie. If he could see her now, she'd be exposed.

"Don't play games with me." Anger cracked his voice.

"At least give me a hint. There's a world of possibilities and I have to get this right." Panic made her hands shake. *Breathe.*

Caleb covered her hand with his. His touch calmed her rising pulse.

"Your sister knew exactly what I was talking about. My bet is you do, too."

"Is that why you tried to kill me?" Katherine railed against the urge to scream. She suppressed her need to tell him what he could do with his file. She had to think about Noah. Nothing mattered more than bringing him home safely. "I'm afraid I'm at a disadvantage here. My sister and I weren't that close. She didn't tell me much of anything. Just used me as a free babysitter." Katherine hated playing nice with this guy when she wanted to climb through the phone connection and do horrible things to him. "How's my nephew?"

"Not good if you don't get me what I want."

Katherine's heart pummeled her ribs. "How's his breathing?"

"I won't let anything happen to him. Not unless you don't cooperate."

"Let me speak to him. I won't do anything else until I know he's okay. You won't like it if I disappear," she hedged.

The phone went silent. *Damn.* Anger them more and

Noah could pay the ultimate price. She struggled to hold back the tears that were threatening. Let one drop and the avalanche would come.

"Auntie?" His voice sounded small and frail, nothing like his usual boisterous self.

Her heart skipped. "Noah. Baby, listen to me. Everything's going to be okay." He couldn't panic. Not with his condition. "We're going to get your medicine."

"I don't like it here." His sniffles punctured her heart.

"They didn't hurt you, did they?" She struggled to keep her voice calm.

"No. They're nice."

"I need you to be very brave. Can you do that?"

"Uh-huh."

"Be good. Listen to what they say. I promise I'm coming to get you as soon as I can."

Before he could respond, a shuffling noise came through the static on the line.

"Bring the file to the drop alone if you ever want to see him alive again."

Click.

Katherine stared out the window as Max wriggled in her lap.

Caleb took the phone from her and placed it on the console between them. "We'll get him back. He's okay. That's the most important thing right now."

"Why would they call again?"

Caleb shrugged. "Insurance."

"Hearing him...knowing how frightened he is...how brave he's being..." She took a deep breath. "It pains me to sit by like this and feel like I'm doing nothing."

"I understand. He's showing real courage. He got that from you." His words caressed her tired heart. Brought it back to life so that it beat again without painful stabs.

Katherine wanted to cry. To release all the pent-up frustration, anger and worry she'd been holding in throughout this ordeal. *And during her entire life,* she thought as she realized she hadn't really cried in more years than she could count. She'd trained herself to sidestep her emotions after her parents died. She'd needed to be the strong one.

At first, she had tried to reach out for help.

Anthony, her first love, had promised to visit every month after she'd had to leave school to go home and care for her sister. His calls were her saving grace. The two jobs she'd worked were barely enough to keep them fed. It was even harder to keep her grades up when she'd lived on little more than a few hours of sleep. But she'd done it. She'd kept her head above water.

His voice, the eye in the storm, had become her lifeline. Without him, she'd feared everything that was still *her* would wash away in the tide and she'd never be the same person again.

With every reassurance he'd given, her confidence had grown. She could do it. She could make it work. She could take care of her sister and still have something of a life left.

Then the calls stemmed. Excuses about conflicting schedules came. And, eventually, the phone stopped ringing.

She'd learned through the grapevine that he'd been dating someone else.

She'd been devastated.

When she'd needed him the most to lean on, he wasn't there, but she had learned from it. Learned to rely on herself and not to depend on others. Learned that other people were disappointments. Learned to keep her walls high and march on. But had she built walls so high no one could penetrate them?

The men she'd dated since had spent more time at sporting events than with her, and she was fine with it.

Outside the window, the rain started coming down. Big drops fell, making large splotches on the windshield.

"I couldn't put my finger on it before. There's something different about the way the guy speaks. You heard him before when we listened to his message on speaker at your house."

"I don't remember an accent."

"Only certain words." She turned to meet Caleb's gaze, and a well of need sprung inside her.

He stroked the back of her neck, pulling her lips closer to his. He was so strong. Capable.

His dark eyes closed the moment his lips pressed to hers, and she surrendered to the kiss. Completely. Freely. With a need burning so brightly inside her, the flames almost engulfed her.

His tongue pulsed inside her mouth and fire shot straight to the insides of her thighs. How could she want a man so instantly? So absolutely? So thoroughly? Her nipples heightened to pointed peaks, straining for his touch. *More.* She wanted all of him, which was even more reason getting involved with him further would be a bad idea.

Katherine pulled back. "You're hurt. We should check out your injury."

"It's a scratch," he said dismissively, his low gravelly baritone sending another round of sensitized shivers skittering across her nerves.

A pained expression crossed his features, and Katherine knew it was more than from his shoulder. She looked into his gaze and saw something reckless...dangerous...sexy.

Wouldn't he leave when this was all over?

She refused to invest in another relationship, because

they didn't work. She'd wind up hurt, and she didn't have it inside her to go through that pain again.

"Let's check it out anyway. I'd feel better if I knew you were going to be okay."

He rolled up his sleeve, revealing a deep gash in solid muscle. He must've caught the panic in her eyes because he quickly said, "It's not as bad as it looks."

"You need to get that checked out."

"I'm not going anywhere until I see this through." His eyes locked on to her as he gripped the steering wheel. "So forget about that."

She clamped her lips shut. Hope filled her chest.

"We should find somewhere we can clean up. I can get supplies. I'm sure people will be suspicious if we stroll into a café looking like this."

"What about the men in suits? I have no idea what my sister got involved in. I don't think she would steal anything, let alone blackmail, but I don't really know. Based on my recent conversation, I think there's some kind of corporation involved."

Caleb started the engine. "We'll get cleaned up and check the CD first." He played around on his phone before putting the gearshift into Drive. "We might have everything we're looking for in our hands already."

He blended into traffic at the next light.

"Whoever those men are, they aren't here to help. They kidnapped your nephew. Tried to take you, too. They've fired at us in broad daylight. They knew where we were, so they've been following us or someone was waiting, watching your place." He issued a grunt. "It'd take one big secret to bring on what we faced today."

"Or one powerful man."

"Your sister made a big enemy out of someone important. The question is who has this much influence? This Kane guy?"

"I have no idea. It'd have to be someone who has the ability to make permanent accidents happen. Send men at a moment's notice to erase people."

Caleb nodded. "Everything's online now. If we had her computer, we might be able to find an electronic trail."

"I'm scared." The admission came when she least expected to voice it.

"I won't let anything happen to you." Even though the set of his jaw said he meant every one of those words, he couldn't guarantee them.

Katherine didn't respond. What could she say?

"The biggest thing he has going for him is that we don't know who he is. I wish there was some way to flush him out."

"I hope we have everything we need in here to find him." The information she needed *had* to be on that CD or Leann's phone. Anything else was unthinkable.

Caleb parked in front of a hotel and excused himself, returning a few minutes later holding a card key. "Once we clean ourselves up and get supplies, we'll check out that disk. Tuck Max into your sweater."

She hobbled out of the sedan. Her stomach growled, reminding her how long it had been since she'd last eaten. It didn't matter. Food wouldn't go down on her queasy stomach. Her nerves would be fried until she knew what was on that CD.

The room was simple and tasteful. The dark wood furniture was modern with clean lines. Artistically angled framed photos of flowers hung above the king-size bed. There was a desk with chair, a minifridge and microwave.

The card on the bed said it was "Heavenly." Katherine didn't need a note to tell her the fluffy white blanket would feel amazing wrapped around her. Add Caleb's arms to the mix and she could sleep for days in his embrace. She quickly canceled the thought. Didn't need to go there again with thoughts of what Caleb could do for her on a bed.

He held up a towel. "Why don't you clean up first?"

"Okay."

"Do you need help?"

She set Max down. Caleb poured water into a coffee cup and placed it on the floor for the little dog to drink.

"I can handle it," Katherine said as she closed the bathroom door behind her.

"Take care with those cuts. I'll clean Max before I head out to pick up supplies. With any luck, I'll find a charger while I'm out." His voice was so close she could tell he'd stopped at the door. "Keep that foot elevated."

Katherine glanced down at her leg. If she looked anything on the outside like she felt on the inside, she dreaded looking into a mirror. Freshening up suddenly sounded like a good idea.

CALEB RETURNED HALF an hour later with bags of food and supplies. "I found a big-box store and picked up antibiotic ointment and gauze. I located a battery for the cell phone, too. I popped the CD into one of their laptops. Nothing unusual jumped out at me. All I saw were pictures of Noah."

Her violet eyes went wide. "That's it?"

"Maybe we'll find more when we go downstairs to the business center and have more time to look."

She nodded.

"As for the cell, I found an interesting number. Did she ever talk about Bolden Holdings?"

"No."

"Sebastian Kane's the CEO. I don't know why I didn't connect the dots sooner. I've seen him on the cover of

Forbes before. Any chance that accent you picked up on is Canadian?"

Her head rocked back and forth. "Very well could be. But why would my sister be involved with him? Seriously? What issue could a man like that possibly have with her? How could she have information about his company?"

"Someone like Kane would care about money and his reputation. I'm betting she somehow got tangled up with him. She could've been dating him. We don't know anything for sure. Maybe that CD will tell us specifically. Maybe there's a picture of them together. I sent a text to Coleman. He's following the lead."

"Before we go downstairs, I should check your shoulder."

"After I take care of your ankle," he insisted. "But first, I've been thinking. Could your sister have had a job you didn't know about? Did she ever talk about her work?"

"She had a part-time job as a barista at Coffee Hut. Said it allowed her to go in early in the morning before Noah was awake. The neighbor sat with him. Then she could take late-morning classes and still be home for him after lunch."

Didn't sound like the kind of person who would go rogue and steal much of anything. Let alone someone who would have the guts to blackmail a major player. Then again, her money was tight. She might have risked it all to be able to spend more time with her son. "I know she didn't mention the father to you, but what kind of guys did she normally date?"

A throaty laugh came from Katherine. "Before Noah? Every kind. She dated smart guys. Athletes. Ones who grew their hair long and ate nothing but kale. I don't think she was seeing anyone lately. She calmed down considerably since she had a baby. Said she couldn't remember the last time she'd had sex."

A blush reddened her cheeks at the admission. Caleb could feel his heartbeat at the base of his throat. She was sexy when she was embarrassed.

Caleb motioned for her to sit on the bed while he positioned the desk chair in front of her and sat on the edge.

"You think she got mixed up dating Kane? Maybe saw something or found something while she was at his place?"

"Anything's possible. Hard to imagine her in a relationship with the head of a conglomerate. Although, she was beautiful."

"She could've met him at work. Maybe he stopped into the coffee shop where she worked? We could find a way to ask her coworkers."

Katherine had cleaned up and looked even more sexy wrapped in a bath towel. The thought of her naked in the shower sent heat rocketing through him. That was the last thing he *should* be thinking about. But hell, if he were being honest, he'd admit seeing her naked was actually at the top of his list of appealing ideas. He gave in to his appreciation for her body. Looking at those long, lean legs, small waist and smooth hips stirred an immediate reaction. When his gaze slid from the smooth curve of her calves down her slender ankles to her bare feet, his mouth dried.

He forced his gaze to her face.

She slicked her tongue over her lips and damned if the image wasn't even sexier. He lowered his gaze to her neck. Her chest rose and fell with her rapid breathing. He saw her breasts tighten under the thin fabric of the towel.

The need to protect her and kiss her surged. If he didn't get a grip she'd know exactly how badly he wanted to make love to her.

Max's bark crashed him back to reality.

He forced himself to think rationally. She was in trouble. He was there to help.

He'd have to work harder to contain his growing attraction.

"Let's get a look at those." He hated the idea of causing her more pain, but her cuts needed tending to, and she needed antibiotic ointment. He'd have to get her to a clinic soon for a tetanus shot, too.

"What about your injuries? We should make sure you're okay," she said, her lips set in a frown.

"I'll live. Do you always put others first?" He wasn't used to that. Wasn't he always the one saving the day? Rescuing others? Denying himself?

"What if something happens to you? Is there anyone I should notify? Girlfriend?"

"Not now. A few before."

She gifted him with her first real smile of the day.

"I told myself I didn't have time for them when I moved into the Dust Bowl Ranch outside San Antonio as a kid. I was busy working and trying to stay under the radar."

"I'm sure they made time for you."

He shrugged. "I dated around. Couldn't find anyone special enough to marry." Caleb figured he'd rather spend his time building his empire than on an evening out with a woman who made him want to stick toothpicks in his eyes for how dull the conversation was. Waiting for the right girl had taken too long. He'd dated here and there. He'd all but given up when Cissy showed up. "Almost got married once."

"What happened?"

"Didn't work out. She left. Said life on the ranch was boring." He didn't want to get into the details about the little girl she'd taken with her. Savannah had been all smiles and freckles. Her heart was bigger than the land. Caleb still wondered if Cissy was taking good enough care of the little angel.

"How long ago was that?"

"Couple of months, I guess." Caleb tucked the remaining gauze back into the box and closed the lid. "Leg's looking better. Swelling's going down. I thought it might get worse after all the running today. Take these." He handed her a couple of ibuprofen and a bottle of water.

"Not sure if I'll know what to do without pain," she said with a weak smile.

He liked that she was relaxing with him. Her sticking around was an idea he could get used to. He mentally slapped himself. Nothing personal, but the last thing Caleb needed to do was to get romantically involved with another woman who needed rescuing. Even if this did feel... different.

Keeping his feelings in check became a bigger priority. Besides, they needed to get dressed and find the business center.

"Took a guess at your size." He tossed the bag onto the bed. "Think you'll find a few things in there you can wear. Can't promise they'll be fashionable."

Katherine took out the cotton shorts and pink T-shirt, blushing at the underwear and bra. "These will work fine."

Caleb fed Max, and then moved to the sink in the bathroom. He unbuttoned his shirt and shrugged it off.

In the mirror, he saw Katherine, now dressed, approaching. She stopped when she saw his shirt was off. Her gaze drifted across his bare torso.

A lightning bolt of heat spread through him, flowing blood south.

Not one woman had brought instant lust like this before. The closest he'd ever been to this was with Michelle and that still paled in comparison. She'd appeared at his doorway broke, asking for work. She'd had no money and no place to live.

He'd taken her in and helped her find a job. It hadn't taken her long to figure out where his bedroom was.

The sex had been hot. Chemistry outside the bedroom, not.

She'd moved her things in though, and seemed intent on staying for a while.

Caleb had started working longer hours than usual, looking for excuses to stay out of the house. Eventually, she'd left. No note.

He'd learned his lesson. He didn't do sex for sex's sake anymore.

Sex with Katherine would be amazing. No, mind-blowing. He had no doubt they'd sizzle with chemistry under the sheets.

Connecting in the everyday world would be no different than his past relationships. At least that's what he told himself. The thought this could be anything deeper or more real scared the hell out of him.

Katherine cleared her throat. "Here. Let me help you with that."

She moved next to him without making eye contact, took a clean washcloth from the counter, rinsed it under the tap and wrung it out. Dabbing his gash, she pressed her silken fingers to his shoulder. Contact sent his hormones into overdrive. Need for her surged faster than he could restrain. His erection pulsed, reminding him of all the things he'd like to do to her and with her. He wanted to be inside her. Now.

"Get ready. This might hurt," she said with a tentative smile, scooting in front of him.

"I'm fine." But was he? His head might be screwed on straight, but his body had ideas of the sexual variety. Damned if he wasn't thinking about sex with Katherine again.

She rubbed the wound with the washcloth until it was clean. Next, she gently dabbed antibiotic ointment on the cut.

He wasn't used to hands like hers. Soft and tender. It felt like a caress.

A crack appeared in his mind, like light in a small dark tunnel. His exterior armor threatened to splinter. He couldn't figure out why he'd told Katherine about Cissy. Weren't those wounds still fresh? Didn't they sting worse than the exterior cut on his shoulder?

Shouldn't he feel guilty for being this close to a woman in a hotel room given that Cissy had walked out so recently?

He didn't.

Instead he felt the strange sensation of warmth and light that accompanied allowing someone to take care of him for a change.

The whole concept was foreign to him. He'd taken care of himself and everyone around him for as long as he could remember.

Her touch, the way it seemed so natural to have her hands on him, suddenly felt more dangerous than the men with guns. All they could do was end a person's life. A woman like Katherine could make it not worth living without her.

Caleb eradicated the thought.

She was a woman in trouble. He was there to help. When this was all over, she'd go back to her life and he'd return to his.

He backed away and slipped on a new T-shirt.

"Let's see about that CD."

Chapter Seven

Katherine tucked Max inside her handbag and followed Caleb downstairs. The business center was a small room adjacent to the lobby. A wall of desks and two computers occupied the space. The wall between the business center and the lobby was made of glass. There wasn't much in the way of privacy, but it would have to do.

Katherine fished the CD out of her bag and handed it to Caleb.

Max squirmed and whimpered.

"Poor little guy. You miss her, don't you?" A wave of melancholy flooded Katherine as she stroked his fur. "He lost his home."

"He can come to the ranch. Unless you want him."

"Might be too sad to go home with me. Although when this ordeal is settled, I'll be looking for a new place to live. Can't imagine going back to my apartment after…"

"Either way, he'll have a new home."

"Poor little guy might need to go out soon after eating and drinking all that water."

"I saw a green space on the side of the building. We can take him there as soon as we see what we're dealing with here."

There was one file on the disk. It was labeled "Katherine."

Caleb's gaze flicked from hers to the computer screen.

"Nothing stood out before. Let's see if a closer look tells us what your sister wanted you to know."

Katherine's pulse raced. She took a deep breath. "Okay."

He clicked on her name as she looked over his shoulder.

"I can't help but wonder why she would send snapshots of Noah through FedEx when she was meeting me to hand him off."

"She must've realized she was being followed and wanted to be sure they weren't intercepted. Let's look through 'em. See if we can find a clue." Caleb started the slide show.

Katherine watched, perplexed, as picture after picture of Noah filled the screen. There were photographs of him at Barton Creek. He'd been to the zoo. It looked like a montage of his summer activities.

"Check your email. It's possible she sent you a note. Pull up her last few messages and look for anything that might signal the file's whereabouts. There might be hints. A word out of place in a sentence. A location she mentions more than once. See if there's anything we can go on."

She logged on remotely. There was nothing unusual as she scanned the last couple of notes from Leann. No extra emails from her sister mysteriously appearing posthumously, either. Not a single clue.

From the lobby, the TV volume cranked up.

"An elderly woman has been gunned down in front of her neighbor's apartment in a normally quiet suburb. The news has rocked a small North Dallas community. The name of the deceased is being withheld until family can be notified but two persons of interest, Katherine Harper and an unidentified male, are believed to have information that would assist in the investigation. An eyewitness saw them running from the scene with a weapon, and police

are warning citizens not to approach them but to call 9-1-1 if they are spotted..."

Katherine's heart dropped. She glanced around. The man behind the registration desk picked up the phone and stared at her. Was he phoning the police? She nudged Caleb.

He turned around and cursed under his breath.

"How on earth could we be tied to Ms. Ranker's murder?" The feeling of being trapped made her pulse climb. How would they get out of the hotel unseen? And if they did, where would they go? Everyone in the area would be looking for them. If they so much as tried to get coffee or food, they might be spotted. There would be nowhere to hide.

Caleb ejected the CD. "We'll figure this out later. Right now, we've gotta get out of here."

"Do we have time to get back to the room? I left everything in there but my purse and Max."

"I don't know how much time we have, but we need to try. I changed clothes and the car keys are in my old pants."

An uninvited image of Caleb's shirtless chest invaded Katherine's thoughts. Reality crashed fast and hard. She glanced around wildly as Caleb led her out of the business center half afraid the guy working the front desk would give chase.

As soon as they entered the stairwell, he urged her to run. They made it up the couple flights of stairs easily thanks to the ibuprofen tablets she'd taken earlier. The medicine saved her from the pain that would be shooting up her leg otherwise.

Caleb stopped at the door. "I'll grab everything I can. You watch the hall. If anyone darkens that corridor, let me know. A second's notice might be the difference between freedom and jail."

He disappeared.

Not a minute later, the elevator dinged.

Katherine stepped inside the room. "Someone's coming."

"Damn." He threw a bag of supplies over his shoulder and took her hand. His grip was firm as he broke into a full run, leading her to the opposite stairwell.

"Stop!" came from behind.

Katherine glanced back. A man dressed in a suit and wearing dark glasses gave chase. How could they escape? Where would they go?

She and Caleb slipped inside the stairwell. The shuffle of feet coming toward them sounded at the same time Max whimpered. How would they get anywhere quietly with him on board?

"It's okay, boy," she whispered. His big dark eyes looked up at her from the bag, and she realized the little guy was shaking. Max was in a totally foreign environment without his owner. *Poor thing.* She lifted him and cradled him to her chest to calm him.

The door from the third floor smacked against the wall at almost the same time as the one from the floor below them. With men coming in both directions, they were sandwiched with no way out.

"Stick close to me," Caleb said, squeezing her hand.

He entered the second floor.

Halfway down the hall, the maid's cart framed a door. "In here," he said, urging her toward it.

"We'll be cornered in there. I don't see another way out."

"Trust me." Caleb darted toward the room as he glanced back.

She saw more than a hint of recklessness in his eyes

now—a throwback to his misspent youth? "How did you get so good at evading people?"

"I told you, I had a rough childhood. Learned a lot of things I didn't want to need to know as an adult." Caleb ducked into the room and shooed out the cleaning lady as doors opened from both ends of the hallway. He slid the dead bolt into place.

Shots were fired and Katherine ducked. Oh. God. She was going to die right there.

Before she could scream, Caleb pulled her to the floor and covered her with his body. His broad, masculine chest flush with her back, she felt the steady rhythm of his heartbeat.

More shots were fired; bullets pinged through the walls. She had the split-second fear her life was about to end and all she could think about was her family. The memories brought a melancholy mix of pain and happiness coursing through her.

What did Caleb have?

Other than his mother, hadn't he been alone most of his life? Her heart ached for him. Maybe that's why he'd gotten so good at taking care of others.

Because of her, he'd end up in jail or dead today.

His exterior was tough. Tall, with dark brown eyes she could look into for days. With his broad shoulders, lean hips, stacked muscles, he was physical strength personified. His substantial presence would affect anyone. He was like steel. But what did he have to fortify from within?

Katherine felt herself being pulled to her feet as she held tight to Max. He'd stopped whimpering. "What are we doing?"

He made quick work jimmying the window open. "Escaping."

A bullet pinged near Katherine's head. Caleb pulled

her to the floor and covered her again before she had a chance to react.

The bullets stopped as a thump sounded against the door. Could they kick it in?

"From here on out, we've got to stay off the grid." His carved-from-granite features were stone.

Katherine took a moment to absorb his words. He was saying they couldn't show their faces again in public. They'd go into hiding and then what? How would they eat? And worse yet, what would happen to Noah? How would she make it to the drop? The center of a mall was about as public of a place as she could imagine.

The crack of an object slamming into the door wrenched her from her shock.

"You climb out first. I'll hold you as long as I can." He set Max on the floor. "I'll toss him down to you, and then I want you to run. Don't wait for me. You hear?"

Not wait for him? Was he kidding? Katherine wouldn't make it two steps without Caleb.

"But—"

"No time."

She sat on the edge of the window for a second to gather her nerves. Caleb helped her twist onto her belly to ease the impact to her leg. He lowered her.

"Ready?"

She nodded, bracing for the impact on her hurt leg. She landed hard. Her legs gave out. As soon as she turned, Caleb was half hanging out the window, making himself as low to the ground as he could before he made sure she was ready and then he let Max drop.

Catching him with both hands, she breathed a sigh of relief when Caleb followed almost immediately after.

"Aren't we near Mockingbird and 75?" he asked as he broke into a run.

"Yeah, but my car's the other direction." Katherine pointed west.

"We have a better shot of getting lost if we can get to the train."

Then what?

Before Katherine could wind up a good anxiety attack, a flurry of men in dark suits came pouring out of the building.

She powered her legs forward to the edge of the lot with the adrenaline thumping through her, ignoring the throbbing pain coursing up her leg. Caleb pushed them forward until they disappeared into a tree line.

The roar of the train sounded nearby.

"If we can get across the tracks, we can make it." He lifted her as if she weighed nothing and sprinted toward the station.

The train was coming fast. Too fast. They'd never make it in time, especially with him carrying her. "I can run."

"Not a chance." Caleb picked up speed, clearing the rail with seconds to spare.

The train car doors opened and he hopped inside, placing Katherine in the first available seat. She prayed the Dallas Area Rapid Transit police or fare-enforcement officers wouldn't be checking passengers for tickets. The last thing they needed was to give someone a reason to notice them, and she remembered reading the rail had increased security after a series of recent murders.

She tucked Max in her purse and watched out the window as the buildings blurred. "Think they saw us?"

"It's a pretty good bet. We'll jump off at the next stop. Get lost somewhere on the Katy Trail."

The engine slowed and the light rail train stopped. They hopped off.

She didn't want to weigh them down. His shoulder was

bleeding again from carrying her. He'd never admit it, but he had to be exhausted by now. He was going on no sleep as it was. "I can make it."

"You sure?"

Katherine nodded. They ran for a few minutes before her leg gave out. "I'm sorry. I need a rest."

He found a small clearing and stopped to catch their breath. "Squeeze into these bushes. This should provide enough cover to hide us for now."

Katherine was beginning to wonder if she'd ever feel secure again.

He took Max from her arms. "Better let him stretch his legs."

Max scuttled to a nearby bush and relieved himself.

"C'mon, boy," Caleb said, patting his leg. His breathing was hardly accelerated whereas Katherine's lungs burned.

The sound of pounding footsteps broke the quiet.

Peering through the leaves, Katherine's heart skittered when she saw the men in suits. They were staring at something in their hands.

Caleb backed out of the underbrush and urged her on the move again as he scooped up Max.

The men seemed to be a few feet behind everywhere they went.

"It's no use," she said, panting. The pain in her leg was staggering.

"Dammit. I didn't even think about this before. It makes sense now."

"What are you talking about?"

"Give me your phone." He held out his free hand.

She dug it out of her purse and placed it on his flat palm.

"Hold Max."

She did.

He pulled out the battery and smashed the phone under

the heel of his cowboy boot. Did the same to his own. Then picked up the pieces and tossed them.

Panic gripped her as it felt like icy fingers had closed around her chest and squeezed. All the air sucked out of her lungs in a whooshing sound. "They can't contact me now. What have you done?"

"They can't find us anymore, either." He took her hand in his. "They've been following us using the GPS tracking in the phone. It's the only way they could always be a step behind."

"How can they do that unless they work for the government?"

"It's surprisingly easy. Anyone can buy the program online." He urged her forward as he took Max, and then ran for what seemed like half an hour before stopping. "We should be safe now."

She hobbled a few feet and settled onto a large rock, stroking Max and fighting waves of tears from exhaustion and panic. "Any idea where we are?"

Caleb shook his head.

He sat beside her and braided their fingers together. "You don't have to keep it together all the time."

Yes, she did. He didn't understand. She had to be strong for Noah. She'd had to be strong her entire life. "I have a lot of responsibility, and the last thing I can afford to do is break down." She sniffed back a tear.

"It's okay to cry. I'm right here, and I'm not going anywhere."

Her heart skipped a beat when she realized those words comforted her far more than she should allow. She shivered and raised her gaze to meet his. Warmth spread through her body.

His chest moved up and down rhythmically, whereas her breathing was ragged. And not just because she'd outrun bullets and scary men with guns. Her pulse rose for a different reason. His body was so close she could breathe in his masculinity. Her arms were full of goose bumps. She knew the instant her body shifted from fear to awareness…

Awareness of his strong hands on her. Awareness of the unique scent of woods and outdoors and virility that belonged to him. Awareness of everything that was Caleb. A sensual shiver raced up her spine.

Being close to him, drinking in his powerful scent was a mistake. Katherine needed a clear head. Especially because she could so vividly recall the way his lips tasted. How soft they were when they moved with hers.

Katherine's heart beat somewhere at the base of her throat, thumping wildly.

Wisps of his sandy-blond curls moved in the wind. His rich brown-gold eyes were fixed on her, blazing. In that moment she wanted nothing more than to explore the steel muscles under the cotton fabric of his T-shirt. Her hands itched to trace his jawline to the dimple in his chin.

Guilt slammed into her. How could she allow herself to become distracted? Noah was the only person who mattered. He needed her now more than ever. Nothing could ever happen between her and Caleb. *Not now. Not ever.* She had a family to think about, and a drop spot to get to. *Refocus.*

"I still can't believe my sister would have had anything to do with a man like Kane."

"I've read he has his hand on everything that crosses the borders from Canada to Mexico."

"Which makes even less sense to me. How would my sister be connected to a man like that? She didn't have any money. She worked at a coffee shop, for God's sake. I know she could keep a secret, but she didn't run in circles like that." Katherine gripped the tree branch tighter. "Wish we could've had more time to check out that CD. Maybe there's a hidden file or something? All I could see were pictures of Noah. Which would make a person think that's all she was sending, but we both know it can't be right."

"Especially when she sent them 'signature required.'" Caleb redressed one of her injuries.

"You said you got into trouble when you were young. What happened?"

He didn't look up. He put away supplies as he finished with them and rolled them into a ball, placing them in a backpack. He patted Max on the head. "I told you. I had a few run-ins with the law when I was younger. Gave my mom a hard time. Stopped when I saw what it was doing to her. End of story."

"Did you act out because of your father?"

He scratched behind Max's ears. The little dog had stopped shaking and sat at Caleb's feet.

"He'll need to eat again soon." The subject had been changed.

All she knew about the handsome cowboy was that he saved cats, dogs and women in trouble. Katherine wished he would open up more.

"You hungry, too?" His jaw did that tick thing again.

She figured the subject of his father was closed.

CALEB NEEDED TO find safe shelter for Katherine. He needed to protect her from everyone and everything bad more than he needed air. Help her, yes, but where had this burning need to banish all her pain come from? He could feel her anguish as if it were his own.

A crack of thunder in the distance threatened a storm.

By tying them to Ms. Ranker's murder, everyone would be on the lookout for him and Katherine now. No place would be safe. They were wanted. Had no transportation.

If they ducked their heads inside the wrong building, they'd be shot at or captured.

The police wouldn't believe their story, so going to them was out.

He and Katherine would need to change their appearance and figure out a place to bed down tonight. But where? He could think of a dozen or so places he could hide her on the ranch.

A lone thought pounded his temples. What would Kane have to gain by getting them arrested?

Dammit. Was there a mole in the police station? A man like Kane could buy a lot of goodwill. Could he ensure they didn't make it out of jail, too?

The DART rail system could get them as far as Plano. The hike back would be dangerous. If anyone spotted them, they would most likely call 9-1-1. How much longer could they outrun a man with Kane's resources?

He had no idea how he'd survive this, let alone keep Katherine and Noah safe. That little boy deserved a life. He had a right to be loved and to have the kind of family she would provide. He deserved Katherine.

She'd be a better mother than she thought. She was risking her life for the child. That kind of dedication and love would ensure Noah had an amazing childhood.

The boy had already lost the one person he was closest to in the world. A pang of regret sliced through Caleb. He knew exactly what it was like to lose a mother. The overwhelming pain that came with realizing he was all alone in the world.

An urge to protect Noah surged so strongly inside he was completely caught off guard.

He refocused on Katherine. Watching her as she tried to be brave would wear down his resolve not to touch her. He fought like hell against the urge to take her in his arms and comfort her already. A little question mark lingered in the back of his mind. Did she want him the way he wanted her?

He could feel her body react to him every time he touched her. Yet she pulled away.

Dammit.

Under another set of circumstances, he would like to take his time to get to know her. Take her out somewhere nice for dinner. Learn about where she went to college and more about the kind of software company she worked for. Date. Like normal people.

Caleb almost laughed out loud.

His life had been anything but *normal*. And this impossible situation was only getting worse. The more time he spent with her, the louder his danger alarms sounded. She was already under his skin, and he wanted to get closer.

His biggest fear was that he wouldn't be able to protect her when the time came, and he would lose her forever. They'd narrowly escaped several times in the past few hours.

Her resolve was weakening.

He could go a few more days without sleep, and his only injury came from his shoulder. He could fix it with a sterile needle and thread. Neither of those was on him at present. He was running out of options for places to hide.

He'd take her to the only place he'd ever truly felt safe, his ranch…and figure out a way to get a message to Matt. Then he'd have to find a way to keep his family safe.

Chapter Eight

Katherine's chestnut hair had been pulled up loosely in a
ponytail. Caleb's fingers itched from wanting to feel the
stray strands that framed her face. The desire to reach out,
touch her, be her comfort, was an ache in his chest. But he
couldn't be her shelter now and still walk away later when
this whole ordeal had passed. No use putting much stock
in the emotions occupying his thoughts. He checked the
area and deemed it safe. For the moment. "I need to get
back to TorJake."

"Why? Won't they be all over the ranch?" Her violet
eyes were enormous. "Isn't that the last place we should
go?"

"They'll be watching at the very least. And we're out
of options."

He glanced around, keeping an eye on a homeless man
curled up near the underbrush. "Out here, there are too
many factors outside of my control."

"What if they're already there waiting? With everything
that's happened so far, they will be all over the place. If
the police don't catch us first."

"It's a big ranch. I know a place we can hide for a while
as long as we can get supplies."

"You think they have the police in their pockets?"

Caleb scratched behind Max's ears. "There could be an officer on Kane's payroll, not the entire force. Rich, connected people use any means to get what they want. Doesn't matter. He has his own personal army of security to command. I can't watch our backs out here."

"What if the sheriff is there? What if he's waiting to arrest us?"

"He believes you're being set up, too."

Shock widened her eyes. "He said that?"

"Yes."

"How can we be sure he's telling the truth? I mean, he could set a trap to make us feel safe so he can arrest us. Or Kane might have gotten to him, offering cash."

Caleb paused for a beat. "I believe the sheriff is honest. I've known him long enough to vouch for him." Caleb and Coleman might have had a good relationship in the past. But that was before Caleb was wanted for questioning in a murder. It'd be risky to trust Coleman now that they were on the run and wanted for questioning, but he didn't want to tell her that. They couldn't risk being delayed at the station and losing time in their search for Noah. Her fingers were interlocked. "If this guy is as big as you say he is, who can really protect us? Where can we go? Even if we make it to the ranch by some miracle, how will we survive? We'll be in hiding forever."

"Only until we come up with a better plan. I can connect with Matt and the boys. They'll be able to help."

"And Noah will end up dead. I heard him wheeze on the phone. If these men are as heartless as you say, then they won't take him to the hospital. They'll just let him die and dump him somewhere."

"We'll figure out a way to get medicine to the drop. Then we have to hide. I didn't see anything on the CD that will help us."

She folded her arms across her chest. Her hands gripped her elbows until her knuckles went white. "They can't contact me now, remember? Not after you trashed my cell. If I don't show up to the drop and stay, they will kill him. There's no other way to reach me."

"We don't know that. If you go, they'll shoot you on the spot. Then what?"

She looked as though she needed a moment to digest his words. "Why do you think they went from trying to make contact with us to trying to kill us?"

"My guess is whatever Leann had over them, they think you've seen it."

"Will they hurt Noah now anyway?"

"I believe they'll keep him alive until…"

"They finish the job. Meaning, erase both of us. Then they'll kill him."

Caleb looked into her vivid gaze. The hurt he saw nearly did him in. He leaned toward her and rested his forehead against hers.

Her hand came up to his chin and guided his lips to hers.

Those lips, soft and slick, pushed all rational thought aside. The bulge in his jeans tightened and strained. The thought of how good she would feel naked and underneath him crashed into his thoughts like a rogue wave, making him harder. He wanted to lay her down and give her all the comfort she could handle.

Was this a bad idea? How could it be when it felt this right? She was almost too much for him. Too beautiful. Too impossible to resist. Were her emotions strapped on a roller coaster she didn't sign up to ride? Was she afraid? Acting on primal instinct?

She needed confirmation of life. Could he hope for more? That she wanted him as badly as he wanted to feel her naked skin against his?

Her tongue dipped in his mouth, and his control obliterated. Blood rushed in his ears, overshadowing rational thought.

His body was tuned to hers. Every vibration. Every quick breath. Every sexy little moan. The thin cotton material of her shirt was the only barrier to bare skin. He slipped his hand up her shirt, sliding under her lacy bra where he found her delicate skin. Her nipple pebbled. A whoosh sounded in his ears. His muscles clenched.

He wanted her. *Now.* He pushed deeper into the vee of her legs. Her legs wrapped around his waist. He was so close to her sweetness, he nearly blew it right there.

She flattened her hands against his back, pulling him closer.

His chest flush with hers sent heat and impulse rocketing through him.

Much more and he couldn't stop himself from ripping her clothes off right then and there.

She needed him to think clearly. Not like some teenager drunk on pheromones. Besides, she already wore the weight of the world on her shoulders. He didn't need to add to her guilt.

With a shudder, he pulled back. "I'm sorry."

"Me, too."

"I don't think this is a good idea."

"Oh." Embarrassment flushed her cheeks.

He hadn't meant for that to happen. "Believe me, I *want* this."

"No. You're right. I should definitely not have done that." Her solemn tone of voice sent a ripple through him.

He stood to face her. "I didn't mean to hurt you. All I want to do is help."

She stalked to a tree, putting distance between them.

Her beautiful face, the pout of her lips, stirred another inappropriate sexual reaction. Didn't she realize his restraint took Herculean effort at this point?

Dammit that he wanted nothing more than to lay her down right then and make love to her until she screamed his name aloud over and over again. It was all he could do not to think about the pink cotton panties she wore. He hadn't dared buy her another pale blue silky pair.

Hell, the need to hold her and to protect her surged so strongly, he'd almost blown it. He was trying to be a better person and show self-discipline. Last thing he wanted was to take advantage of her vulnerability and have her regretting anything about the time they spent together.

When they made love—correction, *if* they made love—it would be the best damn thing either of them had ever done. She wouldn't walk out of his life afterward. It wouldn't be temporary. *Where the hell did that come from?* The admission shocked him.

What was he thinking exactly?

That he didn't want a convenient relationship with her. Wouldn't she leave when the heat was off and she could return to her normal life? She was used to living in a busy major metropolitan city. Life on TorJake was simple. Hard work. Long days. Lots of paperwork.

Caleb didn't get out much. He didn't hit the bars or see the need to sit at white-tablecloth restaurants.

He loved a hard day's work. A cool shower. A down-home meal. And to wrap his arms around the woman he loved. Life didn't get any better than that.

Simply put, their worlds were too different and when she got her life back—and she would get her life back—wouldn't she walk out like the others and move on? Just like Cissy had? One look at Katherine made his heart stir. Not to mention other parts of his body.

He grunted.

This time, his heart might not recover. He felt more for Katherine in the few days he'd known her than he'd ever felt for his ex-girlfriend.

And that scared the hell out of him.

KATHERINE RUBBED TO ease the chill bumps on her arms. Her attraction to Caleb was a distraction. His square jaw. Those rich brown-gold eyes reminded her why fall was her favorite season. He was so damn sexy. With his body flush to hers, everything tingled and surged.

The wind had picked up and the threat of rain intensified. There was a breeze blowing now with pockets of cooler air blasting her. The temperature between her and Caleb had shifted, too. The question was why?

Not that any of this mattered. Those men would find them. They were going to kill her, Caleb and Noah.

She glanced at her watch. "If we're going to make the drop, we'd better get going."

He shook his head. "Not a good idea."

"I don't have a choice. Noah won't survive without his medicine. I have to get it to him."

"You can't save him if you're dead. You have to know it's a setup. I won't allow them to hurt you."

She bristled. "I have to go."

"I don't like it. They've set a trap."

"At least I'll be in the middle of a busy mall."

"That won't stop them. It's absolutely out of the question. They won't allow anything to happen to Noah as long as you're alive. They know it's the only leverage they have. They let him die and there's no deal."

Katherine had to figure out a way to drop the medicine, especially since she didn't have the file. Didn't he understand she had to take the risk? Those jerks may very well be setting her up. What could she do about it? Bottom line? If she didn't show, what chance did Noah have?

She couldn't allow that to happen. She would have to convince Caleb.

"I need to find a phone so I can make contact with Matt. He'll give me a pulse on the sheriff."

"You can use Leann's."

"Lost the power cord. Besides, they don't know we have it yet. Best leave it that way."

Katherine stood and wobbled. "My ankle hurts. I don't think I can walk anymore." She sat on the nearest rock.

Caleb took a knee in front of her. "Let me see what we have here."

"No. You go on." She glanced around and propped her leg on a big rock. "I need a few minutes."

Trepidation and concern played out over his features. "I guess you'll be okay while I scout the area. I'll leave supplies in case you need anything while I'm gone."

Good. She needed to think. "I'll be fine until you get back. Besides, we have a long journey ahead of us later when we head back to the ranch."

He issued a sharp sigh. "Fine." He looked down at Max. "C'mon, boy."

The little dog scampered to Caleb's feet.

"I'll take him so he doesn't make any noise or draw attention to you. We'll be right back. In the meantime, I want you to stay put. No one can track you here. Stay low and hidden." He motioned toward the thicket. "You'll be safe until I get back."

Safe was a word Katherine figured could be deleted

from her vocabulary. Without Caleb, she feared she would never be safe again.

As soon as Caleb was out of sight, she organized supplies.

The sound of Noah wheezing on the phone earlier hammered through her. Time was running out for both of them.

Chapter Nine

Caleb tugged the ball cap he'd bought low on his forehead and put on sunglasses, hooding his eyes. An ache had started in his chest the moment he left Katherine. The memory of her kiss burned into his lips.

It was too early to have real feelings for her. Wasn't it? Protectiveness was a given with her circumstances. His desire to help would be strong. She was in serious trouble. But real feelings?

Not this soon.

Katherine was at the right place at the right time. His wounds from Cissy were still too exposed. She'd got him thinking about what it would be like to have little feet running around the TorJake.

Except that he never missed Cissy the way he was missing Katherine.

Even so, Cissy must've primed him for thinking about having his own family someday and a woman like Katherine by his side. He couldn't deny how right her hands had felt on his body back there.

Hell's bells.

Katherine wasn't interested in a relationship with him. She'd been clear on that.

Maybe this was his twisted way of missing his ex-girlfriend.

Caleb redirected his thoughts as he broke through the tree line and located a phone two blocks away in heavy traffic.

He looked up in time to see a young blonde in tattered jeans and a blouse heading straight toward him. Her backpack had been tossed over her shoulder and her keys were clipped to the strap. A college student? He was most likely in the West Village near the main Southern Methodist University campus. He thought for a second about how close they were to the drop spot and glanced around to see if anyone looked suspicious. Kane could have men stationed anywhere. And they could look like anyone. Even the pretty young woman standing in front of him, stroking the dog, could be a threat. Caleb eyed her.

"Awww. What a cute puppy," she said.

Last thing he wanted was to attract attention. He kept his head low and nodded.

"What's his name?"

"Max." Caleb tensed. His gaze fixed on her, looking for any hint of a weapon. If she had a gun tucked somewhere, he'd see it.

Then again, Kane hadn't exactly been subtle so far.

"He's a sweetie." She bent down and nuzzled Max's nose. "Aren't you?"

Caleb scanned the area, watching for anything that stood out. The street was busy. The sidewalk cafés were full. This section of Dallas teemed with life. It would be so easy to blend in here.

Her gaze came up, stopping on Caleb's face. "You look familiar. Do I know you?"

"Don't think so." He smiled and paused for a beat. "I better get him back to his mom." An image of Katherine waiting in his bed popped into his thoughts. *Not the time. Or the place.*

The girl smiled and walked away.

Caleb picked up the phone and called Matt.

His buddy answered on the first ring.

"I don't have much time to talk, so I'll make this quick—"

"Caleb? What the hell's going on? Where are you?" Matt was silent for a beat. "Never mind. Don't answer that. We probably have company on the line."

Caleb hadn't thought about the line being tapped. It made sense someone would be listening in and trying to locate him by any means possible. Katherine's little sister had done far worse than take a bat to a hornets' nest. She'd written death warrants for everyone she loved and anyone else who tried to help them. Finding a hiding spot was next to impossible when Kane seemed to have so many people in his pockets. "What's happening at the ranch?"

"The men in suits have been here twice. Whatever she stirred up has gone downright crazy."

"Did you catch the news?"

"Sure did. I know you didn't have anything to do with what they're saying. You couldn't have. I don't care what the witness says," Matt said solemnly.

"Thanks for the confidence. It all happened right in front of me."

"You were there?"

"Unfortunately, yes. One minute I was talking to her. The next, bullets were flying. Surely the investigators will be able to figure out which direction the bullets were fired."

"We'll do whatever we have to, to clear your name." Matt issued a sigh. "There's something I should tell you."

"What's that?"

"A man came by the other day. Said he was a U.S.

Marshal. He's offering witness protection to her," Matt whispered. "Said he'd already offered it to her sister."

"What else did he say?"

"He can work out a deal for you, too. Put you both in the program."

"You know I won't leave my ranch," Caleb said, steadfast.

"Well, you might have to. This thing has blown up beyond big."

"Did Coleman meet with him?"

"Yes."

He knew the sheriff was honest to a fault. If he trusted the stranger, then Caleb could risk a little faith, too. Not even a man with Kane's pull could persuade Coleman to switch teams. "What did he think?"

"Said the guy checked out. Thinks you should talk to him. And, Caleb, I do, too."

Then again, the guy working for a legitimate agency didn't mean he was clean. Maybe Caleb could get a better feel if he spoke to Coleman directly. "Tell the sheriff I'll be in touch."

"Not a good idea. He has a tail. Besides, you're wanted. He said to warn you if he sees you he'll have to detain you."

Caleb should've seen that coming. "I don't have much time. How's the ranch?"

"To hell with that, how are you?"

"I'm good. Don't worry about me. Just take care of my horses until I return."

"You know I will."

"Make sure you check out the property, too. The teenagers have been hitting the north fence hard. The acreage in the east needs to be checked for coyotes."

"Jimmy's been on it."

"Won't he be off for his daughter's surgery soon?"

"Yeah."

Caleb needed to drop a hint. Tell Matt where he was going. But how? "You better take over for him. And make sure someone's exercising Dawn. Can't have her too restless like before, when Cissy left. No one's been watching that trail she rode and I might not be back for a long time."

"Don't talk like that." He listened carefully for the telltale rise of Matt's voice when he caught on. "We'll get this figured out, and you'll be home before you know it."

Nope. Matt hadn't picked up on the clue. "I wouldn't count on it."

"It will all work out."

Maybe he could send Matt on a mission? "Do me a favor?"

"Name it."

"Find a picture of Sebastian Kanc."

"The businessman?"

"Yes. Call the manager of the Coffee Hut in Austin and send him the picture. Find out if he came into the shop much, or spent any time with one of the employees by the name of Leann Foster."

"Consider it done."

"I'll be in touch."

"Be safe, man."

Caleb ended the call. He prayed he'd disconnected before his location had been tagged. Being away from Katherine gave him an uneasy feeling, like dark clouds closing in around him, threatening to take away all that was light and good. He needed to get back and make sure she was all right. With her damaged ankle, she might not be able to run. He'd never forgive himself if anything had happened while he'd been gone.

Keeping his head low, he circled back to the brush where he'd tucked her away.

What the hell?

"Katherine," he called into the nearby shrubbery. He searched branches and bushes. Nothing. No answer.

Fear and anger formed liquid that ran cold in his veins. Had he been careless? Had he left her vulnerable and alone with no way to defend herself? Had the cops picked her up?

The bag of supplies was left leaning against the rock. He checked it. The pain relievers were missing as were several bottled waters.

He called her name again, louder.

"Caleb." Her voice came from his left.

He rushed to the bushes at the edge of the hill. His heart thumped in his throat. "What happened?"

"I slipped on a rock." She was on all fours, climbing up.

He picked her up and carried her to the rock. Relief filled his chest. He didn't want to acknowledge how stressed he'd been a minute ago. "What were you doing over there?"

"Looking for you. My leg gave out and I slipped over the edge."

Glancing at his watch, he swore under his breath. "The drop."

"I'm fine. I can make it."

"You wait here. I'll figure something out."

"No. Please. I can do this." She tugged at his hand. Her eyes pleaded.

Looking into her determined eyes, he knew he couldn't leave her behind. She'd be safer if he kept her within arm's reach until he could get her back to TorJake. "Okay."

Caleb retraced his route to West Village, going as slowly as she needed to.

If memory served, NorthPark Center wasn't far. In fact, it should be on the other side of Highway 75. Easy walk for him. Nothing was easy for Katherine right then.

If they thought she'd showed up alone, and weren't expecting him, the element of surprise would be on his side. The thought of anyone touching her or hurting her sent white-hot anger coursing through him.

Why was she so stubborn?

Didn't she realize she might be walking right into their arms? Being in the open was good. Crowds hid a lot of things.

He didn't know if this was the best play. They were walking into a situation set up by Kane. They didn't have the file. Should he turn and walk away while they still could? Meet with the marshal who'd seemed legit? Because nothing about his current situation was going to turn out the way he wanted. She was far too willing to put herself in harm's way to protect everyone around her. Except this burning desire to help Katherine, to keep her safe, kept his feet moving anyway.

People didn't accidently get mixed up with a man like Kane. What was the connection?

Caleb chewed on that thought as he led Katherine a few blocks, near the meeting site.

"Let me go first. Get a good read." Caleb ran ahead and entered the grassy area, leaving her at the perimeter. He blended in with the noisy lunch crowd.

Scanning the area, he could see at least five shooters in position.

Kane had come prepared to do anything necessary to erase Katherine.

If she took a couple more steps, she'd be right where they wanted her.

An imposing figure made a move toward her.

Caleb crouched low. When she stepped into his sight, he sprang forward and clutched her hand. She was shaking.

He pulled her into the crowd.

Glancing around, the shooters didn't seem to notice the small commotion. He turned to a teen and tapped his shoulder. "Hey, kid."

The teen glanced up, looking annoyed at the interruption. When he saw Caleb, the teen straightened his back and pulled out his earbuds.

"Sorry to bother you while you're listening to your music, buddy. I was wondering if you'd like to make a quick twenty bucks."

The kid eyed Caleb suspiciously.

"I need to deliver this stuff to the bronze statue." Caleb took the medicines from Katherine's tight grip. She stroked Max.

The boy's face twisted, giving the universal teenage sign for, *Have you lost your mind?* "Mister, that's only, like, twenty feet away."

Caleb smiled and winked. "It's a dollar a step basically. You want the job or not?"

"Sure. I'd kiss your mother for twenty bucks."

"Deliver the medicine. And leave my mother out of it."

The teen palmed the pill bottle and inhaler. "That's it?"

Caleb nodded.

"Deal."

"Be inconspicuous and I'll make it forty."

A wide smile broke across the teen's face. "Then I'll be stealth."

He rocked his head back and forth as he walked to the sculpture. His gaze intent on the music device in his hand, he plopped down next to the statue.

Caleb never saw the kid slip the medicine under the bronze, but as soon as he popped to his feet and strolled away the package stood out. Amazing.

"Nice job, kid." Caleb handed him a pair of twenties.

He had no idea what Kane and his men would do when they realized there was no file.

"Pleasure doing business with you," he said as he turned and then sauntered off.

With his hand on Katherine's shoulder, he guided her toward a tour group. "Let's get out of here before anyone gets hurt."

"I—I can't. Not without knowing if they got his med—"

"See that baby over there?" He pointed to a mother nursing an infant. "They both could die if we don't leave now."

A mix of emotions played across her features. Worry. Guilt. Her stubborn streak was visible on the surface as her chin lifted. "You're right."

No sooner had the words left her mouth than a scuffle-like noise moved toward them. People ran in different directions, parting faster than the Red Sea, as a serious-looking man walked down the middle. Sunglasses hooded his eyes, but his intention was clear. His face didn't veer from Katherine.

Caleb grabbed her by the arm and pushed her ahead of him, placing himself in between her and the suit. If he could get her toward the flagship store, maybe they could get lost in the rows of clothing.

As they neared the wide-open door, two similar-looking men in suits flanked the entrance.

They were trapped. The man from behind was closing in on them fast. Glancing from left to right, Caleb looked for another way out. One side was a brick wall. Nothing there.

A police radio broke the silence from the left-hand side. Not good.

Except.

Wait a minute.

That would work.

Caleb ducked toward the officer and waved his hands wildly. "I'd like to turn myself in."

"What are you doing?" Katherine's expression was mortification personified.

"Trust me," was all he said.

The look she gave him said she thought he'd snapped. Lost his mind. Her concern that this would make Kane kill Noah was written in the worry lines on her face. The thought crossed Caleb's mind, too. He had to take the chance or they would all be dead. Besides, Kane would most likely bide his time. If he killed Noah too soon, he would lose all his leverage.

Caleb squeezed her hand. "I know what I'm doing."

Too late. The officer was next to them in a beat. "Katherine Harper?"

"Yes, sir," Caleb said.

Katherine's bewildered expression must've robbed her of her ability to speak, too.

"I believe we're wanted for questioning." Caleb glanced around.

The men had disappeared.

Caleb didn't realize until that moment that he'd been holding his breath.

KATHERINE ALLOWED CALEB to lead her outside the police station. Being detained for the past twenty-four hours heightened her fatigue. "You didn't say anything about Noah, did you?"

"No. I didn't figure you wanted me to. Thought about it, though."

"So did I. I actually expected to be arrested."

"That might come next. They're still gathering and analyzing evidence. What did you tell them?"

"That we didn't do anything wrong. I explained exactly

how it all happened back at my apartment. Said it must be some mistake. A random act of violence."

"So did I. The crime scene evidence should corroborate our story."

"There's no way they'll let Noah go if I involve the police. Kane will be furious at me for evading him at the drop for sure now. He warned me to come alone."

"Yes. But Noah will be alive and so will you." Caleb's forehead was etched with worry. Lines bracketed his mouth as he set Max down in a patch of grass.

"You're right. I probably haven't seemed very appreciative. I hope you know how very grateful I am. None of this would have happened without you. Noah and I would probably both be dead by now."

He squeezed her hand reassuringly. He didn't speak. His focus shifted from face to face as though he was evaluating threats.

Katherine exhaled deeply.

He wrapped his arms around her. She was flush with his chest before she could blink.

He pressed a kiss to her forehead. "It was stupid of us to walk into Kane's trap. I thought, for a second, I might lose you. Turning ourselves in was a risk I had to take to get us out of there and keep us alive."

Panic came off his frame in palpable waves. Fear dilated his pupils. His dark brown eyes sliced through her pain. Her loneliness. Katherine didn't realize how alone she'd been until Caleb. "I'm here. I'm not going away. Not unless you want me to."

"No. I don't. I want you right here with me."

She felt comforted by his strong presence. One hand slipped up his shirt onto his chest, rubbing against his skin in the hope of calming him.

She pressed her face against his cotton T-shirt before placing a kiss on his chest. "I'm right here."

He smiled. His fingers tangled in her hair, stroking it off her face.

He splayed his hand on her bottom, lighting fires from deep inside her. He lowered his face to hers and kissed her. His lips skimmed across hers and lit nerve endings she didn't know existed. Her body zinged to life, tantalized, pulsing volts of heat. A little piece of her heart wished he'd said forever.

A car alarm sounded.

He took a step back and scanned the parking lot, picking up Max. "I spoke to Matt."

Katherine tried to regain her mental balance because for a moment she got lost...lost in his gaze...lost in all that was Caleb. "What did he say?"

"Apparently your sister was talking to the Feds. There's a guy who seems legit. He's offering witness protection to you."

"What about you?"

Caleb shrugged. "Don't need it."

"You would never leave TorJake, would you?"

"It's the only home I've ever known."

Katherine hadn't felt home in so many years she couldn't count. Except that lately, home felt a lot like wherever Caleb was. But that was ridiculous. They'd only just met. It took years of getting to know someone before a bond like that could be created. Running for her life, trying to beat bullets, defying death probably had toyed with her emotions. No doubt, she had feelings for Caleb. That couldn't be denied. But the kinds of feelings that could last a lifetime? Real love? Wouldn't he let her down like the others had?

"Can't say I know what you mean," she lied. "How do we know this man can be trusted?"

Caleb's expression was weary. "I thought about that, too. I don't know. It might be the best chance we have."

"What about Noah? What will they do for him?"

"Good question. This guy said he was trying to help your sister before her accident. If they safely tuck you away, he can go after Noah."

"What do you think I should do?" Katherine turned the tables.

His pupils dilated for a split second as the muscles in his jaw clenched. It was the look he got when he was holding back what he really wanted to say.

"Whatever it takes to stay alive," he said, deadpan.

"So you think I should just turn myself in. Let the government handle this?" How could he say this to her? Hadn't he just told her to stay with him? Why had his gaze suddenly cooled?

"I didn't say that. You have to make the decision for yourself. I tried to drop a hint to Matt of where we'd be. We won't survive long without supplies and neither one of us knows how many of Kane's men are out there. Matt didn't get it."

"Where can we go? The police aren't looking for us right now. But Kane's men won't let up."

"I still think the ranch is the best place. There's a spot no one checks on the far side of the property."

"Then I want to go with you."

"Does that mean you won't turn yourself over to federal protection?"

She crossed her arms over her chest. "No. And it's not up for discussion right now."

"I told Matt to talk to Leann's boss to see if Kane visited the coffee shop."

"Good idea." As she turned to walk away, she could feel Caleb's presence right behind her. She was tempted to lean back against his chest and allow him to wrap his arms around her. She didn't.

Whatever Leann had gotten involved with had to have been by accident. No way had her sister known this Kane person. She didn't get involved with known criminals or men with this kind of influence. Leann could keep a secret but she wouldn't drag herself and Noah into a mess like this. "She must've seen something horrible to cause all this."

"I was thinking the same thing. She was a witness to a crime. It's the only reason she'd be offered federal protection that I know of," he said quietly. "We need to make contact with the marshal to figure out what exactly."

Relief and vindication washed over Katherine. The emotions were followed by a deep sense of sadness.

Caleb stroked Max's fur. "I recognized one of the men earlier from photographs in the newspaper at the police station. He was definitely one of Kane's entourage."

"They'll keep coming until they find us, won't they?"

"I believe so."

Tears stung her eyes. What kind of horrible man had her nephew? And yet, Noah had sounded okay on the phone. "Think they picked up his medicine?"

"He's of no value dead. They kill him and you'll go into witness protection. They might have found out Leann was considering the program."

"Do you think they killed her? And they had to get to her before she disappeared with the evidence?" A chill raced up Katherine's arms. "Why not kill me and Noah, too?"

He shrugged. "They think you have evidence. Two sisters and a little boy dead in a short time would sound alarms."

"I just can't figure out why she didn't go right in. Why would she wait?" A beat passed. "For Noah, I guess. She didn't want him to have that life. Kane must not have known about him before."

"Or she didn't think he did."

Reality dawned on her. "Leann was planning to leave him with me before she disappeared. She wanted to make sure he was safe. I'll bet she was ready to turn herself in."

"She must've figured they wouldn't connect the two of you. But why?"

"Leann changed her name when she left all those years ago, so we had different last names. It was her way of cutting all ties." She paused. "Still want to go to your ranch?"

"Yes."

"Then let's go."

"First, we need to change your appearance," Caleb said solemnly, tugging on his hat.

"Good idea. I almost didn't recognize you when you showed up. Max gave you away." She scratched him behind the ears, grateful the police hadn't taken him from her as she recognized the area as their original hiding spot.

"The ball cap. Small changes can make a big difference." He pulled a scarf from the bag of supplies.

She covered most of her hair and tied a knot in the back to hold the material in place. "How's this?"

He tucked a stray strand inside the fabric. "I wouldn't say better. You'd be beautiful no matter what you wore. This is different. Different is good. We want different."

His touch connected her to the memory of his hands on her before. His urgency. Ecstasy. She had no doubt those big hands could bring her pleasures she'd never known.

She ignored the sensitized shivers skittering across her nerves. "A man like Kane won't give up easily, will he?" She lowered her gaze.

He lifted her chin until she was looking him in the eye again. "Don't be sorry for any of this. I'm not. You didn't ask for this any more than Noah did. I'm sure your parents would be proud of you right now. You're risking your life to save your sister's boy. There's no shame in that."

"Except I feel like a coward."

His rich brown gaze trained on her. "Then you don't see what I do."

"Then what am I?"

"Strong. Brave. Intelligent."

She felt a blush crawl up her neck to her cheeks. "You make me sound like so much more than I feel right now."

"Sometimes the brain plays tricks on us. We don't have to buy into it. That's our choice."

She looked him dead in the eye. "You think we'll be safe at your ranch?"

He nodded. "For a while anyway."

Katherine was certain they'd be caught.

If not by Kane's men, then eventually by the Feds. The government wouldn't give a free pass to fugitives. Murderers. If Kane had his way, that would be the label put on them by everyone. Police. Reporters. Citizens. Anyone and everyone.

Strangers would be afraid of them.

Her life was shattered. There'd be no going back.

A new identity didn't sound like a bad idea. She doubted she'd have a job left to go back to when all this was said and done anyway. Would her friends and boss believe she'd had nothing to do with the murder of her landlady?

Friends? That was a joke. Katherine kept to herself most of the time. She worked and read and kept people at a distance, didn't she?

Except for her cowboy.

How could he push her toward the program? Didn't that mean they'd never see each other again?

Her lip quivered, but she ignored it. "I'm tired of running scared. They always seem a step ahead of me anyway."

A mischievous twinkle intensified his gold-brown eyes. "Are you saying what I think you are?"

"I'm ready to fight back."

Caleb's face brightened with anticipation. His eyes glittered an incredible shade of brown. "It's risky."

Risky didn't cover the half of it to Katherine. And yet, waiting, not knowing what would happen next, giving the other guys all the advantage wasn't an option, either. She'd been letting Kane and his men hold the cards for too long. Time to take control. "I know."

"You're sure about this?"

"I've never been more certain of anything in my life. I'm not sure what the plan is yet. Just that we need one."

"Then let's give 'em hell."

He got a sexy spark in his eye when he was being bad. How could someone become so special to her in such a short time span?

She couldn't imagine doing any of this without Caleb. Her cowboy protector...friend...*lover?*

Chapter Ten

Caleb needed transportation. Walking around outside exposed wasn't good, especially after Katherine's fall. Her ankle was swelling again. Kane's men would be all over the place now that they'd managed to get away from them. He was half surprised no one had waited outside the police station earlier. Could he get Katherine out of the city safely before Kane figured out they'd been released?

Even though they'd been questioned and released, being identified by a random person could put them both in danger. Especially if one of Kane's men was around. Attracting attention wasn't good.

He located the nicest restaurant in the area; intently watched where the valet parked cars. He scanned the parking garage for witnesses. A family stepped out of the elevator. He froze. A stab of guilt hit him. He didn't like the idea of taking someone else's property, but there was no other choice. Steal or die.

When the valet parked an SUV with the windows blacked out, he waited for the family to unload their minivan and the valet to jog out of sight.

Caleb figured the owner would be in the restaurant for a good hour. That should give them enough time to get out of the city before anyone knew the sport utility was missing. He could ditch the SUV in a field or alley outside of Allen. If he could get that far, he'd be close enough to get home on foot. The less walking the better for Katherine. Even with a modest amount of pain reliever, she had to be hurting.

He put on a pair of sterile gloves and felt the back tire on the driver's side. Jackpot. The keys were there. A trick he'd learned back in the day before he'd gone on the straight and narrow.

The ignition caught and he drove the SUV to pick up Katherine and Max a minute later.

"I don't want to know where you got this, do I?" She slid into the passenger seat next to him.

"Probably not."

"Then I won't ask." She smiled. Her violet eyes darkened, reflecting her exhaustion. She was putting up a brave front. He could see the fear lurking behind her facade.

He merged the SUV into traffic a few moments later, disappearing onto Highway 75. "Why don't you put the seat back and rest?"

She eyed him warily. "How did you find this so easily?"

There was no use lying to her. "I have a record. Got into trouble as a kid. Had reasons to know how to lift a car quickly." He looked at her more intently, needing to know if his admission bothered her. "I did all that stuff a long time ago. I would never do it now. Hank helped me straighten up."

She didn't blink. "Seems like he also taught you some useful skills for staying alive."

"Any decent man would help a woman in this situation."

"Am I just any woman?"

Was she?

He wanted to continue to compare her to Cissy, the others, needing something to tamp down the out-of-control reaction his body was having. "I never said that."

"Never mind. You've been my knight in shining armor. Which falls into the 'any decent man' category." Her smile didn't reach her eyes.

He wanted to be more to her than "any decent man." But he couldn't ignore the realities. Katherine was a woman in trouble. Cissy had been in dire straits when she'd showed up at his door, too. She'd cried and begged him to help. He would've done anything to save that little girl of hers. Cissy hadn't needed to grovel. And yet, she'd begged to stay at the ranch. Said Savannah loved it out there. When he'd arranged all the doctor visits and taken over her medical care, Cissy had become even more attached.

She'd played a good hand. Turned on the tears when he hadn't immediately returned the sentiment.

Caleb had been convinced her feelings were real. Even though he'd believed getting involved would be a bad idea, she'd eventually worn him down. One thing was certain, he'd do it all again if it meant saving Savannah.

Did he have a deep-down need to save women?

He figured a shrink would have a field day with his psyche. They'd probably say he rescued women because he hadn't been able to save his mom. They'd be right about the last part. Caleb hadn't been able to stop the bastard who'd fathered him from hurting his mother. If Caleb had been older…gotten his bare hands around that man's neck… Caleb would have ripped the guy's head off.

He'd been too young. Too weak. The old man was bigger. Stronger.

Caleb saw too much of the jerk in himself when he looked into the mirror. Let the bastard show his face now. Why did they have to look so much alike?

He couldn't go back and change what made him the

man he was today any more than he could stop himself from doing what he thought was right.

Katherine's delicate hand on his arm redirected his attention.

Caleb couldn't ignore the bolt of heat shooting through him from where she touched. She stirred emotions he'd sworn not to feel again. And yet, how could he stop himself?

Cissy hadn't been gone long. She'd left a hole. Was he trying to fill it with Katherine?

"Where'd you go just now?"

"I'm right here."

"You're not getting off that easily, buster. You know all about my situation. Now it's your turn. Talk."

"You don't want to know what I was thinking."

Her violet eyes widened as she sat up. "Why not? Does it have to do with me?"

Katherine was brave and caring. Even when she was afraid, she faced it. She hadn't asked for his help. In fact, she'd been leery of accepting any aid. Every step of the way, she thought of others, not considering herself during this entire ordeal. When they were both hurt, she wanted to attend to his wounds first. The guilt she carried was a heavy weight on her back. She didn't use tears as a weapon. No, she refused to cry. She held everything on her shoulders and rarely let him in. When he really thought about it, the comparison to Cissy didn't hold water.

Katherine was nothing like Cissy.

He didn't have any plans to tell Katherine how much she occupied his thoughts.

"Maybe I should drive. You haven't slept in a couple of days now. All the adrenaline must be wearing off, too. I'm sure your body's as worn down as mine," she said.

"Probably more so since you haven't so much as closed your eyes since this whole ordeal started."

"I'm fine."

"Still, I'd feel much better if you got some rest. You have dark circles under your eyes. Let me take the wheel for a while."

"I appreciate your concern." She had no idea how much he meant those words.

The back of her hand came up to press against the stubble on his face. Desire pounded him, tensing his muscles and demanding release. A dull ache formed at his temples.

No way was he acting on it in the car.

Maybe soon…

"Besides, we have to ditch the sport utility," he said.

She moved to the backseat. He noticed her taut legs and sweet round behind as she climbed over.

"Here, the least I can do is rub your shoulders."

She worked his tense muscles. Having her hands on him created the opposite effect she desired. Instead of relaxing, his body went rigid. His need for her surged, causing his neck muscles to become more tense.

He glanced in the rearview mirror in time to see her frown.

"You're so tense. That can't be good."

A grin tugged at the corners of his mouth. She had no idea the effect she was having on him. "You touch me much more like that and I can't be held responsible for my actions."

Her eyes widened as reality dawned on her.

Was that a smile he just saw cross her features?

"I DIDN'T MEAN to create an issue for you," Katherine said, quashing the self-satisfied smirk trying to force its way to the surface. She enjoyed the fact a man so strong, so powerful, reacted so intensely to her lightest touch.

"Well you have," he said with a killer grin.

Damn he was sexy.

Katherine forced her gaze away from him and climbed into the front seat.

The sexually charged air hung thickly between them, sending her body to crackling embers. Had she ever felt this way for a man before?

No. Never.

And a tiny piece of her couldn't help but wonder if she'd ever feel this way again. Or if she'd live long enough to see where it could go. Noah. Baby. She prayed he had the life-saving medicine he needed by now.

"This looks like a good place to ditch the SUV," he said, pulling into a corn field.

"Then what?"

"We walk from here. Unless we get lucky and find an ATV."

About the last thing Katherine felt was lucky. "What are the chances of that happening?"

"Pretty good actually. When you know where to look." There came that devilish smile again.

It sent Katherine's heart pounding and her thighs burning to have him nestled against her. She sighed. More inappropriate thoughts. They were becoming more difficult to contain. Caleb was one powerful man. His presence had a way of electrifying her senses and causing her to want. She knew better. Her body wanted nothing more than to get into bed with him and allow his strong physical presence to cover her, warm her and protect her.

Her logical mind knew to rail against those primal feminine urges.

She opened the door, but Caleb was already there. He took Max, and let him run free.

"We'll be okay for a minute. Let me check that ankle before you try to walk on it."

He closed his hand around her ankle and she ignored the fires he lit there, focusing instead on the little dog.

Max piddled on a nearby cornstalk and scurried back to Caleb's feet.

Smart dog. He seemed to know on instinct who the alpha male was.

She took in a deep breath to clear her mind but only managed to breathe in his scent. He was outdoors and masculinity and sex personified. *Bad idea.*

Katherine gripped her purse. "How terrible is it?"

"Are you in pain?"

"A little." She blocked out the true wound. The cavern that couldn't be filled in her chest if anything happened to Noah…or if she couldn't be with Caleb. Her ankle was nothing in comparison to those hurts. "I'll be able to walk on it."

"It's pretty swollen. I'd hate to make it worse."

"Not much choice." She smiled. "We can't hide out in a cornfield forever."

"I was trying to decide if I should let you walk or carry you."

"Oh, don't do that." The very thought of his hands on her sent a sensual chill up her back. The feeling of his arms wrapped around her would be nice. No doubt about it. But if her body was pressed to his, he'd read every bit of physical reaction she had to him. That couldn't possibly help matters.

Katherine squared her shoulders. "No can do, captain. I'm ready and willing to walk the plank."

Her attempt at humor fell flat. *Can't blame a girl for*

trying. Where had that come from? She was becoming delirious. It would do her good to focus. Walking, painful as it would be, would also keep her on track and feeling alive.

Noah's kidnapping came crashing down on Katherine's thoughts.

I won't let you down, baby.

"You mind staying here while I look for transportation?" Caleb asked, breaking through.

"Not at all." She took out a bottle of water and sipped before pouring a little in her curled hand for Max. "Besides, I have company."

Max ignored the water and followed Caleb as he walked away, leaving the water to run off her palm.

Two-timing little puff ball.

Not that she could blame the dog, really. If she had a choice between being protected by her or Caleb, she'd choose the hunky guy with sex appeal to spare, too.

With Caleb by her side, they'd deflected bullets and escaped crazy killers, and yet he'd managed to keep them both alive. If she had money to put on a horse, that Thoroughbred would be named Caleb Snow.

Katherine opened her bag. The pic of Leann with baby Noah she'd taken from the apartment stared up at her. A lump formed in her throat, making it difficult to swallow. She wanted to cry. To feel the sweet release of tears. To liberate all the bottled-up feelings swelling in her chest and let everything go. Nothing came.

Katherine was the emotional equivalent of a drought.

CALEB'S LUCK IMPROVED considerably when he located the ATV at the edge of the field. He roared up with it, enjoying the feeling of making Katherine smile. She looked from Max to Caleb. The little dog had perched its front paws on the steering column and wagged his tail as soon as Katherine came into view.

What could Caleb say? The dog had good taste.

He helped her onto the back and secured her arms around his midsection.

Fifteen minutes into the ride, the ATV stalled. "Out of gas." Going on foot from here would frustrate anyone who was able to follow their tracks.

"Me, too," she said with a brilliant smile. The kind of smile that made a man think she possessed all the stars in the heavens and they reflected like stardust from her face. Wasn't like him to wax poetic.

He made a crutch for her out of a thick tree branch, urging her to put her weight on him as Max tagged along behind, keeping pace.

"Where are we headed?" Katherine asked as they pushed deeper into the woods.

"There's an old building at the back of my property. It's the original homestead. Not much more than a couple of rooms. Been empty for years. No one ever goes there. Hell, few people even know it exists it's so far to the edge of my property. I like it that way, too. I keep a few basic supplies, blankets and such, in the place in case I get out here riding fences and don't want to come back."

"What could you possibly have to hide from? The world? Why? You have a beautiful ranch. Your life looks perfect to me."

Not exactly. There was no one like her waiting for him when he came home every night.

His adrenaline had faded, and he was running out of juice. Especially with the way his mind kept wandering to thoughts of her. What he'd like to do to her.

The rest of the long walk was quiet.

Relief flooded him as the building came into view. A few more steps and he could get Katherine off her bad leg.

He opened the door, and put a thick blanket on top of the wood platform he'd frequently used as a bed. The place had gotten a fair amount of use when Cissy had left. Plenty of times, Caleb hadn't wanted to be inside the main house. She'd disappeared in such a hurry she hadn't packed. Her things were left in the bedroom. Savannah's toys littered the grounds. Reminders of his life with them had been everywhere. They'd been like land mines to Caleb. Each one had detonated a memory…brought out the hollow feeling in his chest. He hadn't been able to look at the color purple again without seeing Savannah's stuffed hippo. It went with her everywhere, tucked under her arm. When she'd watch TV, the hippo was her pillow.

"At least tell me why you have so many things out here. And I don't believe it's just in case you get restless. I'm sure there are plenty of places you could find to soothe yourself." Her violet eyes tore through him.

"My ex had a little girl. They both left. It broke my heart."

"I'm sorry. She wasn't yours?"

He shook his head, stuffing regret down somewhere deep. "No."

"What happened?"

"When they left, it felt like my heart had been ripped from my chest."

She covered his heart with her hand, connecting to the pain he felt.

"Thought I would suffocate inside the house for how empty it felt. Like the air was in a vacuum and I couldn't breathe."

"You must've loved her."

He nodded. "I'd take my horse, Dawn, out after supper.

At times, I couldn't bring myself to go back inside, so I would come here. Guess everyone worried. Matt followed me one night. Margaret probably made him. So, he knows about this place, too."

"Anyone else aware of this place?"

"Me and Matt. Now you."

He settled her onto the blanket and tended to her cuts. He didn't have ice in any of the supplies. There was no electricity at the place. But he'd bought a compression sock at the big-box store and that should help with the swelling. He slipped off her sandal and slid the sock around her foot and up her silky calf. "This should help."

He didn't immediately move his hand. It felt so natural to touch her.

Max circled around a few times before curling up in a ball next to Katherine.

"He lost a lot today. He's probably exhausted," she said.

"So are you." He patted the little puff ball's head.

"I can't help but worry about Noah. I'd close my eyes but I'm afraid of the images my mind will conjure up." The corners of her mouth turned down.

The picture of her when he'd first seen her, all chestnut hair and cherry lips, scared and alone, invaded his thoughts. Her misery was his. He wanted to kiss away her pain. Since he knew he'd never stop there, he went to the small kerosene stove instead and heated water. Margaret had slipped some herbal bags in with his supplies. More of her healing tea no doubt. Caleb was a coffee man, but he was glad for what she'd done. It might provide Katherine with the comfort she needed to relax.

"What's this?" she asked when he handed her a tin cup full of steaming brew.

"Margaret said something about it calming the mind."

"You didn't sleep much after your ex-girlfriend left, did you?" The question caught him off guard.

He shook his head. "I was in bad shape for a while."

He'd rebounded faster than he believed possible thanks to the love and support he received from his second family. Margaret and Matt had been beside him every step of the way until the pain had faded.

He could recall very little about Cissy in detail. He couldn't for the life of him remember what she smelled like, and yet the spring flower bouquet with a hint of vanilla, Katherine's scent, was etched in his memory. Vivid. If she disappeared right then and he never saw her again, he would remember how she smelled for the rest of his life. "I'm better now."

The sound of branches cracking stopped him.

Glancing around, he realized he had nothing to use as a weapon out there. He'd ditched his rifle long ago when he'd run out of ammunition at Katherine's house.

He moved to Katherine and covered her with his body, pulling dusty blankets on top of them to hide.

Even after the outside noise stopped, Caleb held his breath. Matt might have figured out the hint from their earlier phone call, and he could've brought the sheriff with him for all his good intentions. Or it could be an animal.

Katherine lay beneath him, her soft warm body rising and falling with every breath she took, pressing against him. The memory of the way they'd met etched in his thoughts. The way her body felt underneath him. A perfect fit. Her face was so close; he wouldn't have to move far to skim his lips across her jawline, or the base of her throat where he could see her pulse throb. It wouldn't take much movement to lift his chin and kiss her. But he realized he wanted so much more than her kiss.

More than her body.

He wanted all of her. Mind. Body. Soul—if there was such a thing.

Before any of that could happen, he wanted to be able to trust her.

He needed to know that if he opened his heart, she wouldn't stamp her heels all over it and walk away.

The tricky part? To find out, he had to go out on a limb and give the very thing he avoided…trust. Both his father and Cissy had done a number on him in that department. Since history was the best predictor of the future, believing in someone again felt about as easy as skinning a live rattlesnake with a hairbrush.

He wished like hell he'd told Katherine how he'd felt about her when he'd had the chance.

If he could get beyond the pain of his past, could he have a real future with her?

Or would she leave just like the others?

Chapter Eleven

The door to the homestead creaked open slowly. "Caleb, you in here?"

Caleb recognized Matt's voice immediately. He threw the covers off and stood. "Come inside and shut the door."

Worry lines bracketed his friend's mouth. "Damn, I've been worried."

Relief eased Caleb's tense muscles. "I didn't think you'd caught on to my hint on the phone."

"It took me a while. Then it finally clicked."

Caleb helped Katherine into a comfortable sitting position, elevating her swollen ankle. He turned to Matt. "What's going on?"

"You tell me. People are coming out of the woodwork looking for you. Margaret's beside herself with worry."

"No doubt they've been expecting me to come home." Matt nodded.

"What kind of people have been showing up?"

"The marshal for one. He's been checking in every few hours. I didn't tell him you'd made contact, but he seems to know."

"The line must be tapped."

"I guessed as much."

"Speaking of which, you didn't bring your phone with you, did you?"

Matt shook his head. "Figured if they could get to one, they could get to another. Left it in the barn just in case. Sneaked out the back."

"Good thinking. Kane's men followed our movements with the ones we had. I had to ditch them."

"No wonder I kept rolling into voice mail every time I called."

"Who else has been by the ranch?"

"The men in suits have stopped by several times." His lips formed a grim line. "They're staying in town at the Dovetail Inn."

"Did you tell the marshal about them?"

Matt nodded. "He said to ignore them. Truth is I don't know what or who to believe anymore." His gaze traveled from Caleb to Katherine.

"I do," Caleb said firmly. He sensed this whole ordeal would be coming to a head soon, and a big piece of him dreaded the day he would part company with Katherine. It was selfish. He should want everything to be behind them and for normal life to return. Except that she'd imprinted him in ways he could never have imagined a woman could. Being forced to live without her sounded worse than a death sentence. His heart said she wouldn't walk out, but logic forced him to look at his history.

Then again, if the men with guns had their way, he might not live long enough to miss her. And he would. From somewhere deep inside where a little bit of light still lived within him.

"Either way, I can connect with the marshal if you want to go into the program we talked about." Matt shot another weary glance toward Katherine.

Her chin came up proudly, but to her credit she didn't say anything.

She was strong and bold. Another reason Caleb's argument she was just like Cissy didn't hold up. Damn she was sexy, beautiful and strong. Made him want to kick Matt out and do things to her that would remind her she was all woman and not some errant fugitive destined to die by the hands of some criminal jerk.

"They'll have to take me out of here in a box. I have no plans to leave my ranch again." Closure was coming, one way or another, and Caleb regretted the second he realized it also meant their time together would come to an end. He silently pledged to show her just how appealing she was before that happened. "I won't run anymore."

"Is that such a good idea?" Matt's chin jutted out, and he blew out a breath.

Caleb shrugged. "This is my home."

"I can go. I'll draw them away from you," Katherine said, seeming resigned to her fate.

He was touched but not surprised she'd be willing to put herself in more danger for him. Her current situation had come about because she would give her life to protect her nephew. Yet another difference between her and Cissy. Cissy had only thought about herself.

"I don't mean any disrespect, but she brings up a good point. Maybe if she leaves…"

"It won't matter. I'm still a person of interest in a murder, remember?"

"How could I forget?" Matt said with a disgusted grunt. His gaze intensified on Katherine.

"Enough," Caleb barked to his friend. Frustration was getting the best of him. "Did you have a chance to follow up on the mission we discussed?"

"I did." His face muscles pulled taut. "I called the manager, and asked if I could email him a picture of someone I was looking for. I sent him a photo of Kane from a news article I found. He recognized him right away. Said he came in the coffee shop all the time. Or used to when Leann worked there before the accident."

"I wonder why a man like him would get involved with my sister."

"I already know. The manager put one of her coworkers on the line. She was chatty. Said she and Leann used to go climbing together sometimes. She was with her the day of her accident at Enchanted Rock. They all stood by helplessly when she lost her grip and tumbled...."

Matt fixed his gaze on the floor a second before continuing. "The woman said Leann practically dropped out of sight when her old boyfriend showed up a few months ago."

Katherine gasped. "They dated?"

Caleb closed his hand around hers, looping their fingers together, and offering reassurance so she could hear more. She rewarded him with a weak smile.

"Said they were like two lovebirds. He'd visit her at the coffee shop and drop off presents, flowers." Matt looked from Katherine to Caleb and back. "She also said he's Noah's dad."

Katherine's fingers went limp.

"No," came out on a whisper. "Can't be."

"If it's true, if Kane's the father, then Noah's safe," Caleb reassured her.

"But he's a monster. Who knows what he's truly capable of?"

"His company ranks are filled with relatives. I read somewhere that he's devoted to family. Noah's his only child. He'd want to keep him close, but he wouldn't hurt his own son."

"No. He'd just use him as a weapon against me." She released a pained sob but gathered herself quickly.

"This is a game changer. Explains why they didn't kill Noah when they didn't get the file." Anger pierced Caleb for not being able to shield her from pain. "The coworker said she was there that day?"

Matt nodded.

"Then we know it was an accident at least." He turned to Matt. "Wait for me outside?"

"Okay."

He settled Katherine onto the makeshift bed and pressed kisses to her forehead, her eyelids, her chin. He held back the new thought plaguing him. That Kane would realize she would never be able to produce the file, and kill her.

"I'll check the area as Matt leaves. Make sure no one followed him."

Katherine's chest rose on harsh breaths. She nodded.

"I want to give him the CD. See if he can find anything. What do you think?"

Those tormented violet eyes looked up at him. She hesitated. "If you trust him, then I agree."

"Good. Try to get some rest. I'll be right back."

She gazed up at him, confused, tired. "He can't be the father. I'll never see Noah again."

"Don't be afraid. When you close your eyes, I want you to picture me. I'll protect you." She couldn't possibly know just how much he meant those words.

Caleb met his friend on the porch and closed the door. "We need to come up with a plan. But first, we've had a long couple of days, and we need rest."

"It'll be dark soon. You should be all right for tonight. They will figure out where you are eventually. And they'll come with guns blazing. Make no mistake about it," Matt said.

"I know."

"Then what's the game plan? How do you expect to get out of this alive?"

He could see that his friend was coming from a place

of caring. "We'll be ready for them. Tomorrow morning, I want you to tell the men to stay away. Margaret, too. Tell them not to come back to work for a few days. That should give us enough time to handle things. Also, I want to meet with the marshal. First thing before daylight." Caleb held out the CD. "And take a look at this. See if you can find a hidden file, or anything that seems suspicious."

Matt took it and studied the cover for a minute. "What has that woman gotten you into?"

"She didn't." Caleb's jaw muscle tensed. Friend or not, Matt had crossed the line. "Look. My eyes were wide open when I decided to help her. You need to know I plan to see this through no matter what."

"Why? What is she to you?"

"You don't get it." He didn't have a real answer to that question so he said goodbye, checking to make sure no one was in the woods lurking, waiting to make a move. "Keep things quiet tonight. Set up the meeting in the tack room."

Matt agreed before disappearing into the thicket.

Caleb moved inside to find Katherine awake, eyes wide open.

"What did you mean when you said you wouldn't leave the ranch again?"

"Did you get enough to eat? I can open and heat a can of soup." He changed the subject as he lit a Coleman lantern, allowing the soft flame to illuminate the room as the sun retreated, casting a dark shadow to fill the room.

"I'm fine. But you're not thinking straight. I won't let you risk your life for me anymore."

"We going down that path again?" What Matt said must've hurt her feelings. "Matt means well. He doesn't know what he's saying."

"I agree with him. They'll go easy on you. I'll tell everyone I shot Ms. Ranker if I have to." Desperation had the muscles in her face rigid as she stood in front of him, moving closer. A red heat climbed up her neck.

"I can't let you lie." He smiled. "Besides, you're no good at it. And the evidence will clear us."

Defiance shot from her glare. Her stubborn streak reared its head again. "You don't get to decide."

Her gaze was fiery hot. Her body vibrated with intensity as she stalked toward him.

He readied himself for the argument that was sure to come, but she pressed a kiss to his lips instead, shocking the hell out of him. More than his spirits rose.

"There's been enough fighting for one day. I need something else from you."

He locked on to her gaze. "Are you sure this is a good idea?"

"No. Not at all. But I need to do it anyway. I want you. I've never wanted a man more. Do you want me?" She tiptoed up and wrapped her arms around his neck. Her eyes darkened, and she was sexy as hell, gazing up at him. A tear fell onto her cheek.

He kissed it away.

"Sorry. I can't remember the last time I cried."

"Don't be." Caleb knew all about holding in emotion. The way it ate at a person's gut until it felt as though there was no stomach lining left. He dropped his other hand to the small of her back. "There's nothing to be ashamed of."

"I'm being stupid. How could anyone want someone who practically cries all over them?"

"I think it's sweet." Rocking his hips, he pressed his erection against her midsection as he cupped her left breast. Heat shot through his body. "This give you any clue as to the question of whether or not I want you?"

Her face lit up with eagerness, and it nearly did him in. "I need to forget about the danger we're in and the fact

Noah's been kidnapped, just for a little while." She snuggled against him, shifting her stance to wrap her arms around his waist.

Her sensuality was going to his head faster than a shot of hard liquor. "Hold on there."

"What? You don't think this is a good idea?"

"No. It's been a while for me. And I want this to last."

"Either way there's far too much material between us," she said, stepping back long enough to shrug out of her shirt.

Sight of the delicately laced bra she wore caused a painful spasm in his groin. The light color an interesting contrast to her golden skin.

A second later her shorts fell to the ground, revealing matching cotton panties. The panties he'd picked out for her. Pink.

She stood there, arms at her sides, allowing him a minute to really look at her. "Do you still want me?"

He swallowed a groan. "You're beautiful. You're also determined to end this before it gets started."

"Not exactly. I want long and slow." She unhooked her bra and let it drop before shimmying out of her panties.

Caleb ate up the space between them in one quick stride. His thumb grazed her nipple. It pebbled under his touch and a blast of heat strained his erection. His body needed release. He needed to be inside her where she was warm and wet, moving in rhythm with him until they both exploded and she lay melted in his arms. He needed Katherine.

"You want help with those?" She motioned toward his T-shirt and jeans with a teasing smile that stirred his heart.

His shirt came off in one quick motion and joined her clothing on the floor. She didn't wait for him to unzip his jeans, she was already there, her hands on his zip-

per. He aided her in their quick removal along with his
boxer shorts.

Her eyes widened when they stopped on his full erection. "I want to feel you inside me."

Caleb nearly lost control right there. He needed to think
about something else besides the way her honeyed skin
would feel wrapped around him. His passion for her hit
heights he'd never known with a woman, and he hadn't
even entered her yet.

He picked her up and placed her on the bed before re-
trieving a condom from his wallet. His hands shook as he
attempted to sheath himself.

"Here. Let me." She placed it on his tip and rolled her
hand down the shaft.

His muscles went so rigid he felt like an overstrung
cello. "You're sexy...and beautiful."

She lay back, watching him. "Then make love to me."

Her thighs parted and he positioned himself in the V. In
one thrust, he drove inside her warmth. She was so wet,
he nearly exploded. Her body fit him perfectly.

"More," she said through a ragged breath. She gripped
his shoulders.

He wanted to make her scream his name a thousand
times as he rocketed her toward the ultimate release.

He tensed and struggled to maintain self-control. Not
what he was used to. "Not if you want this to last any longer."

He commanded his hips not to move as she traced her
fingers down his arms, then onto his back. Her hands
came up and anchored on his shoulders as he lowered
his mouth over hers, marking her as his. Her silken lips
parted, and his tongue drove into her mouth, tasting her
honeylike sweetness.

Her fingers skimmed along his spine, setting little fires

everywhere she touched. His skin burned with desire only she could release.

Caleb kissed her hard, claiming her mouth as her tongue moved with his. He lightened the kiss softly, allowing her to be in control and to take whatever she needed from him.

In that moment he belonged to her completely, and for as long as she needed him.

And what did he need?

Every needy grasp of her fingertips…every possessive fleck of her tongue…every blast of heat she sent firing through him….

All of her.

She was every bit the woman capable of unleashing his tightly gripped emotions and sending him soaring.

Her tongue delved into his mouth as her fingernails gripped his bottom and he shuddered inside her.

Tremors moved up and down his spine as he pumped her silky heat.

"Caleb," she breathed his name.

He pressed his mouth to the soft curve of her right breast, taking her pointed peak inside his mouth. Her moan was like pouring gasoline on the fire inside him.

He pumped harder as his own desire blazed through his veins.

Hold on…not yet…

He wanted her to explode in his arms into a thousand fragments of light.

He covered her lips, swallowing her next moan and delved his tongue as he bucked his hips.

"Oh, Caleb…"

She tensed her muscles around his erection, and he could feel her nearing the edge.

He pumped faster…harder…deeper…needing to find

her core and tantalize her until the mounting fire inside her detonated.

He teased her nipple between his thumb and forefinger, causing her back to arch. Her chestnut hair blazed across the pillow, her body moved in rhythm with his. Her hips wriggled him deeper inside until he thought he might lose all control. She was on the edge, and he felt it.

Her muscles convulsed, and he thrust deeper, again and again, until he felt her completely come undone in his arms. Only then did he allow himself to think about his own release.

Her tight muscles squeezed around his erection and his body reacted, shivering and quaking. In a sensual burst, he let go. Thundered.

In that instant, there was no Caleb or Katherine. They existed together…as the same person…in one body….

She felt so right in his arms. Would she stay?

Until tomorrow, a little voice said.

Pain gripped him. He couldn't contain his growing feelings for her. This would be over soon. She would be gone. He most likely would never see her again.

Chapter Twelve

The now familiar sounds of the woods, crickets chirping and insects' wings buzzing, broke through the silence in the room. Katherine's sensitized body tingled as Caleb's warm breath moved across her skin. He'd pulled her in tight against him.

Her rapid breathing eventually eased, becoming slow and steady as it found an even tempo. Her heart beat in perfect harmony with his. Everything about the two of them fit together so perfectly. It was so easy to be with Caleb. Being naked with him felt like the most natural thing in the world. She had no insecurities about her body as she lay there. They were like links in a fence, their bond strengthening the whole.

A dumbstruck thought hit her. Their feelings didn't matter anymore. She had Noah to think about. Or did she? She had no idea if he was hurt, or worse. Did Kane even bother to pick up Noah's medication at the drop spot earlier? Would he keep the boy around if he wasn't useful anymore? Logic told her he would, but her heart feared the worst anyway.

If they did survive this nightmare, would she ever see her nephew again? Wouldn't a father trump an aunt? A rich man like Kane could pull strings to ensure she never saw her Noah again.

She recalled the emotions that had drilled through her when she'd found out she'd be responsible for her baby sister. Jealousy. Bitterness. Resentment. They were not the feelings she had about caring for Noah, but she'd known exactly what she was getting into with him. She was older. Ready.

Even though Caleb would never admit it, he would resent her for strapping him down with a ready-made family. If she survived, all her energy had to go toward getting Noah away from Kane.

"Are you sorry?" He broke through her train of thought.

"No. Not for making love. I figured we had to put this attraction behind us so both of us could concentrate. We'll need all our wits about us tomorrow. It was difficult for either one of us to think clearly before."

"And now?" He eyed her suspiciously.

"Everything's crystal clear."

A dark brow lifted. He propped himself up on one elbow. His muscular body glowed in the soft light.

A well of need sprung up inside Katherine so fast and so desperately she had to take a second to catch her breath and allow her pulse to return to normal—whatever "normal" was anymore.

"And what does that mean exactly?" he asked, eyeing her intently.

"It's highly improbable that all three of us will come out of this alive. If what you said about Kane is true, then at least Noah will be safe." If she and Caleb did survive, could they become a family? He'd spoken so fondly of Savannah, could he grow to accept Noah, too? No. Caleb loved Savannah because he loved her mother. He didn't have those feelings for Katherine. Did he?

Her mind was really playing tricks on her. No way could he have fallen in love with her in such a short time. As much as she'd like to believe the possibility, her practical mind brought her back to reality. They'd been running for their lives. Dodging bullets. They'd narrowly escaped death. He'd been her knight in shining armor, showing up at a time when she needed him most. Of course she had strong feelings for her cowboy. But she shouldn't confuse gratitude for keeping her alive with real affection.

"If I have anything to say about it we will." The way he set his jaw said he meant every word, too.

Even a superhero had a weakness. What was the chink in Caleb's veneer?

Women in trouble.

She needed him, just as Cissy had.

Maybe that was the connection.

Katherine shut the thoughts out of her mind. She didn't want to compare what she and Caleb had with his relationship to the other woman. She didn't even want to think about him with another woman.

"What's the plan?" she asked, trying to redirect her internal conversation.

"Our best bet is to make contact with the marshal."

"Why do you think we can trust him?"

He shrugged. "A hunch."

"Why not contact the sheriff?"

"He'll probably put me in jail."

She gasped. "Surely he doesn't believe you had anything to do with the murder."

"Knowing Coleman, he'd detain me to keep me safe until this whole thing blows over."

"You think there's a chance this'll just go away?" Unrealistic hope flickered inside her and then vanished.

"No. I think they'll keep coming until we're both dead."

"Then we should leave. Hide. I'll go with you."

His dark brow arched. "Would you?"

"If it meant you'd be safe."

"And then as soon as I turned my back you'd disappear and try to protect Noah. You're always looking out for those around you, but who looks out for you?"

A tear welled in her eye. "I don't need anyone."

He grunted. "Like hell you don't. I never met anyone who needed people more."

Like Cissy?

Why did the admission hurt so much?

His reasons for helping her were becoming transparent. "Does your cowboy code force you to save all damsels in distress?"

His jaw muscles pulsed and his gaze narrowed. Anger radiated from him. "Being with you has nothing to do with obligation."

"Then what?" She hated feeling so insecure and so vulnerable. Maybe that's why she'd spent so much time blocking out the world? Considering Caleb was about the only true friend she had and they'd just met. She'd been doing a great job of keeping people away to date. Didn't everyone let her down eventually?

He didn't immediately answer.

"I was doing fine by myself before you came along," she lied. She told herself if she could close her eyes, she might even be able to rest.

He pressed a kiss to her forehead. "I know you were. But I wasn't. And I don't know what I'd do without you here."

The thin layer of ice protecting her heart from being broken melted. "We might never know why he's after us." She fell silent. The rock of dread positioned on her chest grew heavier. Her chest walls felt as though they were caving in...as if she was drowning and couldn't get air into her lungs. Leann's secret was a boulder tied around Katherine's neck as she catapulted to the ocean floor.

"Maybe Matt will see something on the CD we over-looked. We didn't exactly have time to dig around on it before they caught up to us," Caleb offered.

"You're sure we can trust him?"

"I'd put my life in his hands."

He just did. And hers, too. Matt didn't hide the fact he didn't have the same dedication to Katherine that he did to Caleb. At least she knew exactly where she stood with him. "He doesn't think you should be around me."

"Just proves he doesn't know what's best for me."

"I can't see a way out of this. Even if you talk to the marshal, you're taking a risk. He might be on Kane's pay-roll. How can we know he'll be of assistance to us?"

Caleb shrugged his shoulders. The light from the lan-tern made his face look even more handsome. "Don't see another choice."

"Me, either. You're right. We need help from someone."

"I can leave before the sun comes up to get Matt. I'll be back before the first light with a few answers. For now, I'd like to try to sleep. Unless you can think of something better to do." He quirked a devastating grin.

One look was all it took for him to stir her sexually. "As a matter of fact, I can. And I think we make love quite well."

"All the more reason for us to keep doing it," he said with one of his trademark looks.

"Unless you're too tired." She repositioned herself bet-ter to kiss him, enjoying the feel of the perfect fit of their naked bodies. His was like pure silk over finely tuned muscle.

"Are you doubting me?"

She kissed his collarbone. "That wouldn't be a wise move on my part. I've seen your stamina. But even you have to sleep sometime."

"After a while," he said, pressing his erection to her thigh. "Right now, I have something else demanding attention."

This time, their lovemaking was slow and tender. Did they both realize each moment together was a precious gift to be savored and enjoyed?

CALEB ROSE BEFORE the sun and heated water for coffee while Katherine slept. He'd had to force himself away from her to get out of bed. Every bone in his body wanted to curl up with her, hold her. He hadn't wanted to leave a second before he had to. He'd managed a few hours of shut-eye, thanks to her being by his side.

He'd expected coming back to the homestead would evoke a hailstorm of bad memories. It didn't.

Katherine had chased away those demons for him, he thought while he let Max outside to take care of his business.

Caleb kept the door cracked open as he opened a can of beef stew and heated it for the pint-size critter. The little guy had been too stressed to eat last night. He'd curled in the corner and slept until he heard Caleb stir. His little ears had perked up and he'd whined until Caleb went to get him.

Time seemed to drip by as Caleb glanced at his watch for the third time in five minutes. Matt was supposed to meet him in the tack room, providing it was safe. He'd been tasked with making contact with the marshal, and trying to figure out what Caleb had missed on the CD.

The unanswered questions in this case weren't helping matters. If he knew what information Kane was looking for, he could provide a better bluff.

One wrong move and boom.

Caleb had not expected to let himself get involved with another woman so quickly. Hell, he was beginning to doubt if he'd ever find true love. What he'd had with Cissy couldn't be classified as such. Real love meant putting others before yourself.

He'd told himself his entire life he hadn't gotten involved with a woman because of his devotion to making a success out of his life.

Was it?

He'd almost made a full-time job of avoiding relationships, hadn't he?

And how much of it had to do with your screwed-up childhood?

In trying to avoid being like his father, had he closed the door to finding anything real in his life?

He'd told himself he didn't have time for women, that all he could afford to focus on was work in order to have a better life. Money didn't buy happiness, but being poor didn't, either. He'd had a ringside seat to that show throughout his childhood.

If his mother could have afforded insurance, she would have been able to take better care of herself.

If his old man had stuck around, she wouldn't have had to be the sole provider.

If they'd had more money, she wouldn't have had to work so hard.

If. If. If.

Was he the one to blame for his relationships not working out? For Cissy? He could tell himself she'd used him till the cows came home, but had he given her anything to hang on to?

He had his doubts.

All his heartache, all his loving memories, had little to do with her and everything to do with the thought of having a real family. His heart ached for the idea of a family, not his ex-girlfriend. And why didn't he really miss her?

Or any of the other dozen women he'd spent time with in the past?

Is it because they weren't Katherine Harper? asked a quiet voice from the back of his mind.

Whether he wanted to acknowledge it or not, if anything happened to her, he would never be the same again.

Chapter Thirteen

Katherine couldn't remember the last time she'd slept so deeply. Dangerous under the circumstances. Caleb's outdoorsy and masculine scent was all over her...the sheets... bringing out a sensual daydream.

She got out of bed, needing to leave this room, this place, as fast as she could. She felt stifled being on his property, in his homestead with reminders of him everywhere, knowing it wouldn't last.

Her ankle tolerated some weight as she hobbled into the makeshift kitchen trying not to think about Caleb's absence.

The possibility he might not come back crossed her mind. Then what?

They hadn't discussed a contingency plan for that.

Katherine struck the thought from her mind. Caleb would return. They would figure out an arrangement. Somehow, some way, they would find a way out of this mess.

She thought about Leann, wondering if her sister had believed the same thing when she'd decided to take these men on by herself.

What file did Leann have that would make Kane turn on her family?

Did she have any idea what she was up against?

Did Katherine?

Kane's twenty-four-hour deadline to produce the file had come and gone. His men were out there, searching for her, ready and waiting. Something told her they'd never give up until she was dead, file or not.

Caleb was out there somewhere, too, putting himself in harm's way for her again. He'd promised to be back before she woke, before sunrise, and yet the sun was blazing in the east. A little piece of her heart died at the thought of anything happening to him.

She stopped at the door and her gaze went to the bed. They'd made love right there last night again and again until their bodies were zapped of strength and they gave in to sleep.

Being near him had made her feel more connected to him than anyone else on the planet. They'd made love intensely, sweetly, passionately, until their bodies became entwined and she could no longer tell where he stopped and she began.

They became one body, one being.

The idea of losing him, losing one more person she loved, was worse than a dagger through the chest.

She sat on the floor, stroking Max's neck absently. The strong coffee revived her. She redressed the wounds on her leg. Some of the gashes were deeper than others but they all looked to be healing rather quickly given the circumstances. The swelling was going down on her ankle. A few more days of rest and she'd be all better.

The external wounds would heal. As for the internal damage, that would depend on how the events of the day progressed.

She sighed deeply. Where was Caleb?

CALEB DIDN'T LIKE the idea of leaving Katherine alone all morning. Matt had been late and that had pushed back the whole morning's timeline.

During the meeting, all Caleb's danger radar fired on high alert. He couldn't figure out if it was because of the marshal or because he'd left Katherine alone in the homestead unguarded.

The meeting with the marshal ran over and Caleb's pulse hammered every extra second he was there. This whole scenario could be a scam to get Katherine alone. That's exactly what the marshal would do if he was on Kane's payroll.

Matt hadn't found any secret files, either, not that he was a computer guru. Caleb needed to talk to Katherine about handing it over to the marshal. The government would have the necessary resources available to uncover anything on the CD. Problem was, they'd have to be able to trust the Feds first. If there was a leak in the department, turning over evidence could be more than a huge mistake. It could be a fatal one.

The idea burned Caleb's gut. He couldn't decide if he wanted to put these guys behind bars or take them out himself. The idea they would threaten an innocent child to get to Katherine fired instant rage in his belly.

There were too many "ifs" to feel good about a decision one way or the other.

He wouldn't make a call without filling her in first.

Climbing onto the porch step, the knot in his gut tightened. Maybe he should've taken her with him and stashed her somewhere close by during the meeting.

No. She was safest right where she was and a part of him knew it. Damn that he was second-guessing himself.

Maybe it was because of the news he had to deliver. Or that a little voice kept reminding him she would leave him. If not now, then later.

Relief hit him faster than a rain shower in a drought

when he stepped inside and saw her on the floor playing with Max.

Her eyes were wide. "Thank God. You're all right."

He moved to her and pressed kisses to her temples. "Matt was late. He thought someone might be following him. I'm sorry you were worried."

"How'd it go?"

"He didn't find anything on the CD. The marshal might be able to if we give him access."

She moved to the counter and then handed him a tin cup filled with coffee. "I can't decide. What's your first instinct?"

"The government can hack into just about anything." He took the disk from his pocket and held it out between them. "If we can trust the bastards, they'll find what we're looking for."

She palmed it. "What if there's nothing on it?"

"We'll have to cross that bridge when we come to it." He paused a beat. "Even if there's enough evidence on this to lock him away forever, there's something else you should know."

Her violet eyes were enormous. "You're scaring me."

"The marshal said Kane has most likely left the United States."

She sat there, looking dumbfounded. "How can that be?"

"It's believed he has a compound across the border in Mexico. The marshal is working on a few leads, gathering more intel."

"What's the use of turning over the CD when everyone, including me, will be dead before they capture him?"

Not if Caleb had anything to say about it. "I know how hopeless this feels."

"Why does he even need the file when he can disappear out of the country with Noah?" She stared blankly at the door. "And I suppose we're just supposed to let the government take its sweet time finding Kane? Meanwhile, he has an assault squad on us."

"They've offered protection."

She blew out a breath. "Like that would do any good. They'd find us eventually."

"Maybe not."

Silence sat between them for a long beat. "I would never see Noah again."

"That's not going to happen."

"Did he say what Kane is after?"

"Said Leann has evidence linking him to a crime."

"I know I haven't painted a great picture of my sister. But she was a good person. I can't imagine why she would get involved with a man like that."

"The marshal said she didn't know. She was young when they met. He swept her off her feet. Spent lots of money on her. He was a successful businessman. Everything looked legit. By the time she figured out his dark side, she was pregnant. She disappeared and had her baby. Never planned to tell him he was the father. Kept the evidence of his crime stashed away just in case he showed up again. And then, one day, he walked into the coffee shop. There she was. She pretended that she missed him and secretly got in touch with the Feds. She was planning to turn state's evidence to keep him away from Noah."

"Explains why she moved around so much before. With Noah getting close to school age, she wanted to put down roots. Do they know what evidence she had against him?"

"She offered to provide pictures to back up her testimony." He issued a grunt. "I think you should take the deal. Let them tuck you away somewhere safe."

"They'll kill Noah."

"Kane won't hurt his son."

"How am I supposed to do that?" Her response was rapid, shooting flames of accusation.

"It'll keep you alive until they can find Kane and Noah."

"And then what? Live out the rest of my life in fear? Alone? Waiting for him to finally figure out where I am? He won't stop until he finds me. I don't know where the picture is. I can't put him away without it. If this guy is as ruthless as they say, Kane won't let up until I'm dead."

She had a good point and Caleb knew it. "It's just an option."

"And what about you, Caleb? Where will you go?"

"I already said it once. I won't leave my ranch."

An incredulous look crossed her features. "They'll find you and kill you. They won't even have to look far."

"I'll be fine. You're not thinking straight."

"Oh, so what am I now? A crazy lunatic? Can you look me in the eyes and tell me I'm wrong?"

He lowered his gaze. "No."

"What's your plan?"

"I'm going to stay and fight. No matter how many men they send, I'll return them in body bags if I have to," he said, determination welling in his chest.

"I shouldn't have to run and hide. I didn't do anything wrong," she said, pacing.

"They'll use Noah as bait to get to you. And you to get to me. You know that, right?"

"Let them. It's obvious they won't let up until I'm dead or Kane's locked away. I may not be able to change the cards I was dealt, but I can decide how to play them."

Her stubborn streak was infuriating. And damn sexy.

"I hear what you're saying, but if anything happens to you, it's game over. At least with you alive, we have cards left to play. He will have a lingering doubt about the file.

He'll have no choice but to hide." Couldn't she see he was trying to save her? Why did she have to be so stubborn?

You'd be the same way, a distant voice said.

Her chin jutted out. "I thought last night meant something. Why would you want me to disappear from your life forever?"

With every part of him, he didn't. But he'd say anything if it meant keeping her safe. "We got caught up in the moment. I think you should go." Damn but it nearly killed him to say those words.

The pure look of hurt in her eyes nearly made him take it back. He couldn't. He wouldn't let her stick around because of him. He told himself she'd be safer in custody.

"Then I will leave. But I'll be damned if you get to tell me where I'll go." Her lips quivered but she didn't cry.

He'd seen that same look of bravery on her how many times now and it still had the same effect on him.

She grabbed her bag and made a start for the door.

Caleb stepped in front of her, blocking passage. "Where exactly are you going?"

"I don't know and you shouldn't care." Katherine was a study in determination.

KATHERINE'S HEART HAD been ripped from her chest. She knew whatever she and Caleb had couldn't last, and yet his words harpooned her. "Get out of my way, I have something to do."

"I shouldn't have pushed you away. I'm sorry. I only said those things because I thought they might influence you to go into protective custody. I didn't mean a word of it. It's killing me that I can't protect you."

Was he lying then or now?

Katherine had no idea. Everything in her heart wanted to believe this was the truth. That whatever they had between them was genuine and real. The physical attraction had to be, she reasoned. No one could fake what had happened between them last night that convincingly. The sex had been complete rapture. No other man had made her feel like that—sexy, beautiful, devoured. He'd drank in every last inch of her and come back for more. Everything about the night was still vivid in her mind. His gorgeous body, bathed in moonlight and the soft glow of the lantern. His cinnamon taste that was still on her lips.

When he'd entered her, she'd felt on top of the world, as though she was soaring above the earth and didn't need air to breathe. She'd felt more alive in that moment than she had her entire life.

Then again, maybe it was purely physical for him.

Sex for sex's sake.

Didn't men view intimacy differently than women?

Maybe the whole experience was food for his sexual appetite. A man like Caleb was surely used to having his way with women. One look at him, his honey-gold skin and brown eyes with their gold flecks, would stir any woman who could see.

The sex had probably been far more special to her than him. Or maybe she refused to acknowledge the possibility he'd love her and could accept her nephew as his own someday. And she would get Noah back.

"I'd like you to move," she said, tears welling in her eyes.

He didn't budge. Instead he stared at her incredulously.

"Now." How dare he? Hadn't he just told her she meant nothing to him? And now he had the audacity to pretend to care.

"I'm not going anywhere until you believe me."

"Then we'll be here all day."

"I can think of a good way to spend 'all day' here."

He got that mischievous look in his eye. The reminder he knew how to take what he wanted.

Katherine's thin veneer was cracking. She folded her arms. "Let me go."

"What's the matter? Afraid you'll run out of excuses to push me away?" He broadened his stance and quirked a devastating smile.

Damn. He knew he was getting to her.

Her hands came up to his chest again to push him away, but he stepped toward her and she ended up gripping his shoulders to steady herself from the physical force that was all Caleb.

Tension crackled in the air between them as he stared at her, his gaze filled with desire. He leaned down and kissed her so tenderly it robbed her ability to breathe.

"I'm sorry I said those things to you. I was a jerk."

The crack expanded like ice defrosting.

"Yes. You were." She leaned into his broad chest.

"Can you forgive me?"

Katherine was startled to realize there wasn't much he could do she wouldn't forgive.

Not that it mattered. Pretty soon, she'd be exactly where Kane wanted her.

Chapter Fourteen

"We need to make contact with Marshal Jones. See if we have anything to work with here." Caleb pointed to the CD.

"How do we do that?"

"Jones gave me this." Caleb pulled a cell from his pocket and held it out. "It's secure."

"Must be. No one has showed up with a gun," she said.

He opened the contacts, touched the name Marshal Jones and then the call button. "Katherine is willing to turn over the CD we discussed," Caleb said, a little weary they were about to hand over their best and only playing card. "But I need some reassurances."

"I'll go with an outside guy to examine it. No one else will see it," Jones said, answering the unasked question.

"I like where you're headed. Go on."

"Served with him in Iraq. He was dishonorably discharged when he punched his sergeant for his stupidity. Let's just say there's no love lost between this guy and the government."

That's exactly what Caleb wanted to hear. "Then he sounds perfect for the job."

"He will be. If there's anything on the CD, you'll know it. We'll catch up to Kane eventually. And we'll have the evidence ready when we do."

Caleb caught Katherine flexing her hands. Was she trying to stop them from shaking? Was she still angry about his harsh words?

He picked up Max and pointed to a wooden chair. When she sat, he handed her the little mutt. The best way to lower her blood pressure was to get her interacting with the dog. It might distract her enough to calm her down. Give her time to think through his actions—actions that would convince her his feelings were real.

"And until then?"

"We need to keep searching. He'll make a mistake, and we'll be there to catch him. He'll know anything we do is most likely a trap. He could just send his minions to do his dirty work, and I can't guarantee anyone's safety if you're not in custody," Jones said.

Caleb walked outside onto the porch. "He'll come for us. This is personal. He'd never planned to hurt his own son. It's always been about taking back evidence and silencing Katherine."

"You may be right. Don't take any chances. I can order extra security."

"Matt will insist on helping, too."

"I don't want to risk any more civilian lives, but I won't stop you. I'll speak to Sheriff Coleman, too. He might be able to provide some assistance. We'll cover all the bases we can," Jones said ominously.

"I feel a lot more comfortable with the odds of keeping her safe at the ranch. It's better than being out there where anything can happen. I can control who has access to the main house. I'll take her there as soon as it's dark. Don't want to move around during the day if I don't have to."

"I'll have the results by morning. If I find what I'm looking for on that CD, we'll arrest him the minute he shows his face in the U.S. again."

"And her nephew?"

"He'll go back to his aunt where he belongs."

"Other than your men, I don't want anyone else knowing we're staying at the ranch," Caleb insisted.

"Agreed. There's no sense inviting more trouble than we already have coming to this party. We'll have our hands full as it is. No additional government agency involvement apart from my men and Coleman. Your location is easy to secure by vehicle with only one road in and out. I'll station someone near the main house and another officer at the mouth of the drive."

"I'll turn over the CD to the officer on duty." Caleb closed the cell, walked back inside and filled Katherine in on the part of the conversation she missed.

Katherine's body language was easy to read. She was curled up with Max in her lap, making herself as small as she could possibly become. She wanted to disappear.

It wasn't cold inside the homestead, but she was shivering slightly. No doubt, she wanted to block out everything that was happening to her.

"IT'LL BE NICE for you to sleep in your own bed for a change," Katherine mused, doing her level best to steer the conversation away from anything stressful. She knew on some level that Caleb hadn't meant to hurt her, but her wounds were still fresh. She needed a minute. Something told her Kane was close by. A man like him would want to finish what he started. No chance he'd walk away and leave her alone.

"No argument there. Except I'll give you the soft bed to sleep on while I keep watch." Caleb moved to the food supplies and opened a can of beans. When they were warm, he offered her first dibs.

"No thanks. I ate a protein bar that was stashed here." The ticking clock was a reminder of how little time she had left. How little time either of them had left. "Did Marshal Jones mention anything about Noah?"

Caleb shook his head.

The pressure was stringing her nerves too tight. A half-desperate laugh slipped out. "I'll just keep hoping for the best then."

He moved to her and kissed her. Warmly. She didn't resist. He tasted like coffee.

"Do you want me to make some more of Margaret's calming tea?" he asked with a wink.

She straightened her shoulders. "God, no. I'm a coffee person through and through."

A white-toothed smile broke across Caleb's face. "You really are determined to hold it together, aren't you?"

"Not on the inside. I'm a wreck." That much was true.

"I'd never be able to tell." He kissed her again.

He pulled her down on his lap as he sat, embracing her as though he might never see her again. He held her as though one of them could be gone tomorrow. Or both.

The gravity of what they were facing hit her hard.

A wave of melancholy washed over her. She'd been so intent on finding a way to bring Kane out into the open, she hadn't really considered the position she was putting herself in or the consequences. "Promise me that if something happens to me, you'll find Noah anyway and get him away from that animal."

His grip tightened around her as his breath warmed her neck. "Don't have to. You'll be around to take care of him yourself."

She turned enough to look into his brown eyes. "Promise me anyway."

His expression was a mix of sadness, regret and sheer grit. "I will not let anything happen to you. That much I can vow."

She could tell from the intensity in his gaze he would take a bullet for her if that was the only way to protect her.

"Drink up." He motioned to her cup. "It'll be dark outside soon. In a short while we can shower and eat a real meal at the main house."

"Both sound almost too good to be true. Although I haven't exactly felt like I've been suffering out here. Not compared to what we've been through." Or the hell she faced at the thought of never seeing Noah again.

Caleb smiled his trademark smile. He rose, let Max out and stood at the open door.

She brought her hand up to his neck. If they survived this ordeal, could the three of them think about a future together? Would he resent having a ready-made family as she had all those years ago?

Or could he love Noah the same way he did Savannah?

CALEB COULDN'T SEE. He didn't have time to let his eyes adjust, either. He knew this trail better than the back of his hand. The path from the homestead to the ranch was thick with trees. They provided much-needed shelter from a sweltering August sun and would afford cover for them now.

He fumbled for Katherine's hand and then slipped through the mesquites in the black, moonless night.

Quietly he made his way through the woods he loved so much. Every tree, every stream, felt so much like a part of him, entwined with his soul. He'd memorized and mentally mapped every inch of his property.

Once inside the house, Caleb bolted the lock. Not that it would do much good against the kind of firepower Kane's men would bring to the fight, but it would make Katherine feel better.

Keeping her as calm and relaxed as he could under

the circumstances became his marching orders. "Which sounds better right now—a hot shower or a good meal while I take the CD to Jones's guy out front?"

She sighed. "I'll take either. Both. But let me take one more look at that before we turn it over."

"You know where the office is. Password is TorJake." He handed her a couple ibuprofen and a bottle of water, shoving the fear he could lose her down deep. "Then you get cleaned up while I see what's in the fridge."

"Deal." She popped the pills in her mouth and downed them with a gulp of water before disappearing down the hall with the disk.

He showered and brushed his teeth in the guest room before returning to the kitchen. The CD sat on the counter near the coffeepot. He could hear the shower going in the master bathroom.

Caleb trucked outside and waved as he neared the cruiser. "Marshal Jones is expecting this. Said you'd know what to do with it."

"Yes, sir," the officer said, opening the door. When he stood, he wasn't more than five foot ten but had a stocky build. "I'll take it to him. There's an officer stationed at the top of the road. He'll keep watch until I return."

Caleb thanked him and returned to the house.

Margaret had stacked several Tupperware containers filled with food in the fridge with a note on top. "This should keep you from getting too skinny until I get back in a couple of days."

The idea of eating Margaret's food was almost enough to bring a smile to his lips again. She'd made several of his favorite meals. There was a roast with those slow-cooked rosemary potatoes he loved, a tub full of sausage mani-cotti, and what looked like smoked brisket. There were mashed potatoes in another container and some greens.

Caleb pulled out the roast, fixed two plates and heated them in the microwave.

Katherine stepped into the kitchen wearing one of his T-shirts and a pair of shorts. Seeing her in his clothes, in his house, stirred his heart. God, he needed her.

She was as beautiful as looking at the endless sky on a clear blue day.

He didn't want this moment to end. For them to end. An ominous feeling it wouldn't last plagued him.

She walked over to him, inclined her head and pressed those sweet lips to his.

The second the kiss deepened, Caleb lifted Katherine and carried her to the bedroom, shooing Max away with his foot.

He made love to her so completely, so thoroughly, she fell asleep in his arms. Right where she belonged.

Chapter Fifteen

Caleb's body warmed Katherine's back. Forget sleep tonight. Her leg hurt. Her throat was dry.

Could she move without waking him?

Even if she managed to slip out of bed undetected, there was Max to deal with. Her nerves were banded so tight, she felt as though one might snap.

Slowly, she rolled away from him until she could feel the edge of the bed. The absence of his touch made her skin cold and her heart ache. She ignored the painful stabs in her chest and slipped off the bed.

Thankfully, Max didn't make a sound. It was too dark to see him, but she figured he was sleeping at the foot of the bed.

She tiptoed out of the room. She'd hoped to feel some relief when they'd come back to the ranch. Instead, the hairs on her neck prickled.

Something brushed against her leg. A yelp escaped before she could suppress it.

Claws?

Katherine squinted. Light streamed in from the window in the hallway. "Here, kitty."

Claws stalked away without looking back.

The kitchen was dark save for the light coming in through the window.

She checked the clock and calculated it had been at least four hours since her last dose of pain medication. She palmed a couple of ibuprofen. Turning the spigot, she scanned the yard.

Where was the officer? His sedan was there. Parked. Doors open. Lights on.

Ice trickled down her spine.

She shook it off.

An officer was parked at the top of the lane and another was right outside the door. It was safe here.

She downed the contents of her glass and set it on the sink.

Where was the officer? If he was walking the perimeter, wouldn't he close the door?

She peeked out the screen door. Nothing stuck out as odd.

The crackle of a radio broke through. She stepped out onto the porch. Outside, every chirp seemed amplified.

The pain in her ankle flared despite the compression sock.

She limped to the edge of the porch. Her mind clicked through a few possibilities. Was the other officer at his post?

Maybe they'd met somewhere in the middle?

Her warning systems flared. She should probably turn and run back into the house. Wake Caleb.

"Anyone here?" she whispered.

The place was quiet. She said a silent protection prayer. Her heart thumped in her throat. Her mouth was so dry she couldn't manage enough spit to swallow.

She checked around the corner.

Nothing.

No one.

Frustration impaled her. Caleb needed sleep. Surely the officer was fine.

It might be a false alarm, but better safe than sorry.

She turned to the back door. Before she could hit her stride, a strong hand crashed down on her shoulder, knocking her backward. The icy fingers were like a vise. She tried to scream. A hand covered her mouth.

"I don't think so, honey," said the male voice.

She recognized it immediately. Scarface.

Using all the force she had, Katherine kicked and threw her elbows into him to break free.

A blast of cold metal hit the back of her head. Blackness.

WAKING TO FIND Katherine out of bed had disturbed Caleb. He'd already checked the house. Hadn't found her. Desperation railed through him. She wouldn't leave him. Would she?

He checked outside.

The officer wasn't at his post, either.

Noise came from the barn before Caleb reached the doors. His stallion was kicking and snorting.

What had Samson riled up?

Caleb didn't like it.

Then again, there wasn't anything about this situation he remotely *liked* so far. The caution bells sounded louder the closer he got to the barn until he couldn't hear his own thoughts anymore.

Katherine was in grave danger. He could feel it in every one of his bones. He sent a text to Marshal Jones. What had happened to his men?

The closer Caleb moved toward Samson, the more intense his fears became.

Caleb slowed his pace, his steps steady, deliberate. "Whoa, boy."

Katherine was missing. His chest nearly caved in at the thought. *Kane.*

His next call was to his friend.

Matt picked up on the first ring.

Caleb let out the breath he'd been holding. "Katherine's gone. I think Kane has her."

"Damn. What do you need me to do?"

"Where are you?"

"Dallas. At the hospital with Jimmy."

"I don't know," Caleb lowered his tone.

From the north side of the woods, a tall man stalked toward him.

"I gotta go. Don't worry about being here," Caleb said, ending the call.

The guy was big, but Caleb had no doubt he could take him down if need be. As he moved into the light, he recognized Marshal Jones.

"Where are your men?"

"Sent one of my guys to deliver the CD. I've been trying to reach the other stationed at the top of the drive with no luck. I wanted to be close by so I parked up the road in the woods."

"Kane's here. It's the only explanation." Caleb glanced at his watch. "I don't know when he got to her." It could have been hours ago.

"My man was here fifteen minutes ago. They can't have gotten far. I'll radio again. There's no other way out of here by car, is there?" Jones fell into step with Caleb, who pointed his flashlight at the ground.

"One road in. One road out. There's countless ways to reach the house through the woods. None of which a car would fit through." Caleb glanced up. "Think they got to your guy?"

"Must've. He would answer his radio otherwise."

"Bastards." The white dot illuminated the yellow-green grass as Caleb moved closer to the tree line. "They used ATVs before. They're smart. They've studied the terrain."

He trained his flashlight on a spot on the ground.

"Hold on." He dropped to his knees.

"A woman's footprint."

"It's hers." He shone the light east. "The footprint stops here." He glanced around on the ground. "See that?"

"A man's shoe print."

"Which means someone carried her." Caleb followed the imprints to the tree line. "They went this way."

"They most likely have a car stashed somewhere," Jones said as he turned toward the lane. "I'll head to the main road."

"You said you heard from one of your guys fifteen minutes ago?"

"Yes."

"It would take about that long to run to the nearest place they could've hid a car. You take the road." Caleb ran toward the barn. "I can cut them off on horseback."

KATHERINE'S EYES BLURRED as she tried to blink them open. The crown of her head felt as though someone had blasted her with a hammer. Her thoughts jumbled. Thinking clearly through her pounding headache would be a challenge.

In a flash, she remembered being outside before someone grabbed her and then the lights went out. Didn't seem like anyone had turned them back on, either. Pitch-black wasn't nearly good enough to describe the darkness surrounding her. Where was she? Where was Caleb? Terror gripped her.

Chill bumps covered her arms. She reached out and hit surface in every direction without extending her arms. Was she in some kind of compartment? Whatever she was in moved fast. She bounced, bumping her head.

She lay on a clothlike material. The whole area couldn't measure more than three or four feet deep and she couldn't stretch out her legs.

Realization dawned. Icy fingers of panic gripped her lungs and squeezed.

She was in the trunk of a car.

Oh, God. How would she get out? Wasn't there a panic lever somewhere?

At least her arms and legs were free. She felt around for something—anything—to pop the trunk. Was there a weapon? A car jack?

Her mind cleared and she recalled more details. Scarface's voice.

Katherine listened carefully to the sounds around her. The engine revved. Brakes squealed as the car flew side to side.

A thump sounded. A gunshot rang out.

Her throat closed as fear seized her.

The car roared to a stop.

She repositioned herself so her feet faced the lid. She'd be ready to launch an attack at whoever opened the trunk.

Her heart hammered in her chest. She held her breath, fighting off sheer terror. *Patience.*

The trunk lid lifted and she thrust her feet at the body leaning toward her. She made contact at the same time she recognized the face. "Caleb?"

His arms reached for her, encircled her, while her brain tried to catch up. He lifted her and carried her to his horse.

His face was a study in concentration and determination. He didn't speak as he balanced her in his arms and popped her into the saddle. He hopped up from behind just in time for her to see that his jeans were soaked with blood on his right thigh. Her heart skipped a beat. She told herself he'd be fine. He had to be okay. His arms circled her as he gripped the reins.

Scarface hadn't fared so well. He was slumped over the steering wheel. "Is he dead?"

"No." Caleb urged his horse forward as lights and sirens wailed from behind. "But he'll wish he was after the marshal gets hold of him."

The feel of Caleb against her back, warming her, brought a sense of rightness to the crazy world. "You found me."

She could feel every muscle in his chest tense.

Samson kept a steady gallop until they reached the barn. Caleb took care of his horse, then, keeping Katherine by his side, headed for the house.

"I walked outside to check on the officer. I turned around to come get you when I heard his voice. Then everything went black. I'm so sorry."

"Don't be. I'm just glad I found you." He pressed kisses to her forehead, then her nose before feathering them on her cheeks. "I can't lose you."

His lips pressed to hers with bruising need.

She loved him. There was no questioning that. But what was he offering? A commitment? Her heart gave a little skip at the thought. He'd already proved he would be there for her no matter what. When the chips were down, he'd come through for her, comforting her, saving her. He was the one person in the world she trusted. "I heard a gunshot and panicked. What happened while I was in the trunk?"

"Scarface took aim. There were too many twists in the road for him to be able to steer and shoot, or…"

"Oh, God. Did he hit you?" She scanned his jeans for a bullet hole, panicked when she noticed the blood.

"Grazed my leg. Flesh wound. I'm fine. I caught up to him before he got off another round."

She couldn't hold back the sob that broke free. She couldn't even think about something happening to Caleb.

"I'm okay. I promise."

She buried her face in his chest, her body shaking. His arms tightened around her.

"Let's get you inside."

"We should get back on the road. Follow Scarface. Maybe he can lead us to Noah?"

"I doubt it. Scarface should be in custody by now. Unless the marshal let him go to follow him. Putting yourself in danger again won't help that little boy."

"This isn't about him anymore, is it?" A chill ran down her spine at the realization. "Kane is after me now."

"For his own freedom. He wants to erase you and the file." Caleb's gaze scanned the trees. "Let's get you inside."

CALEB CLEANED HIS injuries. He dabbed water on his leg, thinking how much he needed to keep his head clear. He dressed the cut on his thigh and changed into clean jeans.

"They might be out there right now," Katherine said as she sat down on his bed. "That's what you were just thinking, wasn't it?"

"Yes."

She glanced at the windows, her tentative smile replaced by a look of apprehension. "What do we do now?"

"I'll reconnect with the marshal and then go after the son of a bitch as soon as we figure out the next step. Until then, we wait here. I won't let him hurt the woman I love again."

"Love?" She rewarded him with a smile. "I love you, too."

By the time Matt eased in the back door, Katherine's nerves were sizzling. "I thought you were in Dallas."

"Came back to help you."

"Why would you do that?"

"When Caleb said he'd found you, I came to stop them from doing anything else." He excused himself, saying he needed to find Caleb.

She made a pot of coffee in the dim light, having allowed her eyes to adjust to the darkness, surprised Matt would want to come to her aid. She glanced out the window. Were they out there watching? Who else would Kane send?

They could be anywhere right now. Even standing outside, looking right at her. A chill ran up her spine. She had to figure out a way to get Caleb to let her come with him to find Kane.

A noise from behind shattered what was left of her brittle nerves. She turned to find Matt standing there. Her hand came up to her chest.

"Didn't mean to scare you," he said.

"It's fine. I'm jumpy." She held up a mug. "Coffee?"

"I can get it. You should sit down. Caleb said you have to be careful on that ankle."

"Believe it or not, it was much worse yesterday." She eyed him warily. He looked determined to say something. She filled a mug and handed it to him. "How about I let you get your own cream and sugar?"

"I take mine black."

There was another thing to like about him. Under ordinary circumstances, she figured they might actually get along. She reminded herself they weren't really friends and he likely hadn't sought her out to talk about the coffee.

"Me, too," she said anyway, figuring he also didn't want to hear about how much they had in common—such as how much they both cared for Caleb. But that was another common bond between them, whether Matt like it or not.

"I'm not good at this sort of thing...." He paused.

She took a sip, welcoming the burn and the warmth on her throat.

Another beat passed as he shifted his weight onto his other foot.

Whatever he had to say, Katherine figured she wasn't about to be showered with compliments. She braced herself for what would come next. She'd stared down worse bulls than a protective friend.

Didn't he realize she had Caleb's best interests at heart?

When he looked as though saying the words out loud might actually cause him physical pain, she said, "I can save you the trouble. I know you don't like me. But if you gave me half a chance, I think we could be friends."

There. She'd said it. She put it out there between them, and he could do what he wanted with it.

She crossed her arms and readied herself for his response.

"That isn't what I came here to say."

"Okay."

"I need to apologize."

"No, you don't." The tension in her neck muscles eased.

His stance was firm and unmoving. "I appreciate you saying that, but I do."

"If the tables were turned and it was me, I'd probably feel the same way as you. I can see how this looks. A stranger shows up on his property and he puts his life in danger to help her. I wouldn't like it, either."

The corner on one side of his mouth lifted. "There is that."

"You must love him a lot."

"Like the brother I never had."

"But I do, too." Had she just admitted her true feelings for Caleb to the one man who could stand her the least? It was one thing to say it to Caleb. Damn. It had come out so fast and yet sounded so natural. Felt natural. Her heart was so full it might burst that he'd said it to her first. But to make the declaration to a friend? To let everyone else know took the relationship to a new level. Was she ready?

Katherine steadied her nerves. Her admission would probably spark a rebellion anyway. Why couldn't she just leave it alone? Why did she need Matt to understand her feelings for Caleb?

Because Matt was like family to him. He was important. She secretly wished for his approval.

"I know," Matt said softly. "He feels the same way. I knew it the first time I saw him with you."

Katherine stood stunned. "I had no idea."

"It's half the reason I've been so…worried," Matt said, leaning against the counter.

"I realize you know him best. You must've seen that look before?"

"No. Never. Not with anyone else." His tone was dead-pan.

Katherine's heart skipped a beat. Maybe she could believe his love was real. He wasn't confusing his need to help with true feelings. Maybe this was different than the women in his past.

Caleb strolled in before she could thank Matt for telling her. "Not with any what?"

Chapter Sixteen

Katherine held out a mug. "Coffee's fresh."

Caleb arched his brow. The corners of his lips turned up and he winked. He walked to her and wrapped his arms around her waist. "You're not getting out of this so easy. What were the two of you talking about?"

Matt made an excuse about walking the perimeter and slipped outside.

"I remembered something that might help. I'd completely forgotten about Leann's phone. I can contact Kane if we can get another power cord and a battery."

"You brought up a good point, but I don't want you doing anything with that phone. Stay inside the house. No matter what. Promise me?"

She folded her arms. "This is the worst. At least when we were on the run, we had distractions. Waiting around with no way to make contact, doing nothing is killing me."

Caleb's pocket vibrated. He pulled Jones's cell from his pocket and glanced at the screen. "It's Jones."

Katherine's heart went into free fall with anticipation.

As soon as Caleb ended the call, he turned to her. "They found it. They found the proof. Leann had pictures linking Kane to murder. He must've had no idea she had evidence until recently."

"Doesn't do any good if they can't find Kane. Can't he

live out the rest of his life in Mexico? With Noah? How will I ever get him back? I can't imagine leaving him to grow up with a monster like that." Panic thumped a fresh course of adrenaline through Katherine's veins. She didn't want to think about never seeing her nephew again.

"We don't know that. Jones has men in Dallas all over it."

His words were meant to be comforting. They weren't. A jagged rock ripped through her chest. Breathing hurt. She'd wait like a sitting duck for how long? Kane's men would never leave her alone. He wouldn't be satisfied until she was dead. "What about Scarface? Did he talk?"

"That's the best part. He did. Kane has been hiding in a warehouse downtown in the garment district. He's believed to be there right now. Jones is going after him. Coleman is on his way with reinforcements."

A myriad of emotions ran through her. Fear for Noah gripped her. Could they get to him in time? A trill of hope rocketed. This whole ordeal could be behind them by morning's light.

A disturbance out front caught their attention.

"Wait here." Caleb moved to the cabinet and pulled out a handgun.

He crossed to her and placed it in her hand. Katherine's hand shook as she recoiled. "Not a good idea. I'm scared to death of those things."

"I won't leave you here without a way to protect yourself. It's a .38. You have to cock it to fire. Like this." He pressed her thumb to the hammer. "Then you point and pull the trigger. Wait here for me, but if someone comes through that door you don't recognize, shoot."

A lump in Katherine's throat made swallowing difficult. Her breathing came in spasms and her chest hurt.

Be strong. Refuse to be defeated. She gripped the handle tighter. "Okay."

"I better check on Matt." Caleb kissed her forehead. He turned and headed toward the front of the house. "Don't be afraid to use the gun if you need to. Look before you shoot."

All her danger signals were flaring, and she knew on instinct something very bad was about to go down. They'd found her. Fear crippled her, freezing every muscle of her body even though she had the very real sense she was shaking on the outside. Sweat beaded and dripped down her forehead like the trickle of melting ice cream.

She couldn't let Caleb go alone.

Her eyes had already adjusted to the darkness, so finding her way around outside the house wasn't a problem. At the last corner, she crouched low, making herself as small as possible, and moved behind the Japanese boxwoods in the front landscaping. Caleb stepped out the front door with his right arm extended, gun aimed.

Matt was on his knees in front of the house with his arms and legs bound. A man the size of a linebacker stood behind him, his gun pointed at his head.

Oh. God. No.

She turned away for an instant, unable to look. Guilt this was all her fault gripped her.

"He has nothing to do with this. Let him go." Caleb's voice was surprisingly even. He was calm under pressure whereas Katherine's nerves were fried.

The sound of gravel crunching underneath tires brought her focus to the road where a blacked-out SUV barreled down the path.

"Doesn't seem like your friend here wants to get up," said the linebacker, kicking Matt from behind.

Katherine prayed Caleb wouldn't react to the taunting.

A thousand ideas ran through her head. Should she slip into the house and call 9-1-1? Wasn't Coleman on his way? She crouched low, rooted to her spot as two men stepped out of the SUV. One she recognized from Noah's kidnapping, the other was new. He was smaller than the others, but wore an expensive suit. His hair was dark, curly and slicked back. Kane?

"Put your gun down on the porch, and we'll consider sparing your life," the familiar one said.

Caleb didn't budge.

"Fine. Then your buddy here gets a bullet in the head." He lowered the barrel toward Matt.

Caleb put up both hands in the universal sign for surrender. "No need to do that." He lowered his gun to the porch and kicked it forward with the toe of his boot.

"Where is she?" the man with the slicked-back dark hair asked, his tone clipped; there was that telltale albeit subtle difference in the way he pronounced his vowels.

Katherine knew exactly who he was. Kane.

"I'm afraid it's just us guys here," Caleb responded.

"Don't insult me. I happen to know you were with her. She must be here somewhere." Kane glanced around. "Come out. Come out. Wherever you are."

Kane walked closer to Caleb, eyeing him up and down. He turned to his henchmen and pointed to Matt. "Show them we're serious."

The crack of a bullet split the night air.

Katherine's heart plummeted. A gasp escaped before she could squash it. She fought the urge to vomit. Make a noise and Kane had what he wanted. *Her.* Game over.

She forced herself to peer through the bushes at him, expecting to see blood splattered on the men. There was none. If they hadn't shot Matt, what had they hit?

The bullet must've pinged the ground instead. Thank God. No one was hurt.

A wicked grin crossed Kane's attractive features. Authority and power radiated from him. Underneath that good-looking exterior, this man was the devil reincarnate. How horrible was he? Leann was a good person. How could she have gotten involved with such evil?

Katherine remembered the practiced, cool voice she'd first heard on the phone. Was that the one he'd used to lure Leann? If she'd seen the other side to him, no wonder she'd wanted to escape. She must've innocently believed she could keep him away from Noah. That definitely had to be why she'd moved around so much. It all made sense now. She'd kept the evidence quiet, waiting until the day he showed up again. And when he'd found her? She'd decided to play him while she'd gone to the Feds for help. A new life. A new identity. She and Noah would be hidden forever.

The cost?

She would have to cross the father of her child.

That couldn't have been easy. Sadness and anger burned Katherine's chest, firing heat through her veins. Why hadn't Leann confided in her?

She didn't want to bring you down with her, a little voice said.

Oh, sister.

Kane glanced around wildly. "Still not wanting to come out and play. Well let's see if this changes your mind." He opened the back door to the SUV and lifted a small figure into his arms.

Noah?

Katherine's heart faltered. She feared it would stop beating altogether if her nephew was dead. Kane was a horrible man. Would he hurt his own son?

No. A man who made sure the boy had his medicine wouldn't harm him.

But he would kill Matt. Possibly even Caleb.

She had to stop him.

Without thinking, she tucked the gun into the band of her shorts and stepped out of the boxwoods. There was no way she could hit him from this far. Not with the way her hands were shaking. If she could get close enough, she'd take that bastard out with one shot. His henchmen might retaliate, but at least Kane would die. "I'm right here, you son of a bitch. You don't have to hurt any more innocent people."

Caleb made a move toward her but backed off when Kane aimed his gun at Noah's temple.

"Don't be a hero, cowboy," Kane said, smooth and practiced. "I've been waiting for this day for a long time. You won't ruin it for me, will you? No one's going to wreck my plans. No one sends me to jail." He turned to face Katherine. "Not that bitch sister of yours. And sure as hell not you. She said she loved me. All the time she was sneaking around behind my back. Talking to the Feds. How could she love me when she stabbed me in the back? What about you? Will you betray him, too? Let's see how much you care about your cowboy." He nodded toward his henchman, who moved behind Caleb and pressed a gun to his back.

"Hurt him if you want. It won't bother me," Katherine lied.

She needed Kane to believe those words even though she could feel warmth traveling up her neck to her cheeks. She ignored it.

Convincing Kane she didn't love Caleb might be his only chance to live.

If she could distract Kane long enough to pull the gun, and then fire, she'd stop him from hurting anyone else.

He wasn't more than five feet away. So close she could smell his musky aftershave. Too far to make a move before Kane's guy had a chance to pull the trigger and end Caleb's life.

She couldn't get a clear shot while Kane held Noah anyway. Thank God he was sleeping. She had to get that monster away from her nephew and focused on her.

"Besides, he doesn't know anything. But I do. And I'll testify. You'll rot in jail with all the other scum who think they're above the law."

"Scum?" Kane's voice raised another octave. "That's what your sister said about me?" The pained look on his face said he still loved Leann.

"Don't believe her. I know exactly what you did. I can point authorities to the evidence, too, and she can't," Caleb said quickly.

Damn him. Didn't he see what she was trying to do? He was going to get himself killed.

"He's wrong. This is between you and me. Let Noah get out of here. Matt can take him. And I'll do anything you want." Noah blinked up at her. Fear filled his brown eyes. He couldn't possibly know how much she loved him. And if they saw how important Caleb was to her, he'd be dead, too.

"Let my son go? My son? Your sister tried to keep him from me. No one will ever keep me from my boy again." Kane's voice bordered on hysteria. The high-pitch sound echoed in the night. "Do something to the friend."

The linebacker hit Matt with the butt of his gun.

Matt crumpled forward. Didn't move again.

Was he unconscious? Alive? He had to be.

Tears welled in her eyes. She sniffed them back. She couldn't afford to let her emotions take control.

A bolt of lightning raced sideways across the sky. A clap of thunder followed moments later.

If she were going to stop Kane, she had to act fast.

Caleb spun around and disarmed the man on him. The pair tumbled onto the ground in a twist of arms and legs.

Katherine used the distraction to slip her hand behind her and grip the gun. She fired a shot and the linebacker went down. Before she could locate Kane, he was next to her, his hand gripping her neck, and it felt like her eyes might pop out.

Another shot rang out.

Chapter Seventeen

Katherine forced herself to look at Caleb, expecting her own exploding pain to register at any moment. Everything had happened so fast, her brain almost couldn't catalog the sequence. Both he and the man on him lay still. Blood. There was so much blood. *Please move, Caleb. Get up.*

He didn't.

Hopelessness engulfed her. If he was dead… Oh, God… She couldn't even think what she would do without him.

Tears sprang from her eyes. She doubled over. Her world imploded around her. She'd finally invested herself and fallen in love. Now he was dead. Just like her parents. Just like her sister.

Leann.

Noah was sick. Would he die, too?

A hand gripped her shoulder, pulling her upright. Cold metal poked her back. She jerked away, spun around and stared into the blackest set of eyes she'd ever seen. "You killed him. This is your fault. You caused me to drop my son, too. That won't be forgiven."

Through blurry eyes she searched for Noah. He'd been placed on a seat in the SUV. The door was open.

Her gaze flew to Matt's lifeless body.

"He's still alive. For the moment. Make another move and he'll be dead, too," Kane said into her ear, disarming her. "You're going to pay for what that bitch sister of yours tried to do to me. I loved her. I treated her like a queen. Look what she did." He waved his gun around, and then pressed the metal barrel against Katherine's temple. "I never would've known if she hadn't gone and gotten herself killed. I pieced it together when I was going through her things. Nobody betrays me and gets away with it."

She squeezed her eyes shut.

"Now move," he growled.

Every muscle in her body stiffened as she forced herself by sheer will to walk. He pushed her toward the barn. The man behind her directed her actions. This was something new to fear. A crazed psychopath who wanted to do more than kill her. He needed to see her suffer.

"You won't get away with this," she said in the dark. His icy fingers gripped her neck. Her body convulsed. She could feel his hot breath on her.

"I'm going send you to meet that bitch sister of yours in death. But first, you're going to watch that boyfriend of yours burn."

Katherine's heart shriveled. The air thinned. She struggled to take a breath. She refused to believe Caleb was gone and her life would end like this. That Noah would be brought up by this monster. There had to be a way out.

He tossed her into a stall and on top of a bale of hay. She popped up. "The cops are coming. They'll arrest you. Hurting me won't help your case. It'll only make it worse. If you leave now, you can disappear. They won't find you if you stay out of the country."

"Be still, kitten." He knocked her down, forced her hands behind her back and tied them together. "I have no plans to rot in jail. Time to get rid of the evidence."

Her body shuddered at his touch. She kicked as hard as she could, connecting with his shin multiple times.

He flinched and slapped her across the left cheek. Katherine's head jolted. It felt as though her eye would explode. A fresh course of adrenaline pumped through her.

"You're about to learn something." A wicked grin spread across his lips. "Look at me."

He touched her cheek with the back of his hand. "She favored you. So beautiful." He shook his head. "She could have had anything she wanted. I would have given her the world."

His lips thinned. His gaze narrowed. "Now you all die." He shook his head. "What a waste."

Katherine struggled against her bindings. The rope cut through her flesh. She ignored the pain, trying to loosen the ties.

A hysterical laugh brought her focus back to Kane.

"Stay here, little one. I'll be right back."

Maybe Katherine could free herself before he returned. Her body convulsed. Yet she couldn't budge the ropes. Kicking did no good, either.

It felt as though Kane had been gone for eternity when he finally showed up, dragging a bloody lifeless body.

Her heart beat against her ribs in painful stabs.

Caleb.

"One more to go and I'll finally be rid of you all," Kane said before he disappeared again.

Where was the sheriff? His men?

Katherine's gaze frantically searched for any sign of life in Caleb. She knew it was too much to hope he was still alive. Yet she had to be sure. She watched his chest for signs of movement. His broad chest rose and fell.

Or was she seeing what she wanted to?

Was he unconscious?

Katherine could've sworn she just saw Caleb surveying the area. Were his eyes open?

Yes. Definitely so. Her heart soared at the realization Caleb was alive. He brought a finger to his lips, the universal sign to keep quiet.

Matt was dragged in next. Katherine wanted to scream. She fought harder against the ropes.

Kane positioned Matt next to Caleb and threw a few fistfuls of hay on top of them. Her pulse beat in her throat. She was sure a red heat crawled up her neck. She put all her focus toward Caleb.

Kane hovered over Katherine. She kicked and threw her arms at him, trying to fight. He held out a match over the heap.

She looked toward the man she loved one more time. One wrong move and Kane would shoot. She needed to stall. To get his attention. She looked up at him. "Leann wouldn't want this. She never meant to hurt you. The Feds must've forced her to turn against you. I know she loved you."

Kane's laugh was haughty and arrogant. He trailed his finger along her jawline, and she saw Caleb's hands fist. Hope filled her chest.

"You are almost as beautiful as Leann," Kane said. "She was a free spirit. You, on the other hand, are a bit uptight. Even so, I could make you moan. The things I would like to do to you before I watch you burn...."

Allowing him to touch her and talk about her sister in that way nearly killed her.

He smoothed his hand across her red cheek. "I wish you hadn't made me do that to you."

Kane's dark eyes homed in on her. He brought a match to life with a flick of his nail and dropped it next to Caleb.

The moment Katherine moved, Caleb was on top of Kane. With a few quick jabs to the head, Kane's body slumped on top of her, pinning her to the ground. He was unconscious, but for how long?

A scream escaped before she could get her bearings and push him off. "I thought you were…"

"I'll be fine. I took a blow to the head. Scrambled a few things. Took a minute to shake. By the time I got my bearings again, I was being dragged to the barn."

She struggled against the ropes on her wrists, tears falling down her cheeks. When Caleb helped free her, they pulled Matt to his feet. He shook his head. Disoriented, he didn't seem able to hold his own weight.

"Help him outside." Caleb handed over Jones's cell. "Call 9-1-1. I have to put out the fire before it spreads."

Katherine dialed the emergency number as she bore some of Matt's heft, and walked outside the barn.

After giving her location and details to the operator, she helped Matt ease onto the ground.

A moment later, Caleb dashed to her side, a fire extinguisher in his hands. "It was contained. Didn't take much to put it out."

"The police are on their way." Katherine looked to Matt. "He's hurt, but conscious."

Max was at the door to the tack room. He stood sentinel, barking wildly.

Caleb's autumn-brown eyes pierced through her as he set the extinguisher down and told her to wait for him.

"No. I'm going with you," she insisted with a glance toward Matt.

He motioned for her to go.

Kane was moving toward the back of the tack room, trying to escape. He rounded on them.

Caleb shielded her with his body, pulling a gun from his waistband. Kane launched himself toward them. The gun fired as the two landed on the ground.

In a quick motion, Caleb straddled Kane. Blood was everywhere.

Panic momentarily stopped her heart. "Are you shot?"

He shook his head.

Kane gurgled blood before his gaze fixed and his expression turned vacant.

She dropped to her knees. Max ran to her. She cradled him. "It's over."

Caleb guided her to her feet where the little dog followed. "Let's get Noah."

His hand closed on hers as he led her outside.

Matt stood, still weak, and Caleb took some of his weight.

Another bolt of lightning cut across the sky as a droplet of rain fell.

An SUV was gone. Only the man who'd been shot remained, lifeless on the ground.

By the time they reached Noah, his face was pale. Katherine picked him up and hugged him. He let out a yelp.

Katherine embraced him tighter. "Oh, baby. You're safe."

His brown eyes were wide and tearful.

Caleb stood next to her. "Okay, little man. We're going to get you to the hospital."

Noah nodded. His bottom lip quivered as tears welled. He was too tired to cry. Not a good sign.

"Did the men bring your medicine, baby?"

He shook his head.

His breathing was shallow, and Katherine realized it was probably the reason he wasn't bawling. He didn't have the energy, which meant he needed medicine right away.

"You're safe," she repeated over and over again, hugging him tightly into her chest. He was fading, and she knew it. "Can you check the car for his medicine, Caleb?"

They searched the vehicle, pulling out the contents of the console and glove box, looking for the life-saving drugs.

Rain starting coming down in a steady rhythm as Katherine held on to her nephew, whispering quiet reassurances that he would be okay.

He *had* to be fine.

She glanced at Caleb and tensed at his worried expression. Noah's eyes rolled back in their sockets; he was losing his grip on consciousness.

"An ambulance is on its way. So is Coleman," Caleb said.

Katherine's tears mixed with rain, sending streaks down her face. "Come on, baby. Stay with me."

Her shoulders rocked as she released the tears she'd been holding far too long. They came out full force now. "When will that damn ambulance be here?"

She kissed Noah's forehead. His face was paler than before. His skin was cool and moist to the touch. Her heart thudded in her chest. "Caleb. Oh, God. Nothing can happen to him. Not now."

"The keys are still in the ignition." He hopped in the driver's side and motioned for her to climb in the passenger seat.

The SUV started on the first try. He glanced back at Matt. "Wait here for the sheriff?"

"Yes. Now go," Matt said.

Caleb glanced at his friend again.

"I'm fine. Get out of here."

The engine roared as Caleb gunned it.

Sirens and lights brought the first spark of hope.

Caleb flashed the headlamps as they cut off the ambulance at the top of the drive.

He hopped out of the driver's seat and crossed his arms

over his head to signal they needed help. A paramedic scrambled out of the passenger seat as Katherine ran toward him with Noah in her arms. "Help him, please. He's not breathing. He has asthma and may not have had medicine in a few days."

A paramedic took him from her arms and ran to the back of the ambulance as she followed. His hands worked quickly and efficiently.

"Has the patient been to the emergency room or used EMS in the past twenty-four to forty-eight hours?" he asked, not looking up.

"No. He was kidnapped. His skin was pale and his breathing shallow when I found him." A flood of tears spilled out of Katherine's eyes and into the rain.

Caleb's arm came around her, reassuring her. Protecting her.

The paramedic shot a sympathetic look toward her. "I'm going to administer a dose of epinephrine."

Another ambulance whirred past. *Matt.*

She turned to Caleb. "Go. Be with your friend. I have this covered. I know how worried you are about him."

Caleb's head shook emphatically. "I won't leave you to deal with this all by yourself."

There was that cowboy code again. "He's your best friend. And I need to know if he's going to be okay. I want you to check on him for both of us."

She could almost see the arguments clicking through his mind. How torn he had to be. "I'm serious. Go. I'm safe and Noah's getting the help he needs."

The paramedic started an IV and bagged him. "We've got to get the boy to the hospital. You can ride in the front," he said to Katherine before turning to Caleb. "You can follow behind in your vehicle."

"I'll go with Noah. You stay with Matt. I'll meet you

at the hospital," Katherine said, determined. She was fine with Noah and he needed to make sure his friend was okay.

"I know that stubborn look. I'd rather stay with you but I won't argue," Caleb agreed, looking more than reluctant.

She gave him a quick kiss as he helped her into the passenger seat.

CALEB DROVE LIKE a bat out of hell down the drive. He parked the SUV and went to his friend.

Matt had an oxygen tube under his nose, and his forehead had been cleaned up from all the blood. His cut wasn't as bad as it had first looked.

Matt blinked up at Caleb. "What the hell are you doing here?"

"Checking on you."

Matt issued a grunt. "I'm not the one who needs you."

"Try telling her that," Caleb quipped.

Sheriff Coleman roared up and jogged toward them. "Sorry I'm late. I got called away to another county on an emergency. Got there and they said they never made the call."

"I'm sure you'll need a statement, but I have to get to the hospital and check on the little boy," Caleb said.

Coleman took Caleb's outstretched hand and shook it. "I can always drop by tomorrow if you'd like. Sounds like you guys have had one hell of a night already."

He nodded.

"I spoke to Dallas PD to make sure you were no longer a person of interest in their murder investigation," Coleman said with a tip of his hat. "You're fine. I'll get this mess cleaned up and be out of here before you return."

"Much obliged, Sheriff." The last thing Caleb wanted to do was to bring Katherine home to reminders of the horrors she and Noah had endured.

Coleman patted Caleb on the back. "You need a ride to the hospital?"

"No, thanks." He said goodbye and climbed into the cab of his pickup.

HE MADE IT to the hospital in record time and found Katherine sitting next to Noah's bed.

She looked up at him with those expressive eyes. "He's going to be fine. His skin is already pink and dry."

Relief flooded him as he pulled up a chair next to her. "Did they say when he'll be released?"

"Could be as early as tomorrow. They want to keep him overnight for observation."

"That's the best news I've heard today."

"It is."

He cupped her cheek. "Then why the sad face?"

"Nothing. How's Matt?"

"He'll be fine. They're bringing him in. Not that he likes the idea."

A knock at the door interrupted their conversation. Marshal Jones poked his head inside. "Katherine Harper?"

"Yes. That's me."

"Marshal," Caleb said, nodding.

Jones returned the acknowledgment.

"Could I have a word with Ms. Harper in the hallway?"

"As long as he can come with me." She moved to the door alongside Caleb who was already in motion.

"Not a problem," Jones said.

"Is everything all right, Marshal?" Her hand was moist from nerves.

Caleb gave it a reassuring squeeze.

"I didn't mean to worry you," Jones said. "I wanted to let you know what we found on the CD." He glanced from her to Caleb.

Katherine's hand came up to her chest. "What?"

"Turns out your sister videotaped Kane murdering a business associate. We've been watching him for years trying to gather evidence against him for other crimes. He was slick. Anytime we got close, witnesses disappeared."

Katherine's head bowed.

"Your sister outsmarted him. She went to great lengths to hide the evidence. She disappeared. Then he found her."

"I wonder why she didn't run straight to the police or you guys," Katherine said, wiping a tear from her eye.

Caleb pulled her close.

"She'd been on the run, trying to keep her son safe. She was young and scared," Jones said. "All she wanted was to give her son a life. When I finally made contact with her, she told me that if anything happened, she wanted Noah to be with you. Said you'd be the best mother he could possibly have."

Tears rolled down Katherine's cheeks.

"For what it's worth, I'm sorry. She was brave to do what she did," he said. "If not for the accident, she would've brought Kane to justice."

Katherine's gaze lifted, her chin came up. "Thanks. It means a lot to hear you say that."

He inclined his chin. "Emergency personnel tried to revive Kane at the scene. You should know he didn't survive. He'll never be able to hurt you or Noah again. We apprehended an SUV with his associates, and they'll be locked away for a long time."

"Thank you." Relief washed through her.

Jones excused himself as Caleb walked her back into Noah's room.

Katherine checked on her nephew before taking a seat next to Caleb on the sofa.

"You need anything? Coffee?" he asked.

"No. I want to be right here in case Noah wakes in this strange place." Her eyes were rimmed with tears when she said, "I'm sorry you couldn't stay with your friend."

"Are you kidding? He was pissed at me for leaving you."

Confusion knitted her eyebrows. "I didn't want you to have to choose between us and him. He's your best friend."

"And he always will be. Did you think you were doing me some kind of favor pushing me away like that?"

"Yes. Noah was fine, and I needed to know how Matt was doing."

"That so?"

"Yes." She looked at him as if he had three eyes. "Besides, you don't know what it's like to have a family thrust on you before you're ready."

"As a matter of fact, I do. And guess what? It doesn't scare me. You make a decision and then adjust your life to adapt to it. I'm a grown man." He pulled her into his arms and felt her melt into his chest. "And I want you."

Tears spilled from her eyes, dotting his T-shirt. "I want you, too," she admitted.

"Let's make a deal."

She arched an eyebrow. "I'm listening."

"Let me tell you what I can and can't handle when we go home."

"Okay." Her smile didn't reach her eyes.

"You gonna explain the long face?"

"You have the ranch. Where's *home* for me and Noah? We can't go back to my apartment. Not after what happened."

"I was getting to that. I want you both to come to live with me. I love you. My life was empty until you came along. If you don't like the ranch, we'll buy a new place. I belong wherever you are."

"Are you serious?" She looked as though she needed a minute to let his words sink in. Her head shook. "You love that place."

"Not as much as I love you."

"I love you, too. Believe me. I do. But what about Noah? I'm the only family he's got and I don't want to confuse him."

"Then let's change that."

Her expression made him think the three eyes she'd seen on his forehead had grown wings. "All I'm saying is let's make it permanent. *Us.* I want to become a family."

She looked up at him wide-eyed as he stood.

He got down on one knee. "If I live another hundred years, I know in my heart I won't meet anyone else like you. You fit me in every possible way that matters. I don't want you to leave. Ever. I want to spend my life chasing away your fears and seeing every one of your smiles. I'm asking you to be my wife."

Tears fell from her eyes.

He leaned forward and thumbed one away as it stained her cheek, and he waited for her answer.

She kissed him. Deep. Passionate. And it stirred his desire. "Keep that up, and I'll show you what we can do with the bed on the other side of that curtain while little man sleeps."

She smiled up at him and his heart squeezed.

"You haven't answered my question."

"Yes, Caleb, I will marry you."

"Good, because I want to start working on a new project."

"A project?" she echoed, raising her brow.

He pulled her into his chest and crushed his lips against

hers. "I want Noah to have a little brother or sister running around soon."

She smiled. "I want that, too."

"And I'm going to spend the rest of my life loving you."

* * * * *

A sneaky peek at next month...

INTRIGUE...

BREATHTAKING ROMANTIC SUSPENSE

My wish list for next month's titles...

In stores from 21st February 2014:

❏ The Girl Next Door — Cynthia Eden

& Rocky Mountain Rescue — Cindi Myers

❏ Snowed In — Cassie Miles

& The Secret of Cherokee Cove — Paula Graves

❏ Bridal Jeopardy — Rebecca York

& The Prosecutor — Adrienne Giordano

Romantic Suspense

❏ Deadly Hunter — Rachel Lee

Available at WHSmith, Tesco, Asda, Eason, Amazon and Apple

Just can't wait?

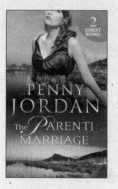

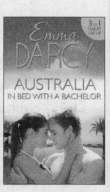

Join the Mills & Boon Book Club

Want to read more **Intrigue** books?
We're offering you **2 more** absolutely **FREE!**

We'll also treat you to these fabulous extras:

- Exclusive offers and much more!

- FREE home delivery

- FREE books and gifts with our special rewards scheme

Get your free books now!

visit www.millsandboon.co.uk/bookclub
or call Customer Relations on 020 8288 2888

The World of Mills & Boon®

There's a Mills & Boon® series that's perfect for you. We publish ten series and, with new titles every month, you never have to wait long for your favourite to come along.

By Request
Relive the romance with the best of the best
12 stories every month

Cherish™
Experience the ultimate rush of falling in love
12 new stories every month

Desire
Passionate and dramatic love stories
6 new stories every month

nocturne™
An exhilarating underworld of dark desires
Up to 3 new stories every month

For exclusive member offers go to
millsandboon.co.uk/subscribe